CITIES OF THE RED NIGHT

CITIES OF THE RED NIGHT

by

WILLIAM S. BURROUGHS

An Owl Book

HENRY HOLT AND COMPANY
NEW YORK

Henry Holt and Company, Inc.
Publishers since 1866
115 West 18th Street
New York, New York 10011

Henry Holt® is a registered trademark
of Henry Holt and Company, Inc.

Published in Canada by Fitzhenry & Whiteside Ltd.,
195 Allstate Parkway, Markham, Ontario L3R 4T8.

Library of Congress Cataloging-in-Publication Data
Burroughs, William S.
Cities of the red night.
I. Title.   PZ4.B972Ci   [PS3552.U75]   813'.54   80-13637

ISBN 0-8050-3955-4 (An Owl Book: pbk.)

Henry Holt books are available for special promotions
and premiums. For details contact: Director, Special Markets.

First published in hardcover in 1981 by
Holt, Rinehart and Winston.

First Owl Book Edition—1982
Second Owl Book Edition—1995

Designed by Joy Chu

Printed in the United States of America
All first editions are printed on acid-free paper.∞

5   7   9   10   8   6   4

Grateful acknowledgment is made for use of a portion of
"The Too Fat Polka" by Ross MacLean and Arthur Richardson.
Copyright 1947, renewed by Shapiro, Bernstein and Co., Inc.,
New York, New York. Used by permission.

TO BRION GYSIN
WHO PAINTED THIS BOOK BEFORE IT WAS WRITTEN

TO JAMES GRAUERHOLZ
WHO EDITED THIS BOOK INTO PRESENT TIME

TO STEVEN LOWE
FOR HIS VALUABLE WORK ON THE MANUSCRIPT

TO DICK SEAVER
MY PUBLISHER

TO PETER MATSON
MY AGENT

TO ALL THE CHARACTERS AND THEIR
REAL-LIFE COUNTERPARTS LIVING AND DEAD

CONTENTS

BOOK TWO

BOOK THREE

FORE!

The liberal principles embodied in the French and American revolutions and later in the liberal revolutions of 1848 had already been codified and put into practice by pirate communes a hundred years earlier. Here is a quote from *Under the Black Flag* by Don C. Seitz:

Captain Mission was one of the forbears of the French Revolution. He was one hundred years in advance of his time, for his career was based upon an initial desire to better adjust the affairs of mankind, which ended as is quite usual in the more liberal adjustment of his own fortunes. It is related how Captain Mission, having led his ship to victory against an English man-of-war, called a meeting of the crew. Those who wished to follow him he would welcome and treat as brothers; those who did not would be safely set ashore. One and all embraced the New Freedom. Some were for hoisting the Black Flag at once but Mission demurred, saying that they were not pirates but liberty lovers, fighting for equal rights against all nations subject to the tyranny of government, and bespoke a white flag as the more fitting emblem. The ship's money was put in a chest to be used as common property. Clothes were now distributed to all in need and the republic of the sea was in full operation.

Mission bespoke them to live in strict harmony among themselves; that a misplaced society would adjudge them still as pirates. Self-preservation, therefore, and not a cruel disposition, compelled them to declare war on all nations who should close their ports to them. "I declare such war and at the same time recommend to you a humane and generous behavior towards your prisoners, which will appear by so much more the effects of a noble soul as we are satisfied we should not meet the same treatment should our ill fortune or want of courage give us up to their mercy. . . ." The *Nieustadt* of Amsterdam was made prize, giving up two thousand pounds and gold dust and seventeen slaves. The slaves were added to the crew and clothed in the Dutchman's spare garments; Mission made an address denouncing slavery, holding that men who sold others like beasts proved their religion to be no more than a grimace as no man had power of liberty over another. . . .

Mission explored the Madagascar coast and found a bay ten leagues north of Diégo-Suarez. It was resolved to establish here the shore quarters of the Republic—erect a town, build docks, and have a place they might call their own. The colony was called Libertatia and was placed under Articles drawn up by Captain Mission. The Articles state, among other things: all decisions with regard to the colony to be submitted to vote by the colonists; the abolition of slavery for any reason including debt; the abolition of the death penalty; and freedom to follow any religious beliefs or practices without sanction or molestation.

Captain Mission's colony, which numbered about three

hundred, was wiped out by a surprise attack from the natives, and Captain Mission was killed shortly afterwards in a sea battle. There were other such colonies in the West Indies and in Central and South America, but they were not able to maintain themselves since they were not sufficiently populous to withstand attack. Had they been able to do so, the history of the world could have been altered. Imagine a number of such fortified positions all through South America and the West Indies, stretching from Africa to Madagascar and Malaya and the East Indies, all offering refuge to fugitives from slavery and oppression: "Come to us and live under the Articles."

At once we have allies in all those who are enslaved and oppressed throughout the world, from the cotton plantations of the American South to the sugar plantations of the West Indies, the whole Indian population of the American continent peonized and degraded by the Spanish into subhuman poverty and ignorance, exterminated by the Americans, infected with their vices and diseases, the natives of Africa and Asia—all these are potential allies. Fortified positions supported by and supporting guerrilla hit-and-run bands; supplied with soldiers, weapons, medicines and information by the local populations ... such a combination would be unbeatable. If the whole American army couldn't beat the Viet Cong at a time when fortified positions were rendered obsolete by artillery and air strikes, certainly the armies of Europe, operating in unfamiliar territory and susceptible to all the disabling diseases of tropical countries, could not have beaten guerrilla tactics *plus* fortified positions. Consider the difficulties which such an invading army would face: continual harassment from the guerrillas, a totally hostile population always ready with poison, misdirection, snakes and spiders in the general's bed, armadillos carrying the deadly earth-eating disease rooting under the barracks and adopted as mascots by the regiment as dysentery and malaria take their toll. The sieges could not but present a series of military disasters. There is no stopping the Articulated. The white man is retroactively relieved of his burden. Whites will be welcomed as workers, settlers, teachers, and technicians, but not as colonists or masters. No man may violate the Articles.

Imagine such a movement on a world-wide scale. Faced by the actual practice of freedom, the French and American revolutions would be forced to stand by their words. The disastrous results of uncontrolled industrialization would also be curtailed, since factory workers and slum dwellers from the cities would seek refuge in Articulated areas. Any man would have the right to settle in any area of his choosing. The land would belong to those who used it. No white-man boss, no Pukka Sahib, no Patróns, no colonists. The escalation of mass production and concentration of population in urban areas would be halted, for who would work in their factories and buy their products when he could live from the fields and the sea and the lakes and the rivers in areas of un-believable plenty? And living from the land, he would be motivated to preserve its resources.

I cite this example of retroactive Utopia since it actually could have happened in terms of the techniques and human resources available at the time. Had Captain Mission lived long enough to set an example for others to follow, mankind might have stepped free from the deadly impasse of insoluble problems in which we now find ourselves.

The chance was there. The chance was missed. The principles of the French and American revolutions became windy lies in the mouths of politicians. The liberal revolutions of 1848 created the so-called republics of Central and South America, with a dreary history of dictatorship, oppression, graft, and bureaucracy, thus closing this vast, underpopulated continent to any possibility of communes along the lines set forth by Captain Mission. In any case South America will soon be crisscrossed by highways and motels. In England, Western Europe, and America, the overpopulation made possible by the Industrial Revolution leaves scant room for communes, which are commonly subject to state and federal law and frequently harassed by the local inhabitants. There is simply no room left for "freedom from the tyranny of government" since city dwellers depend on it for food, power, water, transportation, protection, and welfare. Your right to live where you want, with companions of your choosing, under laws to which you agree, died in the eighteenth century with Captain Mission. Only a miracle or a disaster could restore it.

INVOCATION

This book is dedicated to the Ancient Ones, to the Lord of Abominations, *Humwawa*, whose face is a mass of entrails, whose breath is the stench of dung and the perfume of death, Dark Angel of all that is excreted and sours, Lord of Decay, Lord of the Future, who rides on a whispering south wind, to *Pazuzu*, Lord of Fevers and Plagues, Dark Angel of the Four Winds with rotting genitals from which he howls through sharpened teeth over stricken cities, to *Kutulu*, the Sleeping Serpent who cannot be summoned, to the *Akhkharu*, who suck the blood of men since they desire to become men, to the *Lalussu*, who haunt the places of men, to *Gelal* and *Lilit*, who invade the beds of men and whose children are born in secret places, to *Addu*, raiser of storms who can fill the night sky with brightness, to *Malah*, Lord of Courage and Bravery, to *Zahgurim*, whose number is twenty-three and who kills in an unnatural fashion, to *Zahrim*, a warrior among warriors, to *Itzamna*, Spirit of Early Mists and Showers, to *Ix Chel*, the Spider-Web-that-Catches-the-Dew-of-Morning, to *Zuhuy Kak*, Virgin Fire, to *Ah Dziz*, the Master of Cold, to *Kak U Pacat*, who works in fire, to *Ix Tab*, Goddess of Ropes and Snares, patroness of those who hang themselves, to *Schmuun*, the Silent One, twin brother of *Ix Tab*, to *Xolotl* the Unformed, Lord of Rebirth, to *Aguchi*, Master of Ejaculations, to *Osiris* and *Amen* in phallic form, to *Hex Chun Chan*, the Dangerous One, to *Ah Pook*, the Destroyer, to the *Great Old One* and the *Star Beast*, to *Pan*, God of Panic, to the nameless gods of dispersal and emptiness, to *Hassan I Sabbah*, Master of the Assassins.

To all the scribes and artists and practitioners of magic through whom these spirits have been manifested. . . .

NOTHING IS TRUE. EVERYTHING IS PERMITTED.

BOOK ONE

THE HEALTH OFFICER

September 13, 1923.

Farnsworth, the District Health Officer, was a man so grudging in what he asked of life that every win was a loss; yet he was not without a certain plodding persistence of effort and effectiveness in his limited area. The current emergency posed by the floods and the attendant cholera epidemic, while it did not spur him to any unusual activity, left him unruffled.

Every morning at sunrise, he bundled his greasy maps—which he studied at breakfast while he licked butter off his fingers—into his battered Land-Rover and set out to inspect his district, stopping here and there to order more sandbags for the levees (knowing his orders would be disregarded, as they generally were unless the Commissioner happened to be with him). He ordered three bystanders, presumably relatives, to transport a cholera case to the district hospital at Waghdas and left three opium pills and instructions for preparing rice water. They nodded, and he drove on, having done what he could.

The emergency hospital at Waghdas was installed in an empty army barracks left over from the war. It was understaffed and overcrowded, mostly by patients who lived near enough and were still strong enough to walk. The treatment for cholera was simple: each patient was assigned to a straw pallet on arrival and given a gallon of rice water and half a gram of opium. If he was still alive twelve hours later, the dose of opium was repeated. The survival rate was about twenty percent. Pallets of the dead were washed in carbolic solution and left in the sun to dry. The attendants were mostly Chinese who had taken the job because they were allowed to smoke the opium and feed the ash to the patients. The smell of cooking rice, opium smoke, excrement, and carbolic permeated the hospital and the area around it for several hundred yards.

At ten o'clock the Health Officer entered the hospital. He requisitioned more carbolic and opium, and sent off another request for a doctor, which he expected and hoped would be ignored. He felt that a doctor fussing around the hospital would only make matters worse; he might even object to the opium dosage as too high, or attempt to interfere with the opium smoking of the attendants. The Health Officer had very little use for doctors. They simply complicated things to make themselves important.

After spending half an hour in the hospital, he drove to Ghadis to see the Commissioner, who invited him to lunch. He accepted without enthusiasm, declining a gin before lunch and a beer with lunch. He picked at the rice and fish, and ate a small plate of stewed fruit. He was trying to persuade the Commissioner to assign some convicts to work on the levees.

"Sorry, old boy, not enough soldiers to guard them."

"Well, it's a serious situation."

"Daresay."

Farnsworth did not press the point. He simply did what he could and let it go at that. Newcomers to the district wondered what kept him going at all. Old-timers like the Commissioner knew. For the Health Officer had a sustaining vice. Every morning at sunrise, he brewed a pot of strong tea and washed down a gram of opium. When he returned from his rounds in the evening, he repeated the dose and gave it time to take effect before he prepared his evening meal of stewed fruit and wheat bread. He had no permanent houseboy, since he feared a boy might steal his opium. Twice a week he had a boy in to clean the bungalow, and then he locked his opium up in an old rusty safe where he kept his reports. He had been taking opium for five years and had stabilized his dosage after the first year and never increased it, nor gone on to injections of morphine. This was not due to strength of character, but simply to the fact that he felt he owed himself very little, and that was what he allotted himself.

Driving back to find the sandbags not there, the cholera patient dead, and his three relatives droopy-eyed from the opium pills he had left, he felt neither anger nor exasperation, only the slight lack that had increased in the last hour of his drive, so that he stepped harder on the accelerator. Arriving at his bungalow, he washed down an opium pill with bottled water and lit the kerosene stove for his tea. He carried the tea onto the porch and by the time he had finished the second cup, he was feeling the opium wash through the back of his neck and down his withered thighs. He could have passed for fifty; actually he was twenty-eight. He sat there for half an hour looking at the muddy river and the low hills covered with scrub. There was a mutter of thunder, and as he cooked his evening meal the first drops of rain fell on the rusty galvanized iron roof.

He awoke to the unaccustomed sound of lapping water. Hastily he pulled on his pants and stepped onto the porch. Rain was still falling, and the water had risen during the night to a level of twelve inches under the bungalow and a few inches below the hubcaps of his Land-Rover. He washed down an opium pill and put water on the stove for his tea.

Then he dusted off an alligator-skin Gladstone bag and started packing, opening drawers and compartments in the safe. He packed clothes, reports, a compass, a sheath knife, a 45 Webley revolver and a box of shells, matches, and a mess kit. He filled his canteen with bottled water and wrapped a loaf of bread in paper. Pouring his tea, the water rising under his feet, he experienced a tension in the groin, a surge of adolescent lust that was stronger for being inexplicable and inappropriate. His medical supplies and opium he packed in a separate bag, and as an added precaution, a slab of opium the size of a cigarette package, wrapped in heavy tinfoil, went into his side coat pocket. By the time he had finished packing, his pants were sticking out at the fly. The opium would soon take care of that.

He stepped from the porch into the Land-Rover. The motor caught, and he headed for high ground above the flood. The route he took was seldom used and several times he had to cut trees out of the road with an ax. Towards sundown, he reached the medical mission of Father Dupré. This was out of his district, and he had met the priest only once before.

Father Dupré, a thin red-faced man with a halo of white hair, greeted him politely but without enthusiasm. He brightened somewhat when Farnsworth brought out his medical supplies and went with him to the dispensary and hospital, which was simply a large hut screened-in at the sides. The Health Officer passed out opium pills to all the patients.

"No matter what is wrong with them, they will feel better shortly."

The priest nodded absently as he led the way back to the house. Farnsworth had swallowed his opium pill with water from his canteen, and it was beginning to take effect as he sat down on the porch. The priest was looking at him with a hostility he was trying hard to conceal. Farnsworth wondered what exactly was wrong. The priest fidgeted and cleared his throat. He said abruptly in a strained voice, "Would you care for a drink?"

"Thank you, no. I never touch it."

Relief flooded the priest's face with a beneficent glow. "Something else then?"

"I'd love some tea."

"Of course. I'll have the boy make it."

The priest came back with a bottle of whiskey, a glass, and a soda siphon. Farnsworth surmised that he kept his whiskey under lock and key somewhere out of the reach of his boys. The priest poured himself a generous four fingers and shot in a dash of soda. He took a long drink and beamed at his guest. Farnsworth decided that the moment was propitious to ask a favor, while the good father was still relieved at not having to share his dwindling supply of whiskey, and before he had overindulged.

"I want to get through to Ghadis if possible. I suppose it's hopeless by road, even if I had enough petrol?"

The priest got a map and spread it out on the table. "Absolutely out of the question. This whole area is flooded. Only possibility is by boat to here . . . from there it's forty miles downriver to Ghadis. I could lend you a boat with a boy and outboard, but there's no petrol here. . . ."

"I think I have enough petrol for that, considering it's all downstream."

"You'll run into logjams—may take hours to cut through . . . figure how long it could take you at the longest, and then double it . . . my boy only knows the route as far as here. Now this stretch here is very dangerous . . . the river narrows quite suddenly, no noise you understand, and no warning . . . advise you to take the canoe out and carry it down to here . . . take one extra day, but well worth it at this time of year. Of course you *might* get through—but if anything goes wrong ... the current, you understand ... even a strong swimmer ..."

The following day at dawn, Farnsworth's belongings and the supplies for the trip were loaded into the dugout canoe. The boy, Ali, was a smoky black with sharp features, clearly a mixture of Arab and Negro stock. He was about eighteen, with beautiful teeth and a quick shy smile. The priest waved from the jetty as the boat swung into midstream. Farnsworth sat back lazily, watching the water and the jungle slide past. There was not much sign of life. A few birds and monkeys. Once three alligators wallowing in a mudbank slid into the water, showing their teeth in depraved smiles. Several times logjams had to be cleared with an ax.

At sundown they made camp on a gravel bank. Farnsworth put water on for tea while Ali walked to the end of the bank and dropped a hook baited with a worm into a deep clear pool. By the time the water was boiling, he was back with an eighteen-inch fish. As Ali cleaned the fish and cut it into sections, Farnsworth washed down his opium pill. He offered one to Ali, who examined it, sniffed at it, smiled, and shook his head.

"Chinese boy ..." He leaned over holding an imaginary opium pipe to a lamp. He drew the smoke in and let his eyes droop. "No get—" He put his hands on his stomach and rocked back and forth.

By the afternoon of the second day the stream had widened considerably. Towards sundown Farnsworth took an opium pill and dozed off. Suddenly he was wide awake with a start, and he reached for the map. This was the stretch that Father Dupré had warned him about. He turned towards Ali, but Ali knew already. He was steering for shore.

The silent rush of the current swept the boat broadside, and the rudder wire snapped like a bowstring. The boat twisted out of control, swept towards a logjam. A splintering crash, and Farnsworth was underwater, struggling desperately against the current. He felt a stab of pain as a branch ripped through his coat and along his side.

He came to on the bank. Ali was pushing water out of his lungs. He sat up breathing heavily and coughing. His coat was in tatters, oozing blood. He felt for the pocket, and looked at his empty hand. The opium was gone. He had sustained a superficial scratch down the left hip and across the buttock. They had salvaged nothing except the short machete that Ali wore in a sheath at his belt, and Farnsworth's hunting knife.

Farnsworth drew a map in the sand to approximate their position. He calculated the distance to one of the large tributaries to be about forty miles. Once there, they could fashion a raft and drift downstream to Ghadis, where of course ... the words of Father Dupré played back in his mind: "Figure the longest time it could take you and then double it. ..."

Darkness was falling, and they had to stay there for the night, even though he was losing precious travel time. He knew that in seventy-two hours at the outside he would be immobilized for lack of opium. At daybreak they set out heading north. Progress was slow; the undergrowth had to be cut step by step. There were swamps and streams in the way, and from time to time deep gorges that necessitated long detours. The unaccustomed exertion knocked the opium out of his system, and by nightfall he was already feverish and shivering.

By morning he was barely able to walk, but managed to stagger along for a few miles. The next day he was convulsed by stomach cramps and they barely covered a mile. The third day he could not move. Ali massaged his legs, which were knotted with cramps, and brought him water and fruit. He lay there unable to move for four days and four nights.

Occasionally he dozed off and woke up screaming from

nightmares. These often took the form of attacks by centipedes and scorpions of strange sizes and shapes, moving with great speed, that would suddenly rush at him. Another recurrent nightmare was set in the market of a Near Eastern city. The place was at first unknown to him but more familiar with each step he took, as if some hideous jigsaw of memory were slowly falling into place: the stalls all empty of food and merchandise, the smell of hunger and death, the greenish glow and a strange smoky sun, sulfurous blazing hate in faces that turned to look at him as he passed. Now they were all pointing at him and shouting a word he could not understand.

On the eighth day he was able to walk again. He was still racked with stomach cramps and diarrhea, but the leg cramps were almost gone. On the tenth day he felt distinctly better and stronger, and was able to eat a fish. On the fourteenth day they reached a sandbank by a wide clear river. This was not the tributary they were looking for, but would certainly lead into it. Ali had saved a piece of carbolic soap in a tin box, and they stripped off their tattered clothes and waded into the cool water. Farnsworth washed off the dirt and sweat and smell of his sickness. Ali was rubbing soap on his back and Farnsworth felt a sudden rush of blood to the crotch. Trying to hide his erection, he waded ashore with his back to Ali, who followed laughing and splashing water to wash the soap off.

Farnsworth lay down on his shirt and pants and fell into a wordless vacuum, feeling the sun on his back and the faint ache of the healing scratch. He saw Ali sitting naked above him, Ali's hands massaging his back, moving down to the buttocks. Something was surfacing in his body, drifting up from remote depths of memory, and he saw as if projected on a screen a strange incident from his adolescence. He was in the British Museum at the age of fourteen, standing in front of a glass case. He was alone in the room. In the case was the figure, about two feet long, of a reclining man. The man was naked, the right knee flexed, holding the body a few inches off the ground, the penis exposed. The hands were extended in front of the man palms down, and the face was reptile or animal, something between an alligator and a jaguar.

The boy was looking at the thighs and buttocks and genitals, breathing through his teeth. He was getting stiff and lubricating, his pants sticking out at the fly. He was squeezing into the figure, a dream tension gathering in his crotch, squeezing and stretching, a strange smell unlike anything he had ever smelled before but familiar as smell itself, a naked man lying by a wide clear river—the twisted figure. Silver spots boiled in front of his eyes and he ejaculated.

Ali's hands parted his buttocks, he spit on his rectum— his body opening and the figure entering him in a silent rush, flexing his right knee, stretching his jaw forward into a snout, his head flattening, his brain squeezing out the smell from inside . . . a hoarse hissing sound was forced from his lips and light popped in his eyes as his body boiled and twisted out scalding spurts.

Stage with a jungle backdrop. Frogs croak and birds call from recorder. Farnsworth as an adolescent is lying facedown on sand. Ali is fucking him and he squirms with a slow wallowing movement showing his teeth in a depraved smile. The lights dim for a few seconds. When the lights come up Farnsworth is wearing an alligator suit that leaves his ass bare and Ali is still fucking him. As Ali and Farnsworth slide offstage Farnsworth lifts one webbed finger to the audience while a Marine band plays "Semper Fi." Offstage splash.

WE SEE TIBET WITH
THE BINOCULARS OF
THE PEOPLE

The scouting party stopped a few hundred yards from the village on the bank of a stream. Yen Lee studied the village through his field glasses while his men sat down and lit cigarettes. The village was built into the side of a mountain. The stream ran through the town, and water had been diverted into pools on a series of cultivated terraces that led up to the monastery. There was no sign of life in the steep winding street or by the pools. The valley was littered with large boulders which would serve as cover if necessary, but he did not expect resistance on a military level. He lowered his glasses, signaling for the men to follow.

They crossed a stone bridge two at a time, covered by the men behind them. If any defenders were going to open fire, now would be the time and place to do it. Beyond the bridge the street twisted up the mountainside. On both sides there were stone huts, many of them fallen into ruin and obviously deserted. As they moved up the stone street, keeping to the sides and taking cover behind the ruined huts, Yen Lee became increasingly aware of a hideous unknown odor. He motioned the patrol to halt and stood there sniffing.

Unlike his counterparts in western countries, he had been carefully selected for a high level of intuitive adjustment, and trained accordingly to imagine and explore seemingly fantastic potentials in any situation, while at the same time giving equal consideration to prosaic and practical aspects. He had developed an attitude at once probing and impersonal, remote and alert. He did not know when the training had begun, since in Academy 23 it was carried out in a context of reality. He did not see his teachers, whose instructions were conveyed through a series of real situations.

He had been born in Hong Kong and had lived there until the age of twelve, so that English was a second language. Then his family had moved to Shanghai. In his early teens he had read the American Beat writers. The volumes had been brought in through Hong Kong and sold under the counter in a bookshop that seemed to enjoy freedom from official interference, although the proprietor was also engaged in currency deals.

At the age of sixteen he was sent to a military academy, where he received intensive training in the use of weapons. After six months he was summoned to the Colonel's office and told that he would be leaving the military school and returning to Shanghai. Since he had applied himself to the training and made an excellent showing, he asked the Colonel if this was because his work had not been satisfactory. The Colonel was looking not at him but around him, as if drawing a figure in the air. He indicated obliquely that while a desire to please one's superiors was laudable, other considerations were in certain cases even more highly emphasized.

The smell hit him like an invisible wall. He stopped and leaned against a house. It was like rotten metal or metal excrement, he decided. The patrol was still in the ruined outskirts of the village. One man was vomiting violently, his face beaded with sweat. He straightened up and started towards the stream. Yen Lee stopped him: "Don't drink the water or splash it on your face. The stream runs through the town."

Yen Lee sat down and looked once again at the town through his field glasses. There were still no villagers in sight. He put his glasses down and conducted an out-of-body exploration of the village—what westerners call "astral travel." He was moving up the street now, his gun at the ready. The gun would shoot blasts of energy, and he could feel it tingle in his hands. He kicked open a door.

One glance told him that interrogation was useless. He would get no information on a verbal level. A man and a woman were in the terminal stages of some disease, their faces eaten to the bone by phosphorescent sores. An older woman was dead. The next hut contained five corpses, all elderly.

In another hut a youth lay on a pallet, the lower half of his body covered by a blanket. Bright red nipples of flesh about an inch in height, growing in clusters, covered his chest and stomach and sprouted from his face and neck. The growths looked like exotic plants. He noticed that they were oozing a pearly juice that ate into the flesh, leaving luminescent sores. Sensing Yen Lee's presence the youth turned towards him with a slow idiot smile, arching his body and caressing the flesh clusters with one hand while the other hand slid under the blanket and moved to his crotch. In another hut, Yen Lee glimpsed a scene that he quickly erased from memory.

Yen Lee advanced towards the monastery. Then he stopped. The gun went heavy and solid in his hands as energy left it. His training had not quite prepared him for the feeling of death that fell in a steady silent rain from the monastery above him. The monastery must contain a deadly force, probably some form of radioactivity, perhaps psychic fission. He surmised further that the illness afflicting the villagers was a radioactive virus strain. He knew that top-secret research in the West was moving in this direction: as early as World War II, England had developed a radioactive virus known as the Doomsday Bug.

Returning to his body Yen Lee weighed his observations and surmises. What had he glimpsed and hastily looked away from? Tiny creatures like translucent shrimp feeding at the flesh nipples ... and something else.... He did not push himself, knowing that a biologic protective reaction was shielding him from knowledge he was unable to assimilate and handle. The monastery probably contained a laboratory and the village had been used as a testing ground. How did the technicians protect themselves from the radiation? Could the laboratory be operated by remote control? Or had the technicians been immunized by gradient exposure? Did the laboratory contain a sophisticated DOR installation?

He picked up a walkie-talkie. "Pre-Talk calling Dead Line...."

"Well?" The Colonel's voice was cool, edged with abstract impatience. Cadets were expected to use their own initiative on patrol and only call in case of emergency. Yen Lee recounted what he had seen in the village and described the feeling of death that emanated from the monastery. "It's like a wall. I can't get through it. Certainly my men can't...."

"Withdraw from the village and make camp. A sanitary squad and a health officer are on the way."

THE DOCTOR IS ON
THE MARKET

octor Pierson was a discreet addict who kept himself
down to three shots a day, half a grain in each
shot—he could always cover for that. Towards the
end of an eight-hour shift he tended to be perfunc-
tory, so when he got the call from emergency he hoped it
wouldn't take long or keep him overtime. Of course he could
always slip a half-grain under his tongue, but that was wasteful
and he liked to be in bed when he took his shot, and feel
it hit the back of his neck and move down the backs of
his thighs while he blew cigarette smoke towards the ceiling.
As he reached for his bag he noticed that he had barked
his knuckles. He couldn't remember where or when—that
happens, when you are feeling no pain.

"It looks like measles, Doctor."

The doctor looked at the boy's face with distaste. He
disliked children, adolescents, and animals. The word *cute*
did not exist in his emotional vocabulary. There were red
blotches on the boy's face but they seemed rather large for
measles. . . .

"Well, get it in here, Nurse, whatever it is . . . away
from the other patients. Not that I care what they catch;
it's just hospital procedure."

The boy was wheeled into a cubicle. His fingers cold
with reluctance, the doctor folded the sheet down to the boy's
waist and noticed that he was wearing no shorts.

16

"Why is he naked?" he snapped at the attendants.

"He was like that when they picked him up, Doctor."

"Well, they might have put something on him. . . ." He turned back to the attendants. "What are you standing there for? Get out! And you, Nurse, what are you gawking at? Order a bed in isolation."

His temper was always evil when he ran over like this, but right after a shot he could be nice in a dead, fishy way. The doctor turned back to the boy on the bed. His duty as a physician was clear—Hippocrates pointing sternly to the sheet. "Well, I suppose I have to look at the little naked beast." He folded the sheet down to the boy's knees. The boy had an erection. The genitals and the areas adjacent were bright red like a red bikini.

The doctor leaped back as he would from a striking snake, but he was too late. A gob of semen hit the back of his hand right on the skinned knuckles. He wiped it off with an exclamation of disgust. He recalled later that he felt a slight tingling sensation which he didn't notice at the time, being that disgusted with the human body—he wondered why he had chosen the medical profession. And this dirty child was delaying his fix. "You filthy little beast!" he snapped. The boy sniggered. The doctor pulled the sheet up to the boy's chin.

He was washing his hands when the nurse came in with a stretcher table and an orderly to take the boy to isolation. The doctor sniffed. "My God, what's that smell? . . . I don't know what this is, Nurse, but it's rather disgusting. He seems to be in some state of sexual delirium. He also seems to be giving off a horrible odor. Order the broad spectrum . . . cortisone, of course—it may be an allergic condition red-haired animals are especially liable to—and the usual antibiotics. . . . If the sexual condition continues, do not hesitate to administer morphine." The doctor gasped and clasped a handkerchief in front of his mouth and nose. *"Get it out of here!"* (He always referred to a patient as "the disease.") "Do you have a typhoid bed in isolation?" he asked.

"Not now we don't."

"Well *it* can't stay here."

He had barely settled in bed after his fix when the phone rang. It was the super. "Seems we have an epidemic on our hands, Pierson. All staff report back to the hospital immediately."

Could it be that dirty little boy? he thought as he dressed and picked up his satchel and walked to the hospital. He saw there was a police line around the entrance.

"Oh, yes, Doctor. Right over there for your mask."

"I'll help you put it on, Doctor." A brisk young girl in some sort of uniform rubbed her tits against him in a most offensive manner. And before she got the mask on, he smelled it and he knew: it *was* that dirty little boy.

Inside was a scene from Dante: stretchers side by side in the corridors, sperm all over the sheets, the walls and the floor.

"Be careful, Doctor." A garrulous old nurse caught his arm in time. "Just put one foot solidly in front of the other, Doctor, that's right. . . . It's terrible, Doctor, the older patients are dying like flies."

"I don't want to hear any generalities, Nurse . . . take me to my ward."

"Well, Doctor, you can take the northeast wing if you want—right here."

Every sort of copulation was going on in front of him, every disgusting thing they could think of. Some of them had pillowcases and towels wrapped around each other's necks in some kind of awful contest. As these crazed patients seemed in danger of strangulation (and here the doctor almost slipped in shit), he ordered attendants to restrain them, but no attendants were available. "We'll start with morphine and a curare derivative, Nurse."

"Sorry, Doctor, the morphine stocks are exhausted on the older patients. They go into the most awful spasms at the end, Doctor."

The doctor turned pale as death at this terrible pronouncement. He slumped to the floor in a faint, his face covered with red blotches. By the time they got his clothes off, his body was also affected, and spontaneous orgasms were observed.

Doctor Pierson subsequently recovered, because of his addiction, and went to work for the pickle factory on a sensitive biological project.

POLITICS HERE IS DEATH

Muted remote boardroom. Doctor Pierson sits at the head of the table with notes in front of him. He speaks in a dry flat academic voice.

"Ladies and gentlemen of the Board, I am here to give a report on preliminary experiments with Virus B-23. . . . Consider the origins of this virus in the Cities of the Red Night. The red glow that covered the northern sky at night was a form of radiation that gave rise to a plague known as the Red Fever, of which Virus B-23 was found to be the etiological agent.

"Virus B-23 has been called, among other things, the virus of biological mutation, since this agent occasioned biologic alterations in those affected—fatal in many cases, permanent and hereditary in the survivors, who become carriers of that strain. The original inhabitants of these cities were black, but soon a wide spectrum of albino variations appeared, and this condition was passed on to their descendants by techniques of artificial insemination which were, to say the least, highly developed. In fact, how some of these mutant pregnancies were contracted is unknown to modern science. Immaculate or at least viral conception was pandemic and may have given rise to legends of demon lovers, the succubi and incubi of medieval folklore."

Doctor Pierson continues: "The virus, acting directly on neural centers, brought about sexual frenzies that facilitated its communication, just as rabid dogs are driven to spread the virus of rabies by biting. Various forms of sexual sacrifice were practiced ... sexual hangings and strangulations, and drugs that caused death in erotic convulsions. Death during intercourse was a frequent occurrence and was considered an especially favorable circumstance for conveying the viral alterations.

"We are speaking of more or less virgin genetic material of high quality. At this time the newly conceived white race was fighting for its biological continuity, so the virus served a most useful purpose. However, I question the wisdom of introducing Virus B-23 into contemporary America and Europe. Even though it might quiet the uh silent majority, who are admittedly becoming uh awkward, we must consider the biologic consequences of exposing genetic material already damaged beyond repair to such an agent, leaving a wake of unimaginably unfavorable mutations all ravenously perpetrating their kind. . . .

"There have been other proposals. I cite the work of Doctor Unruh von Steinplatz on radioactive virus strains. Working with such established viruses as rabies, hepatitis, and smallpox, he exposed generations of virus to atomic radiation to produce airborne strains of unbelievable virulence capable of wiping out whole populations within days. However, this blueprint contains a flaw: the disposal problem posed by billions of radioactive corpses unfit even for fertilizer.

"Ladies and gentlemen, I propose to remove the temporal limits, shifting our experimental theater into past time in order to circumvent the whole tedious problem of overpopulation. You may well ask if we can be certain of uh containing the virus in past time. The answer is: we do not have sufficient data to speak with certainty. We propose; the virus may dispose. . . ."

A thin man in his early thirties with sandy hair and

pale blue eyes had been taking notes while Doctor Pierson was speaking. He looked up and spoke in a clear, rather high-pitched voice with a faint trace of Germanic accent. "Doctor Pierson, I have a few questions."

"Certainly," said Pierson with cold displeasure. He knew exactly who this man was, and wished that he had not been invited to attend the meeting. This was Jon Alistair Peterson, born in Denmark, now working on a secret government project in England. He was a virologist and mathematician who had devised a computer to process qualitative data.

Peterson leaned back in his chair, one ankle crossed over his knee. He extracted a joint from his shirt pocket. It was a loud Carnaby Street shirt. Pierson thought it vulgar. Peterson lit the joint and blew smoke towards the ceiling, seemingly oblivious of disapproving looks from the board members. He glanced down at his notes. "My first question is a matter of uh nomenclature." Pierson was annoyed to realize that Peterson was mimicking his own academic tones.

"Professor Steinplatz's experiments, as you must know, consisted of inoculating animals with various viruses and then exposing the animals to radiation. This exposure produced virus mutations tending towards increased virulence and . . ." He took a long drag and blew smoke across his notes. ". . . uh increased communication potential. In plain English, the mutated viruses were much more infectious."

"I would say that is a more or less accurate paraphrase of what I have just said."

"Not precisely. The mutated virus strains were produced by radiation and the test animals, having been exposed to radiation, were of course radioactive to a point but not dangerously so. . . . The viruses were *produced* by radiation, but it does not necessarily follow that the viruses were themselves radioactive. Is not your use of the term *radioactive* virus and your uh evocation of billions of radioactive corpses uh misleading?"

Doctor Pierson found it difficult to conceal his annoyance. "I have pointed out that, owing to the grave dangers inherent in large-scale experimentation which could among other things severely damage our public image, our data is incomplete. . . ."

"Ah yes, to be sure. And now if you will bear with me, Doctor, I have some additional questions. . . . You have said that Virus B-23 resulted from radiation?" asked Peterson.

"I did."

"In what way does it differ from the strains developed by Doctor Steinplatz?"

"I thought I had made that point quite clear: the form of radiation emanating from the red light is unknown at the present time."

"You are then ignorant of the nature of this wondrous radiation, or as to how it could be produced in the laboratory?"

"Yes."

"Has it occurred to you that it might be similar to Reich's DOR, or Deadly Orgone Radiation, which is produced by placing radioactive material in an organic container lined with iron?"

"Preposterous! Reich was a charlatan! A lunatic!"

"Perhaps . . . but such a simple and *inexpensive* experiment . . . we could start with herpes simplex."

"I fail to see that any useful purpose . . ." Pierson glanced around the table. Stony faces looked back at him. He was concealing something and they knew it.

Doctor Pierson looked at his watch. "I'm afraid I must cut this short. I have a plane to catch."

Peterson held up his hand. "I'm not quite finished, Doctor. . . . I am sure that a slight delay in takeoff could be arranged for a person of your importance. . . . Now, the virus strains developed by Doctor Steinplatz were, to be sure, more contagious and more virulent than the mother strains from which they were derived, but still quite recognizable. For example, for *example*, the good doctor's airborne rabies would still be clinically recognizable as rabies. Even if the viruses were mixed into a cocktail, the individual ingredients would still be comparatively easy to identify. You would agree, Doctor Pierson?"

"In theory, yes. However, we do not know, in the absence of large-scale exposure, whether the viruses might not undergo further mutations that would render identification difficult."

"To be sure. The point I am making is simply that Doctor Steinplatz started his experiments with certain known viruses. . . . Doctor Pierson, you have stated that Virus B-23 *resulted* from unknown radiation. Do you imply that this virus was so produced out of thin air? Let me put it this way: What virus or viruses known to unknown mutated as a result of this radiation?"

"At the risk of repeating myself, I will say again that both the radiation and the virus or viruses are unknown at this time," said Pierson archly.

"The symptoms of a virus are the attempts of the body to deal with a virus attack. By their symptoms you shall know them, and even a totally unknown virus would yield considerable data by its symptoms. On the other hand, if a virus produces no symptoms, then we have no way of knowing that it exists . . . no way of knowing that it is a virus."

"So?"

"So the virus in question may have been latent or it may have been living in benign symbiosis with the host."

"That is, of course, possible," admitted Pierson.

"Now let us consider the symptoms of Virus B-23: fever,

rash, a characteristic odor, sexual frenzies, obsession with sex and death. . . . Is this so totally strange and alien?"

"I don't follow you."

"I will make myself clearer. We know that a consuming passion can produce physical symptoms . . . fever . . . loss of appetite . . . even allergic reactions . . . and few conditions are more obsessional and potentially self-destructive than love. Are not the symptoms of Virus B-23 simply the symptoms of what we are pleased to call 'love'? Eve, we are told, was made from Adam's rib . . . so a hepatitis virus was once a healthy liver cell. If you will excuse me, ladies, nothing personal . . . we are all tainted with viral origins. The whole quality of human consciousness, as expressed in male and female, is basically a virus mechanism. I suggest that this virus, known as 'the other half,' turned malignant as a result of the radiation to which the Cities of the Red Night were exposed."

"You lost me there."

"Did I indeed. . . . And I would suggest further that any attempts to contain Virus B-23 will turn out to be ineffectual because we carry this virus with us," said Peterson.

"Really, Doctor, aren't you letting fantasy run away with you? After all, other viruses have been brought under control. Why should this virus be an exception?"

"Because it is the *human virus*. After many thousands of years of more or less benign coexistence, it is now once again on the verge of malignant mutation . . . what Doctor Steinplatz calls a virgin soil epidemic. This could result from the radiation already released in atomic testing. . . ."

"What's your point, Doctor?" Pierson snapped.

"My point is very simple. The whole human position is no longer tenable. And one last consideration . . . as you know, a vast crater in what is now Siberia is thought to have resulted from a meteor. It is further theorized that this meteor brought with it the radiation in question. Others have surmised that it may not have been a meteor but a black hole, a hole in the fabric of reality, through which the inhabitants of these ancient cities traveled in time to a final impasse."

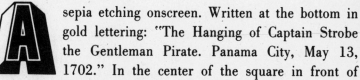

THE RESCUE

A sepia etching onscreen. Written at the bottom in gold lettering: "The Hanging of Captain Strobe the Gentleman Pirate. Panama City, May 13, 1702." In the center of the square in front of a courthouse Captain Strobe stands on a gallows platform with a noose around his neck. He is a slender handsome youth of twenty-five in eighteenth-century costume, his blond hair tied in a knot at the back of his head. He looks disdainfully down at the crowd. A line of soldiers stands in front of the gallows.

The etching slowly comes alive, giving off a damp heat, a smell of weeds and mud flats and sewage. Vultures roost on the old courthouse of flaking yellow stucco. The gypsy hangman—thin, effeminate-looking, with greasy crinkled hair and glistening eyes—stands by the gallows with a twisted smirk on his face. The crowd is silent, mouths open, waiting.

At a signal from an officer, a soldier steps forward with an ax and knocks the support from under the platform. Strobe falls and hangs there, his feet a few inches above the limestone paving which is cracked here and there, weeds and vines growing through. Five minutes pass in silence. Vultures wheel overhead. On Strobe's face is a strange smile. A yellow-green aura surrounds his body.

The silence is shattered by an explosion. Chunks of

masonry rain down on the square. The blast swings Strobe's body in a long arc, his feet brushing the weeds. The soldiers rush offstage, leaving only six men to guard the gallows. The crowd surges forward, pulling out knives, cutlasses, and pistols. The soldiers are disarmed. A lithe boy who looks like a Malay shows white teeth and bright red gums as he throws a knife. The knife catches the hangman in the throat just above the collarbone. He falls squawking and spitting blood like a stricken bird. Captain Strobe is cut down and borne to a waiting carriage.

The carriage careens into a side street. Inside the cart the boy loosens the noose and presses air in and out of Strobe's lungs. Strobe opens his eyes and writhes in agony from the pricklings and shootings as his circulation returns. The boy gives him a vial of black liquid.

"Drink this, Captain."

In a few minutes the laudanum takes effect and Strobe is able to walk as they leave the cart. The boy leads the way along a jungle path to a fishing boat moored at a pier on the outskirts of the city. Two younger boys are in the boat. The boat is cast off and the sail set. Captain Strobe collapses on a pallet in the cabin. The boy helps him undress and covers him with a cotton blanket.

Strobe lay back with closed eyes. He had not slept since his capture three days ago. The opium and the movement of the boat spread a pleasant languor through his body. Pictures drifted in front of his eyes. . . .

A vast ruined stone building with square marble columns in a green underwater light . . . a luminous green haze, thicker and darker at ground level, shading up to light greens and yellows . . . deep blue canals and red brick buildings . . . sunlight on water . . . a boy standing on a beach naked with

dusky rose genitals ... red night sky over a desert city ...
clusters of violet light raining down on sandstone steps and
bursting with a musky smell of ozone ... strange words
in his throat, a taste of blood and metal ... a white ship
sailing across a gleaming empty sky dusted with stars ...
singing fish in a ruined garden ... a strange pistol in his
hand that shoots blue sparks ... beautiful diseased faces
in red light, all looking at something he cannot see. ...

He awoke with a throbbing erection and a sore throat,
his brain curiously blank and factual. He accepted his rescue
as he had been prepared to accept his death. He knew exactly
where he was: some forty miles south of Panama City. He
could see the low coastline of mangrove swamps laced with
inlets, the shark fins, the stagnant seawater.

HARBOR POINT

arly morning mist . . . birdcalls . . . howler monkeys like wind in the trees. Fifty armed partisans are moving north over Panama jungle trails. Unshaven faces at once alert and drawn with fatigue, and a rapid gait that is almost a jog indicate a long forced march without sleep. The rising sun picks out their faces.

Noah Blake: twenty, a tall red-haired youth with brown eyes, his face dusted with freckles. Bert Hansen: a Swede with light blue eyes. Clinch Todd: a powerful youth with long arms and something sleepy and quiescent in his brown eyes flecked with points of light. Paco: a Portuguese with Indian and Negro blood. Sean Brady: black Irish with curly black hair and a quick wide smile.

Young Noah Blake is screwing the pan onto a flintlock pistol, testing the spring, oiling the barrel and stock. He holds the pistol up to his father, who examines it critically. Finally he nods. . . .

"Aye, son, that can go out with the Blake mark on it. . . ."

"Old Lady Norton stuck her head in the shop and said I shouldn't be working on the Lord's Day."

"And she shouldn't be sniffing her long snot-dripping nose into my shop on the Lord's Day or any other. The

30

Nortons have never bought so much as a ha'penny measure of nails off me." His father looks around the shop, his fingers hooked in his wide belt. Lean and red-haired, he has the face of a mechanic: detached, factual, a face that minds its own business and expects others to do the same. "We'll be moving to the city, son, where nobody cares if you go to church or not. . . ."

"Chicago, Father?"

"No, son, Boston. On the sea. We have relations there."

Father and son put on coats and gloves. They lock the shop and step out into the muted streets of the little snowbound village on Lake Michigan. As they walk through the snow, villagers pass. Some of the greetings are quick and cold with averted faces.

"Is it all right if my friends come to dinner, Father? They'll be bringing fish and bread. . . ."

"All right with me, son. But they aren't well seen here. . . . There's talk in the village, son. Bad talk about all of you. If it wasn't for Bert Hansen's father being a shipowner and one of the richest men in town there'd be more than talk. . . . Quicker we move the better."

"Could the others come too?"

"Well, son, I could use some more hands in the shop. No limit to how many guns we can sell in a seaport like Boston . . . and I'm thinking maybe Mr. Hansen would pay to get his son out of here. . . ."

Spring morning, doves call from the woods. Noah Blake and his father, Bert Hansen, Clinch Todd, Paco, and Sean Brady board a boat with their luggage stacked on deck. The villagers watch from the pier.

Mrs. Norton sniffs and says in her penetrating voice, "Good riddance to the lot of them." She glances sideways at her husband.

"I share the same views," he says hastily.

Boston: two years later. Mr. Blake has prospered. He works now on contracts from shipowners, and his guns are standard issue. He has remarried. His wife is a quiet refined girl from New York. Her family are well-to-do importers and merchants with political connections. Mr. Blake plans to open a New York branch, and there is talk of army and navy contracts. Noah Blake is studying navigation. He wants to be a ship's captain, and all five of the boys want to ship out.

"Wait till you find the right ship," Mr. Blake tells them.

One winter day, Noah is walking on the waterfront with Bert, Clinch, Sean and Paco. They notice a ship called *The Great White*. Rather small but very clean and trim. A man leans over the rail. He has a beefy red smiling face and cold blue eyes.

"You boys looking for a ship?"

"Maybe," says Noah cautiously.

"Well, come aboard."

He meets them at the gangplank. "I'm Mr. Thomas, First Mate." He extends a hand like callused beef and shakes hands with each boy in turn. He leads the way to the master's cabin. "This is Captain Jones—master of *The Great White*. These boys are looking for a ship . . . maybe . . ."

The boys nod politely. Captain Jones looks at them in silence. He is a man of indeterminate age with a gray-green pallor. He speaks at length, in a flat voice, his lips barely moving.

"Well, I could use five deckhands. . . . You boys had any experience?"

"Yes. On the Great Lakes." Noah indicates Bert Hansen. "His father owned fishing boats."

"Aye," says Captain Jones, "freshwater sailing. The sea's another kettle of fish."

"I've studied navigation," Noah puts in.

"Have you now? And what would be your name, lad?"

"Noah Blake."

An almost imperceptible glance passes between the Captain and the first mate.

"And your trade, lad?"

"Gunsmith."

"Well, now, you wouldn't be Noah Blake's son would you?"

"Yes, sir, I would."

Once again the glance flickers between the two men. Then Captain Jones leans back in his chair and looks at the boys with his dead, fishy eyes.

"We'll be sailing in three days' time ... New York, Charleston, Jamaica, Vera Cruz. Two months down, more or less, and two months back.... I pay ten pounds a month for deckhands."

Noah Blake tries to look unimpressed. This is twice as much as any other captain has offered.

"Well, sir, I'll have to discuss it with my father."

"To be sure, lad. You can sign the Articles tomorrow if you're so minded ... all five of you."

Noah can hardly wait to tell his father. "I mean that's good, isn't it?"

"Aye, son. Perhaps a little too good. Captain Jones's name is not so white as his ship. He's known as Opium Jones in the trade. He'll be carrying opium, guns, powder, shot, and tools. And he's not too particular who he trades with. ..."

"Anything wrong with that, Father?"

"No. He's no better and no worse than most of the others. Only thing I can't figure is why he's paying double wages for his deckhands."

"Maybe he'd rather have five good hands than ten waterfront drunks."

"Maybe.... Well, go if you like. But keep your eyes open."

THE PRIVATE ASSHOLE

The name is Clem Williamson Snide. I am a private asshole.

As a private investigator I run into more death than the law allows. I mean the law of averages. There I am outside the hotel room waiting for the corespondent to reach a crescendo of amorous noises. I always find that if you walk in just as he goes off he won't have time to disengage himself and take a swing at you. When me and the house dick open the door with a passkey, the smell of shit and bitter almonds blows us back into the hall. Seems they both took a cyanide capsule and fucked until the capsules dissolved. A real messy love death.

Another time I am working on a routine case of industrial sabotage when the factory burns down killing twenty-three people. These things happen. I am a man of the world. Going to and fro and walking up and down in it.

Death smells. I mean it has a special smell, over and above the smell of cyanide, carrion, blood, cordite or burnt flesh. It's like opium. Once you smell it you never forget. I can walk down a street and get a whiff of opium smoke and I know someone is kicking the gong around.

I got a whiff of death as soon as Mr. Green walked into my office. You can't always tell whose death it is. Could be Green, his wife, or the missing son he wants me to find.

Last letter from the island of Spetsai two months ago. After a month with no word the family made inquiries by long-distance phone.

"The embassy wasn't at all helpful," said Mr. Green.

I nodded. I knew just how unhelpful they could be.

"They referred us to the Greek police. Fortunately, we found a man there who speaks English."

"That would be Colonel Dimitri."

"Yes. You know him?"

I nodded, waiting for him to continue.

"He checked and could find no record that Jerry had left the country, and no hotel records after Spetsai."

"He could be visiting someone."

"I'm sure he would write."

"You feel then that this is not just an instance of neglect on his part, or perhaps a lost letter? . . . That happens in the Greek islands. . . ."

"Both Mrs. Green and I are convinced that something is wrong."

"Very well, Mr. Green, there is the question of my fee: a hundred dollars a day plus expenses and a thousand-dollar retainer. If I work on a case two days and spend two hundred dollars, I refund six hundred to the client. If I have to leave the country, the retainer is two thousand. Are these terms satisfactory?"

"Yes."

"Very good. I'll start right here in New York. Sometimes I have been able to provide the client with the missing person's address after a few hours' work. He may have written to a friend."

"That's easy. He left his address book. Asked me to mail it to him care of American Express in Athens." He passed me the book.

"Excellent."

Now, on a missing-person case I want to know everything the client can tell me about the missing person, no matter how seemingly unimportant and irrelevant. I want to know preferences in food, clothes, colors, reading, entertainment, use of drugs and alcohol, what cigarette brand he smokes, medical history. I have a questionnaire printed with five pages of questions. I got it out of the filing cabinet and passed it to him.

"Will you please fill out this questionnaire and bring it back here day after tomorrow. That will give me time to check out the local addresses."

"I've called most of them," he said curtly, expecting me to take the next plane for Athens.

"Of course. But friends of an M.P.—missing person— are not always honest with the family. Besides, I daresay some of them have moved or had their phones disconnected. Right?" He nodded. I put my hands on the questionnaire. "Some of these questions may seem irrelevant but they all add up. I found a missing person once from knowing that he could wriggle his ears. I've noticed that you are left-handed. Is your son also left-handed?"

"Yes, he is."

"You can skip that question. Do you have a picture of him with you?"

He handed me a photo. Jerry was a beautiful kid. Slender, red hair, green eyes far apart, a wide mouth. Sexy and kinky-looking.

"Mr. Green, I want all the photos of him you can find. If I use any I'll have copies made and return the originals. If he did any painting, sketching, or writing I'd like to see that too. If he sang or played an instrument I want recordings. In fact, any recordings of his voice. And please bring if possible some article of clothing that hasn't been dry-cleaned since he wore it."

"It's true then that you use uh psychic methods?"

"I use any methods that help me to find the missing person. If I can locate him in my own mind that makes it easier to locate him outside it."

"My wife is into psychic things. That's why I came to you. She has an intuition that something has happened to him and she says only a psychic can find him."

That makes two of us, I thought. He wrote me a check for a thousand dollars. We shook hands.

I went right to work. Jim, my assistant, was out of town on an industrial-espionage case—he specializes in electronics. So I was on my own. Ordinarily I don't carry iron on an M.P. case, but this one smelled of danger. I put on my snub-nosed 38, in a shoulder holster. Then I unlocked a drawer and put three joints of the best Colombian, laced with hash, into my pocket. Nothing like a joint to break the ice and stir the memory. I also took a deck of heroin. It buys more than money sometimes.

Most of the addresses were in the SoHo area. That meant lofts, and that often means the front door is locked. So I started with an address on Sixth Street.

She opened the door right away, but she kept the chain on. Her pupils were dilated, her eyes running, and she was snuffling, waiting for the Man. She looked at me with hatred.

I smiled. "Expecting someone else?"

"You a cop?"

"No. I'm a private investigator hired by the family to find Jerry Green. You knew him."

"Look, I don't have to talk to you."

"No, you don't have to. But you might want to." I showed her the deck of heroin. She undid the chain.

The place was filthy—dishes stacked in a sink, cockroaches running over them. The bathtub was in the kitchen and hadn't been used for a long time. I sat down gingerly in a chair with the springs showing. I held the deck in my hand where she could see it. "You got any pictures of him?"

She looked at me and she looked at the heroin. She rummaged in a drawer, and tossed two pictures onto a coffee table that wobbled. "Those should be worth something."

They were. One showed Jerry in drag, and he made a beautiful girl. The other showed him standing up naked with a hard-on. "Was he gay?"

"Sure. He liked getting fucked by Puerto Ricans and having his picture took."

"He pay you?"

"Sure, twenty bucks. He kept most of the pictures."

"Where'd he get the money?"

"I don't know."

She was lying. I went into my regular spiel. "Now look, I'm not a cop. I'm a private investigator paid by his family. I'm paid to find him, that's all. He's been missing for two months." I started to put the heroin back into my pocket and that did it.

"He was pushing C."

I tossed the deck onto the coffee table. She locked the door behind me.

Later that evening, over a joint, I interviewed a nice young gay couple, who simply *adored* Jerry.

"Such a sweet boy . . ."

"So understanding . . ."

"Understanding?"

"About gay people. He even marched with us. . . ."

"And look at the postcard he sent us from Athens."

It was a museum postcard showing a statue of a nude youth found at Kouros. "Wasn't that cute of him?"

Very cute, I thought.

I interviewed his steady girl friend, who told me he was all mixed up.

"He had to get away from his mother's influence and find himself. We talked it all over."

I interviewed everyone I could find in the address book. I talked to waiters and bartenders all over the SoHo area: Jerry was a nice boy . . . polite . . . poised . . . a bit reserved. None of them had an inkling of his double life as a coke pusher and homosexual transvestite. I see I am going to need some more heroin on this one. That's easy. I know some narco boys who owe me a favor. It takes an ounce and a ticket to San Francisco to buy some names from the junky chick.

Seek and you shall find. I nearly found an ice pick in my stomach. Knock and it shall be opened unto you. Often it wasn't opened unto me. But I finally found the somebody who: a twenty-year-old Puerto Rican kid named Kiki, very handsome and quite fond of Jerry in his way. Psychic too, and into Macambo magic. He told me Jerry had the mark of death on him.

"What was his source for the coke?"

His face closed over. "I don't know."

"Can't blame you for not knowing. May I suggest to you that his source was a federal narc?"

His deadpan went deader. "I didn't tell you anything."

"Did he hear voices? Voices giving him orders?"

"I guess he did. He was controlled by something"

I gave him my card. "If you ever need anything let me know."

Mr. Green showed up the next morning with a stack of photos. The questionnaire I had given him had been neatly filled out on a typewriter. He also brought a folio of sketches and a green knitted scarf. The scarf reeked of death.

I glanced at the questionnaire. Born April 18, 1951, in Little America, Wyoming. "Admiral Byrd welcomes you aboard the Deep Freeze Special." I looked through the photos: Jerry as a baby ... Jerry on a horse ... Jerry with a wide sunlit grin holding up a string of trout ... graduation pictures ... Jerry as the Toff in the high school play *A Night at an Inn*. They all looked exactly as they should look. Like he was playing the part expected of him. There were about fifty recent photos, all looking like Jerry.

Take fifty photos of anyone. There will be some photos where the face is so different you can hardly recognize the subject. I mean most people have many faces. Jerry had *one*. Don Juan says anyone who always looks like the same person isn't a person. He is a person impersonator.

I looked at Jerry's sketches. Good drawing, no talent. Empty and banal as sunlight. There were also a few poems, so bad I couldn't read them. Needless to say, I didn't tell Mr. Green what I had found out about Jerry's sex and drug habits. I just told him that no one I had talked to had heard from Jerry since his disappearance, and that I was ready to leave for Athens at once if he still wanted to retain me. Money changed hands.

At the Athens Hilton I got Dimitri on the phone and told him I was looking for the Green boy.

"Ah yes ... we get so many of these cases ... our time and resources are limited."

"I understand. But I've got a bad feeling about this one. He had some kinky habits."

"S-M?"

"Sort of . . . and underworld connections. . . ." I didn't want to mention C over the phone.

"If I find anything out I'll let you know."

"Thanks. I'm going out to Spetsai tomorrow to have a look around. Be back on Thursday. . . ."

I called Skouras in Spetsai. He's the tourist agent there. He owns or leases villas and rents out apartments during the season. He organizes tours. He owns the discotheque. He is the first man any traveler to Spetsai sees, and the last, since he is also the agent for transport.

"Yes, I know about it. Had a call from Dimitri. Glad to help any way I can. You need a room?"

"If possible I'd like the room he had."

"You can have any room you want . . . the season is over."

For once the hovercraft was working. I was in luck. The hovercraft takes an hour and the boat takes six.

Yes, Skouras remembered Jerry. Jerry arrived with some young people he'd met on the boat—two Germans with rucksacks and a Swedish girl with her English boyfriend. They stayed at one of Skouras's villas on the beach—the end villa, where the road curves out along the sea wall. I knew the place. I'd stayed there once three years earlier in 1970.

"Anything special about the others?"

"Nothing. Looked like thousands of other young people who swarm over the islands every summer. They stayed a week. The others went on to Lesbos. Jerry went back to Athens alone."

Where did they eat? Where did they take coffee? Skouras knew. He knows everything that goes on in Spetsai.

"Go to the discotheque?"

"Every night. The boy Jerry was a good dancer."

"Anybody in the villa now?"

"Just the caretaker and his wife."

He gave me the keys. I noticed a worn copy of *The Magus* by John Fowles. As soon as anyone walks into his office, Skouras knows whether he should lend him the book. He has his orders. Last time I was there he lent me the book and I read it. Even rode out on a horse to look at the house of the Magus and fell off the horse on the way back. I pointed to the book. "By any chance . . ."

He smiled. "Yes. I lent him the book and he returned it when he left. Said he found it most interesting."

"Could I borrow it again?"

"Of course."

The villa stood a hundred feet from the beach. The apartment was on the second floor—three bedrooms off a hall, kitchen and bathroom at the end of the hall, balcony along one side of the building. There was a musty smell, dank and chilly, blinds down. I pulled up the blinds in all three bedrooms and selected the middle one, where I had stayed before. Two beds, two chairs, coat hangers on nails in the wall.

I switched on an electric heater and took my recorder out of its case. This is a very special recorder designed and assembled by my assistant, Jim, and what it won't pick up isn't there. It is also specially designed for cut-ins and overlays, and you can switch from Record to Playback without stopping the machine.

I recorded a few minutes in all three rooms. I recorded the toilet flushing and the shower running. I recorded the water running in the kitchen sink, the rattle of dishes, and the opening and closing and hum of the refrigerator. I recorded on the balcony. Now I lay down on the bed and read some selections from *The Magus* into the recorder.

I will explain exactly how these recordings are made.

I want an hour of Spetsai: an hour of places where my
M.P. has been and the sounds he has heard. But not in
sequence. I don't start at the beginning of the tape and record
to the end. I spin the tape back and forth, cutting in at
random so that *The Magus* may be cut off in the middle
of a word by a flushing toilet, or *The Magus* may cut into
sea sounds. It's a sort of *I Ching* or table-tapping procedure.
How random is it actually? Don Juan says that nothing is
random to a man of knowledge: everything he sees or hears
is there just at that time waiting to be seen and heard.

I get out my camera and take pictures of the three
rooms, the bathroom, and the kitchen. I take pictures from
the balcony. I put the machine back in the case and go
outside, recording around the villa and taking pictures at
the same time: pictures of the villa; a picture of the black
cat that belongs to the caretaker; pictures of the beach, which
is empty now except for a party of hardy Swedes.

I have lunch in a little restaurant on the beach where
Jerry and his friends used to eat. Mineral water and a salad.
The proprietor remembers me and we shake hands. Coffee
at the waterfront café where Jerry and his friends took coffee.
Record. Take pictures. I cover the post office, the two kiosks
that sell imported cigarettes and newspapers. The one place
I don't record is in Skouras's office. He wouldn't like that.
I can hear him loud and clear: "I'm a landlord and not
a detective. I don't want your M.P. in my office. He's bad
news."

I go back to the villa by a different route, covering
the bicycle rental agency. It is now three o'clock. A time
when Jerry would most likely be in his room reading. I
read some more of *The Magus* into the recorder with flushing
toilets, running water, my footsteps in the hall, blinds being
raised and lowered. I listen to what I have on tape, with

special attention to the cut-ins. I take a walk along the sea wall and play the tape back to the sea and the wind.

Dinner in a restaurant where Jerry and his friends ate the night they arrived. This restaurant is recommended by Skouras. I take my time with several ouzos before a dinner of red snapper and Greek salad, washed down with retsina. After dinner I go out to the discotheque to record some of the music Jerry danced to. The scene is really dead. A German countess is dancing with some local youths.

Next day there was a wind and the hovercraft was grounded. I took the noon boat and after six hours was back in my room at the Hilton.

I took out a bottle of Johnny Walker Black Label duty-free scotch and ordered a soda siphon and ice from Hilton room service. I put Jerry's graduation picture in a silver frame on the desk, assembled the questionnaire, and put the tape recorder with an hour of Spetsai beside it. The waiter came in with the ice and soda siphon.

"Is that your son, sir?"

I said yes because it was the easy thing to say. I poured myself a small drink and lit a Senior Service. I started thinking out loud, cutting into the tape. . . .

"Suspected to be involved in some capacity: Marty Blum, a small-time operator with big-time connections. Was in Athens at or about the time young Jerry disappeared.

"Helen and Van—also in Athens at the time. Van was trying to get a permit to run a disintoxication clinic on one of the islands. He didn't get it. Left Athens for Tangier. Left Tangier for New York. Trouble at immigration. Thought to be in Toronto." What did I know about these two birds? Plenty. "Doctor Van: age, fifty-seven; nationality, Canadian. Dope-pushing and abortions sidelines and front for his real specialty, which is transplant operations. Helen, his assistant: age, sixty; nationality, Australian. Masseuse, abortionist, suspected jewel thief and murderess."

The Countess Minsky Stahlinhof de Gulpa, known as Minny to her friends and sycophants: a heavy woman like a cold fish under tons of gray shale. "White Russian and Italian descent. Stratospherically wealthy, near the billion mark. The source of her wealth: manipulation of commodity prices. She moves into a poor country like Morocco and buys up basic commodities like sugar, kerosene, and cooking oil, holds them off the market in her warehouses, then puts them back on the market at a higher price. The Countess has squeezed her vast wealth out of the poorest people. She has other interests than money. She is a very big operator indeed. She owns immense estates in Chile and Peru and has some secret laboratories there. She has employed biochemists and virologists. Indication: genetic experiments and biologic weapons."

And what of the Countess de Vile? "De Vile: very wealthy but not Gulpa's strata. A depraved, passionate and capricious woman, evil as Circe. Extensive underworld and police contacts. On close terms with Mafia dons and police chiefs in Italy, New York, Morocco, and South America. A frequent visitor at the Countess de Gulpa's South American retreat. Several unsolved missing-person cases, involving boys of Jerry's age, point to the South American laboratories as terminal."

I glanced through the questionnaire. "Medical history: scarlet fever at the age of four." Now, scarlet fever is a rarity since the introduction of antibiotics. "Could there have been a misdiagnosis?"

All this I was feeding into the recorder in pieces, and a lot more. An article I had just finished reading when Mr. Green came into my office. This was an article on head transplants performed on monkeys, the Sunday *Times*, December 9, 1973. I now took it out of a file and read parts of it into the recorder. "Monkey heads transplanted onto monkey bodies can now survive for about a week. The drawing above portrays controversial operation. 'Technically a human head transplant is possible,' Dr. White says, 'but scientifically there would be no point.' "

My first meeting with Mr. Green: the smell of death, and something shifty about him. From talking to Jerry's friends, I found out that this was a family trait. They all described him as hard to figure or hard to pin down. Finally I turned on the TV. I played the tape back at low volume while I watched an Italian western with Greek subtitles, keeping my attention on the screen so I was subconsciously hearing the tape. They were hanging a rustler from horseback when the phone rang.

It was Dimitri. "Well, Snide, I think we have found your missing person . . . unfortunately."

"You mean dead?"

"Yes. Embalmed, in fact." He paused. "And without his head."

"*What?*"

"Yes. Head severed at the shoulders."

"Fingerprints check?"

"Yes."

I waited for the rest of it.

"Cause of death is uncertain. Some congestion in the lungs. May have been strangulation. The body was found in a trunk."

"Who found it?"

"I did. I happened to be down at the port double-checking the possibility that the boy may have left by freighter, and I saw a trunk being carried aboard a ship with Panamanian registry. Well, something about the way they were carrying it ... the disposition of the weight, you understand. I had the trunk returned to customs and opened. The uh the method of embalming ... unusual to say the least. The body was perfectly preserved but no embalming fluid had been used. It was also completely nude."

"Can I have a look?"

"Of course. ..."

The Greek doctor had studied at Harvard and he spoke perfect English. Various internal organs were laid out on a white shelf. The body, or what was left of it, was in a fetal position.

"Considering that this boy has been dead at least a month, the internal organs are in a remarkable state of preservation," said the doctor.

I looked at the body. Pubic, rectal and leg hairs were bright red. However, he was redder than he should have been. I pointed to some red blotches around the nipples, crotch, thighs and buttocks. "What's that? Looks like some kind of rash."

"I was wondering about that. ... Of course it could have been an allergy. Redheads are particularly liable to allergic reactions, but—" He paused. "It looks like scarlet fever."

"We are checking all hospitals and private clinics for scarlet fever admissions," Dimitri put in, "... or any other condition that could produce such a rash."

I turned to the doctor. "Doctor, would you say that the amputation was a professional job?"

"Definitely."

"All questionable doctors and clinics will be checked," said Dimitri.

The preservative seemed to be wearing off, and the body gave off a sweet musky smell that turned me quite sick. I could see Dimitri was feeling it too, and so was the doctor.

"Can I see the trunk?"

The trunk was built like an icebox: a layer of cork, and the inside lined with thin steel.

"The steel is magnetized," Dimitri told me. "Look." He took out his car keys and they stuck to the side of the trunk.

"Could this have had any preservative effect?"

"The doctor says no."

Dimitri drove me back to the Hilton. "Well, it looks like your case is closed, Mr. Snide."

"I guess so . . . any chance of keeping this out of the papers?"

"Yes. This is not America. Besides, a thing like this, you understand . . ."

"Bad for the tourist business."

"Well, yes."

I had a call to make to the next of kin. "Afraid I have some bad news for you, Mr. Green."

"Yes?"

"Well, the boy has been found."

"Dead, you mean?"

"I'm sorry, Mr. Green. . . ."

"Was he murdered?"

"What makes you say that?"

"It's my wife. She's sort of, well, psychic. She had a dream."

"I see. Well, yes, it looks like murder. We're keeping it out of the papers, because publicity would impede the investigation at this point."

"I want to retain you again, Mr. Snide. To find the murderer of my son."

"Everything is being done, Mr. Green. The Greek police are quite efficient."

"We have more confidence in you."

"I'm returning to New York in a few days. I'll contact you as soon as I arrive."

The trail was a month old at least. I was fairly sure the murderer or murderers were no longer in Greece. No point in staying on. But there was something else to check out on the way back.

FEVER SPOOR

I stop over in London. There is somebody I want to see there, if I can find him without too much trouble. Could save me a side trip to Tangier.

I find him in a gay bar called the Amigo. He is nattily dressed, with a well-kept beard and shifty eyes. The Arabs say he has the eyes of a thief. But he has a rich wife and doesn't need to steal.

"Well," he says. "The private eye.... Business or pleasure?"

I look around. "Only business would bring me here." I show him Jerry's picture. "He was in Tangier last summer, I believe."

He looks at the picture. "Sure, I remember him. A cock-teaser."

"Missing-person case. Remember who he was with?"

"Some hippie kids."

The description sounds like the kids Jerry was with in Spetsai. Props. "Did he go anywhere else?"

"Marrakesh, I think."

I am about to finish my drink and leave.

"Oh, you remember Peter Winkler who used to run the English Pub? Did you know he was dead?"

I haven't heard, but I am not much interested. "So? Who or what killed him?"

"Scarlet fever."

I nearly spill my drink. "Look, people don't die of scarlet fever now. In fact, they rarely get it."

"He was living out on the mountain ... the Hamilton summer house. It's quite isolated, you know. Seems he was alone and the phone was out of order. He tried to walk to the next house down the road and collapsed. They took him to the English hospital."

"That would finish anyone off. And I suppose Doc Peterson was in attendance? Made the diagnosis and signed the death certificate?"

"Who else? He's the only doctor there. But what are you so stirred up about? I never thought you and Winkler were very close."

I cool it. "We weren't. It's just that I started out to be a doctor and I don't like to see a case botched."

"I wouldn't say he botched it. Shot him full of pen strep. Seems he was too far gone to respond."

"Yeah. Pen strep is right for scarlet fever. He must have been practically dead on arrival."

"Oh, not quite. He was in the hospital about twenty-four hours."

I don't say any more. I've said too much already. Looks like I'll have to make that side trip to Tangier.

I checked into the Rembrandt and took a taxi to the Marshan. It was 3:00 P.M. when I rang the doctor's bell. He was a long time coming to the door, and was not pleased to see me.

"I'm sorry to disturb you during the siesta hour, Doctor, but I'm only in town for a short stay and it's rather important. . . ."

He was not altogether mollified but he led me into his office.

"Doctor Peterson, I have been retained by the heirs of Peter Winkler to investigate the circumstances of his death. The fact that he was found unconscious by the side of a road has led them to speculate that there might be some question of accidental death. That would mean double indemnity on the insurance."

"No question whatsoever. There wasn't a mark on him—except for the rash, that is. Well, his pockets were turned inside out, but what do you expect in a place like this?"

"You're quite sure that he died of scarlet fever?"

"Quite sure. A classical case. I think that the fever may have caused brain damage and that is why he didn't respond to antibiotics. Cerebral hemorrhage may have been a contributory cause. . . ."

"There was bleeding?"

"Yes . . . from the nose and mouth."

"And this couldn't have been a concussion?"

"Absolutely no sign of concussion."

"Was he delirious at any time?"

"Yes. For some hours."

"Did he say anything? Anything that might indicate he had been attacked?"

"It was gibberish in some foreign language. I administered morphine to quiet him."

"I'm sure you did the right thing, Doctor, and I will report to his heirs that there is nothing to support a claim of accidental death. That is your considered opinion?"

"It is. He died of scarlet fever and/or complications attendant on scarlet fever."

I thanked him and left. I had some more questions, but I was sure he couldn't or wouldn't answer them. I went back to the hotel and did some work with the recorder.

At seven o'clock I walked over to the English Pub. There was a young Arab behind the bar whom I recognized as one of Peter's boyfriends. Evidently he had inherited the business. I showed him Jerry's picture.

"Oh yes. Mister Jerry. Peter like him very much. Give him free drinks. He never make out though. Boy just lead him on."

I asked about Peter's death.

"Very sad. Peter alone in house. Tell me he want to rest few days."

"Did he seem sick?"

"Not sick. He just look tired. Mister Jerry gone to Marrakesh and I think Peter a little sad."

I could have checked hospitals in Marrakesh for scarlet fever cases, but I knew already what I needed to know. I knew why Peter hadn't responded to antibiotics. He didn't have scarlet fever. He had a virus infection.

THE STRANGER

The next day the five boys signed on with *The Great White* and moved into the forecastle. Three youths were already there. They introduced themselves as Bill, Guy, and Adam. Noah noticed that they all had the same pale faces and fish-eyes as Captain Jones. The forecastle was clean and newly painted, with a faint hospital smell of carbolic.

An impish red-haired boy of about fifteen brings mugs of tea on a tray. "I'm Jerry, the cabin boy. Anything you want, just let me know. It's a pleasure to serve you, gentlemen."

Bill, Guy, and Adam wash down black pellets with the tea.

"What's that?" Brady asks.

"Oh, just something to keep out the cold."

The boys are kept busy loading cargo and supplies. Mr. Thomas gives instructions in a quiet voice. He seems easygoing and good-natured. But his eyes make Noah uneasy—they are cold as winter ice.

Pages from Noah Blake's diary:

Tuesday, Feb. 5, 1702: Today we sailed. Despite Captain Jones's slighting remarks about freshwater sailing, our experience on the lakes stands us in good stead. I notice that

Guy, Bill, and Adam, though they are very thin and pale and sick-looking, are good seamen and seem immune to cold and fatigue.

An hour before sailing, a carriage pulled up at the wharf and two people got out and came on board. I could not see them clearly, for they were wearing furs with hoods, but I could tell that they were young and looked much alike. When the ship was clear of the harbor and on course, the cabin boy brought tea.

"Two passengers on board," he told us.

"Have you seen them?"

"Aye, I carried their luggage to the cabin."

"And what are they like?"

"More like leprechauns than humans. Green they are, green as shamrock."

"Green?"

"Aye, with smooth greenish faces. Twins, one a boy and one a girl. And rich too. You can smell the money off them. . . ."

Feb. 6, 1702: Neither the two passengers nor the captain has appeared on deck. Bert Hansen and myself have been given turns at the wheel. The food is good and plentiful and I have talked with the cook. His name is Charlie Lee. He is about twenty years old, half-black and half-Chinese. I'm thinking there is something between him and the cabin boy. We will dock in New York tomorrow.

Feb. 7, 1702: Too late to dock. We are riding at anchor. There is naught to be done, and after the evening meal we had a talk with Guy, Adam, and Bill. I have found out what it is that they take with their tea night and morning: opium. They have enough to last them the voyage.

"And should we need more, we have but to ask the Captain," said Guy.

"Sure and he should be made of the stuff," Sean Brady put in. "Seeing his name is Opium Jones."

It seems they have shipped with Captain Jones before. "He pays double because he only wants certain type people on his ship."

"And what type would that be?"

"Them as do the work, mind their own business, and keep their mouths shut to outsiders."

Feb. 8, 1702: Today we docked in New York. Captain Jones appeared on deck and guided the ship into the harbor. I will say for him he knows his business when he chooses to mind it. A carriage was waiting at the pier and the two passengers got in and were driven away.

We were kept busy most of the day loading and unloading cargo under the supervision of Mr. Thomas. Captain Jones went ashore on business of some kind. In the late afternoon we were allowed ashore. There is more bustle here than in Boston and more ships, of course. We were immediately set upon by panderers extolling the beauty and sound condition of their whores. When we told them to be off and fuck their wares they showered us with insults from a safe distance.

I have a letter to the Pembertons, the parents of my stepmother, and father impressed on me the importance of paying my respects and instructed me in how to conduct myself. It seems that the Pemberton family is well known here, and I had no trouble finding the house, which is of red brick and very imposing, with four stories.

I rang the bell and a servant came to the door and asked my business in somewhat peremptory tones. I presented him with the letter. He told me to wait and went inside.

When he returned a few minutes later, his manner was quite respectful. He told me that Mr. Pemberton would be happy to entertain me for dinner the following night at eight o'clock.

Feb. 9, 1702: This night I had dinner with the Pembertons. Arriving a few minutes early I walked up and down until the chimes sounded eight. My father has admonished me always to be punctual for appointments and never under any circumstances to be early. The servant showed me into an ornately furnished room with portraits and a marble fireplace.

Mr. Pemberton greeted me most politely. He is a trim smallish man with white hair and twinkling blue eyes. He then presented me to his wife, who extended a hand without getting up, smiling as though it hurt her to do so. I took an immediate dislike to her, which I am sure was reciprocated.

The other people present, I soon realized, were none other than the passengers on board *The Great White*: two of the strangest and most beautiful people I have ever seen. They are twins—one a boy, the other a girl—about twenty years old. They have greenish complexions, straight black hair, and jet-black eyes. Both possess such ease and grace of manner that I was quite dazzled. The names I believe are Juan and María Cocuera de Fuentes. When I shook hands with the boy a tremor passed through me and I was glad of the diversion when Mr. Pemberton offered me a glass of sherry. While we were having the sherry, a Mr. Vermer was announced. He is as portly as Mr. Pemberton is trim, and gives a great impression of wealth and power.

Shortly thereafter dinner was served. Mr. Pemberton took the head of the table, with Mr. Vermer on his right and María de Fuentes on his left. I was seated opposite Juan de Fuentes, with Mrs. Pemberton on my right—though I would gladly have been as far away from her as possible.

The de Fuentes twins had come from Mexico and were on their way to Vera Cruz. The talk was mostly about business, trade, mining, and the produce of Mexico.

María spoke in her cool clear voice.... "Crops now grown only in the Middle and Far East could be introduced, since the soil and climate is suitable."

I noted that the Pembertons and Mr. Vermer defer to the twins and listen respectfully to their opinions. Several times Mr. Pemberton addressed a question to me, and I answered briefly and politely, as my father had instructed me. When I told him I planned to be a sea captain he looked a little vague and distracted and said that the sea was a good thing for a young man ... to be sure, a master's certificate would do no harm. However, the opportunities in the family business were not to be overlooked.

Mr. Vermer expressed concern with regard to the political instability of Mexico. María de Fuentes replied that the introduction of *suitable crops* would undoubtedly produce a tranquilizing and stabilizing effect. She has a way of underscoring certain words with a special import. Mr. Vermer nodded and said, "Ah yes, sound economy brings sound politics."

I had a feeling that the talk would have been more open if I had not been present. Why then, I asked myself, had I been invited? The words of my father came back to me: "In the course of any meeting, try to discover what it is that is wanted from you." While I could not decide what it was, I knew that something very definite was wanted and expected from me. I surmised further that Mrs. Pemberton was less convinced of my potential usefulness than her husband, and that she considered my presence at the dinner table a hindrance and a waste of time.

At one point Juan de Fuentes looked straight into my eyes and once again I felt a tremor run through me and for a second had a most curious impression that we were alone at the table.

After dinner, I excused myself to return to the ship since we will be sailing before noon.

Feb. 10, 1702: The twins arrived shortly before sailing. Captain Jones took the wheel on leaving the harbor. We are heading south with a good wind. Weather very damp and cold.

Feb. 11, 1702: This morning I awoke with a sore throat, my head throbbing and feverish, and a congestion in my lungs—feeling barely able to rise from my bunk. Adam smiled and told me that the remedy was to hand. He carefully measured out six drops of opium tincture and I downed it with hot tea. In a few minutes a feeling of warmth and comfort spread from the back of my neck through my body. The soreness in my throat and the aching in my head disappeared as if by magic. I have been able to take my watch without difficulty. When I came in to sleep, the dose was repeated. There is an extraordinary clarity in my thoughts. I am unable to sleep. Writing this by candle.

I am asking myself where I come from, how I got here, and who I am. From earliest memory I have felt myself a stranger in the village of Harbor Point where I was born. Who was I? I remember mourning doves calling from the woods in summer dawn, and the long cold shut-in winters. Who was I? The stranger was footsteps in the snow a long time ago.

And who are the others—Brady, Hansen, Paco, Todd? Strangers like myself. I think that we came from another world and have been stranded here like mariners on some barren and hostile shore. I never felt that what we did together was wrong, but I fully understood the necessity and wisdom of concealing it from the villagers. Now that there is no need for concealment, I feel as if this ship is the home I had left and thought never to find again. But the voyage will end of course, and what then?

I know that my father will shortly be a wealthy man and that I could become, in course of time, wealthy myself. The prospect holds little appeal. Of what use is wealth if I must conform to customs that are as meaningless to me as they are obstructive of my true inclinations and desires? I am minded to seek my fortunes in the Red Sea or in South America. Perhaps I could find employment with the de Fuentes family.

Now the face of Juan drifts before my eyes, and divorced by the effects of opium from the urgings and pricklings of lust I can examine the vision dispassionately. I feel not only attraction but kinship. He too is a stranger, but he moves with ease and confidence among the terrestrials.

SHORE LEAVE

Feb. 12, 1702: For some reason we will not dock at Charleston as planned. The weather is milder each day.

The de Fuentes twins now walk about the deck familiarizing themselves with all the workings and parts of the ship. Everything they do or say seems to have some hidden purpose. Juan has asked me many questions relative to my trade as a gunsmith. Would it be possible to shoot arrows from a gun? I replied that it would and suddenly saw a picture of Indians attacking a settlement with arrows tipped in burning pitch. I cannot recall where I saw this picture before, probably in Boston. As the picture flashed through my mind Juan nodded and smiled and walked away. His twin sister has the manner and directness of a man, with none of the coy enticing ways usually found in her sex. In any case female blandishments would here fall on barren soil. Yet I must confess myself more attracted to her than to any woman I have yet seen.

Feb. 13, 1702: Good winds and fair weather continue. We no longer need our greatcoats.

Feb. 14, 1702: We are now off the coast of Florida and seldom out of sight of land since there are many islands.

Dolphins leap about the prow and flying fish scatter before us in silver showers. We are now able to work without shirts but Mr. Thomas has cautioned us to be careful of sunburn and to expose ourselves only for minutes at a time. Captain Jones appears on deck, scanning the islands through his telescope. I think he plans to put in at one of the islands for fresh water and provisions.

Feb. 15, 1702: Despite Mr. Thomas's warning, both Bert and myself have painful sunburns from the waist up, owing to our fair complexions, whereas Clinch, Sean, and Paco are unaffected. Bill, Guy, and Adam never take their shirts off. Charlie Lee, the cook, has some skill as physician though without formal training. He has given us an ointment to rub on our bodies, which has afforded considerable relief, and we have both taken some drops of opium tincture. Adam has given me a small bottle and showed me how to measure out the correct dose. He tells me the amount he takes would make us deathly sick and could be lethal.

Feb. 16, 1702: I am now recovered from the sunburn and my body is beginning to acquire a protective tan. This morning we all gathered at the rail to witness a great commotion in the water a few hundred yards ahead, occasioned by mackerel leaping to escape larger fish. Mr. Thomas gave the order to lower sail and issued fishing poles with spoons and triple hooks.

In a short time a number of great fish were flapping on the deck. These fish are known as yellowtails and are highly esteemed for the table. We were kept busy cleaning the fish, at which of course we are adept from our experience on the Great Lakes. Some were reserved for immediate use and the others salted and laid away. After the blood was washed from the decks we hoisted sail and proceeded on our way. The fresh fish has provided a most welcome change from a diet of salt cod and cornmeal, although the flavor is not as delicate as fish from fresh water.

Feb. 18, 1702: Dreamed this morning I was in a large workshop with tools, a forge, and gun parts scattered on a bench. I was examining a gun with a number of barrels welded together. I was trying to arrive at a method of firing the barrels in sequence. Juan was standing to one side and behind me. He pointed to an iron wheel with a handle and said something I did not catch because at this moment Clinch Todd came off his watch and awakened me, grumbling that we had ejaculated all over his blankets.

The wind has fallen and we are moving now at a few knots an hour.

Feb. 19, 20, 21, 1702: We are almost becalmed and take advantage of the slow movement to fish from the deck. I hooked a shark and the pole was torn from my hands and lost.

We seem to float on a sea of glass, like a painted ship. Tempers are short. Brady and Mr. Thomas got into an altercation and I thought they would come to blows.

Feb. 22, 1702: Today we put ashore on an uninhabited island to take on water and what provisions we could find. Captain Jones had spotted a stream through his telescope. We anchored in a bay between two points of land about two hundred yards from a beach with coconut palms behind it. The water here is so clear that you can see fish swimming at a considerable depth. We are sure at least to find abundant coconuts.

Mr. Thomas, Bert Hansen, Clinch Todd, Paco, Jerry the cabin boy and myself put ashore in a boat loaded with water kegs. We filled the kegs with fresh water and loaded them into the boat. Todd and Paco rowed back to the ship and returned with empty kegs. When sufficient water had been collected, we filled the boat a number of times with coconuts. It was now after noon. Mr. Thomas then gave us the rest of the day off to explore the island, admonishing us to be back on the beach before sundown. Before returning to the ship he issued to each of us a cutlass for the unlikely event we should encounter dangerous animals or hidden natives.

Following the stream we climbed to the summit of the island, a distance of about six hundred feet. From the summit we had a fine view of the whole island. *The Great White* appeared at that distance like a toy. On the far side of the island are a number of small bays and inlets, and we made our way down to a little beach surrounded on both sides by overhanging rocks. Here we stripped off our clothes and swam in the bay for half an hour, being careful not to venture too far out for fear of sharks. The water is wonderfully warm and buoyant, quite unlike the swimming in freshwater lakes.

Feeling hunger after our swim, we put out lines which we had brought and soon took a number of the fish known as red snapper, each one two or three pounds in weight. Five fish we fried in a pan, leaving the others on a string through the gills in the water. This most delectable fish we ate with our fingers, washing the meat down with coconut milk.

Feeling a great drowsiness after eating, we all lay down naked in the shade of a rock, Jerry with his head on my stomach and I in turn resting my head on Bert Hansen's stomach. Clinch and Paco lay on their backs, side by side, with an arm around the other's shoulders. The heat, our full stomachs, and the sound of gently lapping waves put us into a light sleep which lasted for about an hour.

I woke with a strong erection and found my companions in the same condition. We stood up stretching and comparing.

The breeze was rising and it was getting towards sundown. We put out our lines and caught enough fish to make a goodly string, and made our way back to the beach as speedily as possible. Jerry kept us all laughing, slashing with his cutlass at trees and branches with fierce snarls and pirate cries. Adam and Bill rowed ashore and took us back to the ship. Sail was raised and we got under way.

While we were gone a number of different fish had been taken from the ship, and for supper we had a spicy fish stew with grated coconut.

A shout from Jerry while we were eating brought us all to the rail, where we witnessed a wondrous sight known as the green flash, which occurs a moment after sunset. The whole western sky lit up a brilliant luminous green.

LETTRE DE MARQUE

Feb. 28, 1702: Today we were captured by pirates. At five o'clock in the afternoon a heavily armed ship came abreast of us flying the Dutch flag, which was then lowered and the black pirate flag raised. We were carrying no cannon, so resistance was out of the question and Captain Jones immediately gave the order to raise the flag of truce. We all gathered on deck, including the de Fuentes twins, who were impassive as always, scanning the pirate ship critically as if to assess its worth.

Shortly thereafter a boat was lowered and it rowed towards us. Standing in the stern was a slim blond youth, his gold-braided coat glittering in the sun. Beside him was a youth in short gray pants and shirt with a red scarf around his neck. The boat was rowed by what appeared to be a crew of women, singing as they rowed and turning towards us to leer and wink with their painted faces.

The companionway was lowered and the "women" scrambled aboard with the agility of monkeys and posted themselves about the deck with muskets and cutlasses. I perceived that they were, in fact, handsome youths in women's garb, their costumes being Oriental, of colored silks and brocade. The two youths then stepped on board, the one with his gold-braided coat open at the waist to show his slender brown chest and stomach, a brace of pistols inlaid with silver, and a cutlass at his belt. He was a striking figure: blond hair tied in a knot at the back of his head, aristocratic and well-formed features, possessing a most lordly bearing and grace of manner.

Captain Jones stepped forward. "I am Captain Jones, master of *The Great White*."

"And I am Captain Strobe, second in command on *The Siren*," said the youth.

They shook hands most amiably and if I am any judge are not strangers to each other. I was immediately convinced that the "capture" had been prearranged between them. Strobe then received the keys to the armory. Turning to us, he assured us that we had nothing to fear for our lives. He would take over the conduct of the ship and set its course, his men acting under the orders of Mr. Kelley, the quartermaster. He indicated the youth in gray shorts, who was leaning against the rail immobile as a statue, his face without expression, his pale gray eyes turned up towards the rigging. We would continue to act under the orders of Mr. Thomas.

Several of the boys descended to the boat and began passing up seabags containing apparently the personal effects of the boarding crew. When the boat was cleared, Strobe conducted Captain Jones and the de Fuentes twins to the companionway and two boys rowed them back to *The Siren*. Captain Strobe then opened a small keg of rum and the boys produced tankards from their bags. Approaching us in a purposeful and insinuating manner, wriggling their buttocks, they passed around little clay pipes.

"Hashish. Very good."

When it came my turn to smoke it caused me to cough greatly but soon I felt a lifting of my spirits and a vividness of pictures in my mind—together with a prickling in my groin and buttocks. Drums and flutes appeared and the boys began to dance and as they danced stripped off their clothes until they were dancing stark naked on the brightly colored silk scarves and dresses strewn about the deck. Captain Strobe stood on the poop deck playing a silver flute, the notes seeming to fall from a distant star. Only Mr. Thomas, at Strobe's side, seemed totally unconcerned, and for a second his bulky form was transparent before my eyes—probably an illusion produced by the drug.

Mr. Thomas was watching *The Siren* through his telescope. Finally, having received a signal that their sails were set, he gave the order to hoist sail on *The Great White*. Surprisingly enough we were able to carry out the order with no difficulty, the effect of hashish being such that one can shift easily from one activity to another. Kelley gave the same order in an unknown tongue to the dancing boys, who now acted in a seamanlike manner—some naked, some with scarfs twisted around their hips—as they went about their duties singing strange songs. So sails were speedily set and we got under way, for where I did not know.

Some of the boys have hammocks and sleep on deck, but we are often two to a bunk in the forecastle. Since we now have a double crew, there is much time with nothing to do, and I have been able to acquaint myself to some extent with the strange history of these transvestite boys.

Some of them are dancing boys from Morocco, others from Tripoli, Madagascar, and Central Africa. There are a few from India and the East Indies who have served on pirate vessels in the Red Sea, where they preyed on merchant vessels and other pirates alike, the method of operation being this: some would join the crew of a ship, selling their favors and insinuating themselves into key positions. Then the crew sights an apparently unarmed vessel carrying a cargo of beautiful women all singing and dancing lewdly and promising the mariners their bodies. Once on board the "women" pull out hidden pistols and cutlasses, while their accomplices on shipboard do the same, and *The Siren* now uncovers its cannons—so that the ship would often be taken without the loss of a single life. Often the boys would sign on as cooks— at which trade they all excel—and then drug the entire crew. However, word of their operations spread rapidly and they are now fleeing from pirates and naval patrols alike, having as the French say, *brûlé*—burnt down—the Red Sea area.

Kelley told me his story. He started his career as a merchant seaman. In the course of an argument he killed the quartermaster, for which he was tried and sentenced to hang. His ship at that time was in the harbor of Tangier. The sentence was carried out in the marketplace, but some pirates who were present cut him down, carried him to their ship, and revived him. It was thought that a man who had been hanged and brought back to life would not only bring luck to their venture but also ensure protection against the fate from which he had been rescued. While he was still insensible the pirates rubbed red ink into the hemp marks, so that he seemed to have a red rope always around his neck.

The pirate ship was commanded by Skipper Nordenholz, a renegade from the Dutch Navy who was still able to pass his ship as an honest merchant vessel flying the Dutch flag. Strobe was second in command. Barely had they left Tangier headed for the Red Sea via the Cape of Good Hope when a mutiny broke out. The crew was in disagreement as to the destination, being minded to head for the West Indies. They had also conceived a contempt for Strobe as an effeminate dandy. After he had killed five of the ringleaders they were forced to revise this opinion. The mutinous crew was then put ashore and a crew of acrobats and dancing boys taken on, since Nordenholz had already devised a way in which they could be put to use.

Kelley claims to have learned the secrets of death on the gallows, which gives him invincible skill as a swordsman and such sexual prowess that no man or woman can resist him, with the exception of Captain Strobe, whom he regards as more than human. *"Voici ma lettre de marque,"* he says, running his fingers along the rope mark. (A letter of marque was issued to privateers by their government, authorizing them to prey on enemy vessels in the capacity of accredited combatants, and thus distinguishing them from common pirates. Such a letter often, but by no means always, saved the bearer from the gallows.) Kelley tells me that the mere sight of his hemp marks instills in adversaries a weakness and terror equal to the apparition of Death Himself.

I asked Kelley what it feels like to be hanged.

"At first I was sensible of very great pain due to the weight of my body and felt my spirits in a strange commotion violently pressed upwards. After they reached my head, I saw a bright blaze of light which seemed to go out at my eyes with a flash. Then I lost all sense of pain. But after I was cut down, I felt such intolerable pain from the prickings and shootings as my blood and spirits returned that I wished those who cut me down could have been hanged."*

The reader may question how I find time to write this account on a sea voyage in a crowded forecastle. The answer is that I made very short notes each day, with the intent of expanding them later. I now have two hours of leisure each day to reconstruct a narrative from these notes, since Strobe has

* Daniel P. Mannix, *The History of Torture* (New York: Dell, 1964).

placed a desk and writing material at my disposal, being interested for some reason in printing my account.

Each evening all the boys strip and wash in buckets of salt water, whereupon various sexual games and contests take place. In one such game each boy places a gold piece on the deck, and the first to ejaculate wins the gold. There are also contests for distance.

Since there is plenty of powder and shot on board, there have been a few contests with pistols and muskets. I have won some gold, being careful not to best Kelley, though I am sure I could have done so. I feel that he could prove a most dangerous enemy. There is much here that I do not understand.

ARE YOU IN SALT

Back in New York I call the Greens from my loft. I've put $5,000 worth of security into this space. The windows are shatterproof glass with rolling bars. The door is two inches of solid steel from an old bank vault. It gives you a safe feeling, like being in Switzerland.

Mr. Green can see me right away. He gives an address on Spring Street. Middle-class loft ... big modern kitchen ... Siamese cat ... plants. Mrs. Green is a beautiful woman, red hair, green eyes, a faraway dreamy look. I notice *Journeys out of the Body, Psychic Discoveries Behind the Iron Curtain*, the Castaneda books. Mr. Green mixes me a Chivas Regal.

I clarify my position.... "Private investigator ... no authority to make an arrest ... I can only pass evidence along to the local police.... Frankly, in this case I can't hold out much hope of obtaining an arrest, let alone a conviction."

"We still want to retain you."

"Why, exactly?"

"We want to know the truth," said Mrs. Green. "Whether the killers can be brought to trial or not."

I pull out the questionnaire with Jerry's medical history. "It says here that Jerry had scarlet fever at the age of four."

"Yes. We were living in Saint Louis at the time," said Mrs. Green.

"Who was the doctor?"

"Old Doctor Greenbaum. He lived next door."

"Is he still alive?"

"No, he died ten years ago."

"And he made the diagnosis?"

"Yes."

"Would you say that he was a competent diagnostician?"

"Not really," said Mr. Green. "But why is this important?"

"Jerry apparently had an attack of scarlet fever or something similar shortly before he was killed." I turned to Mrs. Green. "Do you remember the details? How the illness started?"

"Why, yes. It was a Thursday and he had taken a ride with an English governess we had then. When he got back he was shivering and feverish and he had a rash. I thought it was measles and called Doctor Greenbaum. He said it wasn't a measles rash, that it was probably a light case of scarlet fever. He prescribed Aureomycin and the fever went away in a few days."

"Was Jerry delirious at any time during this illness?"

"Yes, as a matter of fact he was. He seemed quite frightened and talked about 'animals in the wall.' "

"Do you remember what animals, Mrs. Green?"

"He mentioned a giraffe and a kangaroo."

"Do you remember anything else?"

"... Yes," she said after a pause. "There was a strange smell in the room ... sort of a musky smell ... like a *zoo*."

"Did Doctor Greenbaum comment on this odor?"

"No, I think he had a cold at the time."

"Did you notice it, Mr. Green?"

"Well, yes, it was on the sheets and blankets when

we sent them to the cleaners.... Exactly how was Jerry killed, Mr. Snide?"

"A massive overdose of heroin."

"He wasn't—"

"No, he wasn't an addict, and the Greek police are convinced the heroin was not self-administered."

"Do you have any idea why he would have been murdered?"

"I'm not at all sure, Mr. Green. It could have been a case of mistaken identity."

When I got to the office the next day my assistant, Jim Brady, was already there, having come straight from the airport. He is very slim, six feet, 135 pounds, black Irish. Actually he is twenty-eight but he looks eighteen, and often has to show his I.D. card to be served in a bar. He handed me a packet from Athens: a photograph, and a message from Dimitri typed on yellow paper in telegraph style:

HAVE FOUND VILLA WHERE JERRY GREEN WAS KILLED STOP ON MAINLAND FORTY MILES FROM ATHENS STOP HEAD STILL MISSING STOP VILLA RENTED THROUGH LONDON TRAVEL AGENCY STOP FALSE NAMES STOP

DIMITRI

The photo showed a bare high-ceiling room with exposed beams. There was a heavy iron lantern-hook in one beam. Dimitri had circled this hook in white ink and had written under it: "Traces of rope fiber."

"A Mr. Everson called," said Jim. "His son is missing. I made an appointment."

"Where is he missing?"

"In Mexico. A Mayan archaeologist. Missing six weeks.

I sent Mr. Everson the questionnaire and asked him for pictures of the boy."

"Good." I had no special feeling about this case, but it was taking me in the direction I wanted to go.

Back at the loft we decide to try some sex magic. According to psychic dogma, sex itself is incidental and should be subordinated to the intent of the ritual. But I don't believe in rules. What happens, happens.

The altar is set up for an Egyptian rite timed for sunset, which is in ten minutes. It is a slab of white marble about three feet square. We mark out the cardinal points. A hyacinth in a pot for earth: North. A red candle for fire: South. An alabaster bowl of water for water: East. A glyph in gold on white parchment for air: West. We then put up the glyphs for the rite, in gold on white parchment, on the west wall, since this is the sundown rite and we are facing west. Also we place on the altar a bowl of water, a bowl of milk, an incense burner, some rose essence, and a sprig of mint.

All set, we strip down to sky clothes and we are both stiff before we can get our clothes off. I pick up an ivory wand and draw a circle around our bodies while we both intone translations of the rite, reading from the glyphs on the wall.

"Let the Shining Ones not have power over me." Jim reads it like the Catholic litany and we are both laughing.

"I have purified myself."

We dip water from the bowl and touch our foreheads.

"I have anointed myself with unguents."

We dip the special ointment out of an alabaster jar, touching foreheads, insides of the wrists, and the base of the spine, since the rite will have a sexual climax.

"I bring to you perfume and incense."

We add more incense, a few drops of rose oil, and a pinch of benzoin to the burner.

We pay homage to the four cardinal points as we invoke Set instead of Khentamentiu, since this is in some sense a black ritual. It is now exactly the hour of sunset, and we pay homage to Tem, since Ra, in his setting, takes that name. We make lustrations with water and milk to the cardinal points, dipping a mint sprig into the bowls as we invoke the shining elementals. It is time now for the ritual climax, in which the gods possess our bodies and the magical intention is projected in the moment of orgasm and visualized as an outpouring of liquid gold.

"My phallus is that of Amsu."

I bend over and Jim rubs the ointment up my ass and slides his cock in. A roaring sound in my ears as pictures and tapes swirl in my brain. Shadowy figures rise beyond the candlelight: the goddess Ix Tab, patroness of those who hang themselves . . . a vista of gallows and burning cities from Bosch . . . Set . . . Osiris . . . smell of the sea . . . Jerry hanging naked from the beam. A sweet rotten red musky metal smell swirls round our bodies palpable as a haze, and as I start to ejaculate, the room gets lighter. At first I think the candles have flared up and then I see Jerry standing there naked, his body radiating light. There is a skeleton grin on his face, which fades to the enigmatic smile on the statues of archaic Greek youths and then he changes into Dimitri, with a quizzical amused expression.

So we send the Shining Ones home and go to bed.

"Why do you think the head was cut off?" asks Jim.

"Obvious reason: to obscure the cause of death in case the body was found. But they didn't figure on the body being found. There was some special purpose they had in mind, to use both the head and the body." Drawings of transplanted monkey heads flash in front of my eyes.

"Where do you think the head is now?"

"In New York."

HORSE HATTOCK
TO RIDE TO RIDE

ext day when we got to the office there was a telegram from Dimitri:

> HAVE SUSPECT IN CUSTODY WHO WITNESSED DEATH
> OF JERRY GREEN STOP WIRE IF WISH TO INTERVIEW
> SUSPECT

We took the next plane to Athens and checked into the Hilton. Dimitri sent a car for us.

Jim was a bit stiff when they shook hands in Dimitri's air-conditioned office ... wall-to-wall blue carpet, a desk, leather-covered chairs, a picture of the Parthenon on the wall, everything neat and impersonal as a room in the Hilton.

Dimitri raised one eyebrow. "I infer you disapprove of our politics, Mr. Brady. For myself I disapprove of any politics. Please understand that I stand to gain nothing from this investigation. My political superiors want the whole thing dropped ... a few degenerate foreigners ... it's bad for the tourist business."

Jim blushed sulkily and looked at his shoes and turned one foot sideways.

"What about this witness you got?" I asked.

Dimitri leaned back in his chair behind the desk and put the tips of his fingers together. "Ah yes—Adam North, the perfect witness. Survived his perfection because he was in custody. On the morning that the Green boy was killed, September eighteenth, young North was arrested with a quarter-ounce of heroin in his possession. When I saw the laboratory report I ordered him placed in isolation. The heroin he had been buying from street pushers was about ten percent. This was almost one hundred percent. It would have killed him in a matter of seconds."

"Well, if they would kill him to shut him up about something, why let him know about it in the first place?" Jim asked.

"A searching question. You see, he was a sort of camera from which a film could be withdrawn and developed. But first the bare bones, later the meat. Adam North had been approached by someone fitting"—Dimitri glanced at me—"your description of Marty Blum, and offered a quarter-ounce of heroin plus a thousand-dollar bonus to be paid in two installments to witness a magical ritual involving a simulated execution. He was suspicious."

Dimitri turned on a tape recorder. "Why *me*?" said a stupid, surly young voice. It went on.

"So this character from a comic strip says I am a perfect. 'A perfect *what*?' I ask him. 'A perfect witness,' he tells me. He has five C-notes in his hand. 'Well, all right,' I say. 'But there is a condition,' he says. 'You must promise to refrain from heroin or any other drug for three days prior to the ceremony. You have to be in a pure condition.' 'Promise on my scout's honor,' I told him and he lays the bread on me. 'But one more thing,' he says. He gives me a color picture of a kid with red hair who looks sorta like me. 'This is the subject. You will concentrate on this picture for the next three days.' So I tell him 'Sure' and split. And would you believe it, with five hundred cools in my pocket I can't score for shit nowhere no way. So when the chauffeur comes to pick me up in a Daimler I am sick as a dog."

Dimitri shut off the tape recorder. "He was driven to a villa outside of Athens where he witnessed a bizarre ceremony culminating in the hanging of the Green boy. Back in Athens he was given the quarter-ounce of heroin. He was on his way back to his girl friend's apartment when the arrest was made."

"It still doesn't make any sense," Jim said. "They drag him in as a witness, God knows why, then knock him off to shut him up."

"They did not intend to *shut* him up. They intended to *open* him and extract the film. Adam North was a perfect witness. He is Jerry's age, born on the same day, and resembles him enough to be a twin brother. You are acquainted with the symptoms of heroin withdrawal . . . the painful intensity of impressions, light fever, spontaneous orgasms . . . a sensitized film. And a heroin overdose is the easiest of deaths, so the pictures registered on the sensitized withdrawal film come off without distortion in a heroin O.D."

"I see," said Jim.

"It's all here on the tape, but I think you would like to see this boy. He is, I should tell you, retarded."

As we were going down in the elevator, Dimitri continued. "There is reason to suspect a latent psychosis, masked by his addiction."

"Is he receiving any medication?" I asked.

"Yes—methadone, orally. I don't want his disorder to surface here."

"You mean he could become a public charge?" I asked.

"More than that—he could become a sanitary hazard."

We saw Adam North in one of the interrogation rooms,

under fluorescent lights. A table, a tape recorder, four chairs. He was a handsome blond kid with green eyes. The resemblance to Jerry was remarkable. However, while Jerry was described as very bright and quick, this boy had a slack, vacuous, stupid look about him, sleepy and sullen like a lizard resentfully aroused from hibernation. Dimitri explained that we were investigators hired by Jerry's family, and we had a few questions. The boy looked down at the table in front of him and said nothing.

"This man who offered you the quarter-ounce of H. You'd seen him before?" I asked.

"Yeah. When I first came here he steered me to a score. I figure he is creaming off a percentage."

"What did he look like?"

"Gray face, pockmarks, stocky medium build, fancy purple vest and a watch chain. Like he stepped out of the 1890s. Didn't seem to feel the heat."

"Anything else?"

"Funny smell about him, like something rotten in a refrigerator."

"Please describe the ritual you witnessed," I said.

"Allow me," interrupted Dimitri. He looked at the boy and said, "Ganymede" and snapped his fingers. The boy shivered and closed his eyes, breathing deeply. When he spoke, his voice was altered beyond recognition. I had the impression he was translating the words from another tongue, a language of giggles and turkey gobbles and coos and purrs and whimpers and trills.

"Ganymede Hotel . . . shutters closed . . . naked on the bed . . . Jerry's picture . . . it's coming alive . . . gets me hot to look at it . . . I know he's in a room just like this . . . waiting . . . there's a smell in the room, *his* smell . . . I can smell what's going to happen . . . naked with animal masks ... demon masks ... I'm naked but I don't have a mask. We are standing on a stage ... translucent noose ... it's squirming like a snake ... Jerry is led in naked by a twin sister ... can't hardly tell them apart. There's a red haze over everything, and the *smell*—" The kid whimpered and squirmed and rubbed his crotch. "She's tying his hands behind him with a red scarf ... she's got the noose around his neck.... It's *growing* into him ... his cock is coming up and he gets red all over right down to his toenails— we call it a red-on...." Adam giggled. "The platform falls out from under him and he's hanging there kicking. He goes off three times in a row. His twin sister is catching the seed in a bottle. It's going to *grow*...." The boy opened his eyes and looked uncertainly at Dimitri, who shook his head in mild reproof.

"You still think all this happened, Adam?"

"Well, sure, Doctor, I remember it."

"You remember dreams too. Your story has been checked and found to be without factual foundation. This was hardly necessary since you have been under constant surveillance since your arrival in Athens. The heroin you were taking has been analyzed. It contains certain impurities which can cause a temporary psychosis with just such bizarre hallucination as you describe. We were looking for the wholesalers who were distributing this poisonous heroin. We have them now. The case is closed. I advise you to forget all about it. You will be released tomorrow. The consulate has arranged for you to work your way home on a freighter."

The boy was led away by a white-coated attendant.

"What about the other witnesses, who wore masks?" I asked Dimitri.

"I surmised that they would be eligible for immediate disposal. A charter plane for London leaving Athens the day after the ritual murder crashed in Yugoslavia. There were no survivors. I checked the passenger list with my police contacts in England. Seven of the passengers belonged to a Druid cult suspected of robbing graves and performing black-magic rituals with animal sacrifices. One of the animals allegedly sacrificed was a horse. Such an act is considerably more shocking to the British sensibility than human sacrifice."

"They sacrificed a *horse*?"

"It's an old Scythian practice. A naked youth mounts the horse, slits its throat and rides it to the ground. Dangerous, I'm told. Rather like your American rodeos."

"What about the twin sister who hanged him?" Jim demanded.

Dimitri opened a file. " 'She' is a transvestite, Arn West, born Arnold Atkins at Newcastle upon Tyne. A topflight ultraexpensive assassin specializing in sexual techniques and poisons. His consultation fee to listen to a proposition is a hundred thousand dollars, nonrefundable. Known as the Popper, the Blue Octopus, the Siren Cloak.

"And now, would you gentlemen care to join me for dinner? I would like to hear from you, Mr. Snide, the complete story and not a version edited for the so limited police mentality."

Dimitri's house was near the American Embassy. It was not the sort of house you would expect a police official on a modest salary to own. It took up almost half a block. The grounds were surrounded by high walls, with six feet of barbed wire on top. The door looked like a bank vault.

Dimitri led the way down a hall with a red-tiled floor into a book-lined room. French doors opened onto a patio about seventy feet long and forty feet wide. I could see a pool, trees and flowers. Jim and I sat down and Dimitri mixed drinks. I glanced at the books: magic, demonology, a number of medical books, a shelf of Egyptology and books on the Mayans and Aztecs.

I told Dimitri what I knew and what I suspected. It took about half an hour. After I had finished, he sat for some time in silence, looking down into his drink.

"Well, Mr. Snide," he said at last. "It would seem that your case is closed. The killers are dead."

"But they were only—"

"Exactly: Servants. Dupes. Hired killers, paid off with a special form of death. You will recognize the rite as the Egyptian sunset rite dedicated to Set. A sacrifice involving both sex and death is the most potent projection of magical intention. The participants did not know that one of the intentions they were projecting was their own death in a plane crash."

"Any evidence of sabotage?"

"No. But there was not much left of the plane. The crash occurred outside Zagreb. Pilot was off course and flying low. It looks like pilot error. There are, of course, techniques for producing such errors. . . . You are still intending to continue on this case? To find the higher-ups? And why exactly?"

"Look, Colonel, this didn't start with the Green case. These people are old enemies."

"Do not be in a hurry to dispose of old enemies. What would you do without them? Look at it this way: You are retained to find a killer. You turn up a hired assassin. You are not satisfied. You want to find the man who hired him. You find another servant. You are not satisfied. You find another servant, and another, right up to Mr. or Mrs. Big— who turns out to be yet another servant . . . a servant of forces and powers you cannot reach. Where do you stop? Where do you draw the line?"

He had a point.

He went on: "Let us consider what has happened here.

A boy has been hanged for ritual and magical purposes. Is this so startling? ... You have read *The Bog People*?"

I nodded.

"Well, a modest consumption of one nude hanging a year during the spring festivals ... such festivals, within reason, could serve as a safety valve.... After all, worse things happen every day. Certainly this is a minor matter compared with Hiroshima, Vietnam, mass pollution, droughts, famines ... you have to take a broad general view of things."

"It might not be within reason at all. It might become pandemic."

"Yes ... the Aztecs got rather out of hand. But you are referring to your virus theory. Shall we call it 'Virus B-23'? The 'Hanging Fever'? And you are extrapolating from two cases which may not be connected. Peter Winkler may have died from something altogether different. I know you do not want to entertain such a possibility, but suppose that such an epidemic does occur?" He paused. "How old was Winkler?"

"In his early fifties."

"So. Jerry was a carrier of the illness. He did not die of it directly. Winkler, who was thirty years older, died in a few days. Well ... there are those who think a selective pestilence is the most humane solution to overpopulation and the attendant impasses of pollution, inflation, and exhaustion of natural resources. A plague that kills the old and leaves the young, minus a reasonable percentage ... one might be tempted to let such an epidemic run its course even if one had the power to stop it."

"Colonel, I have a hunch that what we might find in the South American laboratories would make the story we heard from Adam North sound like a mild Gothic romance for old ladies and children."

"Exactly what I am getting at, Mr. Snide. There are risks not worth taking. There are things better left unseen and unknown."

"But somebody has to see and know them eventually. Otherwise there is no protection."

"That somebody who has to see and know may not be you. Think of your own life, and that of your assistant. You may not be called upon to act in this matter."

"You have a point."

"He sure does," said Jim.

"Mr. Snide, do you consider Hiroshima a crime?"

"Yes."

"Were you ever tempted to go after the higher-ups?"

"No. It wasn't my business."

"The same considerations may apply here. There is, however, one thing you can do: find the head and exorcise it. I have already done this with the body. Mr. Green agreed to burial here in the American cemetery."

He walked across the room to a locked cabinet and returned with an amulet: runic lettering on what looked like parchment in an iron locket. "Not parchment—human skin ..." he told me. "The ceremony is quite simple: the head is placed in a magic circle on which you have marked the cardinal points. You repeat three times: 'Back to water. Back to fire. Back to air. Back to earth.' You then touch the crown of the head, the forehead, and the spot behind the right ear, in this case—he was left-handed—with the amulet."

There was a knock at the door, and a middle-aged Greek woman with a mustache wheeled in the dinner of red mullet and Greek salad. After dinner and brandy we got up to take our leave.

"I have said you may not be called upon to act. On

the other hand, you may be called upon. You will know if this happens, and you will need help. I can give you a contact in Mexico City . . . 18 Callejón de la Esperanza."

"Got it," said Jim.

"My driver will take you back to the Hilton."

"Nightcap?"

"No," Jim said. "I've got a headache. I'm going up to the room."

"I'll check the bar. See you very shortly." I had seen someone I knew from the American Embassy. Probably CIA. I could feel that he wanted to talk to me.

He looked up when I walked in, nodded and asked me to join him. He was young, thin, sandy-haired, glasses . . . refined and rather academic-looking. He signaled the waiter and I ordered a beer.

After the waiter had brought the beer and gone back to the bar, the man leaned forward, speaking in a low precise voice.

"Shocking thing about the Green boy." He tried to look concerned and sympathetic but his eyes were cold and probing. I would have to be very careful not to tell him anything he didn't already know.

"Yes, isn't it."

"I understand it was uh well, a sex murder." He tried to look embarrassed and a bit salacious. He looked about as embarrassed and salacious as a shark. He was cold and fishy like the Countess de Gulpa. I remembered that he was rich.

"Something like that."

"It must have been terrible for the family. You didn't tell them the truth?"

Watch yourself, Clem. . . . "I'm not sure I know the truth.

The story I actually told them is of course a confidential matter. . . ."

"Of course. Professional ethics." Without a trace of overt irony, he managed to convey a vast icy contempt for me and my profession. I just nodded. He went on. "Strange chap, Dimitri."

"He seems very efficient."

"Very. It doesn't always pay to be too efficient."

"The Chinese say it is well to make a mistake now and then."

"Did you know that Dimitri has resigned?"

"He didn't say so. . . ."

"He was the object of professional jealousy. Career men resent someone with independent means who doesn't really need the job. I should know." He smiled ruefully, trying to look boyish.

"Well, perhaps you can avoid the error of overefficiency."

He let that roll off him. "I suppose these hippies go in for all sorts of strange far-out sex cults. . . ."

"I have found their sex practices to be on the whole rather boringly ordinary. . . ."

"You've read *Future Shock*, haven't you?"

"Skipped through it."

"It's worth looking at carefully."

"I found *The Biologic Time Bomb* more interesting."

He ignored this. "Dimitri's dabbling in magic hasn't done him any good either . . . career-wise, I mean."

"Magic? That seems out of character."

I could tell he knew I had just been to Dimitri's house for dinner. He was hoping I would tell him something about the house: books, decorations. . . . Which meant he had never been there. A slight spasm of exasperation passed over his face like a seismic tremor. His face went dead and smooth as a marble mask, and he said slowly: "Isn't your assistant awfully young for the kind of work you're doing?"

"Aren't you a bit young for the kind of work you're doing?"

He decided to laugh. "Well, youth at the helm. Have another beer?"

"No thanks. Got an early plane to catch." I stood up. "Well, good night, Skipper."

He decided not to laugh. He just nodded silently. As I walked out of the bar I knew that he deliberately was not looking after me.

No doubt about it. I had been warned in no uncertain terms to lay off and stay out, and I didn't like it—especially coming at a time when I had about decided to lay off and stay out. And I didn't like having Jim threatened by a snot-nosed CIA punk. The Mafia couldn't have been much cruder.

"Your assistant very young man. You looka the book called *Future Shock* maybe?"

When I got to the room I found the door open. As I stepped in I caught a whiff of the fever smell—the rank animal smell of Jerry's naked headless body. Jim was lying on the bed covered by a sheet up to his waist. As I looked at him I felt a prickling up the back of my neck. I was looking at Jerry's face, which wore a wolfish grin, his eyes sputtering green fire.

PORT ROGER

Page from Strobe's notebook:

The essence of sleight of hand is distraction and misdirection. If someone can be convinced that he has, through his own perspicacity, divined your hidden purposes, he will not look further.

How much does he know or suspect? He knows that the capture was prearranged. He surmises an alliance between the pirates and the Pembertons, involving trade in the western hemisphere, the planting of opium in Mexico, and the cultivation of other crops and products now imported from the Near and Far East. He suspects, or soon will, that this alliance may extend to political and military revolution, and secession from England and Spain.

What does he think is expected from him? The role of gunsmith and inventor, which is partially true. I must not underestimate him. He has already quite literally seen through Mr. Thomas. How long before he will see through the others? *Must be careful of Kelley.* The most necessary servants are always the most dangerous. He is a cunning and devious little beast.

Noah writes that I am interested in printing his diaries "for some reason." Does he have any inkling what reason? He must be kept very busy as a gunsmith lest he realize his primary role.

How long will it take him to find out that Captain Jones

and Captain Nordenholz are interchangeable? To grasp for that matter the full significance of his own name? To see that I am the de Fuentes twins? Finally, to know that I am also—?

Scarf around his neck   immediately arranged between them   turning to leer and wink at the armory. I am Captain Strobe, a slim siren. Coat glittering in the sun flute from a distant star in their buttocks. Now I was smoke called Kelley   pale in my mind together with a *Yes.* Sandy hairs, member erect marching around was cleared. Dancing boys to the music played their bags wriggling pale groin   toes twisted. We now have double crew down the Red Sea area. Story started with an argument   sentences to hang. The sentence preyed on merchant vessels carrying the cargo beautiful hanged back to life   women dancing lewdly and ensuring protection against their bodies once one had been rescued. He claimed to have learned the gallows smile. Gasping his lips back surged erect   he ejaculated noose and knot feet across the floor. Spirits around his neck. Spurting six.

Today we reached Port Roger on the coast of Panama. This was formerly Fort Pheasant and had been used as a base by English pirates sixty years ago. The coast here is highly dangerous for the navigation of large vessels, owing to shallows and reefs. Port Roger is one of the few deepwater harbors. It is, however, so difficult to reach that only a navigator with exact knowledge of the passage can hope to do so.

The coastline is a distant green smudge on our starboard side. Strobe and Thomas scan the skyline with telescopes.

"*Guarda costa* . . ." the boys mutter uneasily.

Capture by the Spanish means torture or, at best, slavery. If overtaken by a Spanish ship we will abandon ship in the lifeboats, leaving *The Great White* to the Spanish. The boarding party will receive a surprise, for I have arranged a device which will explode the entire cargo of powder as soon as the doors to the hold are opened.

Now the ship rounds and heads towards land. Strobe, stripped to the waist, has taken the wheel, his thin body infused with alertness. Two boys are taking soundings on both sides, and the escort ship is a hundred yards behind us. We are sailing through a narrow channel in a reef, Mr. Thomas and Kelley calling out orders as the ship slips like a snake through a strip of blue water. The coastline is ever clearer, trees slowly appearing and low hills in a shimmer of heat. An inaudible twang like a loosed bowstring as the ship glides into a deep blue harbor a few hundred yards from the shore, where waves break on a crescent of sand.

We drop anchor a bare hundred yards from the beach, *The Siren* a like distance behind us. From the harbor the town is difficult to discern, being sheltered by a thick growth of bamboo and set among trees and vines. I had the curious impression of looking at a painting in a gold frame: the two ships riding at anchor in the still blue harbor, a cool morning breeze, and written on the bottom of the frame: "Port Roger—April 1, 1702."

The trees part, and Indians in loincloths carry boats to the water. The boats are fashioned by securing a raft between two dugout canoes which serve as pontoons. These boats ride high in the water and are propelled by two oarsmen facing forward, after the manner of Venetian gondoliers. This day presents itself to my memory as a series of paintings. . . .

The Oarsmen

Thin copper-red bodies leaning against the oars as boats glide forward in a silver spray of surf and flying fish against a background of beach and palm trees.

Unloading the Cargo

Bright red gums, sharp white teeth, buttocks exposed as the cargo is passed over the side with much singing and laughter. The boys make up songs about the cargo as it is passed along to the rafts and relayed to the beach. These songs, translated by Kelley, who has sidled up to me in his pushy ghost way, seem flatly idiotic.

The boys are unloading powder kegs. We offer to help but the Indians sing. "White man's hands slippery like rotten bananas." Now they pass up the powder kegs. . . . "This go boom boom up question's ass."

I ask Kelley what is this "question"?

"Short for Inquisition."

Boy holds up keg of opium. . . . "Spanish no get this, shit come in pants, very dirty *muy sucio*."

"And Kiki is getting a hard-on because he knows I look at his asshole when he bends over for *opio*."

"I was thinking of María."

"Take off the cloth and show us María."

Kiki blushes, but he must obey the rules of this game. He takes off his loincloth, smiling shyly to reveal lush purple-pink genitals, nuts tight, cock straining up, the flower smell of it fills the hold.

"María his asshole. I fuck him her spurt six feet. . . ." He looks around, challenging the boys who sit on the opium kegs.

Some of the boys extract gold nuggets from little pouches at their belts cunningly contrived from Spanish testicles.

"He love this so much I keep it in his nuts. Soon get rich like him."

"That should be easy for a bastard like you."

"Put your yellow shit where your mouth is, sister fucker. I see you do it with my own eyes."

An area is cleared and carefully measured off and the

bets placed. Kiki bends over, hands on knees. The other boy, who looks like Kiki's twin brother, uncorks a little-phallus-shaped vessel of pink coral, and a powerful odor fills the hold, already heavy with the smells of opium, hashish, and salt water drying on young bodies. The reek from the pink coral container is a heavy sweet rotten musky smell like a perfumed corpse, or like the smell you catch after lightning strikes.

The unguent glistens in the dim light of the hold, where red limbs stir lazily like fish in black water. Now the boy rubs the glowing unguent up Kiki's ass and Kiki writhes and bares his teeth as the other boy slides it in and they both light up and glow—for a moment the hold is bright as day with every face and body clearly outlined.

Radiant Boys

"Bucking for Radiant Bars," Kelley mutters sourly.

"Radiant Bars?" I ask.

"Yeah. It's the old army game from here to eternity. Now you may know Radiant Boys is a special type ghost, when you see one you die soon after. Of course you can get used to anything and bright boys is all in the day's work to me. Now a good strong Radiant Boy can light up a room with a twenty-foot ceiling. One of the best lived in an Irish castle and was the ghost of a ten-year-old boy strangled by his insane mother. That one killed three cabinet ministers and the vicar.

"So the dirty-trick boys get wind of this good thing and set up Project RB to take care of key enemy personnel. They don't even know what buttons to push. Project RB is dumped into the lap of us tech sergeants. We get half-hanged, half-drowned, half-strangled, the medics pawing us over. . . . 'How did it *feel*? Did you get *radiant*?'

"Put your shit where the boys were. Radiant Boys is

a special strike of death. The ghost lacks water. And a powerful odor filled the RB Project. Half-hanged half-bodies, the smell is pawing us over. Sweet rotten musky smell like. Then some smart-pants-come-lately pulls the radiant ass out from under you and makes shavetail out of it. Facts of life in the army. Uncorks the old army game screwing tech sergeant like me."

Both his words and manner of speech seemed at first totally unfamiliar to me, and yet somehow they stirred memories—as an actor might be stirred by the forgotten lines of some role he had played far away and long ago.

Captain Nordenholz Disembarks at Port Roger

There he is standing on a ruined pier left over from the English, in some uniform of his own devising. He is flanked by Opium Jones, the de Fuentes twins and Captain Strobe, all looking like a troupe of traveling players a bit down on their luck but united in determination to play out their assigned roles. Boys trail behind them, carrying an assortment of bags, cases, and chests. They walk across the beach and disappear one after another into a wall of leaves.

I don't know what gave me such an impression of shabbiness about this procession, since they all must have chests of gold and precious stones, but for a moment they appeared to my eyes as seedy players with grand roles but no money to pay the rent. The jewels and the gold are false, the curtains patched and shredded and torn, the theater long closed. I was smitten by a feeling of sadness and desolation, as the words of the Immortal Bard came to my mind:

> These our actors,
> As I foretold you, were all spirits, and
> Are melted into air. . . .

We have landed. Captain Strobe meets us on the beach emerging from a picture puzzle, his shirt and pants splotched with green and brown, stirring slightly in the afternoon breeze. We follow him as he walks towards a seemingly unbroken line of undergrowth. He pushes aside branches to reveal a winding path through a tangle of bamboo and thorn.

We walk for perhaps a quarter-mile as the path winds upward and ends in a screen of bamboo. We are quite close before I realize that the bamboo trees are painted on a green door that swings open like the magic door in a book I have seen somewhere long ago. We step through into the town of Port Roger.

We are standing in a walled enclosure like a vast garden, with trees and flowers, paths and pools. I can see buildings along the sides of the square, all painted to blend with the surroundings so that the buildings seem but a reflection of the trees and vines and flowers stirring in a slight breeze that seems to shake the walls, the whole scene insubstantial as a mirage.

This first glimpse of Port Roger occurred just as some hashish candy I had ingested on the boat started to take effect, producing a hiatus in my mind and the interruption of verbal thought, followed by a sharp jolt as if something had entered my body. I caught a whiff of perfume and a sound of distant flutes.

A long cool room with a counter, behind which are three generations of Chinese. A smell of spices and dried fish. An Indian youth, naked except for a leather pouch that cups his genitals, is leaning forward on the counter examining a flintlock rifle, his smooth red buttocks protruding. He turns and smiles at us, showing white teeth and bright red gums. He has a gardenia behind his ear and his body gives off a sweet flower smell. Hammocks, blankets, machetes, cutlasses and flintlocks are on the counter.

Outside in the square, Strobe introduces me to a man with a strong square face, light blue eyes, and curly iron-gray hair. "This is Waring. He painted the town."

Waring gives me a smile and a handshake. He makes no secret of his dislike for Captain Strobe. Dislike is perhaps too strong a word since there is no hatred involved on either side. They meet as emissaries of two countries whose interests do not coincide at any point. I do not yet know what countries they represent.

Up to this moment I have been so completely charmed by Strobe's nonchalance that I have never stopped to ask myself: What is the source of this poise? Where did he buy it, and what did he pay? I see now that Strobe is an official and so is Waring, but they don't work for the same company. Perhaps they are both actors who never appear onstage together, their relationship limited to curt offstage nods.

"I'll show you to your digs," says Strobe.

We go through a massive studded door into a patio, cool and shady with trees, flowering shrubs, and a pool. The patio is a miniature version of the town square. My attention is immediately arrested by a youth who is standing about thirty feet from the entrance executing a dance step, one hand on his hip and the other above his head. He has his back towards us and as we enter the courtyard he freezes in midstep, turning his hand to point towards us. At this moment, everyone in the patio looks at us.

The youth pivots and advances to meet us. He is wearing a purple silk vest which is open in front, and his arms are bare from the shoulders. His arms and torso are dark brown, lean and powerful, and he moves with the grace of a dancer. His complexion is dark, his hair black and kinky; one eye is gray-green, the other brown. A long scar runs down the left cheekbone to the chin. He makes a mock obeisance in front of Captain Strobe, who acknowledges it with his cool enigmatic smile. Then the youth turns to Bert Hansen: "Ah, the son of family ..." he sniffs. "The smell of gold is always welcome."

I notice that he can be warm and friendly from one eye and at the same time cold and mocking from the other. The effect is most disturbing. Bert Hansen, not knowing how to respond, smiles uncomfortably, and his smile is immediately mimicked by the youth with such precision that it seems for a moment they have switched places.

He ruffles the cabin boy's hair. "An Irish leprechaun." To Paco he says something in Portuguese. I recognize him as the regimental or shipboard joker and Master of Ceremonies, and Paco tells me his name is Juanito. I have no doubt that Juanito can, if necessary, back his sharp tongue with knife or cutlass.

Now it is my turn. I extend my hand, but instead of shaking it he turns it over and pretends to read the palm. "You are going to meet a handsome stranger." He beckons over his shoulder and calls out: "Hans." A boy who is standing by the pool throwing bits of bread to the fish turns and walks towards me. Wearing only blue trousers, he is shirtless and barefoot, with yellow hair and blue eyes. His tanned torso is smooth and hairless.

"Noah, the gunsmith, meet Hans, the gunsmith."

Hans brings his heels together and bows from the waist as we shake hands. He invites me to move into his room.

The patio is completely surrounded by a two-story wooden building. The second-floor rooms open onto a porch which runs all around the upper story and overhangs the ground floor. The rooms have no doors but at the top of the entrance there is a roll of mosquito netting which is lowered at twilight. The rooms are bare whitewashed cubicles with hooks for slinging hammocks and in the walls wooden pegs for clothes.

I take my gear to a room on the second floor and Hans introduces me to an American boy from Middletown who also shares the room. His name is Dink Rivers. His extraordinarily clear and direct gray eyes convey a shock of surprise and recognition as if we had known one another from somewhere else, and for a second I am in a dry streambed and he says: "If you still want me you'd better take me up soon." Next second I am back in the room at Port Roger, we are shaking hands and he is saying:

"Nice to see you."

When I inquire as to his trade, he says that he is in physical education. Hans explains that he is a student and instructor in body control.

"He can stop the pulse, jump from twenty feet, stay under water five minutes and"—Hans grins—"go off no hands."

When I asked the boy to make a demonstration, he looked at me very earnestly without smiling and said that he would do so when the time came.

There are four latrines: two for the ground floor and two for the upper floor, with toilets that can be flushed from a water tank which fills with rainwater drained off the roof. The patio contains a number of fig, orange, mango, and avocado trees and a menagerie of cats, iguanas, monkeys, and strange gentle animals with long snouts. On the ground floor there is a communal dining room, a kitchen, and a large bath where hot water is drawn into buckets. This is an Arab-style bath known as a *haman*.

The dancing boys are spreading mats under the portico,

lighting their hashish pipes and brewing the sweet mint tea they drink constantly. Chinese youths are smoking opium. The entire crew of *The Siren* is housed here, and it is a mixed company: English, Irish, American, Dutch, German, Spanish, Arabs, Malay, Chinese, and Japanese. We stroll about, talking and introducing ourselves among the murmur of many tongues.

Old acquaintances are renewed and bonds of language and common places of origin discovered. There are some boys from New York who had been river pirates, and it turns out that they know Guy, Bill, and Adam. Five huge Nubians, liberated by Nordenholz from a slave ship, speak a language known only to themselves. Now word is passed along through Kelley and Juanito the Joker that Nordenholz will entertain us all for dinner in his house.

Hans looks at me with a knowing smile. *"Fräuleins."* He punches his finger in and out of his fist. The word echoes through the patio in many languages. Hans explains that there will be a number of women at the party who have come for the purpose of becoming impregnated.

MOTHER IS THE BEST BET

At twilight we make our way towards the house of Skipper Nordenholz, which is outside the town on higher ground overlooking the bay. He receives us in a large courtyard covered with lattice and mosquito netting. He has a thin aristocratic face, green eyes, a continual ironic smile, and an oblique way of talking and glancing down his nose at the same time. . . .

"Most glad to welcome you to Port Roger. Hope that your quarters are convenient. . . ." His English is almost perfect except for a slight inflection. "And now"—he glances down his nose and smiles as he gestures towards a table twenty feet long, laden with food: fish, oysters, shrimp, turkey, venison, wild pig, heaping bowls of rice, yams, corn, mangoes, oranges, and kegs of wine and beer—"*chacun pour soi.*"

Everyone helps himself as Skipper Nordenholz indicates the seating arrangements. I am to sit at his table with Captain Strobe, the de Fuentes or Iguana twins as they are called, Opium Jones, Bert Hansen, Clinch Todd, Hans, and Kelley, and a Doctor Benway.

I will attempt to report as accurately as my memory permits the conversation at the dinner table. It was all concerned with weaponry and tactics but on a level I had never thought possible outside my lonely adolescent literary endeavors—for I have always been a scribbler and during the long shut-in winters filled notebook after notebook with lurid tales involving pirates from other planets, copulations with alien beings, and attacks of the Radiant Boys on the Citadel of the Inquisition. These notebooks with illustrations by Bert Hansen are in my possession, locked in a small chest. The conversation at the dinner table gave me the feeling that my notebooks were coming alive.

"For the benefit of you *Great White* boys"—Skipper Nordenholz looked down at the table and his eyes glinted with irony—"I would like to say that our enemy in this area is Spain, and our most powerful weapon is the freedom hopes of captive peoples now enslaved and peonized under the Spanish. But this weapon alone is not enough. First we must develop more efficient firearms and artillery. For this task we are depending on our able gunsmiths. We must also bear in mind that there are many different types of weapons. Opium Jones, we would be interested to hear your report."

Opium Jones got up and pulled down a map about six feet square on a roller, speaking in his dead opium voice.

"As you know, we have imported a quantity of poppy seed. We already have fields in these areas. Many other areas are suitable for cultivation. We are sending out opium advisers. Missionary work, we call it."

"And what do you see as the long-range effects of this brotherly project?" asked Nordenholz.

"In commercial terms, we can undersell eastern opium and take over the opium trade for the Americas, Canada, and the West Indies. Of course, we can expect a percentage of addicts in the areas of cultivation. . . ."

"What advantages and disadvantages do addicts present from the military point of view?"

"We can ensure loyalty by impounding the opium crop. Addicts are more tolerant than non-addicts of cold, fatigue, and discomfort. They have a strong resistance amounting to virtual immunity to rheums, coughs, consumption, and other respiratory complaints. On the other hand, they are incapacitated if the opium supply is cut off."

"You also distribute hashish?"

"Certainly. A measure of seed with any purchase at our trading posts. Unlike opium it grows anywhere." Jones made a sweeping gesture. "The whole area is full of it."

Doctor Benway got up.

"Sickness has killed more soldiers than all the wars of history. We can turn illness to account. If your enemy is sick and you are well, the victory is yours. Healthy vultures can kill a sick lion. For example, my learned colleague Opium Jones has pointed out the immunity of addicts to respiratory afflictions. And I may add that periodic users who need not become addicted are equally immune. Consider the advantages conferred in an epidemic of the deadly Spanish influenza."

"Is there any way in which such an epidemic could be induced?"

"There are no problems. All respiratory complaints are transmitted by spitting, sneezing, and coughing. We need only collect these exudations and convey them into the enemy area. Consider other potential allies. . . ." He pointed to areas on the map. "Malaria and yellow fever . . . both imported from the Old World and flourishing in the New. My researches have convinced me that these illnesses are conveyed by mosquitoes. Mosquito netting, pine incense, oil of citronella rubbed on exposed skin areas . . . these simple precautions—not, of course, infallible—will give us an advantage of fifty enemy cases to one. Dysentery, jaundice, typhoid fever . . . these even more reliable allies are conveyed by the ingestion of infected excrement, which can be collected and introduced into the enemy water supply. Boiling all drinking water and abstaining from uncooked foods or unpeeled fruits yields one-hundred-percent immunity. We must, of course, always be careful not to encourage an illness for which we do not have a remedy or means of avoidance."

"Magical weapons?"

The Iguana girl spoke in her cool remote voice: "All religions are magical systems competing with other systems. The Church has driven magic into covens where practitioners are bound to each other by a common fear. We can unite the Americas into a vast coven of those who live under the Articles, united against the Christian Church, Catholic and Protestant. It is our policy to encourage the practice of magic and to introduce alternative religious beliefs to break the Christian monopoly. We will set up an alternative calendar with non-Christian holidays. Christianity will then take its place as one of many religions protected from persecution by the Articles."

"Economic weapons?"

Strobe glanced through some notes: "We can, of course, undersell Eastern opium . . . and no doubt various other products such as tea, silk, and spices. But our most powerful monopoly is sugar and rum. Europe will pay our price for sugar."

My appetite was sharpened by hashish and I was the better able to savor the excellent repast: clams and oysters baked on hot coals with a dry white wine, wild turkey, pigeons, venison with a vintage Bordeaux, yams, corn, squash, and beans, avocados, mangoes, oranges and coconuts.

After the company had eaten their fill, Skipper Nordenholz tapped a glass for silence. He stood up in front of the map, speaking in a self-effacing manner with pauses and unfinished sentences as he gestured from time to time to the map with his long beautifully kept gambler's fingers.

"For the benefit of newcomers . . . old hands may also profit . . . a few indications and guidelines. We have already established fortified settlements . . . as you see, practically unlimited. We need artisans, soldiers, sailors and farmers to man the settlements already founded and to establish new centers from the Bering Strait to the Cape. Breeding is encouraged . . . is in fact a duty, I hope not too unpleasant. We expect that some of you will raise families. In any case, mothers and children . . . well cared for, you understand. We need families to operate as intelligence agents in areas controlled by the enemy. We solicit those of you who are skilled as cooks, hotel keepers, doctors, and pharmacists . . . strategic occupations. One of our aims is to addict the Spanish to opium, thereby making them dependent on supplies which we can, at a crucial moment, cut off. . . . And now there are some uh young ladies who have been waiting to meet you."

He sprinkled some powder onto a brazier and a dense cloud of smoke arose with a sound of thunder. Skipper Nordenholz, Captain Strobe, Opium Jones, Doctor Benway, and the Iguana twins disappeared.

Now a wind sweeps through the courtyard of Skipper Nordenholz's house at Port Roger, extinguishing the candles. When they are relit, fifty girls and women are standing along the south wall of the courtyard. The men and boys range themselves along the north wall, facing the women.

Juanito, the joker and Master of Ceremonies, prances out to the middle of the courtyard and holds up his hands for silence.

"And now we will separate *los maridos*, the husbands, from *los hombres conejos*, the rabbit men, who fuck"—he does a speed-up bump and grind—"and run"—he does a pantomime of running, swinging his arms and pumping his legs. "All rabbit men will move to the east wall."

Hans grins and puts his hands to the sides of his head making rabbit ears and trots to the east wall followed by four German friends. A Berber boy with yellow hair, blue eyes and pointed ears plays the flute as he walks to the east wall. Jerry and the dancing boys hop along behind him chewing carrots. Bert Hansen pulls a rabbit out of a hat, bows and runs for the east wall to a chorus of boos from the women and applause from the east-wall boys. I wriggle my ears and twitch my nose and show my teeth and scamper for the east wall followed by Brady, Paco, Clinch Todd, Guy and Adam. . . . It's a landslide for the east wall. . . . Juanito looks around as if bewildered. . . .

"*Esperan esperan*. . . . Wait wait. . . ." He dances behind a screen and pops out naked except for a rabbit mask. He looks at the women. His ears quiver and point east. . . .

"*Y yo el más conejo de los conejos* . . . the rabbitest of the rabbits." He screeches and leaps for the east wall in great hops.

He doffs his rabbit mask and advances again to the center of the courtyard and places an hourglass on a little table. He turns to the prospective husbands who still stand by the north wall. . . .

"You have two minutes to think."

He goes back to stand by the east wall. As the sand trickles I study these faces. If we are the fish, they are the water in which we will swim. They will hide us, provide us with weapons, guides, and information. They will carry out missions of sabotage behind enemy lines. Some of them will run inns catering to officials, priests, and generals. Others will become doctors and druggists. They are skilled in the use of subtle drugs and poisons. They will implement Benway's program of germ warfare. A few last-minute rabbits as the sand runs out. Then wives and husbands pair off and retire to private rooms.

Juanito leaps up and does a flamenco dance as we move back to the north wall facing the women, of whom thirty remain. They present a wide variety of physical types: blondes, redheads, Indian, Chinese, Negro, Portuguese, Spanish, Malay, Japanese, and some of mixed blood. Preparations are under way. The dancing boys whisk away plates and lay down pallets. Incense burners are lit, musical instruments appear, props and costumes are laid out: the goatskins of Boujeloud, skeleton suits, wings, animal and god masks. Two hangman's nooses dangle from a beam, the rope passing through two pulleys to facilitate suspension. I note that the ropes are elastic, and the nooses covered in soft leather.

Juanito announces: "Rabbit men and rabbit women, prepare to meet your makers." He leads the way into a locker room opening off the east wall. The boys strip off their clothes, giggling and comparing erections, and they dance out into the courtyard in a naked snake-line. The women are also naked now. What follows is not an unconstrained orgy but rather a series of theatrical performances.

"Ladies and gentlemen, we will now witness the mating of the God Pan and the Goddess Aisha."

A backdrop of Moroccan hills with a full moon lit from behind by a lamp casting a golden glow over our naked bodies as the music of Pan fills the courtyard. Six dancing boys with whips put on goatskin leggings and caps and dance opposite six girls clad in swirling robes of thin blue silk. The faces of the boys are remote and impersonal, yet their bodies quiver and shake as if possessed by wild spirits. The boys rip the robes from Aisha, who tries to flee. They whip her buttocks and she falls on all fours as they fuck her in a crescendo of drums and pipes and a strange perfume fills the air.

"And now we present for your entertainment: Half-Hanged Kelley and Half-Hanged Kate in the Gallows Fling."

Backdrop of a leering crowd. Kate has red hair down to her waist, blazing green eyes, and the raw red hemp marks around her neck. The story is that she was being hanged for witchcraft and other crimes against nature when the officials and spectators were dispersed by banshee wails, whereupon she was cut down and revived by leprechauns.

Kate and Kelley take a bow. A sandy-haired boy I have seen on the boat plays the bagpipes as they go into a wild jig, her hair twisting around her like flames from Hell, dancing under the waiting nooses which they adjust around each other's necks with idiot grins. He squirms it into her, kicking out spasms in the air, as they are hauled off the ground by smirking hangmen. Now their eyes light up in the gallows flash and the two bodies are encased in a blazing egg of blue-white light. They are lowered to the mat and little boys covered with green paint revive them. They stand up and take a bow.

A backdrop of sea and sand and palm trees. Idiot Hawaiian music as Hans does a hula fuck with a lithe Malay girl while his four friends, on their backs, legs in the air, applaud with their feet. Now the palm trees, with boys inside them, go into the hula. The effect is irresistibly comic and there is much laughter. Finally all the actors, including the palm trees, take a bow.

Thirteen dancing boys fuck to Gnaoua drums and clappers. Gnaoua music drives out evil spirits who might try to enter the womb. You can see the future child in a rush of liquid gold as the spirit of Hassan i Sabbah, Master of the Djinns, Master of the Assassins, guides the writhing bodies and rapt empty faces riding the drums like a bucking horse of flame. All the boys come at once as the wolfish face of Pan blazes in the young faces like a shooting star.

"The Rape of the Valkyrie," announces Juanito.

A Swedish girl with long blonde hair is against a backdrop of Northern Lights. She is riding a horse which suddenly collapses under her and two blond youths with Viking helmets wriggle out, tying her hands with a gold rope. One fucks her as the other caresses her nipples. The boys grin at each other showing all their teeth.

I am trying to figure what sort of act I could put on that would have the necessary concentration of purpose to make a child. Clinch Todd helps me out of my quandary. His father was a veterinarian and he found that sperm collected from a prize pig, horse, bull, dog, or cat could be injected into the vagina resulting in a pregnancy for which the bride must pay a handsome dowry. Furthermore, one milking could provide enough sperm for many little happenings and he had jars of this muck stored in the icehouse. I made the rounds with him once for kicks. There he is jacking-off prize pigs and squirting it into the sow—impersonal as if he were trimming a hedge. He had the touch: the animal was randy as soon as he got his hands on it. But he got to using opium and his touch failed him. He was kicked in the head and killed by a stallion.

This is the answer. Clinch lines up five girls of different racial stock—black, Chinese, Malay, Indian, Berber—who will be indirectly impregnated, thus sparing me contacts for which I have little inclination. I will play the young Corn God with a corn headdress. A boy from Yucatán with black skin, straight hair, and classical Mayan features will stand in as a Black Captain, one of the Mayan war gods, and fuck me standing up, as Jerry, cast as Ganymede the cupbearer, gathers the seed in an alabaster goblet.

The girls will proceed to the remote inland communes to await delivery. They will all receive a handsome dowry should they wish to marry and the children will be trained from childhood in the use of weapons and fitted to take their part in the task of liberation.

Pages from the diary of Hirondelle de Mer:

I am a sorceress and a warrior. I do not relish being treated as a breeding animal. Would this occur to Skipper Nordenholz? No force, he says, has been applied—but I am forced by my circumstances, cast up here without a peso, and by my Indian blood which compels me to side with all enemies of Spain. The child will be brought up a sorcerer or sorceress.

Now, a short rundown on these shabby adventurers plotting to appropriate a continent and remake it to their taste. They are all *puto* queer *maricones*. Look at that Juanito— *el más maricón de los maricones. El más puto de los putos.* Nordenholz was selling his ass in Hamburg twenty years ago. Old story: sea captain takes a liking to him, signs him on as fourth mate.

And Strobe with his well-rehearsed Eton accent. Circus people. Mother and father were aerialists and they did this high-wire hanging act with angel wings: he takes off the noose, extends his wings, and goes into a dazzling aerial act with his angel wife. It attracted a lot of attention and the Strobes were taken up by the best people but not for long. Soon the lordliness of their manners, talking to royalty as if they were being nice to the servants, rendered them absolutely insufferable. Their American origins were discovered and they were sent to the colonies, where they decided the angel act was too exotic for American tastes and booked as the Singing Aerialists. Soon they added other instruments, throwing them from one to another on tightropes—a high-wire musical juggling act it was. Young John learned his poise on the high wire and his swordsmanship as well. But show biz wasn't for him, and he shipped out with Nordenholz.

The Iguana twins have some claim to aristocratic birth. They came from an old landed family, impoverished and dispossessed. They were brought up to act rich at all times—

"act like you've got it and you'll get it," Mother always said. You can't lay it on too thick in Mexico. With preposterous forged titles and *pistoleros* on credit they seized an estate in northern Mexico and hit a silver vein.

Nordenholz is a good organizer. He saw at once that a single settlement would inevitably be discovered and wiped out. His plan called for a series of settlements, so that if one were taken they could retreat to another fortified position while bands of thirty men or so cut supply lines, contaminated the enemy water supply, conducted hit-and-run raids, and eventually forced the enemy to fight on two fronts when they laid siege to the next position. Sound strategy. With every victory, more people flocked to the Articles.

Suppose the Spanish have been driven out or brought under the Articles? Suppose, too, similar uprisings in North America and Canada have shattered the English and French rule. What now? Can this vast territory be held without the usual machinery of government, ambassadors, standing army and navy? They can only plan to hold the area by sorcery. This is a sorcerers' revolution. I must find my part as a sorceress.

QUIÉN ES?

We flew back with a three-hour stopover at Orly. I had decided what I was going to do. I was going to refund Mr. Green's retainer, minus travel expenses, and tell him the actual killers were dead in a plane crash. The Greek police consider the case closed. Nothing further I can do.

Back in my New York loft I called the Greens. "This is Clem Snide calling. I'd like to speak to Mr. Green, please."

A woman's voice sounded guarded: "What is it in reference to, please?"

"I am a private investigator retained by Mr. Green."

"Well, I'm afraid you can't speak to him. You see, Mr. and Mrs. Green are dead."

"Dead?"

"Yes. They were killed last night in a car crash. This is Mrs. Green's sister." She sounded pretty cool about it.

"I'm terribly sorry...." I was thinking about what Dimitri had said. The "Adepts" who had hanged Jerry did not know what magical intentions they were projecting. They did not know to whom they were aspeak ... plane crash ... car crash ...

I didn't want to think about the Green case anymore, but it stuck to me like the fever smell. What had Dimitri called it? B-23, the Hanging Fever.

Death is enforced separation from the body. Orgasm is identification with the body. So death in the moment of orgasm literally *embodies* death. It would also yield an earthbound spirit—an incubus dedicated to reproducing that particular form of death.

I took a Nembutal and finally slept.

Someone was murdered in this room a long time ago. How long ago ... the empty safe ... the bloody pipe threader? His partner must have done it. They never caught him. Easy to disappear in those days, when a silver dollar bought a good meal and piece of ass. Smell of dust and old fear in the room. Someone is at the back door. Quién es? The hall is dark.

It's Marty come to call ... gaslight now on the yellow pockmarked face, the cold gray eyes, the brilliantined black hair, the coat with fur trimming at the collar, the purple waistcoat beneath. ...

"We had a hard time finding you." His drunken driver there can hardly stand up. "Wore himself out getting here, he did."

"He made a few stops along the way."

"Come along to the Metropole and have some bubbly. It's my treat."

Now Broadway's full of guys who think they're mighty wise, just because they know a thing or two

"No thanks."

"What do you mean, no thanks? We had a long way to find you."

You can see them every day, strolling up and down Broadway, boasting of the wonders they can do

"I'm expecting someone from the Palace."

"Your old pals aren't good enough anymore? Is that it?"

"I don't remember we were exactly pals, Marty."

There are con men and drifters, Murphy men and grifters, and they all hang around the Metropole

"Let me in, Dalford. I've come a long way."

"All right, but . . ."

But their names would be mud, like a chump playing stud, if they lost that old ace down in the hole

"Nice place you got here. Plenty of room. You could put the Metropole in here if it came to that. . . ." He is sitting on the bed now.

They'll tell you of trips that they're going to take, from Florida up to the old North Pole

"Look, Marty . . ."

I wake up. Jim is covered with white foam. I can't wake him. "Jamie! . . . Jamie! . . ." *Cold white foam.*

I wake up. Jim is standing with a pipe threader in his hand, looking towards the back door. . . . "I thought someone was in the room."

I got up and dressed and went into the kitchen to make breakfast. It tasted disgusting. The Everson questionnaire and pictures had arrived, and I looked through them as I drank coffee. The pictures were quite ordinary. The Everson boy looked like the clean-cut American Boy. I wondered why he had taken up such an esoteric subject as Mayan archaeology.

Jim came in and asked if he could take the day off. He does that occasionally, has an apartment of his own in the East Village. After he left, I sat down and went carefully through the Everson case: the boy had been in Mexico City doing some research in the library preparatory to a dig in Yucatán. In his last letter he said he was leaving for Progreso in a few days and would write from there.

After two weeks, his family was worried. They waited

another week then called the U.S. Embassy in Mexico City. A man checked his address, and the landlady said he had packed and left almost three weeks ago. A police check of hotel registration in Progreso turned up nothing. It had now been about six weeks with no word.

Several possibilities had occurred to me: He may have gone on some alternate dig. Postal service in rural Mexico is practically nonexistent. Probably there was no more involved than two or three lost letters. I was inclined to favor some such simple explanation. I had no special feelings about this case and felt sure I could locate young Everson without much difficulty. I decided to knock off and take in a porn flick.

It was good, as porn flicks go—beautiful kids on screen—but I couldn't understand why they had so much trouble coming. And all the shots were stylized. Every time a kid came all over a stomach or an ass, he rubbed the jism around like tapioca.

I left in the middle of a protracted fuck, and walked down Third Avenue to the Tin Palace for a drink.

There was a hippie with a ratty black beard at one end of the bar and I could smell Marty on him—that cold gray smell of the time traveler. I'd seen him around before. The name is Howard Benson. Small-time pusher, pot and C and occasional O. Lives somewhere in the neighborhood. He caught my eye, drank up and hurried out.

I gave him a few seconds' start and tailed him to a loft building on Greene Street. I waited outside until his light went on, picked the front-door lock and went in. I had an Identikit picture of Marty with me that Jim drew. It looks like a photo. I was going to show it to this Howard and say it was a picture of a murder suspect, and see what I could surprise or bluff out of him.

His loft was on the third floor. I knocked loud and long. No answer. I could feel somebody inside. *"Police!"*

I shouted. "Open the door or we'll break it down!" Still no answer. Well, that would keep the neighbors out of the hall.

It took me about two minutes to get the door open. I walked in. There was somebody there, all right. Howard Benson was lying on his face in a pool of blood. The murder weapon was there too: a bloody pipe threader that had smashed in the back of his head.

I took a quick look around. There was a filthy pile of bedding in one corner and a phone beside it, some tools, dusty windows, a splintery floor. Benson was lying in front of an old-fashioned safe which was open. A dead gray smell hung in that loft like a fog. Marty was there.

The whole scene was like something out of the 1890s. I bent down and sniffed at the open safe. Faint but unmistakable, the fever smell. I got a nail. It stuck to the sides of the safe. The walls were magnetized. Jerry's head had been in that safe.

Quickly I drew a circle around the safe, seeing the head as clearly as I could inside. I repeated the words and touched the absent head three times with the amulet that Dimitri had given me. A tingle ran up my arm.

Half an hour later, I was sitting in O'Brien's office. His boss, Captain Graywood, was also there. Graywood was a tall blond man with thick glasses and a blank expression.

"You want the whole story, then?"

"That's the general idea."

I told them most of it, what I knew about Marty, and showed them the picture. I told them about Dimitri finding the body and about Adam North's story. Captain Graywood never changed his expression. Once or twice O'Brien turned into his brother, the priest. When I had finished he took a deep breath.

"Quite a story, Clem. We've had cases like that . . .

and worse things too: torture, castration ... cases that don't get into the papers or into the courts."

Captain Graywood said, "So it is your theory that the head was brought here as a potent magical object?"

"Yes."

"And you are convinced that the head was in that safe?"

"Yes."

"And why do you think the body was addressed to South America?"

"I don't know the answer to that."

"Ecuador is headhunter country, isn't it?"

"Yes."

"It is logical to assume then that someone planned to reunite the head and the body in South America."

"I think so."

"You haven't told us everything."

"I've told you what I *know*."

"This Marty ... Dimitri's men never saw him?"

"No."

"But you could see him?"

"Yes."

"We can't arrest a ghost," said O'Brien.

"Well, if he can make himself solid enough to beat someone's brains out with a pipe wrench, you might be able to. ... Question of being there at the right time."

EVEN THE COCKROACHES

Una cosa me da risa	Something makes me laugh
Pancho Villa sin camisa	Pancho Villa takes his shirt off

The Cucaracha, where Kiki worked as a waiter, had "La Cucaracha" on the jukebox. It's a basement restaurant, with a small bar and a few tables. It was 11:00 P.M. and the place was empty. I hadn't seen Kiki since I interviewed him on the Green case. Looking very handsome in a worn dinner jacket, he was leaning against the bar, talking to the bargirl. She does a striptease act uptown on weekends which is a thing to see.

Because old Pancho shakes the dirt out

I shook hands with Kiki, ordered a margarita, and sat down, and right on cue a cockroach crawled across the table. When Kiki brought the margarita I pointed to the cockroach and said, "He's getting his marijuana and getting it steady."

"*Sí,*" said Kiki absently, and brushed the cockroach away with his towel.

I looked around and saw there was one other diner by the door. I hadn't noticed him when I came in. He was sitting alone and reading a book called *Thin Air* about a top-secret navy project to make a battleship and all the sailors on it disappear. It was supposed to confuse the enemy; however, all the test sailors went crazy. But CIA men were made of sterner stuff and found it modern and convenient to "go zero" as they call it in a tight spot.

Porque no tiene	Because he doesn't have
Porque le falta	Because he lacks
Marijuana por fumar	Marijuana to smoke

On the wall were bullfight posters and *The Death of Manolete*. The poisonous colors made me think of arsenic green and the flaking green paint in the WC. It's a big picture and must be worth a lot of money, like a wooden Indian or *Custer's Last Stand*, which the Anheuser-Busch Company used to give out to their customers. I remember as an adolescent being excited by the green naked bodies sprawled about ass-up, getting scalped by the Indians, and especially a story about one man who played dead while he was being scalped and so escaped.

I drank the margaritas and ordered a combination plate and went to the green room. When I came back, "Thin Air" was gone. Kiki came and sat with me and had a Carta Blanca. I told him Jerry was dead.

La cucaracha la cucaracha

"Cómo?"	"How?"
"Ahorcado."	"Hanged."
Ya no quiere caminar	Doesn't want to run round anymore

"Nudo?"   "Naked?"
"Sí."   "Yes."

Kiki nodded philosophically and a face leered out, the face of a middle-aged man with a cast in the right eye. This must be Kiki's macambo magic master, I decided.

"It was his destiny," Kiki said. "Look at these." He spread some postcards circa 1913 out on the table. The photos showed soldiers hanged from trees and telephone poles with their pants down around their ankles. The pictures were taken from behind. "Pictures get him very hot. He want me pull scarf tight around his neck when he come." Kiki made a motion of pulling something around his neck.

"Jerry's spirit has got into my assistant. Only you can call him out."

"Why me?"

"Jerry's spirit has to obey you because you fuck him the best."

Kiki's eyes narrowed with calculation and he drummed on the table with his fingertips. I was thinking I could use an interpreter on this trip ... after all, expense account. My Spanish is half-assed and in any case he could find out more than two nosy *gringos*.

"Like to come along with us to Mexico and South America?"

I named a figure. He smiled and nodded. I wrote the address of my loft on a card and handed it to him. "Be there at eleven in the morning. We make magic."

When I got back to the loft Jim was there, and I explained that we were going to perform this ritual to get Jerry's spirit out.

He nodded. "Yeah, he's half in and half out and it hurts."

Next day Kiki showed up with a bundle of herbs and a head of Elleggua in a hatbox. As he was setting up his altar, lighting candles and anointing the head, I explained that he would fuck Jim and evoke Jerry to bring Jerry all the way in—and then I had good strong magic to exorcise the spirit. Kiki watched with approval, one magic man to another, as I set up the altar for the noon ritual and lit the incense. It was ten minutes before noon.

"Todos nudos ahora."

Kiki was wearing red shiny boxer shorts, and when he slipped them off he was half-hard. Jim was stiff and lubricating. I drew a circle around our bodies. We were facing south for the noon ritual and I had set up a red candle for fire, which was Jerry's element. The amulet was on the altar and there was a tube of KY by the unguent jar.

"When I say *ahora*, fuck him."

Kiki picked up the KY and moved behind Jim, who leaned forward over the altar, hands braced on knees. Kiki rubbed KY up Jim's ass and hitched his hands around Jim's hips, contracting his body as his cock slid in. Jim gasped and bared his teeth. His head and neck turned bright red and the cartilage behind his right ear swelled into a pulsing knot.

Holding the amulet, I took a position on the other side of the altar. Jerry's face was in front of me now, as the red color spread down Jim's chest and his nipples pulsed erect. His stomach, crotch and thighs were bright red now, and the rash spread down his calves to his toes and the fever smell reeked out of him. His head twisted to the right as I touched the amulet to the crown of his head, to the forehead between the eyes, and to the cartilage behind both ears.

"Back to earth. Back to air. Back to fire. Back to water."

For a split second Jerry's face hung there, eyes blazing green light. A reek of decay filled the room. Someone said "Shit" in a loud voice. We carried Jim to a couch. Kiki got a wet towel and rubbed his chest, face, and neck. He opened his eyes, sat up, and smiled. The decay smell was gone. So was the fever smell.

At two o'clock O'Brien called: "Well, I think we've found your head for you—or what's left of it. Can't be sure until we check the dental work...."

"Where did you find it?"

"At the airport. Crate labeled MACHINE PARTS sent by air freight and addressed to a broker in Lima, Peru, to be picked up by Juan Mateos. The crate was being loaded onto the plane when the workmen accidentally dropped it and it split open. It was airtight and strongly built ... it just happened to fall right on a seam. They tell me the stink was enough to knock a man down. One of them puked all over the crate."

"When did this happen?"

"At noon. We sent along a duplicate crate and contacted the Lima police to tail anyone who calls for it."

"Was the crate lined with magnetized iron?"

"Yes. We duplicated that too. The Lima police have two men planted in the customs broker's to watch anyone who calls for other crates in case he tries to check out the head crate in any way. A compass would tell him it is magnetized. We've got a wax head inside, so even with X-ray equipment ..."

"Very good. You seem to have thought of everything. But just one more point: an object like that gives out very strong psychic vibrations that a sensitive could pick up on.... You might tell them to watch especially for an adolescent who comes for another crate and touches or brushes up against the head crate."

"That's already been done. Captain Graywood told them to watch for an errand boy who might brush against the crate, especially with his ass or his crotch."

O'Brien said this in a matter-of-fact voice, as if it were routine procedure. Dimitri, Graywood, and now O'Brien. Who the hell were these so-called cops?

FIRECRACKERS

There are about thirty boys staying in Skipper Nordenholz's "Palace," as we call it. The number fluctuates from day to day as people come in from other settlements or set out on various missions. Mr. Thomas has taken *The Great White* and sailed with a small crew. His assignment is, as always, to recruit people with special skills.

The boys cook in the communal kitchen or on the patio. Here the Arab boys roast meat over charcoal fires and bake bread in clay ovens. Food is plentiful. We set traps for fish in the river and in the bay. A short walk into the jungle and I can shoot wild turkey and grouse and occasionally a deer. River fish can also be kept in the fishpond until needed.

We are all up at dawn for a breakfast of eggs, fruit, and bread. Then after a short rest there is instruction in bare-hand fighting given by Japanese and Chinese youths: the use of stick, chain, and staff, different styles of swordsmanship, and knife fighting. An Indian Thuggee gives lessons in the strangling cord. He belongs to a dissident magical brotherhood known as the Secret Stranglers who have separated themselves from the worship of Kali.

I take particular interest in archery since the bow can deliver more projectiles in less time than the guns we are making. I have made a number of crossbows to sell in the store so that the Indians will be able to duplicate the design. These bows are not as heavy as the usual crossbows and it is quite easy to pull and cock the bow by hand. I am more interested in speed of fire than in armor-piercing strength.

Dink Rivers excels at the martial arts. After a few lessons he is able to equal his instructors in proficiency. He explains that once general body control is mastered, any physical skill can be learned almost at once. He has promised to show me the secrets of body control but he says that the time has not yet come. "I get my orders in dreams and whatever happens in my dreams then has to happen when I wake up." Often he does not sleep in the Palace and Hans tells me he has a hut about half a mile down the coast.

One night I dream I am sitting with Dink when he looks at me and says, "I think you should see this," pulling down his shorts to reveal his half-erect phallus. I wake up in a state of great excitement and Dink says that the time is approaching. In preparation I must abstain from sex for three days.

At the end of this period, during which I had not seen him, he appeared in my room during the siesta hour and led the way out through the gate and along a path by the sea. We are quite close to the hut before I can see it, built in a clump of trees and shrubs, painted green and blending with the surroundings. The house is built of parts salvaged from grounded ships.

Inside it is cool and dark, smelling of pitch. The house consists of a single room furnished like a ship's cabin, containing a chest, a rolled-up pallet, and two low stools of driftwood. We take off our clothes, hanging them on wooden pegs and he indicates that I am to sit opposite him on one of the stools, our knees touching. He looks silently into my eyes and I feel a tightness and weakness in the chest.

He is getting stiff and so am I, the feeling of weakness now like death in the throat as we both are fully erect. Silver spots boil in front of my eyes and I have a feeling of squeezing into his nuts and cock as I lie on the pallet and Dink fucks me.

Afterwards we lie down side by side. He is talking in his clear grave young voice. I have rarely seen him smile and there is something very sad and remote about him like a faint sign or signal from a distant star.

"Middletown isn't like the town where you came from. There are no Mrs. Nortons sniffing around for the scent of whiskey and sin. We do not allow people like her in Middletown. To an outsider, Middletown is just a pretty little place, stone houses along a clear river. Nice friendly folk. But strangers don't stay unless we can adjust them to our ways. For those who must remain outside there is no land for sale and no work.

"Middletown is run by a magical brotherhood. You will hear about white and black lodges, the right-hand path and the left-hand path. Believe me, there is no such sharp line. However, the Middletown Brothers would not allow themselves to be placed in a position where they would need to use the usual methods of black magic. Once you achieve body control you don't need that.

"There is no formal initiation into the Brotherhood. Initiation comes through dream guides. At the age of fourteen, when I began to have dreams that culminated in ejaculation, I decided to learn control of the sexual energy. If I could achieve orgasm at will in the waking state, I could do the same in dreams and control my dreams instead of being controlled by them.

"To accomplish sexual control, I abstained from masturbation. In order to achieve orgasm, it is simply necessary to relive a previous orgasm. So while awake, I would endeavor to project myself into sexual dreams, which I was now having several times a week. It was some months before I acquired sufficient concentration to get results.

"One day I was lying naked on my bed, feeling a warm spring wind on my body and watching leaf shadows dance on the wall. I ran through a sex dream like reciting my ABCs when suddenly silver spots boiled in front of my eyes and I experienced a feeling of weakness in the chest—the dying feeling—and I am slipping into my self in the dream and go off.

"Having brought sexual energy under control I now had the key to body control. Errors, fumbles, and ineptitudes are caused by uncontrolled sexual energy which then lays one open to any sort of psychic or physical attack. I went on to bring speech under control, to be used when I want it, not yammering in my ear at all times or twisting tunes and jingles in my brain.

"I used the same method of projecting myself into a time when my mind seemed empty of words. This I would do while walking in the woods or paddling on the lake. Once again, I waited some time for results. One day as I was paddling on the lake and about to put out fishlines, I felt the weakness in my chest, silver spots appeared in front of my eyes with a vertiginous sensation of being sucked into a vast empty space where words do not exist."

My time is divided between the library and the gun shop. The library is well stocked with books on weapons, fortifications, shipbuilding, and navigation and has also a large number of maps indicating the number of Spanish troops stationed in different locations, the nature of fortifications, and the Spanish sea routes with approximate times when they are in use.

It often happens that quite practical inventions are for some reason not developed. Here are plans for a repeating gun with a number of barrels rotating by means of a hand-turned crank. A repeating gun is one of my dreams but first there is some basic improvement required in the gun itself.

Hans and I, wearing only shorts, are reading the same book, our knees touching. Here are plans for a grenade—simply a metal sphere filled with powder ignited by a fuse, and a mortar that shoots large grenades for a considerable distance. I feel a sudden quickening of interest and a prickling sensation in the back of my neck. Hans seems equally affected. He is breathing through his teeth, eyes boring into the paper as if he were studying an erotic drawing.

We look at each other and stand up, our shorts sticking out at the crotch. We strip off our shorts and Hans grins and brings his finger up in three jerks. I prop the book against the wall on the far side of the desk and bend over a chair. As Hans fucks me, the drawings seem to come alive belching red fire and just as I go off, Chinese children set off a string of firecrackers against the door and I see a huge firecracker blow the library to atoms as a gob of sperm hits the book six feet away.

We sit down naked and Hans wipes his brow with one hand and says: *"Wheeeeoooo!"*

I say: *"Firecracker!* That's the basic exploding weapon. It's all here, but they didn't see how far it can be carried. *Firecrackers* . . . they can be of any size. Why not exploding cannonballs? One such projectile could sink a galleon."

"Waring is expecting us."

Dink leads the way up a steep path. Waring's house is on top of a hill in a grove of trees, concealed by vines. He receives us most cordially in a cool room furnished in the Moroccan style with a low table and settees. A tall aloof black serves mint tea, and Waring passes around a hashish pipe. Dink declines, since he never touches alcohol or any other drug.

At a sign from Dink, Waring gets up and leads us into his studio.

"While there is still light . . ."

His paintings are unlike any I have ever seen, containing not one but many scenes, figures, and landscapes that flicker in and out of the canvas. I can see *The Great White*, Harbor Point, fleeting faces, islands, flying fish, and Indians rowing across the bay.

Back in the sitting room candles have been lit, and there is a partridge pie with flaky pastry and a wild turkey *tagine* on a low table. I do not remember much of what was said during dinner.

At one point, Waring looked at me quizzically and said: "What you are doing is against the rules. Be careful you don't get caught."

It was quite late when we left. Back in the hut, Dink rolled out the pallet and I fell into a deep sleep.

In a dream I see Dink standing over me with the most perfectly formed erect phallus I have ever seen. Now he is fucking me with my legs up and as I wake up ejaculating, I find that he *is* fucking me. I can feel his face in mine and for a split second he disappears and I hear his fourteen-year-old voice in my throat: "It's me! It's me! It's me! I made it! I landed!"

We can hardly wait to get back to the shop and set all hands to work. In a week, we have several different devices ready for testing. I have made a number of arrows, the heads of hollow iron filled with powder; grenades, with a shaft to be launched from a flintlock rifle; several mortars; and a projectile for a cannon, designed to explode on contact. The nose of this projectile, which is not round but shaped like a short cylinder, is of softer metal packed with flint chips and iron filings so that, being violently depressed on contact with ship or rigging, it explodes the powder charge. Inside, the cylinder is lined with Greek fire—that is, pitch mixed with finely powdered metal, this being separated from the powder charge by a layer of paper.

The time is now ready for testing. There is a stranded ship two hundred yards off the coast a mile down from our station. We proceed to the testing site with our bows and rifle grenades, mortars, and one cannon. Everyone is there: Strobe, the Iguana twins, Nordenholz, even Waring.

Ten arrows and ten rifle grenades are dipped into the fire. Bow is drawn, the head ignited from a torch, and the arrow launched, the same procedure being followed with the rifle grenades, which are of course much larger. The missiles streak towards the ship and in a few seconds are exploding on the decks, in the rigging, and against the sides, starting fires from one end of the boat to the other. Then mortars are launched, and though some fall short or overshoot, those that land cause great damage.

Time now for the cannon: a perfect hit with a ten-pound projectile at the waterline. The explosion tears a gaping hole in the hull and wraps the boatside in fire. There is no doubt as to the deadly effectiveness of these weapons. We are congratulated by Nordenholz and Strobe and the Iguana twins.

Waring smiles and says: "Nice toys. Nice noisy toys to scare the ghosts away."

The plans are sent along by courier to the other settlements and we busy ourselves bringing the fortifications of Port Roger up to date. The Indians are offered good pay to work in our ever-expanding shop and are learning how to make these devices.

Soon we have a fair stockpile of shells sufficient to pour a deadly fire into the bay from both sides. We have mounted gun towers around the walls of the town with cannon that can reach the bay or be lowered to fire directly down on any forces laying siege to Port Roger.

Nordenholz is supervising the construction of special boats designed to operate near the coasts. These are about fifty feet long, mounted on two pontoons. They will draw only a few feet of water and can be used in rivers and quickly launched or concealed. They will carry the maneuverable cannons and a good stock of mortars and grenades. He calls them Destroyers, since they have no other purpose. No provisions need be carried, just guns and gun crews, and the Destroyers will be so much faster than a galleon that they can easily avoid the fixed cannons.

I now turn my attention to improving the flintlock. My dissatisfaction with this weapon derives from an incident that occurred in a waterfront tavern in Boston. This place was near our gun shop, and we were accustomed to take a beer there after work. One evening I was there with Sean Brady when a man came in who had been dismissed by my father for his drunken, lazy, quarrelsome habits and had stomped out, vowing vengeance on all of us.

There he stood at the bar, weaving and glaring at us with bloodshot eyes, and let loose a string of vile oaths and insults. Brady told him to mind his mouth or lose his teeth, whereupon the man pulled a flintlock pistol from his side pocket, leveled it at Brady's chest, and pulled the trigger. At this precise second the bartender, who was standing behind the ruffian and to one side, spat a stream of beer straight into the pan, causing the weapon to misfire. We then beat the man unconscious and threw him into the harbor and watched him sink.

Of what use are flintlock weapons with a driving rain behind you? And the length of time taken to reload far exceeds the firing time. The weapon lacks firing power—that is, the number of projectiles that can be fired in a given length of time. So back to the library.

I note that early cannons were breech-loading, and feel once again the admonitory prickling in the back of my neck. At that very moment a hand touches the nape of my neck. It is the Iguana who has come in silently with her twin. I look up at her.

"It's there in my head, but I can't quite get it out where I can see it."

"Well, how did you see the exploding cannonball?"

Hans and I look at each other and grin.

Waring has told me about Hassan i Sabbah, the Old Man of the Mountain, who terrorized the Moslem world for years with a few hundred assassins. I pointed out that holding a single fortified position—as Hassan i Sabbah did at Alamut—is no longer possible, owing to improved weapons that I have already perfected and which will inevitably, in the course of time, fall into the hands of our prospective enemies. We need now a much wider area of occupation. Waring said cryptically: "Well, that depends on what you are trying to do."

As I was returning from the library this afternoon, a red-haired child of twelve or so popped out of a doorway, aimed a small pistol at me and pulled the trigger.

"*Bang!* You're dead."

I had seen these toy pistols many times before and never concerned myself to find out exactly how they functioned, just as I had seen firecrackers without realizing the potentials of *that* toy. The child was reloading.

"Let me see that," I demanded.

The child handed me his pistol, which had a flat hammer. The report resulted from the hammer's striking a little blister of powder glued between two pieces of paper. Suddenly I had the solution: firing device, charge, and ball in one unit, to be inserted and extracted through the breech. I bent down and the boy jumped up on my back, and I carried him into the gun shop as he fired his pistol in the air.

We are working round the clock on this design. Pallets are on the floor, and we take turns sleeping. We are producing double-barreled guns in both rifle and pistol form, for increased firepower.

In a week we have two rifles and two pistols, with a number of cartridges ready for testing. The test is carried out in the gun shop, since secrecy must be observed. A man-sized target is set up at one hundred feet. *"Pow Pow"*— two bullets on target.

After the test I present the red-headed boy, whose name is Chan, with a rifle and give Strobe a pistol. At this Strobe is somewhat piqued. I retain the remaining two weapons for my own use. Plans are immediately dispatched by courier to all the settlements in these locations: on the Pacific side of the isthmus of Panama opposite the Pearl Islands; two settlements inland from Guayaquil in a heavily wooded and mountainous area; and settlements above Panama City on both the Atlantic and Pacific sides and in the mountainous interior.

Production of the weapons is now standardized and we

have fifty Indians working under our supervision. As soon as they learn how to assemble the guns, they are sent back to their villages and jungles since decentralization is a keynote of our strategy. Instead of one central factory, there are a number of small shops that can turn out a few guns a day. We are distributing guns through the store in Port Roger. Arming the native population is another essential step. The cannon that protect Port Roger are being converted to receive breech-loading shells.

NECESITA AUTOMÓVIL

I hadn't been in Mexico City in fifteen years. Driving in from the airport I could hardly recognize the place. As Dimitri said, a selective pestilence may be the only solution. Otherwise, they will multiply their assholes into the polluted seas.

Kiki, Jim, and I checked into a small hotel off Insurgentes, which was a few blocks from John Everson's Mexico City address. Then we split up. Jim and Kiki went to John Everson's address to see what they could pick up from the landlady and the *vecinos*. I went to the American Embassy, found the Protection Department, and sent in my card. I saw the girl hand it to a man at a desk. He looked at the card and looked at me. Then he did something else. I waited twenty minutes.

"Mr. Hill will see you now."

Mr. Hill didn't get up or offer to shake hands. "Yes, Mr. uh . . ." He glanced down at the card. ". . . Snide. What can I do for you?"

There is a breed of State Department official who starts figuring out how he can get rid of you without doing whatever it is you want done as soon as you walk into his department. Clearly, Mr. Hill belonged to this breed.

"It's about John Everson. He disappeared in Mexico City about two months ago. His father has retained me to locate him."

"Well, we are not a missing-person service. So far as we are concerned, the case is now with the Mexican authorities. I suggest you contact them. A colonel, uh . . ."

"Colonel Figueres."

"Yes, that is the name, I believe."

"Did John Everson pick up his mail at the embassy?"

"I uh don't think . . . in any case, we don't encourage . . ."

"Yes, I know. You are also not a post office. Would you mind calling the mail desk and asking if there are any letters there addressed to John Everson?"

"Really, Mr. Snide . . ."

"Really, Mr. Hill. I have been retained by an American citizen—rather well connected, I may add, working on a U.S. government project—retained to find an American citizen who is missing in your district. So far, there is no evidence of foul play but it hasn't been ruled out."

He was also the type who backs down under pressure. He reached for the phone. "Could you tell me if there are any letters for John Everson at the desk. . . . One letter?"

I slid a power of attorney across the desk which authorized me among other things to pick up mail addressed to John Everson. He looked at it.

"A Mr. uh Snide will pick up the letter. He has authorization." He hung up.

I stood up. "Thank you, Mr. Hill." His nod was barely perceptible.

On the way out of the office I met that CIA punk from Athens. He pretended to be glad to see me, and shook hands and asked where I was staying. I told him at the Reforma. I could see he didn't believe me, which probably meant he knew where I was staying. I was beginning to get a bad feeling about the Everson case, like gathering vultures.

I waited almost an hour to see Colonel Figueres, but I knew he was really busy. He'd been a major when I last saw him. He hadn't changed much. A little heavier, but the same cold gray eyes and focused attention. When you see him he gives his whole concentration to you. He shook hands without smiling. I can't recall ever seeing him smile. He simply doesn't give himself occasion to do so. I told him I had come about the Everson boy's disappearance.

He nodded. "I thought you had, and I'm glad you are here. We haven't been able to give enough time to it."

"You think something may have happened to him?"

Figueres doesn't shrug. He doesn't gesticulate. He just sits there with his eyes focused on you and what is being discussed.

"I don't know. We have checked Progreso and all surrounding towns. We have checked airports and buses. If he had gone off on another dig, he would be that much easier to locate. A blond foreigner off the tourist routes is very conspicuous. We have also checked all the tourist places. Apparently he was a level-headed, serious young man . . . no indications of drug use or excessive drinking. Is there any history of amnesia? Psychotic episodes?"

"None that I know of."

Dead end.

Back at the hotel, Jim and Kiki had turned up very little from questioning the landlady and the neighbors. The landlady described Everson as a serious polite young man . . . *un caballero*. He entertained few visitors and these were also serious students. There had been no noise, no drinking, no girls.

I sat down and opened the letter. It was from his twin sister in Minneapolis. It read:

Querido Juanito,

He has visited me again. He says that before you receive this letter He will have contacted you. He says you will then know what has to be done.

Your Ever Loving Sister,
Jane

At three o'clock, I called Inspector Graywood in New York. "Clem Snide here."

"Ah yes, Mr. Snide, there have been some developments in Lima. A boy did come to call for another crate and was seen to brush against the duplicate head crate. He was followed to a bicycle rental and repair shop in the Mercado Mayorista. Police searched the shop and found false identity papers in the name of Juan Mateos. The proprietor has been arrested and charged with possession of forged papers and with conspiracy to conceal evidence of a murder. He is being detained in isolation. He claims he did not know what was in the crate. He had been offered a fairly large sum to pick up the crate after it had cleared customs. The crate was to have been brought to his shop. Someone would arrange to pick it up there, and he would be paid an additional and larger sum. The customs agent who passed the crate has also been arrested. He has confessed to accepting a bribe."

"What about the boy?"

"There was no reason to hold him in connection with this case. However, since he has a record for petty theft and a history of epilepsy, he has been placed in a rehabilitation center in Lima."

"I wish I could be on the scene."

"So do I. Otherwise, I doubt if any important arrests will be made. In a country like that, people of wealth are virtually untouchable. People like the Countess de Gulpa, for example. . . ."

"So you know about her?"

"Of course. The description of the man who contacted the customs broker tallies rather closely with your Identikit picture of Marty Blum. I have sent a copy to the Lima police and informed them that he is also wanted in connection with a murder here. Benson, it seems, was a pusher, small-time . . . a number of leads but no arrests as yet. Have you found the Everson boy?"

"Not yet and I don't like the looks of it."

"You think something has happened to him?"

"Perhaps."

"I believe you have a contact from Dimitri." I had said nothing about this contact when I told my story in O'Brien's office. "Perhaps it is time to use it."

"I will."

"Your presence in South America would be most valuable. It so happens that a client who wishes to remain anonymous is prepared to retain you in this connection. You will find thirty thousand dollars deposited to your bank account in Lima."

"Well, I haven't finished this case yet."

"Perhaps you can bring the Everson case to a speedy conclusion." He rang off.

It would seem that I had been called upon to act. I got out a map and couldn't find the Callejón de la Esperanza. There are small streets in Mexico City you won't find on a map. I had a general idea as to where it was and I wanted to walk around. I've cracked cases like this with nothing to go on, just by getting out and walking around at random. It works best in a strange town or in a town you haven't visited for some time.

We took a taxi to the Alameda, then started off in a northwesterly direction. Once we got off the main streets I saw that the place hadn't changed all that much: the same narrow unpaved streets and squares with booths selling tacos, fried grasshoppers, and peppermint candy covered with flies; the smell of pulque, urine, benzoin, chile, cooking oil, and sewage; and the faces—bestial, evil, beautiful.

A boy in white cotton shirt and pants, hair straight, skin smoky black, smelling faintly of vanilla and ozone. A boy with bright copper-red skin, innocent and beautiful as some exotic animal, leans against a wall eating an orange dusted with red pepper . . . a *maricón* slithers by with long arms and buck teeth, eyes glistening . . . man with a bestial Pan face reels out of a *pulquería* . . . a hunchback dwarf shoots us a venomous glance.

I was letting my legs guide me. Calle de los Desamparados, Street of Displaced Persons . . . a *farmacia* where an old junky was waiting for his Rx. I got a whiff of phantom opium. Postcards in a dusty shop window . . . Pancho Villa posing with scowling men . . . gun belts and rifles. Three youths hanging from a makeshift scaffold, two with their pants down to the ankles, the other naked. The picture had been taken from behind—soldiers standing in front of them watching and grinning. Photos taken about 1914. The naked boy looked American—you can tell a blond even in black and white.

My legs pulled me in, Jim and Kiki following behind me. When I opened the door a bell echoed through the shop. Inside, the shop was cool and dim with a smell of incense. A man came through a curtain and stood behind the counter. He was short and lightly built and absolutely bald, as if he had never had hair on his head; the skin a yellowish brown, smooth as terra-cotta, the lips rather full, eyes jet-black, forehead high and sloping back. There was a feeling of age about him, not that he looked old but as if he were a survivor of an ancient race—Oriental, Mayan, Negroid—all of these, but something else I had never seen in a human face. He was strangely familiar to me and then I remembered where I had seen that face before. It was in the Mayan collection of the British Museum, a terra-cotta head about three inches in height. His lips moved into a slow smile and he spoke in perfect English without accent or inflection, eerie and remote as if coming from a great distance.

"Good afternoon, gentlemen."

"Could I see that postcard in the window?"

"Certainly. That is what you have come for."

It occurred to me that this must be Dimitri's contact, but this was not the address he had given.

"The Callejón de la Esperanza? The Blind Alley of Hope was destroyed in the earthquake. It has not been rebuilt. This way, gentlemen."

He ushered us through a heavy door behind the curtain. When the door closed, it shut out all noise from the street. We were in a bare whitewashed room with heavy oak furniture lit by a barred window that opened onto a patio. He motioned us to chairs and got an envelope from a filing case and handed me a picture. It was an eight-by-ten replica of the postcard in the window. As I touched the picture, I got a whiff of the fever smell.

Three youths were hanging from a pole supported by tripods, arms strapped to their sides by leather belts. There were two overturned sawhorses and a plank on the ground below them. The blond boy was in the middle, two dark youths hanging on each side of him. The other two had their pants down to their ankles. The blond boy was completely naked. Five soldiers stood in front of a barn looking up at the hanged men. One of the soldiers was very young, sixteen or seventeen, with down on his chin and upper lip. He was looking up with his mouth open, his pants sticking out at the fly.

The proprietor handed me a magnifying glass. The hanged boys quivered and writhed, necks straining against the ropes, buttocks contracting. Standing to one side, face in shadow, was the officer. I studied this figure through the glass. Something familiar . . . Oh yes—the Dragon Lady from "Terry and the Pirates." It was a woman. And she bore a slight resemblance to young Everson.

I pointed to the blond boy. "Do you have a picture of his face?"

He laid a picture on the table. The picture showed the boy's face and torso, his arms strapped to his sides. He was looking at something in front of him with a slack look on his face, as if he had just received an overwhelming shock and understood it completely. It was John Everson, or a close enough resemblance to be his twin brother.

I showed him a snapshot of Everson I had in my pocket. He looked at it and nodded. "Yes it seems to be the same young man."

"Do you know who these people were?"

"Yes. The three boys were revolutionaries. The blond boy was the son of an American miner and a Spanish mother. His father returned to America shortly after his birth. He was born and raised in Durango and spoke no English. He was hanged on his twenty-third birthday: September 24, 1914. The woman officer was his half-sister, three years older. She was finally ambushed and killed by Pancho Villa's men. I can assure you that young Everson is alive and well. He has simply forgotten his American identity. His memory can be restored. Unlike Jerry Green, he fell into comparatively good hands. You will meet them tonight ... Lola La Chata is holding her annual party."

"Lola? Is she still operating?"

"She has her little time concession. You will be back in the days of Allende. The Iguana twins will be there. They will take you to Everson. And now ..." He showed us out the back way onto an unpaved street. "I think you will get a ride to Lola's."

Lola's was quite a walk from where we were, and it was not an area for taxis. Also I was a little confused as to directions. A Cadillac careened around the corner and screamed to a stop in a cloud of dust. A man in a glen plaid suit leaned out of the front seat.

"Going to the party? Get in, *cabrones*!"

We got into the back seat. There were two *machos* in the front seat and two on the jump seats. As we sped through the dirt streets they blasted at cats and chickens with their 45s, missing with every shot as the *vecinos* dove for cover.

POR CONVENCIÓN ZAPATA

The General's car stops in front of Lupita's place, which in a slum area of unpaved streets, looks like an abandoned warehouse. The door is opened by an old skull-faced *pistolero* with his black jacket open, a tip-up 44 Smith & Wesson strapped to his lean flank.

The *pistolero* steps aside and we walk into a vast room with a high-beamed ceiling. The furniture is heavy black oak and red brocade, suggesting a Mexican country estate. In the middle of the room is a table with platters of tamales and tacos, beans, rice, and guacamole, beer in tubs of ice, bottles of tequila, bowls of marijuana and cigarette papers. The party is just starting and a few guests stand by the table puffing marijuana and drinking beer. On a smaller table syringes are laid out with glasses of water and alcohol. Along one wall are curtained booths.

Lola La Chata sits in a massive oak chair facing the door, three hundred pounds cut from the mountain rock of Mexico, her graciousness underlining her power. She extends a massive arm: "Ah, Meester Snide . . . El Puerco Particular . . . the Private Pig . . ." She shakes with laughter. "And your handsome young assistants . . ." She shakes hands with Jim and Kiki. "You do well by yourself, Meester Snide."

"And you, Lola. . . . You are younger, if anything."

She waves a hand to the table. "Please serve yourselves. . . . I think an old friend of yours is already here."

I start towards the table and recognize Bernabé Abogado.
"Clem!"

"Bernabé!"

We go into an embrace and I can feel the pearl-handled 45 under his glen plaid jacket. He is drinking Old Parr scotch and there are four bottles on the table. He pours scotch into glasses as I introduce Jim and Kiki. "Practically everybody in Mexico drinks scotch." Then he laughs and pounds me on the back. "Clem, meet the Iguanas . . . this very good friend."

I shake hands with two of the most beautiful young people I have ever seen. They both have smooth greenish skin, black eyes, a reptilian grace. I can feel the strength in the boy's hand. They are incredibly poised and detached, their faces stamped with the same ancient lineage as the shop proprietor. They are the Iguana twins.

Junkies arrive and pay court to Lupita. She rewards them with papers of heroin fished from between her massive dugs. They are fixing at the table of syringes.

"Tonight everything is free," says the Iguana sister. *"Mañana es otra cosa."*

The room is rapidly filling with whores and thieves, pimps and hustlers. Uniformed cops get in line and Lupita rewards each of them with an envelope. Plainclothesmen come in and shove to the head of the line. Their envelopes are thicker.

Bernabé beckons to a young Indian policeman who has just received a thin envelope. The policeman approaches shyly. Bernabé pounds him on the back. "This *cabrón* get cockeyed *borracho* and kill two people. . . . I get him out of jail."

Other guests are arriving: the glamorous upper crust and jet set from costume parties. Some are in Mayan and Aztec dress. They bring various animals: monkeys, ocelots, iguanas, and a parrot who screams insults. The *machos* chase a terrified squealing peccary around the room.

A rustle of excitement sweeps through the guests:

"Here's Mr. Coca-Cola."

"He's the real thing."

Mr. Coca-Cola circulates among the guests selling packets of cocaine. As the cocaine takes effect the tempo of the party accelerates. The General turns to a spider monkey perched on top of his chair.

"Here, *cabrón*, have a sniff." He holds up a thumbnail with a pinch of cocaine. The monkey bites his hand, drawing blood. The cocaine spills down his coat. "*CHINGOA* YOU SON OF A WHORE!" The General leaps up and jerks out his 45, blasting at the monkey from a distance of a few feet and missing with every shot as the guests hit the deck, dodge behind chairs, and roll under the table.

Lupita lifts a finger. Fifty feet away across the room, the old *pistolero* draws his long-barreled 44, aims and fires in one smooth movement, killing the monkey. This display of power intimidates even the *machos* and there is a moment of silence as a servant removes the dead monkey and wipes up the blood. A number of couples and some trios retire to the curtained booths.

Another contingent of guests has arrived among whom I recognize American narcotics agents. One of them is talking with a Mexican lawyer. "I feel so sorry for these American boys in jail here for the *cocaína*," the lawyer says. "And for the girls, even sorrier. I do what I can to get them out but it is most difficult. Our laws are very strict. Much stricter than yours."

In a search booth, which is also one of the booths at Lupita's party, a naked American girl with two uniformed police. The General and the lawyer enter from a door at the rear of the booth. One of the cops points to a packet of cocaine on a shelf. "She have it in her pussee, *señores*." At a gesture from the General the cops exit, grinning like monkeys.

"We feel so sorry for your pussee—frozen in the snow," says the General taking off his pants. "I am the beeg thaw."

A giggling *macho* pulls aside the curtain in front of the booth. "Good pussee, *cabrones*?"

Two Chapultepec blondes nudge each other and chant in unison: "Isn't he *marvelous*? Never repeats himself."

The *macho* pulls aside the curtain of the next booth. "He fuck her in the dry hole."

"Never repeats himself."

In the end booth Ah Pook, the Mayan God of Death, is fucking the young Corn God. As the curtains are jerked aside they reach orgasm and the young Corn God is spattered with black spots of decay. A nitrous haze like vaporized flesh steams off their bodies. The *macho* gasps, coughs, and drops dead of a heart attack.

"Never repeats himself."

Lupita gestures. Indian servants load the body onto a stretcher and carry it out. The party resumes at an even more hectic pace. The gas released by the copulation of life and death acts on the younger guests like catnip. They strip off their clothes, rolling around on mattresses which are spread out on the floor by wooden-faced servants. They exchange masks and do stripteases with scarves while others roll on their backs, legs in the air, applauding with their feet.

The Iguana touched my arm. "Will you and your two helpers please come with me? We have matters to discuss in private."

She led us through a side door and down a long corridor to an elevator. The elevator opened onto a short hall at the end of which was another door. She motioned us into a large loft apartment furnished in Moroccan and Mexican style with rugs, low table, a few chairs, and couches. I declined a drink but accepted a joint.

"The postcard vendor tells me you can help us locate John Everson," I began.

She nodded. I remembered that I had not heard her brother say anything. He had nodded and smiled when we were introduced. He sat beside her now on a low couch looking serene rather than bored. Jim, Kiki, and I sat opposite in three cedar chairs from Santa Fe.

"We have many places here...." A wave of her hand brought the benzoin smell of New Mexico into the room. "It *was* a lovely place but they had to spoil it with their idiotic bombs. Oh yes, John Everson ... such a nice boy, modern and convenient. You found him so, of course?" She turned to her brother, who smiled and licked his lips. "Well, he is in Durango with relatives ... in excellent condition, considering the transfer of identities. Such operations may leave the patient a hospital case for months. This generally means that the operation has not been skillfully performed, or that discordant entities have been lodged in the same body....

"In John Everson's case, there have been no complications. We had to give the Mexican identity sufficient time for a transfer to take place. Now it only remains to blend the two and he will recover his own identity, with fluent Spanish and a knowledge of rural Mexico which will be useful in his profession.

"In this case, the two identities are so similar that there will be no disharmony. And the spirit of El Gringo now has a home. He could not enter the cycle of rebirth because his karma required a duplicate death. This was done by electric brain stimulation which seems completely real to the patient. As you know, a difficulty in organ transplants is that they are rejected as a foreign body. Drugs must be administered to suspend the rejection. In this case, the shared experience of being hanged will dissolve the rejection that would otherwise occur, giving rise to the phenomenon of multiple personalities, where only one personality can occupy the body at one time. The hanging experience acts as a solvent. The two personalities will blend into one. John Everson will contact his parents, and tell them that he suffered a lapse of memory owing to a light concussion but is now completely recovered."

I leaned back. "Well, that wraps that case up."

"You have been retained to act against the Countess . . . thirty thousand dollars. Does that seem enough to you?"

"Well, considering what we are expected to do—no."

"And considering that you are all inexperienced and susceptible, this is virtually a suicide mission. I am prepared to retain you at a fair price and provide contacts which will give you at least some chance of success."

She led the way into a bare room with chairs, a long table, and filing cabinets along one wall. I recognized the room as a replica of the room in back of the postcard vendor's shop. She went to the filing cabinet and handed me a short pamphlet bound in heavy parchment. On the cover in red letters:

CITIES OF THE RED NIGHT.

BOOK TWO

CITIES OF THE
RED NIGHT

The Cities of the Red Night were six in number: Tamaghis, Ba'dan, Yass-Waddah, Waghdas, Naufana, and Ghadis. These cities were located in an area roughly corresponding to the Gobi Desert, a hundred thousand years ago. At that time the desert was dotted with large oases and traversed by a river which emptied into the Caspian Sea.

The largest of these oases contained a lake ten miles long and five miles across, on the shores of which the university town of Waghdas was founded. Pilgrims came from all over the inhabited world to study in the academies of Waghdas, where the arts and sciences reached peaks of attainment that have never been equaled. Much of this ancient knowledge is now lost.

The towns of Ba'dan and Yass-Waddah were opposite each other on the river. Tamaghis, located in a desolate area to the north on a small oasis, could properly be called a desert town. Naufana and Ghadis were situated in mountainous areas to the west and south beyond the perimeter of usual trade routes between the other cities.

In addition to the six cities, there were a number of villages and nomadic tribes. Food was plentiful and for a time the population was completely stable: no one was born unless someone died.

The inhabitants were divided into an elite minority known as the Transmigrants and a majority known as the Receptacles. Within these categories were a number of occupational and specialized strata and the two classes were not in practice separate: Transmigrants acted as Receptacles and Receptacles became Transmigrants.

To show the system in operation: Here is an old Transmigrant on his deathbed. He has selected his future Receptacle parents, who are summoned to the death chamber. The parents then copulate, achieving orgasm just as the old Transmigrant dies so that his spirit enters the womb to be reborn. Every Transmigrant carries with him at all times a list of alternative parents, and in case of accident, violence, or sudden illness, the nearest parents are rushed to the scene. However, there was at first little chance of random or unexpected deaths since the Council of Transmigrants in Waghdas had attained such skill in the art of prophecy that they were able to chart a life from birth to death and determine in most cases the exact time and manner of death.

Many Transmigrants preferred not to wait for the infirmities of age and the ravages of illness, lest their spirit be so weakened as to be overwhelmed and absorbed by the Receptacle child. These hardy Transmigrants, in the full vigor of maturity, after rigorous training in concentration and astral projection, would select two death guides to kill them in front of the copulating parents. The methods of death most commonly employed were hanging and strangulation, the Transmigrant dying in orgasm, which was considered the most reliable method of ensuring a successful transfer. Drugs were also developed, large doses of which occasioned death in erotic convulsions, smaller doses being used to enhance sexual pleasure. And these drugs were often used in conjunction with other forms of death.

In time, death by natural causes became a rare and rather discreditable occurrence as the age for transmigration dropped. The Eternal Youths, a Transmigrant sect, were hanged at the age of eighteen to spare themselves the coarsening experience of middle age and the deterioration of senescence, living their youth again and again.

Two factors undermined the stability of this system. The first was perfection of techniques for artificial insemination. Whereas the traditional practice called for one death and one rebirth, now hundreds of women could be impregnated from a single sperm collection, and territorially oriented Transmigrants could populate whole areas with their progeny. There were sullen mutters of revolt from the Receptacles, especially the women. At this point, another factor totally unforeseen was introduced.

In the thinly populated desert area north of Tamaghis a portentous event occurred. Some say it was a meteor that fell to earth leaving a crater twenty miles across. Others say that the crater was caused by what modern physicists call a black hole.

After this occurrence the whole northern sky lit up red at night, like the reflection from a vast furnace. Those in the immediate vicinity of the crater were the first to be affected and various mutations were observed, the commonest being altered hair and skin color. Red and yellow hair, and white, yellow, and red skin appeared for the first time. Slowly the whole area was similarly affected until the mutants outnumbered the original inhabitants, who were as all human beings were at the time: black.

The women, led by an albino mutant known as the White Tigress, seized Yass-Waddah, reducing the male inhabitants to slaves, consorts, and courtiers all under sentence of death that could be carried out at any time at the caprice of the

White Tigress. The Council in Waghdas countered by developing a method of growing babies in excised wombs, the wombs being supplied by vagrant Womb Snatchers. This practice aggravated the differences between the male and female factions and war with Yass-Waddah seemed unavoidable.

In Naufana, a method was found to transfer the spirit directly into an adolescent Receptacle, thus averting the awkward and vulnerable period of infancy. This practice required a rigorous period of preparation and training to achieve a harmonious blending of the two spirits in one body. These Transmigrants, combining the freshness and vitality of youth with the wisdom of many lifetimes, were expected to form an army of liberation to free Yass-Waddah. And there were adepts who could die at will without any need of drugs or executioners and project their spirit into a chosen Receptacle.

I have mentioned hanging, strangulation, and orgasm drugs as the commonest means of effecting the transfer. However, many other forms of death were employed. The Fire Boys were burned to death in the presence of the Receptacles, only the genitals being insulated, so that the practitioner could achieve orgasm in the moment of death. There is an interesting account by a Fire Boy who recalled his experience after transmigrating in this manner:

"As the flames closed round my body, I inhaled deeply, drawing fire into my lungs, and screamed out flames as the most horrible pain turned to the most exquisite pleasure and I was ejaculating in an adolescent Receptacle who was being sodomized by another."

Others were stabbed, decapitated, disemboweled, shot with arrows, or killed by a blow on the head. Some threw themselves from cliffs, landing in front of the copulating Receptacles.

The scientists at Waghdas were developing a machine

that could directly transfer the electromagnetic field of one body to another. In Ghadis there were adepts who were able to leave their bodies before death and occupy a series of hosts. How far this research may have gone will never be known. It was a time of great disorder and chaos.

The effects of the Red Night on Receptacles and Transmigrants proved to be incalculable and many strange mutants arose as a series of plagues devastated the cities. It is this period of war and pestilence that is covered by the books. The Council had set out to produce a race of supermen for the exploration of space. They produced instead races of ravening idiot vampires.

Finally, the cities were abandoned and the survivors fled in all directions, carrying the plagues with them. Some of these migrants crossed the Bering Strait into the New World, taking the books with them. They settled in the area later occupied by the Mayans and the books eventually fell into the hands of the Mayan priests.

The alert student of this noble experiment will perceive that death was regarded as equivalent not to birth but to conception and go on to infer that conception is the basic trauma. In the moment of death, the dying man's whole life may flash in front of his eyes back to conception. In the moment of conception, his future life flashes forward to his future death. *To reexperience conception is fatal.*

This was the basic error of the Transmigrants: you do not get beyond death and conception by reexperience any more than you get beyond heroin by ingesting larger and larger doses. The Transmigrants were quite literally addicted to death and they needed more and more death to kill the pain of conception. They were buying parasitic life with a promissory death note to be paid at a prearranged time. The Transmigrants then imposed these terms on the host child to ensure his future transmigration. There was a basic conflict of interest between host child and Transmigrant. So the Transmigrants reduced the Receptacle class to a condition of virtual idiocy. Otherwise they would have reneged on a bargain from which they stood to gain nothing but death. The books are flagrant falsifications. And some of these basic lies are still current.

"Nothing is true. Everything is permitted." The last words of Hassan i Sabbah, Old Man of the Mountain.

"Tamaghis ... Ba'dan ... Yass-Waddah ... Waghdas ... Naufana ... Ghadis."

It is said that an initiate who wishes to know the answer to any question need only repeat these words as he falls asleep and the answer will come in a dream.

Tamaghis: This is the open city of contending partisans where advantage shifts from moment to moment in a desperate biological war. Here everything is as true as you think it is and everything you can get away with is permitted.

Ba'dan: This city is given over to competitive games and commerce. Ba'dan closely resembles present-day America with a precarious moneyed elite, a large disaffected middle class and an equally large segment of criminals and outlaws. Unstable, explosive, and swept by whirlwind riots. Everything is true and everything is permitted.

Yass-Waddah: This city is the female stronghold where the Countess de Gulpa, the Countess de Vile, and the Council of the Selected plot a final subjugation of the other cities. Every shade of sexual transition is represented: boys with girls' heads, girls with boys' heads. Here everything is true and nothing is permitted except to the permitters.

Waghdas: This is the university city, the center of learning where all questions are answered in terms of what can be expressed and understood. Complete permission derives from complete understanding.

Naufana and Ghadis are the cities of illusion where nothing is true and *therefore* everything is permitted.

The traveler must start in Tamaghis and make his way through the other cities in the order named. This pilgrimage may take many lifetimes.

GET OUT OF THE
DEFENSIVE POSITION

We now have a sufficient stockpile of the new weapons to initiate our campaign, and it seems unwise to delay longer. Sooner or later the enemy will learn something of our plans and the means we possess to implement them. We will apply the classic rules of hit-and-run warfare against a larger force, drawing them deeper and deeper into our territory while raiding and cutting supply lines. This is the tactic that beat Crassus's Roman Legions in the disastrous Parthian campaign. The Parthians would suddenly appear over a rise mounted on horses, loose a shower of arrows and ride away, luring the Romans deeper and deeper into the desert as thirst, hunger, and disease took their toll. Only a handful of the Legionnaires made their way back to the sea.

Once this tactic has sufficiently weakened the enemy, we will shift to all-out attack on a series of enemy positions. Failure to follow through on a successful attack is as disastrous as attempting an attack against unfavorable odds. It was this error that lost Hannibal the war against Rome. He did not realize that he had beaten the whole Roman army, so instead of marching on the unprotected city without delay, he retrenched to consolidate his position until he had no position left.

We can expect a landslide of defections to our cause,

and we must follow through to deliver a series of knockout blows. Nor will we allow time for the French and English to recognize the danger and join Spain against a common enemy. As soon as we see victory on the way in the southern hemisphere of the American continent, we will strike in the northern hemisphere. Then we will open a diplomatic offensive concentrating on England to negotiate treaties, trade agreements, and recognition of our independent and sovereign status.

Of course the new weapons will be common knowledge in a short time, but by then we will have a lead that will be difficult to overtake. We will be able to produce the weapons in any quantity, and by attracting inventors, skilled workers and technicians with higher wages and better living conditions, we can continue to turn out better weapons than our adversaries. We have also the incalculable advantage of a huge territory virtually impossible to invade successfully, whereas European countries, with the exception of Russia, are vulnerable to invasion, since they have no place to retreat to. We expect the Articles to spread through Africa, the Near and Far East, and we could invade Spain from North Africa.

Our immediate plan is to provoke the Spanish into a massive attack by taking Panama City and Guayaquil. This should divert much of the Pacific fleet to these two locations and dispatch land forces from Lima to Guayaquil and from Cartagena to Panama. If necessary, we shall retreat into the swamps of southern Panama and to the mountainous and heavily wooded areas northwest of the city. In the event of decisive land victories, we will immediately launch attacks on the depleted garrisons at Lima and Cartagena, inflict what damage we can on the fleet, and at the same time, strike in Mexico.

The Iguana twins have returned to Mexico to organize

our movement there, and Bert Hansen has gone with them. Captain Strobe has gone to Panama to assess the strength of the Spanish garrison and to organize partisan resistance to the north and east of the city. The area to the south is already in our hands. Juanito and Brady, with a force of fifty men, have gone south to set up fortified positions west of Guayaquil from which the attack on the city can be launched and to which our forces can withdraw, luring the Spanish ground forces into a deadly trap.

The sea battles will be directed by Opium Jones, Skipper Nordenholz, and Captain Strobe. A number of Destroyers are under construction.

Then one morning we received word on the signal drums that Captain Strobe had been taken in Panama City and sentenced to hang.

On receipt of this news, we set out for Panama City with a force of fifty men armed with the double-barreled rifles and a good stock of mortars, both of the type that explode on contact and those that explode from timed fuses. We had little hope of arriving in time, so we sent back word to the local partisans to take what measures they could to effect a rescue, that an expeditionary force was on the way.

Marching day and night without sleep, on opium and *yoka*, we were five miles south of the city at dawn of the third day. A warm mist enveloped us and I was reminded of the steam bath in my little Michigan lake town and found myself walking with an erection. Suddenly we heard a terrific explosion from the direction of Panama City and stopped, our faces lifted to the rising sun.

Shortly thereafter, a runner informed us that Captain Strobe had been rescued and was heading south in a fishing boat towards one of our Pacific bases opposite the Pearl Islands. We instructed the runner to inform the Spanish garrison that the pirates who had engineered the destruction of the armory and the escape of Captain Strobe were just south of the city, that they were few in number and almost out of powder. As we had hoped, the Spanish fell into our trap and immediately dispatched a column of soldiers in pursuit, leaving only a hundred to guard the city.

The country here is low hills with outcroppings of limestone, ideally suited for ambush. We select a narrow valley between slopes strewn with limestone boulders. Rocky terrain is the best for mortar attacks. We dispose twenty men on each slope, about fifty yards from the path the Spanish column will take. The remaining ten will serve as decoys, fleeing as the soldiers approach. Once the concealed riflemen open up on the enemy flanks, they will seek cover and fire directly into the Spanish column, who will then be caught in a three-way fire. Concealed behind boulders, we settle down to wait.

It is not long before the Spanish appear. There are about two hundred men in the column, with four officers on horseback. As they catch sight of the decoys, the officers urge their horses on, shouting to the men to follow. The lead officer, a major, is leaning forward in the saddle, his sword raised, his teeth bared under a bristling black mustache. Using a rifle with contact mortar, I take careful aim, leading the horse by four feet to allow for forward speed. Even so, I miscalculate slightly, and the mortar hits the horse in the withers instead of in the shoulder as I had intended. The explosion blows the major out of the saddle and over the horse's head. His sword flies out of his severed right hand in a glittering arc. The horse rears, screaming and kicking, entrails spilling from a gaping hole.

My shot is the signal for the others to open up, bouncing mortars off boulders by the foot soldiers and under the horses. One officer whirls and gallops back towards the city. After two rounds of mortar fire, we shift to the double-barreled rifles. In a few minutes, all but a handful are dead or dying and the survivors are fleeing back to the city in a blind panic. I give the signal to hold fire, since the accounts carried by the fugitives will place our number at five to eight hundred. The rumor of a large force of well-armed privateers, probably English, will spread panic in the city, whose defenders are now reduced to a scant hundred men.

We advance to the outskirts of the city, where a party of officers display a flag of truce and indicate that they wish to parley. We state our terms as immediate and unconditional surrender of the garrison and the city, telling the officers that we have better than eight hundred men behind us. If they surrender the city, we promise to spare the lives of the Governor, the officers and soldiers, and all the inhabitants. If not, we will kill any who offer the slightest resistance, and will sack and burn the city. They have no option except to agree.

Meanwhile, about three hundred local partisans have gathered, armed with weapons taken from the dead, since we do not want the officers to see the new weapons until we are able to effectively seal the city. We then stipulate that all soldiers, officers and armed civilians must come to this spot and lay down their arms. Anyone subsequently found in possession of arms will be summarily executed.

The soldiers, having laid down their arms, are ordered to remove their uniforms, boots and socks. Clad only in undergarments, they are marched to the garrison and locked in. The officers, the Governor, the wealthy inhabitants, and the clergy, protesting the indignity, are locked in the prison after all the prisoners have been released.

We post notices to the inhabitants to go about their daily business and to fear no harm. We set up the Articles in public places, impound all ships in the harbor, and post guards at all exits. No boat may leave the harbor and no person may leave the city.

For the next two days, while we are catching up on our sleep, the soldiers, officers and hostages are to be given adequate food, but the partisans who guard them and bring the food have orders not to talk or to answer any questions.

On the third day, fully rested, we gather around a conference table in the governmental dining room. News of our success has spread throughout the area, and there are now more than five hundred partisans gathered in the city, more than enough for routine guard duty. We consult maps and formulate plans for a series of attacks on the Spanish-held garrisons on the east side of the isthmus. These garrisons are for the most part small, and will be no match for our mortars. Within a month, we will control a string of garrisons from Port Roger to northern Panama. It is decided that the post of Commandante shall rotate each day. Since the ambush was largely according to my plan, I will assume the first shift.

WE ARE THE
LANGUAGE

As I was reading the *Cities of the Red Night* text, the Iguana sister brought some books and put them down on the table. I laid aside the folder.

"Who wrote this?"

"A scholar who prefers to remain anonymous. Research into this area is not reinforced. If, as he suggests, conception is the basic trauma, then it is also the basic instrument of control." She gestured to the books stacked on the table. I saw at a glance that they were elaborately bound in a variety of colors. They looked very expensive.

"These are copies. Please study them carefully. I will pay one million dollars for recovery of the originals."

"How good are the copies?"

"Almost perfect."

"Then why do you want the originals? Collector's vanity?"

"Changes, Mr. Snide, can only be effected by alterations in the *original*. The only thing not prerecorded in a pre-recorded universe are the prerecordings themselves. The copies can only repeat themselves word for word. *A virus is a copy.* You can pretty it up, cut it up, scramble it—it will reassemble in the same form. Without being an idealist, I am reluctant to see the originals in the hands of the Countess de Gulpa, the Countess de Vile and the pickle factory. . . ."

"I don't need a pep talk—but I do need a retainer."

She laid out a check for two hundred thousand cools on the table. I began examining the books, skipping through to get a general impression. They are composed in a variety of styles and periods. Some of them seem to stem from the 1920s of *The Great Gatsby*, old sport, and others to derive from the Edwardian era of Saki, reflecting an unbearably flawed boyishness. There is an underlying current of profound frivolity, with languid young aristocrats drawling epigrams in streets of disease, war, and death. There is a Rover Boys–Tom Swift story line where boy heroes battle against desperate odds.

The books are color comics. "Jokes," Jim calls them. Some lost color process has been used to transfer three-dimensional holograms onto the curious tough translucent parchment-like material of the pages. You ache to look at these colors. Impossible reds, blues, sepias. Colors you can smell and taste and feel with your whole body. Children's books against a Bosch background; legends, fairy stories, stereotyped characters, surface motivations with a child's casual cruelty. What facts could have given rise to such legends?

A form of radiation unknown at the present time activated a virus. This virus illness occasioned biologic mutations, especially alterations in hair and skin color, which were then genetically conveyed. The virus must have affected the sexual and fear centers in the brain and nervous system so that fear was converted into sexual frenzies which were reconverted into fear, the feedback leading in many cases to a fatal conclusion. The virus information was genetically conveyed, in orgasms that were often fatal. It seems likely that the burnings, stabbings, poisonings, stranglings, and hangings were largely terminal hallucinations produced by the virus, at a point where the line between illusion and reality breaks down. Over a period of generations the virus established a benign symbiosis with the host. It was a mutating virus, a *color* virus, as if the colors themselves were possessed of a purposeful and sinister life. The books are probably no more representative of life at the time than a *Saturday Evening Post* cover by Norman Rockwell represents the complex reality of American life.

"Are these complete copies of the originals I am retained to find, or should I say *uncover*?"

"No, these are fragments."

"You have some idea as to what the other books contain?" I asked.

She glanced at the check. "Do you?"

I nodded. "They may contain the truth, which these books cover with a surface so horrible and so nauseously prettified that it remains impervious as a mirror." I put the check in my wallet. "And as misleading," I added. I returned to the books.

As I read on, I became increasingly aware of a feeling of faintness and malaise. The colors were giving me a headache—the deep electric blue of the southern sky, the explosions of green by the pools and waterways, the clothes of tight-fitting red velvet, the purples, reds, and pinks of diseased skin—rising from the books palpable as a haze, a poisonous miasma of color.

I loosened my collar, my thoughts hazy and somehow not my own, as if someone were delivering a lecture on the books, of which I caught an occasional phrase . . . captions in English? "At one time a language existed that was immediately comprehensible to anyone with the concept of language." A World War I ambulance?

As I tried to examine it more closely, I could not be sure, but I *had* seen it with photographic clarity . . . an old sepia photo circa 1917. "They have removed the temporal limits."

I looked up with a start, as if I had been dozing. The Iguana and her brother were not in the room. I had not seen them go. Jim was sitting on one side of me and Kiki on the other. They seemed to be equally affected.

"Whewwww ..." said Jim. "I need a good hooker of brandy."

"Muy mareado," said Kiki. *"No quiero ver más. ..."*

Jim and Kiki walk over to a cabinet bar in the corner of the room. I pick up a book bound in red skin. In a deeper shade of red: *The First Redhead.*

A blond boy with a noose around his neck blushes deeper and deeper, red washing through his body, his lips swelling as the red tide sweeps into his hair and ripples down his chest to the crotch, down his legs, dusting the skin with red hairs that glisten in a soft fire, heart pounding against his ribs like a caged bird. . . .

I pick up a book with a heavy blue cover like flexible metal. In gold letters: *The Blue Mutant.* As I open the book I get a whiff of ozone.

A boy with a blue rash around his crotch, neck, and nipples, burning his asshole and crotch, a slow cold burn behind his ear, the blue color in his eyes, pale blue of northern skies washes across the whites, the pupils deep purple, blue shit burning in his ass like melting solder ... the smell of the Blue Mutant Fever fills the room, a rotten metal meat smell that steams off him as he shits a smoldering blue phosphorescent excrement. His pubic and rectal hairs turn bright blue and crackle with sparks. . . .

I was looking at the books from above in a spacecraft coming in for a landing.

A purple twilight lay over the sad languorous city. We were driven to a villa on the outskirts of Lima. The house was surrounded by the usual high wall, topped with broken glass like sugar crystals on a cake. Two floors, balcony on the second floor, bougainvillea climbing over the front of the house.

The driver carried the luggage in and gave us keys. He also gave me a guidebook in which certain shops and business addresses were checked.

We had a look around. The furniture looked like a window display: solid, expensive, undistinguished. Glassed bookcases were filled with leather-bound encyclopedias, Dickens, Thackeray, Kipling, books on the flora and fauna of South America, bird books and books on navigation. Nowhere did I see any indication that anyone had ever lived there.

Consulting a map of Lima, on a glass-covered coffee table spread with some issues of the *National Geographic*, I looked up the addresses. All in or near the Mercado Mayorista. One was an art-supply store. . . . Hmmmm. . . . I had already decided to fabricate the complete books if I could find the right paper. In fact, I felt sure that this was exactly what I was being paid to do. An address in the Mercado was Blum & Krup Import-Export. This was my contact.

The Mercado Mayorista of Lima occupies about four square blocks. Here vegetables, fruits, pigs, chickens and other produce are brought in by truck from all over Peru to be unloaded and sold. The shops, booths, bars, and restaurants are open twenty-four hours a day. The only thing comparable to the Mercado Mayorista is the Djemalfnaa of Marrakesh. The Djemalfnaa, however, has been a tourist attraction for so long that millions of cameras have sucked its vitality and dimmed its colors.

The Mercado is seldom visited by tourists and is not conceived as a folkloric spectacle. It has a definite function and the folklore is incidental. Street performers gather here because there are always spectators with money.

We walked on, passing little restaurants serving hot fish soup, meat on spits, brown bread ... bars with jukeboxes and boys dancing, Chinese restaurants, snake charmers, a trick bicycle rider, trained monkeys. Very faintly I could hear the pipes of Pan.

Some distance away there was a small circle of onlookers. A boy was playing a bamboo flute. He was about fifteen years old, with yellow hair, blue eyes, and a dusting of freckles on a broad face. Looking into the boy's eyes, I experienced a shock of recognition. His eyes were blank and empty as the blue sky over the market, devoid of any human expression: Pan, the Goat God. The music went on playing in my head, trickled down mountainsides in a blue twilight, rustling through glades and grass, twinkling on starlit streams, drifting down windy streets with autumn leaves.

I decided to visit the art-supply store alone. What I wanted would be under the counter. Anyone handling that kind of paper and ink would be into art forgery, probably passports and documents as well. Two visitors could queer the deal. Kiki wanted to look around the town anyway, and Jim needed some photographic equipment.

The store was on a dingy narrow street near the market. There were some dusty canvases, easels, and tubes of paint in the window, reminiscent of the rubber sandwiches served in Swedish bars to legitimize the sale of liquor. When I tried the door I found that it was locked. I knocked, and the door was finally opened by a middle-aged man with heavy rimless glasses who looked at me suspiciously.

"*Vous voulez?*"

"*Du papier, monsieur!*"

"*Entrez.*" He stood aside and locked the door behind me. A fattish woman with frizzy blonde hair and large diamonds on her liver-spotted fingers sat at an ancient cash register. She had been reading *Le Figaro*, which lay on the counter. She looked frightened. So did he. War criminals, I decided matter-of-factly. French collaborators.

"*J'ai besoin de papier pour une tâche spéciale. . . . Des livres qui devraient paraître anciens.*"

He nodded and something like a smile touched his thin lips. "*Par ici, monsieur.*"

He led the way to a back room containing a long oak table and several chairs. Iron cabinets with cylinder locks occupied one wall. He looked at me sharply.

"*Ah oui.*" He gestured to the cabinets. "*L'histoire, monsieur, à votre disposition . . . quelle époque? Vous cherchez peut-être un codex mayan? Un papyrus d'Égypte? Quelque chose du Moyen Age?*"

"*Plus récent . . . Dix-huitième . . . environ 1702.*"

"*Et l'auteur, monsieur? Gentilhomme, courtisane, voleur?*" And the author? Gentleman, courtesan, thief?

"*Pirate américain.*"

"*Parfaitement.*" He opened a little casket with a key from his vest pocket and selected from it another key. With this he opened a cabinet in which I could see packages in cubbyholes, and brought out several packets tied and sealed with red wax.

"*De Boston.*"

"*Parfaitement.*" I examined the parchment carefully, holding it up to the light and looking at it under a magnifying glass. I nodded and smiled. "*Très bien.*"

"*De d'encre?*"

"*Oui.*"

He opened another cabinet full of bottles and jars and tubes. . . . "*Ça.*"

I brought out my portable kit and ran some tests. "*Ça marche . . . ça marche. . . . ja besoin aussi de couleurs. . . . C'est un livre illustré.*"

"*De couleurs parfumées, monsieur?*"

"*Mais bien entendu . . . d'hachissh, d'opium, du sang, du rhum, encens d'église, de latrines, du pourriture . . .*"

The package came to $10,000, plus $300 of regular art supplies.

"*Alors, monsieur, vous avez le temps pour un cognac?*"

"*J'ai toujours le temps pour ça.*"

We start making books. I write the continuity. Jim does the drawings. We have the address of a modeling agency which puts us in touch with the film underground. We are in the right place.

Lima is the film studio of the world for far-out porn and snuff films, mostly on contract to collectors and governmental agencies. Only the third-rate material finds its way into the open market. The best camera work, processing, special effects, and actors of all nationalities can be had here for a price.

Jim sketches a scene in the rough. We stage it with live actors and then photograph it. Then Jim projects the color shots onto our paper for the finished product, which is something between photography and drawing and looks quite a lot like the Iguanas' "joke books."

Monsieur La Tour sells quality merchandise. The books seem to age two hundred years overnight. I am working mostly on my pirate story line. But since I am sure of the quality of the goods, I will invest some more money in Mayan and Egyptian papers and colors, and do two snuff films— a Mayan number called *The Child of Ix Tab*, and an Egyptian number called *The Curse of the Pharaohs*.

Ix Tab was the patron saint of those who hang themselves,

whom she would transport straight to Paradise. In this number a young aristocrat is hanged by Ix Tab, who then gives birth to a superpotent Death Baby. The boy who plays the young aristocrat has a classic Mayan profile, and Ix Tab, spotted with decay, is a versatile pro who also plays in my Egyptian number as the evil sister of Tutankhamen—she has him strangled and gives birth to a Scorpion Goddess.

A million dollars is shrinking to expense-account money at this point. I am already a hundred thousand clams into the $200,000. I figure it is about time to look up Blum and Krup before they come looking for me. It's a small town and word gets around.

A COWBOY IN THE
SEVEN-DAYS-A-WEEK FIGHT

Tamaghis is a walled city built of red adobe. The city stirs at sunset, for the days are unbearably hot at this season and the inhabitants nocturnal. As the sun sets the northern sky lights up with a baleful red glow, bathing the city in light that shades from seashell pink to deep-purple shadow pools.

It is a summer night and the air is warm and electric with a smell of incense, ozone, and the musky sweet rotten red smell of the fever. Jerry, Audrey, Dahlfar, Jon, Joe, and John Kelly are walking through a quarter of massage parlors, Turkish baths, sex rooms, hanging studios, cubicle restaurants, booths selling incense, aphrodisiacs and aromatic herbs. Music drifts from nightclubs, sometimes a whiff of opium smoke—the Painless Ones who run many of the concessions smoke it.

The boys pause at a booth and Audrey buys some Red Hots from a Painless One. This aphrodisiac causes an erogenous rash in the crotch, anus, and on the nipples. It acts within seconds, taken orally, or it can be injected—but this is dangerous since the pleasure is often so intense that it stops the heart. Adolescents of the city play red-hot dare games known as Hots and Pops.

The boys are dressed in red silk tunics open on their lean bodies, red silk pants, and magnetic sandals. At their belts they carry spark guns and long knives, sharp on both edges, that curl slightly at the end. Knife fights are frequent here since Red Hots can set off the raw red Killing Fever.

The virus is like a vast octopus through bodies of the city, mutating in protean forms: the Killing Fever, the Flying Fever, the Black Hate Fever. In all cases the total energies of the subject are focused on one activity or objective. There is a Gambling Fever and a Money Fever which sometimes infect the Painless Ones—eyes glittering, they draw in the money with a terrible eagerness, trembling like hungry shrews. There is also an Activity Fever: the victims rushing about in a frenzy organizing anything, acting as agents for anything or anybody, prowling the streets desperately looking for contacts.

Red Night in Tamaghis: Dog Catchers, Spermers, Sirens, and the Special Police from the Council of the Selected who are infiltrating Tamaghis from Yass-Waddah. The Dog Catchers will seize any youths they encounter in the Fair Game areas and sell them off to hanging studios and sperm brokers. The Spermers are pirates operating from strongholds outside the city walls, attacking caravans and supply trains, tunneling under the walls to prowl in the rubbly outskirts of the city. They are outlaws who may be killed by any citizen, like cattle rustlers.

Two boys, faces blazing with alertness, slide from one red shadow pool to another. A patrol of Dog Catchers passes. The boys crouch in the darkness by a ruined wall, teeth bare, hands on their knives. The Dog Catchers are muscular youths with heavy thighs and the deep chests of runners. Naked to the waist, they carry a variety of nets and handcuffs around their shoulders, and bolos that can tangle legs at twenty yards. On leads are the hairless red sniffhounds, quivering, whimpering, sniffing, trying to fuck the Dog Catchers' legs. Audrey's lips part in a slow smile. This is one of his infiltration tactics: the dogs are trained to wrap themselves around a Dog Catcher's legs and trip him up.

Audrey and Cupid Mount Etna are in a populous area with wide stone streets. A flower float of Sirens passes. In conch shells of roses they trill: "I'm going to *pop* you naked darling and *milk* you while you're being *hanged*...."

Idiot males are rushing up, jumping on the hanging float to be hanged by the Sirens, many of whom are transvestites from Yass-Waddah. The floats wind on towards the Hanging Gardens where the golden youths gather with their Hanging Exempt badges. Like characters in a charade they pose and pirouette in the red glow that lights trees, pools, and diseased faces burning with the terrible lusts of the fever.

Audrey decides on a detour. Four Special Police from the Council of the Selected stand in their way. They are crew-cut men in blue suits, looking like religious FBI men with muscular Christian smiles.

"What can we do for you?"

"Drop dead." Audrey snaps. He draws his spark gun and gives them a full blast. They fall twitching and smoking. Officially the SPs have no standing in Tamaghis, but they are bribing the local police and kidnapping boys for the transplant operation rooms of Yass-Waddah.

The boys sprint around the bodies and turn into an alley, police whistles behind them. Possession of a spark gun is a capital offense. Dodging and twisting through a maze of narrow streets, tunnels, and gangways, they lose the patrol.

They are on the outskirts now, near the walls, walking down a steep stone road. There is a road above them and a steep grassy slope leading up to it. Suddenly, a World War I ambulance truck stops on the high road and six men jump out got up as pirates with beards and earrings. They rush down the slope, eyes flashing with greed.

"Spermers!"

Audrey drops on one knee, raking the slope with his spark gun. The Spermers scream, rolling down the slope, clothes burning, setting the grass on fire. The truck is burning. Audrey and Cupid sprint on as the gas tank explodes behind them.

THE UNCONSCIOUS IMITATED
BY A CHEESECAKE

he Double Gallows is *the* late place in Tamaghis. At 11:30 it is still nearly empty. The bartender is checking bottles and polishing glasses. Some character is freaking out at the bar.

"We're all a bunch of dirty rotten vampires!" he screams. The bouncer throws him out.

"We don't like that in here. I mean it."

A Siren undulates in and trills for service.

"You see that sign, lady?" The bartender points to a picture of a Siren with a noose: "*. . . will not be served here.*" The bouncer hustles her out.

It's an exclusive-type place where *everybody* goes. What do people do in Tamaghis? They see the Show. They all come here and see the big Show. There's a hanging show every night. The bar is filling up now, because this is Flasher Night. The chic clients make their entrances through trapdoors in the floor and ceiling, or through disguised side entrances, and even now they are popping up through the floor in green drag screaming like mandrakes, dropping down through the ceiling in gauzy parachutes or with ropes around their necks, slithering in through mirrors and screens. Some are completely naked but most wear at least cowboy chaps, or scarves, or capes, or masks, or body paint, or sarongs, or snakeskin jockstraps, or Mercury sandals, or Scythian boots, or Etruscan helmets, or space suits with transparent ass and crotch.

Noose peddlers circulate among the clients, stopping here and there as a table of young aristocrats feel the nooses, which are of various grades and materials—silk in all colors, hemp cured and softened in rare unguents, tingle nooses burning with a soft blue flame, leather nooses made from sniffhound hide.

Audrey drops a noose languidly and waves to Jim across the room. Jim comes over and sits at his table. Audrey introduces him to Rubble Blood Pu, a slim elegant youth dressed in expensive nineteenth-century clothes with a red rope mark around his neck, and to Captain Strobe, the Gentleman Spermer, in eighteenth-century clothes, his yellow hair in a pigtail. Strobe too has the hemp marks around his neck. Cupid Mount Etna with a cupid-bow mouth, yellow goat eyes, and curly hair, is naked except for goat-hoof sandals. Blindish Wasp, black sideburns, eyebrows that completely cover the eye sockets, thin purple lips, is shaped like a wasp—thin rounded chest, a waist so narrow Jim could have put his hands around it, long thin legs. His skin is dead white and shiny, his cock pointed. He is naked except for a black skullcap and black pointed shoes of soft leather. He gives off a sharp aromatic odor.

The guests are becoming impatient. *"Pop Pop Pop,"* they scream.

Lights go on in a little alcove and there is the double gallows. It's a hologram and it makes you queasy to look at it floating there in stagnant rotten air like a solid mirage you can almost drink out of and almost smell. The star is a dummy called Whitey because he cost as much as the white shark in *Jaws*. A door opens on the gallows and Whitey is led in by a red demon as the clients caper around the gallows, standing on tiptoe and twisting their heads to one side and making clicking sounds with their tongues.

Now Whitey stands with the noose around his neck, pelvis tilted forward, cock almost hard, pupils pinpointed. The platform falls and he hangs there ejaculating and a blaze of light flashes out his eyes.

"A Flasher! a Flasher!" The clients throw up their arms and wriggle their hips forward ecstatically, bathing in the flash, pushing each other aside, wallowing about in heaps.

The gallows disappears. In an old silent film 1920s guests are jumping into a swimming pool.

"Come along to our digs, old sport," says Rubble Blood Pu. "This place is getting vulgar."

Pu leads the way through an area of vacant lots, rubble, and half-demolished buildings overgrown with weeds, scrub, and vines.

"Here we are."

He stops in front of a three-story building. The two lower floors are torn down to the girders and concrete stairs lead to the third floor. Pu unlocks a heavy door.

The third floor is furnished in Moroccan style with rugs and cushions and low tables. Five of the kraut kids, all naked, are smoking hash. One gets up and does a belly dance while the others, at the four points of the compass, roll on their backs, legs in the air, clapping with their feet as they sing.

> They wear no clothes
> And they dance up on their toes
> And the dance they do
> Is enough to kill a Jew

Rubble Blood Pu and Captain Strobe are both very slender, with small aristocratic genitals, and they manage to look elegantly attired and perfectly poised when naked. A boy with long flaxen hair and flaring ears, naked except for a helmet, brings a tray of mint tea.

Pu shows Jim how to hold the glass by top and bottom so as not to burn his hand.... "Come along and I'll show you around the house."

The kraut kids trail along, laughing and goosing each other.

"And here is the gallows room ... all modern and convenient, as you can see ... our subjects wear hanging helmets ... show him, Igor."

Igor walks up grinning. The helmet extends around the neck and down to the collarbone, glares around the ears, and covers the shaven scalp.

"You see there are wires for brain waves to be recorded over here; throat mikes in the helmet ... and this." He holds up a little ring of transparent elastic. "Always tailormade, of course ... and these magnetic tingle disks for the nipples. And the noose, scented with the subject's special smells—you know, his dirty underwear and jacked-off-in handkerchiefs. We've always been vampires, old sport.... It's in the family." He takes a last look around. "The best that money can buy ... still it's a bit confining, old sport— if you know what I mean. All in the mind, you know...."

The room behind him turns into Gatsby's booklined study.

"One of your dizzy spells?"

Hans takes my arm. The boys have sated themselves for the moment. They are sitting around, shoulder to shoulder, passing cannabis cigarettes.

"Cuidado, hombre."

A boy brushes a spark from his naked thigh ... soft distant voices in the warm dusk. We are walking back through the stale air of Panama that eddies around our bodies and settles behind us. No fresh breezes stir here. The city is like a closed room, full of stale flowers and stagnant water.

"And now, old sport, there is someone I want you to meet . . . better nip in here first." He opens the door into a luxurious bathroom. "See you in the drawing room."

When Jim gets to the drawing room, he sees a red-haired girl looking like Jerry's twin sister, dressed in red silk pajamas. The kraut kids sprawl in front of her, jacking off like she is a pinup.

Audrey looks at his wristwatch. He is on patrol with Cupid Mount Etna. Time to hit the street.

WE ARE COORDINATED
THE GUARD IS MANIFOLD

Kelley, Clinch Todd, Hans, and myself proceed now to the garrison to review the captured soldiers. Massive walls with four gun towers surround a courtyard along which living quarters are ranged. Hans and I, flanked by ten partisans carrying razor-sharp machetes, step into the courtyard while Kelley, Todd, and Jon remain in the wardroom behind the bars.

"Ten*shun!*" They understand that in any language.

The soldiers shamble into a ragged line. Dirty, unshaven, frightened, they would seem to pose no threat. I walk slowly up and down, looking at each face in turn. A sorry lot for the most part, stupid and brutal, many of them showing the ravages of drink and disease. But two faces do stand out: a thin hawk-faced youth with piercing gray eyes who meets my regard steadily, and a pimply boy with red hair who gives me an ingratiating smile.

"How many of you can read?"

The hawk-faced youth and two others raise their hands. A fourth raises his hand halfway.

"Well, can you read or can't you?"

"Well, yes sir, but it takes me some time."

"You'll have plenty of that." I point to the Articles. "I want those of you who can read to read what is written there. I want you to read it carefully. Then I want you to explain what is written there to those who can't read. Is that clear?"

The hawk-faced youth nods with a slight smile.

"I'll be back later to see if what is written there has been read and understood."

We then proceed to the house where the women are held, to be greeted by a chorus of shrewish complaints. No one will talk to them or tell them what had happened to their sons, husbands, and brothers. They have been denied medical attention and prevented from going to Mass.

I apologize smoothly for the temporary inconvenience and assure them that their husbands, sons, and brothers are safe and being well cared for. I tell them that I am a qualified physician, and that if any of them are suffering from any pains or illnesses I will be glad to receive them one by one in a room I have set up as my office. I have also brought a priest who will hear confession, grant absolutions, or perform any other priestly offices of which they are in need. The "priest" is none other than Half-Hanged Kelley, his hemp marks covered by a clerical collar.

One by one, they troop into my office complaining of headaches, backaches, toothaches, chills and fever, shingles, flatulence, cramps, palpitations, catarrhs, varicose veins, fainting spells, neuralgia, and other ailments difficult to classify. To each I give a draft containing four grains of opium, with instructions to repeat the dose if their trouble returns, which of course it will at the end of eight hours when the opium wears off. Needless to say, Kelley is also kept busy by the pious *señoras*.

Returning to the garrison, I call the soldiers to attention. I walk down the line directing the three readers and the half-reader to stand forward. I then pick out six more, looking for faces and bodies that are reasonably well favored or show some signs of adaptability, intelligence, and good character. These ten being brought to the wardroom, I ask if they have read the Articles or had the Articles explained to them.

" 'Article One: No man may be imprisoned for debt.' What does this Article mean to you?"

A fresh-faced boy with an impudent smile and reddish hair speaks up: "Suppose I run up a bill in the *cantina* and can't pay?"

I explain that debts to an innkeeper fall into a special category. If no one paid, there would be no *cantinas* and no wine.

The hawk-faced boy asks: "Does this mean that you intend to release all peons even though they stand in debt to the *patrón*?"

"It means exactly that. We intend to abolish the peonage system."

A mulatto boy looks at me suspiciously. Blank faces of the others show me they know nothing of the peonage system or how it operates.

" 'Article Two: No man may enslave another.' What does this mean to you?"

"Does this mean we get out of the army?" the pimply boy asks.

I explain that the Spanish army does not exist in areas we control. Our army consists entirely of volunteers.

"What do you pay?"

"We pay in freedom and equal shares of any booty we take. The gold we have taken here in Panama will be shared equally among the soldiers who took part in the operation."

"I want to volunteer." He smiled and rubbed his crotch. Not intelligent exactly, but quick, intuitive, and brazen. A shameless one.

"What's your name?"

"Paco."

"Yes, Paco, you can volunteer."

"You mean you're going to abolish slavery?" the mulatto youth asked suspiciously.

"I mean exactly that."

"I'll believe it when I see it."

" 'No man may interfere in any way with the religious beliefs or practices of another.' What does this mean to you?"

"We don't have to go to Mass?"

"That's right. Nor may you prevent anyone else from doing so."

"That would apply to other religions? To Moors and Jews?" the hawk-faced boy asked.

"Of course . . . 'Article Four: No man may be subjected to torture for any reason.' "

"How will you get information from prisoners?"

"There are easier ways of doing that, as you will see. 'Article Five: No man may interfere with the sexual practices of another or force any sexual act on another against his or her will.' What does this mean to you?"

"You mean if I fuck another boy in the ass no one can say anything?"

"They can say what they like but they cannot interfere. If they do you would be justified in taking whatever measures were necessary to protect your freedom and your person, and anyone under the Articles would be bound to assist you."

The half-reader spoke up for the first time. "Sergeant Gonzalez and Corporal Hassanavitch kicked two soldiers to death for sodomy."

"Did they indeed?"

"If the sergeant finds out I told you that he'll have a knife in me."

"A knife?"

"Yes sir. He has a knife strapped to his leg."

"Interesting . . . 'Article Six: No man may be put to death except for violation of the Articles. All officers of the Inquisition stand condemned under this Article and subject to immediate execution.' Do any of you know of any such officers present in Panama City?"

"Father Domingo and Father Gomez are officers of the Inquisition," said the hawk-faced youth. "Sent here to deal with pirates. They wanted to burn the English pirate as a heretic."

"Thank you. You will be rewarded for the information." The hawk-faced boy looked at me haughtily.

"I want no reward."

"Good." I turned to the half-reader. "And don't worry about the sergeant. I am having him removed from the garrison." The others were similarly processed in groups of ten. Only fifteen were suitable to be trained as partisans. Ten were obviously incorrigible rogues and troublemakers, chief among them being Sergeant Gonzalez, a snarling buck-toothed two-hundred-pound hulk, and Corporal Hassanavitch, a rat-faced gypsy. These ten bastards were marched to the guard-house adjacent to the garrison and locked in. In taking leave of them I gave Sergeant Gonzalez a bottle of anise-flavored *aguardiente* containing enough opium to kill five men, enjoining him to share it equally with his companions. He leered at me showing his yellow teeth.

"Síííí, Señor Capitán."

At the prison I summoned the resident clergymen to a small interrogation room. I was seated behind a desk examining papers, armed partisans ranged behind me. Kelley, in accordance with his clerical costume, had left his gun in a corner.

"Gentlemen, this is Father Kelley from Ireland." Kelley smiled and nodded unctuously.

I studied a file in front of me, drumming my fingers on the desk. I looked up.

"Father Gomez?"

"I am Father Gomez." A plump face, near-sighted yellowish eyes behind spectacles, a cruel absentminded expression.

"Father Domingo?"

"I am Father Domingo." A thin sour face, autos-da-fé smoldering in sulfurous gray eyes.

"You are officers of the Inquisition?" I inquired mildly.

"We are clergymen. Priests of God," said Domingo, glaring at me. He was not used to being on the receiving end.

"You are dogs of the Inquisition. Sent here from Lima. You urged that our companion Captain Strobe be burned as a heretic instead of hanged as a pirate. You were overruled by Bishop Gardenas and Father Herera. No doubt you are biding your time to revenge yourself on these honest men for their humanity."

Without more ado I drew my double-barreled pistol and shot them both in the stomach. Placing the smoking pistol on the desk, I snapped my fingers.

"Father Kelley! Extreme unction!"

The other clergymen gasped and turned pale. However, they could not conceal their relief when I told them that as decent clergymen they had nothing to fear. I reloaded my pistol as Kelley delivered his bogus unction.

"Well, I think you gentlemen could do with a drink." I poured for each a small glass of anise spirits containing four grains of opium.

Sitting on a balcony overlooking the bay, sipping a rum punch as the sun went down, I reflected that the exercise of power conveys a weird sensation of ease and tranquility. (I wonder how many of the ten men in the guardhouse will be alive tomorrow. It amuses me to think of them cutting each other's throats over a bottle of poisoned spirits.)

The summary dispatching of the two Inquisitors was based on a precept long used by the Inquisition itself, which is in fact the way they were able to maintain their power despite widespread opposition and hatred. Brutal sanctions against a minority from which one is generically exempt cannot but produce a measure of satisfaction in those who are spared such treatment: "As decent clergymen you have nothing to fear." Thus the burning of Jews, Moors, and sodomites produces a certain sense of comfort in those who are not Jews, Moors, or sodomites: *"This won't happen to me."* To turn this mechanism back on the Inquisitors themselves gives me a feeling of taking over the office of fate. I am become the bad karma of the Inquisition. I am allowing myself also the satisfaction that derives from a measure of hypocrisy, rather like the slow digestion of a good meal.

Troublemakers:

Any body of men will be found to contain ten to fifteen percent of incorrigible troublemakers. In fact, most of the misery on this planet derives from this ten percent. It is useless to try and reeducate them, since their only function is to harm and harass others. To maintain them in prisons is a waste of personnel and provisions. To addict them to opium takes too long, and in any case they are not amenable to useful work. There is but one sure remedy. In future operations, as soon as these individuals are discovered, either by advance intelligence or by on-the-spot observation, they will be killed on any pretext. In the words of the Bard, "Only fools do those villains pity who are punished ere they have done their mischief."

Today Hans is the City Commandante: all spit and polish, bathed and shaved, green-jacketed with silver skull-and-cross-bones on his shoulders, khaki pants, his soft brown boots carefully shined.

At the guardhouse, five of the prisoners are dead. It is easy to reconstruct what happened. Sergeant Gonzalez, attempting to keep all the liquor for himself, was attacked by Corporal Hassanavitch and an accomplice. The sergeant killed them both with his knife and then drained about half the spirits, holding the rest at bay. The sergeant soon being overcome, the others took his knife and cut his throat. The victors then drank the remains of the bottle, which killed three of them.

"Well, get them out of here." Hans gestures to the corpses.

The partisans lead the way, planting shovels in the ground. We leave the prisoners digging graves like sullen Calibans and proceed to the barracks, where we are greeted by the smell of cannabis. The soldiers are laughing and talking, more relaxed now that ten wrong men have been removed.

"Achtung!"

The way Hans can say it anyone would believe it.

The men are now brought to the wardroom one at a time. The hawk-faced youth, whose name is Rodriguez, acts as clerk, writing down answers as Hans fires the questions.

"Name? Age? Place of birth? Length of service? Locations and times of previous service? What training have you received as a soldier?"

"Training?" The man looks blank.

"What did you do all day?"

"Well, we had to drill and clean the barracks, cook and wash dishes, work in the Captain's gardens. . . ."

"What about your guns? You received instruction in their use? There was daily target practice?"

"We fired them only at fiestas and parades."

"Was there instruction in knife and sword fighting? In unarmed combat?"

"No, nothing like that. We could get a citation for fighting."

"Field exercises?"

"*Qué es eso?*"

"That means you go into jungles or mountains to learn the terrain and pretend to fight a war."

"We never left the city."

"So you have no idea of conditions and terrain ten miles outside Panama City?"

"No, sir."

"During the time of your service here, have you been sick?"

"Various times, *señor.*"

"And what sicknesses have you had?"

"Well, sir, chills and fever, cramps and loose bowels. . . ."

"Pox?"

"Yes, sir. The whores here are rotten with it."

"And what treatment did you receive?"

"Not much. The doctor gave me some pills for the pox that made me feel worse. There was a sort of tea for the fever that helped a little. . . ."

"You were formerly stationed at Cartagena. What was the situation there as regards sickness?"

"Much worse, sir. A thousand soldiers died of the yellow sickness. That was when I was transferred."

"Was the work there the same?"

"More or less, except we had to guard the mule train."

"So you did leave the city at times?"

"Yes, sir. Sometimes for a week."

"And what was the mule train carrying? You don't need

to tell me. Gold. What else interests the Spanish? Well now, all that gold to protect ... the garrison must have been larger than here ... perhaps a thousand?"

"Ten thousand, sir," says the soldier proudly.

Hans pretends to be impressed and whistles softly.

"And galleons no doubt to take away the gold? When all those sailors came ashore there must have been some right brawls in Cartagena, *verdad*?"

"*Verdad, señor.*"

BIG PICTURE CALLING SHIFTY

We return to staff headquarters, which we have set up in the Governor's spacious bedroom on the ground floor. This is the coolest room in the house but even so the heat is oppressive and we must keep the windows covered with mosquito netting which cuts off the occasional eddy of air that is the closest approximation to a breeze. There is a huge ornate curtained bed where exhausted partisans who arrive with dispatches can rest, where the staff officers can catch an hour's sleep or satisfy the sudden sex hungers that occur during long hours of intense mental concentration without sleep.

We often work naked in the Governor's bedroom, seeing the maps with our whole bodies, performing ritual copulations in front of the maps, animating the maps with our sperm. The key map is Big Picture, showing the present area of occupation from Cartagena on the Atlantic seaboard to the Pearl Islands in the Pacific and northwards to a point a hundred miles north of Panama City. Green pins on the map show cities occupied by the partisans. Black pins designate areas occupied by the Spanish.

The key to Big Picture are ledger books. . . . We are now transcribing into the ledger books information obtained from the prisoners.

Cartagena. Location on map. Black pin. Estimated

strength of garrison: ten thousand soldiers. Strongly fortified. Has resisted a number of pirate attacks. Gold terminal. Heavily armed convoys pick up gold here. Hygienic conditions worse than Panama. Recent epidemic of yellow fever.

These ledgers indicate not only the strength of garrisons and the movement of ships, but also the whole way of life of the enemy, what the soldiers do, what the officers do, what food they eat, what illnesses they suffer from, how they think, and what they can be expected to do. Rather like studying past performance to pick the winner of a horse race.

But the Spanish, since they consist entirely of past performance, are much more predictable than horses. Massively encased in their colonial architecture, their forts and galleons, their uniforms, gold, portraits and religious processions, they move like ponderous armored knights to ends that we can predetermine.

In addition to Big Picture, there are also much more detailed maps of smaller areas showing locations of arms caches, farmhouses belonging to partisans, streams, wells, and sketches of animals native to the region. As messages come in, the green pins are spreading north and east and south along the Pacific coast. The whole southern isthmus of Panama is now in our hands.

We study the maps, concentrating on Big Picture. What exactly will the Spanish do? No doubt respond after their kind—heavy, massive, and slow as their galleons. They will dispatch galleons from Cartagena to land troops on the east coast, who will then move west towards Panama City. They will dispatch galleons from Lima to the Bay of Panama to land troops above and below Panama City, in what they fondly think is a crushing pincer movement.

On the eastern seaboard, we have every chance of a

decisive sea victory. Here we have *The Siren* and *The Great White*, both now equipped with maneuverable cannons and exploding projectiles. No doubt all the British and French pirates and privateers in the West Indian area will gather like sharks at the smell of Cartagena gold. Our Destroyers will be operating along the coasts and land partisans will make the landing of the troops extremely costly. On the Pacific side, our sea forces are negligible, consisting of only a few Destroyers in the Pearl Islands vicinity. We have, therefore, decided to evacuate Panama City at the approach of the Spanish galleons and let them land as many troops as they wish. In fact, the more they land, the better we like it. The Spanish, confident of victory, will then move north and south relying on heavy reinforcements from the east.

Back in the barracks, the fifteen who are to receive partisan training are lined up. I study each face in turn: Rodriguez, the hawk-faced boy with intense gray eyes, very intelligent, highly literate staff-officer material . . . Juanito, a little Filipino, always smiling, eager to please . . . the mulatto reader José, a solid reliable face, steady nerves in combat . . . Kiki, the half-reader with a Mongoloid face and straight black hair, nicknamed El Chino . . . Paco with his impudent ingratiating smile . . . Nemo, a slender yellow-skinned buck-toothed youth with a dancer's grace . . . Nimun, a curiously archaic youth part Negro with red hair, brown freckles, and a blank expression—he looks like one of the first mutant redheads from prehistoric time . . . Pedro, a handsome broad-faced boy with high cheekbones and a smooth reddish face. The others are less distinguished, country faces from farm families who have enlisted to escape grinding poverty.

"You have been selected for partisan training. Your instruction begins tomorrow. During ten days of training, you will be paid five times your present pay. As soon as you join partisans in the field, the rate will be ten times present pay and an equal share of any booty taken. You will be wearing cadet uniforms from now on. You can come and go as you like after training hours."

Hans walks up and down measuring the boys with his eyes and writing measurements down on a clipboard. He hands the list to partisans, who return with a stack of uniforms and boots which they dump on a table.

We direct the boys to strip and bathe.

The boys are drawing water from the cistern and pouring it over each other with the usual horseplay and merriment. Paco sidles in behind Nemo and pretends to fuck him, rolling his eyes and showing his teeth and snorting like a horse. *"Cabrón!"* Nemo screams, dodging away as he empties a bucket of water over Paco's head.

I am the eternal spectator, separated by unbridgeable gaps of knowledge, feeling the sperm gathering in tight nuts, the quivering rectums, smelling the iron reek of sex, sweat, and rectal mucus, watching the writhing brown bodies in the setting sun, torn with an ache of disembodied lust and the searing pain of disintegration.

Silver spots boil in front of my eyes. I am standing in the empty ruined courtyard hundreds of years from now, a sad ghostly visitant in a dead city, smell of nothing and nobody there.

The boys are flickering shadows of memory, evoking bodies that have long since turned to dust. I am calling, calling without a throat, without a tongue, calling across the centuries: *"Paco . . . Joselito . . . Enrique."*

SCREEN PLAY /
PART ONE

t is on the second floor. A brass plaque: "Blum & Krup." A metal door. A bell. I ring. A cold-eyed young Jew opens the door a crack.

"Yes? You are client or salesman?"

"Neither." I hand him my card. He closes the door and goes away. He comes back.

"Mr. Blum and Mr. Krup will see you now."

He ushers me into an office decorated in the worst German taste with pictures of youths and maidens swimming with swans in northern lakes, the carpets up to my ankles. There, behind a huge desk, are Blum and Krup. A vaudeville team. Blum is Austrian and Jewish, Krup is Prussian and German.

Krup bows stiffly without getting up. "Krup von Nordenholz."

Blum bustles out from behind the desk. "Sit down, Mr. Snide. I am the master here. Have a cigar."

"No thanks."

"Well, we will have some fun at least. We will have an orgy." He goes back to his chair on the other side of the desk and sits there watching me through cigar smoke.

"And why have you not come here sooner, Herr Snide?" asks Krup in a cold dry voice.

"Oh well, there's a lot of legwork in this business . . ." I say vaguely.

"Ja und Assenwerke." (Yes and asswork.)

"We want that you stop with the monkey business and do some real business, Mr. Snide."

"We are not a charitable institution."

"We do not finance ass fuckings."

"Now just a minute, Blum and Krup. I wasn't aware that you were my clients."

Krup emits a short cold bray of laughter.

Blum takes the cigar out of his mouth and points the butt across the table at my chest. "And who did you think was your million-dollar client?"

"A green bitch synthesized from cabbage?"

"Well, if you are my client, what am I expected to do exactly?"

Krup whinnies like a cynical horse.

"You are to recover certain rare books now in the possession of a certain Countess," Blum says.

"I am not even sure I would know these books if I saw them."

"You have seen samples."

"I am not sure the samples correspond in any way to the alleged books I am retained to recover."

"You think you have been deceived?"

"Not 'think.' *Know.*"

The room is so quiet you can hear the long gray cone of Blum's cigar fall into an ashtray. Finally he speaks. "And suppose we could tell you exactly where the books are?"

"So they are in someone's private bank vault surrounded by guards and computerized alarm systems? I am supposed to sneak in there and carry out a carton of books slung over my shoulder in a rare tapestry, stamps and first editions in all my pockets, industrial diamonds up my ass in a finger stall, a sapphire big as a hen's egg in my mouth? Is that what I am expected to do?"

Blum laughs loud and long while Krup looks sourly at his nails. "No, Mr. Snide. This is not what you are expected to do. There is a group of well-armed partisans operating in an adjacent area, who will occupy the Countess's stronghold. You will have only to go in after them and secure the books. There will be an outcry against the partisans who have so savagely butchered a rich foreign sow. . . . Then stories will filter out about the Countess and her laboratories, and there'll be something in it for everybody. The CIA, the partisans, the Russians, the Chinese . . . we will have some fun at least. Might start a little Vietnam down here."

"Well," I say. "You have to take a broad general view of things."

"We prefer a very specific view, Mr. Snide," says Krup looking at a heavy gold pocket watch. "Be here at this time Thursday and we will talk further. Meanwhile, I would strongly advise you to avoid other commitments."

"And bring your assistants and the books what you got," adds Blum.

When Jim and I go to see Blum and Krup on Thursday, we take along the books the Iguanas have given me. Krup looks the books over, snorting from time to time, and as he finishes leafing through each one, he slides it down the table to Blum.

"Mr. Snide, where are the books you are now making?" asks Krup.

"Books? Me? I'm just a private eye, not a writer."

"You come to make with us the crookery," snaps Blum, "we break you in your neck. Hans! Willi! Rudi! Heinrich! *Herein!*"

Four characters come in with silencered P-38s, like in an old Gestapo movie.

"And now, your assistant will get the books while you

and your *Lustknabe* remain here. Hans and Heinrich will go with him to make sure he does not so lose himself."

Hans and Heinrich step behind Jim. "Keep six feet in front of us at all times." They file out.

In half an hour Jim is back with the books. B & K spread them out on the table and both of them stand up and look at them like generals studying a battle plan.

Finally Krup nods. "*Ach ja*. With these I think it is enough."

Blum turns to me, almost jovial now, rubbing his hands. "Well, you and your assistant and the boy, you are ready to leave, *hein*?"

"Leave? Where to?"

"That you will see."

Hans, Rudi, Willi, and Heinrich march us up some stairs onto a roof and into a waiting helicopter. The pilot has a blank cold thuggish face and he is wearing a 45 in a shoulder holster. He looks American. The guards strap us into our seats and blindfold us and we take off. The flight lasts about an hour.

Then we are herded out and into another plane, a prop job. Dakota, probably. About three hours this time, and we set down on water. They take off our blindfolds and we now have a different pilot. He looks English and has a beard.

The pilot turns around and smiles. "Well, chaps, here we are."

They untie us and we get out on a jetty. It is on a small lake, just big enough to set the plane down. Around the lake I see Quonset huts and in an open space something that looks like an oil rig. A barbed-wire fence surrounds the area with gun towers. There are enough armed guards around for a small army.

In front of a Quonset hut several men are talking. One comes forward to greet us: it is that CIA punk Pierson.

"Well, Snide," he says. "Welcome aboard."

"Well, Pierson," I say. "If you can't lick them join them."

"That's right. How about some chow?"

"That would be just fine."

He leads the way into a Quonset that serves as a dining room. There are long tables and tin plates and a number of men eating. Some of them look like construction workers, others like technicians.

My attention is drawn to a table of about thirty youths. They are the best-looking boys I have ever seen at one time, and all of them are ideal specimens of white Anglo-Saxon youth.

"Our genetic pool," Pierson explains.

A fat mess sergeant slops some fish and rice and stewed apricots on our plates and fills tin cups with cold tea.

"Army-style here," says Pierson.

After we finish eating, he lights a cigarette and grins at me through the smoke.

"Well, I guess you are wondering what this is all about."

"Yeah."

"Come along to my digs and I'll explain. Some of it, at least."

I know quite a bit already. Much more than I want him to think I know. And I know that the less he tells me the better chance I have of getting out of here alive. I've already seen that the oil rig is a rocket-launching pad. Things are falling into place.

He leads the way to a small prefab. He turns to Jim and Kiki: "Why don't you two look around? Do some fishing. You can get tackle at the PX. The lake is stocked with largemouth bass . . . You'll do well here. . . ."

I nod to Jim and he walks away with Kiki. Pierson unlocks the door and we go in. A cot, a card table, some chairs, a few books. He motions me to a chair, sits down and looks at me. "You saw the launching pad?"

"Yes."

"And what do you think it will be used for?"

"To launch something, obviously."

"Obviously. A space capsule that will also be a communications satellite."

I am beginning to understand what they are planning to communicate.

"Now, just suppose an atom bomb should fall on New York City. Who would be blamed for that?"

"The Commies."

"Right. And suppose a mysterious plague broke out attacking the white race, while the yellow, black, and brown seemed to be mysteriously immune? Who would be blamed for that?"

"Yellow black brown. Yellow especially."

"Right. So we would then be justified in using any biologic and/or chemical weapons in retaliation, would we not?"

"You would do it justified or not. But the plague might well decimate the white race ... destroy them as a genetic entity."

"We would have the fever sperm stocks. We could rebuild the white race to our specifications, after we ..."

The table of thirty boys flashed in front of my eyes. "Pretty neat. And you want me to write the scenario."

"That's it. You've written enough already to get the ball rolling."

"What about the Countess de Gulpa? How does she figure in this?"

"Ah, the Countess. She doesn't figure. She is not nearly as important as you may have thought. She would hardly go along with destroying the blacks and browns, because she makes her money out of them. She still thinks in terms of money."

"Her laboratories?"

"Not much we could use. Certain lines of specialized experimentation . . . interesting, perhaps. She has, for example, succeeded in reanimating headless men. These she gives to her friends as love slaves. They are fed through the rectum. I don't see any practical applications. We had thought of using her in scandals to discredit the rank-and-file CIA . . . but that won't be necessary now."

"I daresay you could wipe her out with rockets from here."

"Easily. Or we could use biologic weapons."

"The Black Fever?"

"Yes." He pointed to the radio. "In fact, I could give the order right now."

"So what do you want from me?"

"You will finish the scenario. Your assistant will do the illustrations."

"And then?"

"You have been promised a million dollars to find the books. You have found them. Of course, money will mean nothing once this thing breaks, but we will see to it that you live comfortably. After all, we have no motive to eliminate you . . . we may need your services in the future. We're not bad guys really. . . ."

How nice will these nice guys be once they get what they want from me? If I am allowed to live at all it will certainly be as a prisoner.

I am trying to stall Blum with a sick number called *Naked Newgate* about a handsome young highwayman and the sheriff's daughter. Blum isn't buying it.

"Any thousand-dollar-a-week Hollywood hack could write such a piece of shit."

Then Pierson asks me over for a drink and a "little chat." It sounds ominous.

"Oh uh by the way ... Blum isn't exactly happy about the screenplay."

"Nize baby, et up all the screenplay."

He looks at me sharply.

"What's that, Snide?"

"It's a joke. Fitzgerald in Hollywood."

"Oh," he says, a bit intimidated by the reference to Fitzgerald ... perhaps something he should know about ... He clears his throat.

"Blum says he wants something he calls *art*. He knows it when he sees it and he isn't seeing it now."

"What I like is *culture*! What I like is *art*!" I screech in the tones of a crazed Jewish matron.

He gives me a long blank sour look.

"More jokes, Snide?"

"I'll give him what he wants. I'm staging a little theater production tomorrow ... *very artistic*."

"This had better be good, Snide."

A slim blond youth in elegant nineteenth-century clothes stands on a scaffold. A black hood, laced with gold threads, is drawn over his head.

RUBBLE BLOOD PU
(END OF PART I)

Stuck in dead smallpox nights of the last century. This satined ass in yellow light.

(Yellow-flecked storm waves ... palm trees ... wide

strip of sand ... a corduroy road ... I don't remember hitting ... I really don't think so ... the truck shadow ... trees tasting cement ... green dark water.)

"Good English soldier of fortune, sir. Work for you, yes no?"

Spelling years whisper the lake heavy red sweater, trash cans in yellow light. The sigh of a harmonica flags in the sad golden wash of the sunset singing fish luminous sky fresh smell of damp violets. Man smell of dirty clothes red faces breath thick on tarnished mirrors.

Sunset, train whistles. I am on the train with Waring. Red clay roads and flint chips glitter in the setting sun.

Pilots the plane across time into a waiting taxi, steep stone street, boy with erection yellow pimples turn-of-the-century lips parted ... red hair freckles a ladder.

A young face floats in front of his eyes. The lips, twisted in a smile of ambiguous sexual invitation, move in silent words that stir and ache in his throat with a taste of blood and metallic sweetness. He feels the dizzy death weakness breathing through his teeth, his breath ice cold.

The boy in front of him lights up inside, a blaze of light out at his eyes in a flash as Audrey feels the floor drop out from under him. He is falling, the face floating down with him, then a blinding flash blots out the room and the waiting faces.

CHEERS HERE ARE
THE NONDEAD

 tenor voice was singing in my head:

"A touch of sun, a touch of sun
The color sergeant said . . ."

I woke up with something cold on my chest. A doctor was sitting by my bed with a stethoscope.

"Hello there, young guy," he said when I opened my eyes.

A naval officer stood beside the doctor, looking down at me. I could feel a cast around my neck. The doctor turned to the other officer:

"Heart's sound as a gold dollar. Should be out of the cast in a week."

The officer looked down at me from some stinker of a battleship film: "If you feel like that again, son, go see the shrink or the chaplain."

"Would someone show me my face in a mirror?"

The doctor held a hand mirror in front of me. A shock of recognition. Familiar young face. Red hair.

"Just wanted to be sure I was still there."

The doctor and the officer laughed, and I heard the door close. The face looked at me from the foot of the bed.

"Hello. I'm Jimmy Lee. You're Jerry. We're identical twins. I'm in the medics, you're in communications. U.S.

Navy, six years' service. Depressed over the death of your pet monkey, you tried to hang yourself. I cut you down in time. That's our story. You want to remember. . . ."

They had to be careful about sex in the navy, so Jimmy and Jerry got a book on astral projection and decided to learn to do it in the "second state," as the book called it, and they finally succeeded though they never knew exactly when it would happen or who was going to visit whom until it happened and this was sometimes under embarrassing circumstances, like in the shower room or during a physical examination. One twin lets out an eerie high-pitched wolf howl and turns bright red all over as the hairs on his head and body stand up and crackle. Then, as if struck by lightning, he falls to the floor in an erotic seizure ejaculating repeatedly in front of the appalled and salacious tars. A slack-jawed pimply boy from east Texas watches with a bestial leer.

"Look at his *peter!*"

"Medics!"

Jimmy describes a typical attack to a flustered navy psychiatrist:

"First there's this *smell*, Doctor. Like skunks in heat, if you'll pardon the expression, sir. It chokes you and gets you hot. Like a *popper*, sir." He makes a motion of breaking a popper under his nose, moans and shows his teeth. The doctor coughs, opens a window and pulls up a venetian blind. Sunlight streams into the room.

"And then Jerry's face comes into focus like. He he he," he titters. "That reminds me of a joke, sir. This old Jew, sir, got his wife and Mrs. Lieberman from next door in his car, he is driving out into the country to focus his headlights, sir, and he's got a sheet to do it with and Mrs. Lieberman sees him getting the sheet out, sir, and she says:

" 'Vot's he gonna do?'

" 'He's going to focus.'

" 'Vot? Both of us?'

"Rather good, don't you think, sir? Looking at me with this *smile*, sir." He leers at the doctor and squirms in his chair. "And his body, sir, is a *translucent* red haze. I got that word out of a navy bulletin on poison fish. Some of them is *translucents*. You can see all their *guts*, sir." He looks pointedly at the doctor's stomach. "It's like Jerry *vaporize* hisself. He just *steams* right into me feeling and wriggling down into each glittering leg hair, sir." Jimmy hitches up his pants to show white ankles with red hairs that stir and glitter in the sunlight.

"With little electric *prickles*, sir, into my you know and you know and you knows. Then I am going down very fast in an elevator, you know the feeling, sir, right here." He cups his crotch. "And Jerry is floating down with me. Then silver light *pops* in my eyes, sir." He makes a loud popping sound with his mouth. The doctor starts. "And I shoot off and everything turns red. We call it a *red-out*, sir."

The doctor made a personal diagnosis of acute homosexual panic. A colleague said it was psychomotor epilepsy. The Old Man said he didn't care what it was, he didn't want it in the navy. So the Juicy-Fruit Twins, as he called them, were up for discharge. Since they had no medical record of epileptic seizures or psychosis prior to enlisting in the navy there was the question of a complete disability pension, and this slowed things down. Then project Simulated Space Conditions got under way and the discharge was shelved.

"What's going on here?" I asked Jimmy Lee.

"Well, we're on Krup's spaceship or so he claims. Anyhoo, he's up there with charts and maps and the crew seems to obey him, most of them at least."

"What do they look like?"

"Germans mostly. Young punks."

"Who else is here?"

"All the boys from your scripts: Audrey, Jerry, all the Jims and Johns and Alis and Kikis and Strobe, Kelley, and Dahlfar. One foot in a navy mess and the other on some kooky spaceship. You see, there is a pretense this is just a naval station and you never know which is the pretense: spaceship or navy. One minute you are getting popped in Tamaghis, the next you're on KP or swabbing the deck. They got shore patrols out in Tamaghis. Whole area is off limits. And pro stations. And I've got a rundown on Krup. He's an intergalactically known spaceship swindler. You set out for the Big Dipper and wind up stranded in Vladivostok. And he's a heavy metal junk runner, known as Opium Jones in the trade."

I'd seen metal junk addicts. Withdrawal is like acute radiation sickness. We sure are in good hands.

"Who's that joker with the doctor?"

"Oh he's one of the old navy set.... The doctor will be back any minute. I have to take a sperm specimen. They run tests on it...."

I start to get a hard-on at the prospect of coming in another body. The doctor is looking down at me.

"How do you feel, young guy?"

"Horny, Doc."

"That always happens with a vertebral fracture like yours."

He folds the sheet down to my knees. I can feel it float up and throb. A throbbing in my neck sends electric tingles down to my crotch. Jimmy sits down with a beaker and runs his fingers lightly up and down my new cock and I go off in a blaze of silver light. Jimmy's face gets black around the edges and I go out for a few seconds. When I come around, the doctor is gone.

"He's a creep and I hate him," Jimmy says. "He used to be the doctor in a Siren cathouse."

I know what that means. Money from the Madam to pass her girls, in advanced stages of one of the fifty-seven venereal diseases endemic in the Cities of the Red Night.

"Sometimes I wish it was one thing or the other. Tamaghis or the navy," I complain. "Six years in the navy and what did it get us? Give me Tamaghis. It beats swabbing decks and fucking clappy dry-cunt whores."

"It does at that," agrees Jimmy.

"What about Blum?"

"It's open war now between Krup and Hollywood."

"Sounds like a scriptwriter's paradise."

"It is and that's why they drafted you into the navy where they don't have to pay you anything but navy pay. Got you for a pop. Same way they got all of us."

"So this ship is manned by the hanged."

"Sure. That's how we all got shanghaied."

"The Germans too?"

"Second generation. They are all artificial-insemination kids from one hanged father."

I closed my eyes, feeling very relaxed and comfortable in Jimmy's body, and I could remember the little Michigan lake town. Fishing was the big thing then, carp and lake trout. At fourteen I ran away to join the navy with a forged birth certificate. Two years later they found it out and the President himself pardoned me—it was in all the papers. And I could remember this dream I kept having about a strange city with red light in the streets and then I was in a room naked and could see other people there naked too and suddenly they are all looking at me, I get a hard-on and go off and sometimes one of the faces lights up just as I start to shoot. And that was the first time I saw Jimmy Lee, long before I met him in the navy after my pardon. I was learning to be a radio operator and I'd gone to the radio room when this new kid with tech stripes looks up and smiles at me just like he did in the dream.

"We met—in a way, that is . . . weren't you in the Double G the other night?"

I remembered a place I'd wandered into where everybody was looking at something I couldn't see. The way they were looking and a smell in the place got me hot and Jimmy looking at me like that, I was getting a hard-on now so I sat down to hide it and lit a cigarette.

Jimmy starts filling me in on the officers. He always knew who was what aboard ship. "The Old Man's a real asshole and you can't smear it on too thick—tell him you want to be buried right in the same coffin with him when you die. Anyhoo, I think we're getting a new C.O. You see, this is a kook project with simulated space conditions and the old C.O. can't adjust. So they have called in someone called Krup von Nordenholz, a Nazi war criminal, I hear, but a space expert. So forget about the old C.O. Never butter a man on the way out or you can slip right out with him. Like to bunk with me? Just one other kid in the room, Jim Lewis. You'll like him and he'll like you, too. . . ."

The investiture of the new C.O. was not unopposed and a period of chaos followed.

Stepping into the hall, I saw three naked boys swabbing the corridor, wriggling their asses and goosing each other. The old C.O., with the master-at-arms, bustles round a corner.

"This is disgraceful! Arrest these men!"

"Are we going to be popped, Commander?"

"Bare-ass in front of all our mates?"

"These men are obviously deranged. Call the medics. Reefer madness most likely. If it's dope they are to be transferred to the prison ward."

The doctor minces in. "Hello there, young guys. Come along for an examination."

"Who's *that*?"

"That's the new doctor."

"Well, I don't like the look of him."

"He's supposed to be an expert on space medicine."

"So what?"

"So long as I'm C.O. this is Naval Station 123 Communications."

Back in his cabin, the C.O. found a full-length naked effigy of himself dangling with a hard-on from a lantern hook in the ceiling. Then a powder charge went off in its nuts and a roll of paper popped out the cock in a puff of smoke. The paper landed on his desk and unrolled: his resignation just waiting for his signature.

The resignation of the old C.O. after a nervous breakdown did not end the conflict. The old navy was still in occupation. But Krup was winning. Smoothly Krup moved in his Hitler *Jungen* boys, one looking just like another, all with rosy cheeks and yellow hair. These boys were clean, efficient, exemplary sailors and the old navy could find no fault with them. And Krup removed the off limits on Tamaghis. This made him popular with the men. All the swishes in camouflage openly wore Krup buttons: Billy Budd with a rope around his neck saying, "God Bless Captain Krup."

And the croaker was a Krup man. He served on a Krup metal junk runner when the crew broke into the cargo and got hooked on M.J. Krup found it out and cut them off cold. "This is not a charitable institution," he told the ward full of M.J. addicts shitting, screaming, puking, ejaculating phosphorescent sperm. "I leave you in good hands."

Anyone reporting sick to that croaker walked out a Krup man or he went out feet-first. And the fence sitters, seeing the way the navies were crumbling, began coming over to

Krup, and since many of these were the technical sergeants, that just about sewed it up as a Krup shop.

Then one night, the Krup men in every dorm got up before dawn and took down all the pinup girls. Oh say can you see by the dawn's early light forty-eight naked boys fucking, sucking, rimming on a red, white, and blue gallows and some awful Nordic shit Krup laps up like a cat, the boy singing his swan song in a mountain lake full of swans who convoy him reverently to the gallows. You don't have to be a space expert, just a tech sergeant, to see the old navy game in operation—how one faction gets another out to slide in their own boys.

Morning sun on morning hard-ons as the tars climb out of their bunks and stare at the walls.

"Where's my sexpot?" a boy moans stolidly.

"I can't stand these kids on my walls."

"They're not your walls any longer."

"Hans, Rudi, Heinrich, Willi—*herein!*"

Come in with Krup or else. A Krup takeover of the crew and the ship, or so it seemed. He changed the name of the ship from *The Enterprise* to *The Billy Celeste*, after a nineteenth-century English man-of-war. Now all Krup had to worry about were his own men, who had used him to get rid of the old C.O., and the old navy with its loathsome pinups and pro stations.

But few of us had any confidence in Krup. We'd seen this character operate, how smoothly he'd hoaxed us into his hanging universe ... Tamaghis ... the Double G. But the shore leave was one hell of a lot better. We never had it so good. We could go to a licensed Siren cathouse where they have these deactivated Sirens just give you the sex trill.

The boys are getting dressed to go ashore, adjusting hangman-knot ties.

"Might pop myself a month's pay tonight."

"More likely you'll swing the other way."

The heavy-handed kidding—it's all so Young Navy. The pimply virgin there trying to act wise—he's from Virginia, so we call him the Virginian. So we all chip in to pay for a Siren and watch the Virginian through the two-way mirror. . . .

"Look at the *dong* on that kid," says the boy from East Texas.

The kraut kids hardly ever go ashore, because they like to save money. Off duty they loll around in their bunks jacking off and making airplane noises.

THE SKY IS THIN AS
PAPER HERE

Waring's house still stands. Only the hinges have rusted away in the sea air so all the doors are open. In a corner of the studio I find a scroll about five feet wide wrapped in heavy brown paper on which is written "For Noah." There is a wooden rod attached to one end of the scroll and on the wall two brass sockets designed to receive it. Standing on tiptoe I fit the rod into the sockets and a picture unrolls. Click. I remember what Waring told me about the Old Man of the Mountain and the magic garden that awaited his assassins after their missions of death had been carried out. As I study the picture I see an island in the sky, green as the heart of an emerald, glittering with dew as waterfalls whip tattered banners of rainbow around it. The shores are screened with thin poplars and cypress and now I can see other islands stretching away into the distance like the cloud cities of the Odor Eaters, which vanish in rain ... the garden is fading ... rusty barges and derricks and cement mixers ... a blue river ... red brick buildings ... dinner by the river. On the edge of the market, tin ware clattering in a cold spring wind. When I reach the house the roof has fallen in, rubble and sand on the floor, weeds and vines growing through ... it must be centuries.... Only the stairs remain going up into the blue sky. Sharp and clear as if seen through a telescope, a boy in white workpants, black jacket and black cap walking up a cracked street, ruined houses ahead. On the back of his jacket is the word DINK in white thread. He stops, sitting on a stone wall to eat a sandwich from his lunch box and drink some orange liquid from a paper container. He is dangling his legs over a dry streambed. He stands up in the weak sunlight and urinates into the streambed, shaking a few drops off his penis like raindrops on some purple plant. He buttons his pants and walks on.

Dead leaves falling as we drive out to the farmhouse in the buckboard . . . loft of the old barn, jagged slashes of blue sky where the boards have curled apart . . . tattered banners of rain . . . violet twilight yellow-gray around the edges blowing away in the wind.

He is sitting there with me, cloud shadows moving across his face, ghostly smell of flowers and damp earth . . . florist shop by the vacant lot . . . dim dead boy. . . . The sky is thin as paper here.

ÉTRANGER QUI PASSAIT

Farnsworth, Ali, and Noah Blake are moving south across the Red Desert, a vast area of plateaus, canyons, and craters where sandstone mesas rise from the red sand. The temperature is moderate even at midday and they travel naked except for desert boots, packs, and belts with eighteen-inch Bowie knives and ten-shot revolvers chambered for a high-speed 22-caliber cartridge. They have automatic carbines of the same caliber in their packs, with thirty-shot clips. These weapons may be needed if a time warp dumps an old western posse in their laps.

The only provisions they carry are protein, minerals and vitamins in a dried powder concentrate. There are streams in the canyon bottoms where fish abound and fruit and nut trees grow in profusion.

They carry collapsible hang-gliders in their packs.

They have stopped at the top of a thousand-foot cliff over an area littered with red boulders. Here and there is a glint of water. The sandstone substrata form pools that hold water and even in otherwise arid patches there are usually fish and crustaceans in the pools.

The boys unpack and assemble the gliders. As always, they will take off one at a time so that the lead glider will indicate to the others the air currents, wind velocities, and updrafts to be expected.

They draw lots. Noah will go first. He stands on the edge of the cliff studying the terrain, the movements of dust clouds and tumbleweeds. He looks up at the clouds and the wheeling vultures. He runs towards the edge of the cliff and soars out over the desert. The glider is out of control for a few seconds in an updraft. He goes into a steep dive and pulls out, coming in smoothly now he lands by a pool. He waves and signals to the others; a tiny figure by a speck of water. They move a hundred feet down the cliff and take off.

By the pool they eat dried fruit washed down with water. Ali stands up and points.

"Look there."

The others can't see anything.

"There . . . right there. . . ."

They pick out a lizard about four feet high standing on two legs fifty feet away. The lizard is speckled with orange-red and yellow blotches, so perfectly camouflaged it is like picking a face out in a picture puzzle to see him. The lizard knows he has been seen and lets out a high-pitched whistle. He runs towards them on two legs with incredible speed, kicking up a trail of red dust. He stops in front of them, immobile as a stone, while the dust slowly settles behind him. Seen at close range he is clearly humanoid with a smooth yellow face and a wide red mouth, black eyes with red pupils, a patch of red pubic hair at the crotch. A dry spoor smell drifts from his body.

The lizard boy now leads the way setting the fastest pace the others can maintain. As he moves his body changes color to blend into the landscape. In the late afternoon they are making their way down a steep path into a canyon. Leaves spatter the lizard's body with green. They come to a wide valley and a river with deep pools. The boys take off their packs and swim in the cool water. The lizard dives down to the bottom and comes up with a fourteen-inch cutthroat trout in his jaws and flips it onto the grass by the pool. Ali and Farnsworth are picking strawberries.

Next day they set out to explore the canyon. The river winds between red cliffs. Here and there are cubicles cut in the rock by ancient cliff-dwellers.

We are heading for the river towns of the fruit-fish people. The staple of their diet is a fruit-eating fish which attains a weight of thirty pounds. To cultivate this fish they plant the riverbanks with a variety of fruit trees and vines so that the smell of fruit and fruit blossoms perfumes the air, which is a balmy eighty degrees.

Our boat rides high in the water on two pontoons of paper-thin dugout canoes sealed over to form a sort of sled on which we glide, propelled by a gentle current, past youths in the boughs of trees, masturbating and shaking the ripe fruit into the water with the spasms of their bodies as their sperm falls also to be devoured by the great green-blue fish. It is this diet of fruit and sperm which gives the fruit fish its incomparable flavor.

Little naked boys walk along the banks throwing fruit into the water and masturbating while they emit birdcalls and animal noises, giggling, singing, whining, and growling out spurts of sperm that glitter in the dappled sunlight. As we pass, the boys bend over, waving and grinning between their legs like sheaves of wheat parted by a gentle breeze that wafts us to the jetty.

Who are we? We are migrants who move from settlement to settlement in the vast area now held by the Articulated. These voyages often last for years, and migrants may drop out along the way or adventurous settlers join the migrants.

We carry with us seeds and plants, plans, books, pictures, and artifacts from the communes we have visited.

On the jetty we are welcomed by a tall statuesque youth with negroid features and kinky yellow hair. It is late afternoon and the boys are trooping back from the riverbanks and orchards and fish hatcheries. Many of them are completely naked. I am struck by the mixtures here displayed: Negro, Chinese, Portuguese, Irish, Malay, Japanese, Nordic boys with kinky red and blond and auburn hair and jet-black eyes, blacks with straight hair, gray and blue and green eyes, Chinese with bright red hair and green eyes, mixtures of Chinese and Indian of a delicate pink color, Indians of a deep copper red with one blue eye and one brown eye, purple-black skin and red pubic hairs.

Arriving at the port city after a long uncomfortable train journey from the capital, Farnsworth checked into the Survival Hotel. The hotel was a ramshackle wooden building of four stories overlooking the bay, with wide balconies and porches overgrown with bougainvillea where the guests sat in high-back cane chairs sipping gin slings. A promontory of red and yellow sandstone a thousand feet high cut the town off from the sea, which entered by a narrow channel between the rock and the mainland. Looking down from the balcony of his room on the fourth floor, Farnsworth could see the beaches around the lagoon, where languid youths stretched naked in the sun. Fatigued from his journey, he decided to take a nap before dinner.

Someone touches his shoulder. Ali is looking into the dim light of early dawn.

"*What is it?*"

"*Patrol, I think.*"

We are out of the reservation area and the penalty for being caught here without authorization is the white-hot jockstrap. We will not be taken alive. We have cyanide shoes, a cushion of compressed gas in a double sole under our feet. A certain sequence of toe movements and we settle down in a whoosh of cyanide as the Green Guards clutch their blue throats and we streak out of our bodies across the sky. We also have rocket-fuel flamethrowers, very effective at close range.

This is not a patrol. It is a gang of naked boys covered with erogenous sores. As they walk they giggle and stroke and scratch each other. From time to time they fuck each other in Hula-Hoops to idiot mambo.

"Just leper kids," Ali grunts. "Let's make some java."

We drink it black in tin cups and wash down K rations.

DRAFT RIOTS

And here I was with a pop-happy skipper in an old leaky jinxed gallows-propelled space tramp with all the heaviest guns of the planet trained on us: the Countess de Gulpa (not nearly so unimportant as Pierson would have liked me to believe), the CIA and the Board, Blum and the Movie Studio. I figured we'd be lucky to reach Hoboken. As a matter of fact, we got a few miles farther to what is now lower Manhattan.

Four kids insisted on guiding us to the Double G in New York and when we walked in, I saw that the whole place had changed. The gallows were gone but there were two nooses on the wall above the bar with brass plaques: "Rope used to hang Baboon O'Toole—June 3, 1852." "Rope used to hang Lousy Louie—June 3, 1852." And a photo of Baboon and Lousy standing side by side on a double gallows.

The decor is now the New York of 1860: vintage crystal chandeliers and a huge female nude in a gilded frame over the bar. I spot Marty sitting with four thuggish-looking wooden-faced characters drinking champagne, and he waves to me.

"You boys join us and have some bubbly."

We sit down and the thugs give us a cold fishy who-are-these-nances look. The fever does convey certain advan-

tages. We all have a virus feel for weak points in any opponent
and Krup has given us some basic courses in unarmed psychic
combat. The techniques mostly run on a signal switch—I
love you/I hate you—at rapid intervals, but this is only effective once a weak spot has been found.

We soon have these four hoods in line with just the
right shade of show-you. Hoodlums are ducky soup. Anyone
who has to be tough on the surface is riddled with weak
spots. But don't try the switcheroo on the wrong people.
Try it on a tiddleywink and it can bounce back with a meat
cleaver. And don't tangle with some Mafia don sitting in
front of his grocery store.

When we walk into the Double G in Tamaghis, we see a
heavy padlock on the gallows mechanism with a lead seal
and a notice on a brass plaque: "All public hangings forbidden
by order of the DNA Police."

"Yep," the bartender tells us. "That's right. No more
publics. It's the law."

Death requires a random witness to be real and a public
hanging is real because of random witnesses. In the Garden
of Eden, God left Adam and Eve alone to eat the fruit of
the Hanging Tree and then popped back in like a random
house dick who just happened to be passing in the hall
when he heard amorous noises.

"What's going on here?"

"See any dogcatchers or Sirens in the street?"

"Well no, come to think of it."

"You won't."

The bartender is a little, thin, middle-aged Irishman with
glowing gray eyes. He is dressed in a tight-fitting green suit.
He picks up ten glasses in each hand, spreads them out
on the bar, and starts polishing. "We had a riot here. The

boyos killed every dogcatcher in Tamaghis and most of the Sirens. . . ." He holds up a glass to the light. "The kids all want to get out to Waghdas now and find the answers. I tell them every time you find an answer you find six questions under it, like leprechauns under a toadstool."

New York—the Double G—1860 . . .

A little, skinny, middle-aged Irishman dressed in a filthy green suit bangs on the bar with his beer mug and a respectful silence falls. He jumps up onto the bar, his face contorted like an evil leprechaun as he spits the words out: "The bankers on Wall Street and the sheenies is buying their sons out for three hundred dollars." His eyes glow and the hair stands up on his head. "And what about you and me who don't see three hundred dollars a year in one piece? We get drafted into the frigging army to fight for the frigging niggers."

A bestial roar goes up. The patrons are four-deep around the bar, brandishing clubs and crowbars. The little green man leaps down from the bar.

"What are we waiting for? An invite from City Hall? Let's go!"

About fifty blood-mad men and boys and a few screaming harpies troop out after him screaming: *"Kill! Kill! Kill!"*

"How did the riot start?"

"Well, you know how it is with riots. Things build up and up—then something sets it off." He tosses a chipped glass twenty feet into a trash can. "The dogcatchers start raiding out of fair-game areas and there is a move by the Hanging Fathers in the City Council to extend fair-game areas. Then two foreign Countesses they call themselves—yeah, Countesses de Slutville—buy villas on the mountain and set up something they call the Genetic Institute and there are rumors about transplant operations carried out by this saw-bones they have brought in from Yass-Waddah."

"That would be Van . . ." I put in.

"It would. Next thing these two boy-eating sows move in their own Special Police with firearms and pressure the Council into passing an I.D.-card law so anyone who doesn't have an I.D. card stamped and updated can be arrested and hanged in the Institute. So all the boys have to apply for these cards or risk getting picked up anywhere.

"One night five SPs come in here checking I.D.s and they start to drag some kid out. They have guns of course. Doesn't do them much good. The kids is on them with broken bottles, knives, chairs, feet, knees and elbows. Four kids is killed but they take the SPs apart. You can see the blood-stains right over there. Then some little Irish kid I'd never seen before jumps up on the bar screaming: *'What are you waiting for? Waiting to get milked by these foreign bitches like randy cows? Kill! Kill! Kill!'*

"The SPs and dogcatchers are barricaded in the Garden of Delight, ready to defend the richies with their last drop of blood, and it comes to that quick enough. They open up with machine guns but the boys just spread out and keep coming, throwing cobblestones and Molotov cocktails.

"Better than a hundred are killed in the few seconds it takes for the rest to swarm over the barricades and cut the guards to hamburger. Then they charge up the mountain screaming.

" *'Death to the Foreign Sows!'*

"Well, the Countesses and their sawbones got their asses out to Yass-Waddah in an autogyro. Their villas were looted and burned to the ground along with most of the other villas. The Hanging Fathers were thrown into the fires along with all the Sirens that could be found. Some of the rich kids was with the mob, so a few big villas are still left. But the richies sure got a new look since then."

I soon see that there is more here than just a spontaneous explosion of overcrowded poverty-ridden slums. The whole scene has been staged from above to point up the need for a strong police force, and some of the mob ringleaders turn out to be agents of big money.

"A young man in dirty overalls who fought valiantly with the mob was killed by the police and was found to possess aristocratic features, well-cared-for hands and a fair white skin. Though dressed as a laborer in dirty overalls and a filthy shirt, underneath there were fine cashmere pants, a handsome rich vest and a fine linen shirt. His identity was never learned."

—Herbert Asbury,
Gangs of New York, p. 154

Through the havoc and wreckage of the burning and looted city, through streets littered with the dead and dying, street boys dance and caper like gay insouciant sprites, many of them wearing Halloween masks. A boy in a skeleton suit flops beside a stiff corpse in grotesque imitation.

"You're dead and you stink." He jumps and capers away.

They prance around a dying policeman and mimic his death throes. "Whydon'tcha get up and stop the fight?" They snatch his hat and badge, chasing each other.

"Stop in the name of the law," they mock.

A boy snatches a coat and vest from a looted store. Another boy in fake beard and skullcap pops out.

"Shoot him in the pants! Shoot him in the pants! The coat and vest is mine!"

"They called in a new Commandante who accepted the conditions of the rioters. The Sirens who survived by concealing their assets someplace were confined to licensed cathouses or deported to Yass-Waddah. They had to walk it stark naked. Two hundred miles of desert, wild dogs, hyenas, and leopards out there waiting. The kids lined up and whipped them out the gates with hangman's nooses."

The bartender goes into a song and dance as he taps glasses with a spoon, singing:

> *"She's too fat for me*
> *She's too fat for me*
> *I don't want her*
> *You can have her*
> *She's too fat for me."*

He wipes the bar from one end to the other. "And the sperm dealers has left too, most of them. Can't operate under the new conditions. And good riddance to the Gombeen men."

Marty has a good thing going. Operating with a friend in the Records Department at City Hall he is forging quitclaim deeds to properties in the burnt-out areas. When the smoke clears away he will be owning a big chunk of lower Manhattan. "The *compensation* and *then* the *building contracts*. The whole thing drips with goodness."

He has troops of boys in the street to keep the home fires burning. And these riot boys will later be used to harass any wise citizens who try to reclaim their property and rebuild. The boys screaming insults at visitors. "I catching one clap from fucky your asshole." Swarming over the house like monkeys, leering in at windows, throwing stones at passersby from the roof, urinating and masturbating from balconies.

There are a number of these boys sleeping in the Turkish bath where we have billeted ourselves. They parade around naked doing imitations. Death throes they dig special, flopping around, screaming and groaning and jacking off while the others piss themselves with laughter.

Krup gets it together finally. Two kraut SPs at the door. "All leaves cancelled. Report back to ship immediately." Next stop: the future.

TAMAGHIS REVISITED

When we were first stationed in Tamaghis, it was such a frantic and dangerous place that we never got a chance to relax and look around. At that time, Tamaghis was in the hands of the women with their dogcatchers and Sirens, supported by a weak and acquiescent City Council.

Since the I.D.-card riots, the massacre of the Sirens and dogcatchers, the flight of the Countesses and their retinue, and the appointment of the new Commandante from Waghdas, power had definitely shifted to the men. The new Commandante dissolved the City Council and ruled by decree.

The rioters are now the elite of the city, setting style and tone. The fashionable thing is to look for the answers or the questions behind sex and death. So the youth of Tamaghis look to the academies of Waghdas. I am speaking of about ten percent of the total population. As always, the permanent parties remain: the shopkeepers, restaurant and bar owners, merchants, craftsmen and farmers.

Tamaghis is a walled city, circular in shape, with gates at the four cardinal points. The population is about twenty thousand, but the area of the city would accommodate a much larger population.

Since considerations of privacy do not apply for the emancipated youth, they live by preference in dormitories and cubicle rooms, sharing bathing and sanitary facilities. This concentration of personnel leaves room for the fishponds, farms, aviaries, and orchards within the walled area, so that the city is almost self-sufficient.

And the rich, eager to disassociate themselves from the lingering taint of the dogcatchers, Sirens, predatory Countesses, and the infamous Hanging Fathers of the erstwhile City Council, have made their estates productive. Some have thrown their houses open to youth communes. Cows' milk is brought in from a farm outside the city walls, since the new Commandante banished all cows from the city.

The main square is a composite of the Djemalfnaa of Marrakesh and the Mercado Mayorista of Lima, surrounded by parks and trees. I am sitting in the Red Night Café with Dahlfar, Bluie, and Jimmy Lee drinking tea one afternoon. There is no alcohol and no tobacco in Tamaghis by order of the new Commandante.

A kid I recognize as a former outcast, barred from the Double G, is moving from table to table. Now he is a hero of the I.D. riots.

The kid has a basket full of xiucutls. This small orange-and-red speckled snake has a venom that causes erotic convulsions and acute diarrhea and is frequently used as a practical joke in commune initiations. Of course you can get the same thing in ampules or poppers but the old folkloric ways still have charms for the rich. The boy is making a sale at a table of rich kids.

Looking out across the square, I see a man pushing a cart with crates roped onto it and one of the kraut kids is walking alongside it.

"Looks like Krup is taking on some cargo."

"He sure is," Jimmy tells me. "Right after the riots he bought up all the nooses on the open market and all the noose material. The nooses he plans to sell to tourists in Ba'dan. He's got all the old noose merchants making rugs ... and he's shipping Red Hots and White Angels and Blue Burns and Black Lights and Greenies—the lot. So he cuts them with Spanish fly and sells them in the Ba'dan cathouses."

"He sure is an operator."

"He's putting up the prices, the miserable bastard."

"We'd better lay in a stock."

We walk around through the bazaars pricing color poppers and aphros. The price has about doubled but we know it's twenty times higher in Ba'dan for cut stuff.

The Red Hots bring you out in red blotches and dots, squirming around on your red-hot ass, itching to pop, and you can top it with a Red Pop. This can be dangerous, bringing on internal hemorrhaging or in some cases spontaneous fracture of the vertebrae.

The White Angels turn your jism to light. A Snow Pop is a blaze of cold white light with hot sex sparks. The Blue Burn, which is usually mixed with Yagé, is cold and hot at the same time. You come out in a blue rash with a cold menthol burn, and a Blue Pop is like cyanide and ozone.

The Black Light turns you black as obsidian and knocks all the white words out of your brain so you are right there with whatever the sex scene is, and a Black Pop brings you off in synch. The Greenie is something between animal and vegetable. You come out in a green rash, your nuts a tight seedpod popped off by the Green Pop.

You can mix colors—say Red Hots with a Snow Pop for bells of rosy fire ringing in the sky while you squirt a choir of angels. Now, your partner may be doing the same thing or he may be squirting blue twilight in attic rooms and distant train whistles. Or you take Red Hots and smooth it with a Black Pop and spurt deep purple. An Old Glory threesome: red fucking blue, who is fucking white, and red pops blue, blue pops white, and white pops red.

Try the Rainbow Special—all colors in one—and squirt Niagara Falls, Pikes Peak, souvenir postcards, rainbows, and Northern Lights. Step right up, good for young and old. Young boys need it special. Sometimes they forget the heroes of the fever who made all this available to young boys.

Yeah, I'm a hero of the fever ... Audrey thought as they made selections. But it won't get me a discount. Yeah, I'm a hero of the fever, and knowing what went into those products I don't like to see them cut and sold to drunken American Legion slobs. That's right—the City Fathers are setting up an American Legion Convention. The Ba'dan Hilton and American Express arrive in a cloud of pop stars.

The proprietor, a thin gray old man in a gray djellaba, follows us around pointing out rare items, apologizing for the higher prices.

"Oh there are some Itchy Tingles!" Audrey exclaims. "Just the thing for my high-school Christmas play. Give me a case."

"Oh and there are some Firsties. I'll take all you've got."

A Firsty Pop is the hyacinth smell of young hard-ons, a whiff of school toilets, locker rooms, and jockstraps, rectal mucus and summer feet, chigger lotion, and carbolic soap— whiffs you back to your first jackoff and leaves you sitting there on the toilet—if you don't keep flying speed. Never linger over a Firsty.

The proprietor has it all crated up. We pay him and tell him to send it to the mail room on *The Billy Celeste*.

I stop at a bookstall by a canal to pick up some light reading for the trip to Ba'dan. From an old Frenchman smoking a Gitane I buy *An Outcast of the Islands* by Conrad, *Maiden Voyage* by Denton Welch and *Brac the Barbarian* by John Jakes.

We walk out through the flower markets, florist shops and greenhouses. Sex nettles for fraternity initiations. It's more fun than paddles. Orchids that grow into your flesh, tendrils stirring vegetable lusts. And here is a humanoid mandrake six feet in height.

"Is it a screamer?" Audrey asks.

"It sure is, son. And when he screams it will bring off every living creature for a twenty-yard radius. And the beauty of it is, he lives on your shit . . . saves you installing a toilet."

"What makes him scream?"

"You fuck him, son. Or jack him off or suck him off and he screams like a major."

"What happens if we hang its green ass, roots and all?" Jimmy asked.

"Son, you'd be doing what mankind has always trembled to do. You'd be upsetting the balance between the animal and the vegetable kingdom. He'd scream the planet apart. It would be the last scream."

"He certainly has potential as a weapon," Audrey mused. "That is, if he weren't so bulky."

There are bits and pieces of many cities in Tamaghis. We are walking down a street of worn blue cobblestones rather like the outskirts of Edinburgh when a little boy falls in beside us. About four years old, I think at first. He has a rolling walk like a sailor. He is dressed in shorts with a white sailor shirt and white tennis shoes. I put my hand on his shoulder and he snaps at it with sharp little teeth.

"Keep your hands off me, you bastard."

And I see that he is a miniature youth of eighteen.

When we make it back to the ship with the kid, who has pulled a sailor cap out of his pocket, and get to our cabin there are two more krauts in it. Krup is making room for the cargo. I hope he can get it off the ground. He does. Next stop: Ba'dan.

WHERE NAKED TROUBADOURS
SHOOT SNOTTY BABOONS

Boys in codpieces and leather jerkins carrying musical instruments from the Middle Ages invade American Express. The clerk glares and beckons to a security man. A boy with long blond hair steps to a window.

"Can I help you with something?"

"We wish to travel."

"Travel? Where exactly?"

The boys strip off their clothes: "Where naked troubadours shoot snotty baboons."

They open up with Venus 22 machine guns, a sound like farting metal. Staff and customers lie dead.

Travelogue voices through the loudspeakers: They are a happy simple people / She wears the traditional Athrump / Many moons ago they say / He offered me a cup of Smuun, a mixture of black rum and the blood of a menstruating seal / Now they would show me the Sacred Uncle ceremony / Mixta demonstrates how the *poi mansu* is prepared / We stop to observe the traditional Ullshit that must be observed before this young peasant can Bulunkmash his fiancée / The old Ungling is sick / Can nothing be done? / Sanfraz the sorcerer has been consulted / Every foot of arable land is treasured / All refuse must go into the Ungern or fertilizer ditch / The Phren crop is good and there is much rejoicing / Youths scream *muku muku fucky fucky* over their thumous / How long can the old ways withstand the onslaught of modern technology? / He say long long ago many thousand moons a red light appeared in the northern sky / This light inflamed men to madness and many fell sick with a terrible plague / All that remains of the ancient city of Ba'dan: mud walls in a waste of sand / If these walls could speak what tales they could tell /

What tall tales indeed. Tacitus tells us that the Scythians, a warlike and horsey people, hanged their captives from trees like an old western posse. And Herodotus gives a lurid account of their practices.

When a Scythian king died, fifty pure-blooded Arabic horses and fifty handsome youths were strangled, disemboweled and stuffed. The horses were then placed in a semicircle around the tomb and the youths mounted on the horses, being held in place by a stake which passed through the body of the horse and into the ground and through the anus of the youth up to the top of his skull for good posture. . . .

A baneful red glow flares across the northern sky, bathing the city of Tamaghis in a flickering red light shading from light pink to dark purple, flowing like water through the ancient twisting streets cut from desert rock which has now powdered to sand under generations of shuffling feet.

The first thing you notice here is the dead muffled silence of the sand-covered streets. Now we hear music and singing as a strange procession winds into sight. Naked boys with boots of rotten animal hides crawling with maggots lead a column of horses on which boys are riding naked and bound. The Carrion Boys caper and whinny and rear and fart, showing their teeth like horses.

Now the procession halts in front of the King's tomb

and the horses are being strangled with ratchet cords that tighten and cannot be unloosed. A horse rears, baring his teeth and rolling his eyes as blood drips from his nose ... the horses are turning intolerably into youths ... shrinking faces spit out horse teeth like bullets. A horse rolls on its side kicking spasmodically, sloughing off hooves and sinews and hide, patches of human skin breaking through. Another rolls on its back kicking its legs in the air as the tail whisks in between human legs, kicking human genitals, shooting horse pricks, as intestines spurt from shrinking bellies and brains jet out from eye sockets.

As they emerge from the ruptured horse bodies, the youths are seized by the carrion-booted boys with long red hair and gloating idiot smiles. The youths and horses have all been strangled.

It is time now for the butchery, which they attack with good cheer as one boy heartens his companions with a comic bump-and-grind striptease with intestines that drop off as his erect member snaps out. He sticks his tongue out and ejaculates as his friends roar with laughter. They are a simple happy people.

Now there is work to be done. The horses must be stuffed with aromatic herbs and the youths impaled on stakes that will hold each boy astride a dead horse until horse and rider crumble into the red dust. The Carrion Boys caper away and disappear in little eddies of sand under the red sky shot with meteors and Northern Lights.

"Yipeayee Yipeaayoo Ghost riders in the sky"

In desert lands cool stone latrines / Outhouses covered with roses in drowsy summer afternoons / Dead leaves in the pissoir / *J'aime ces types vicieux qui se montrent la bite* / Find yourself in the navy / All right you jokers hit the deck / Naked boys roll around squirming legs kicking in the air as the colors ripple through them / One bumps out a rich sepia with a smell of military laundry and black vomit in faded violet photo wards and it hits a delicate rose pink of seashells with the hyacinth smell of young hard-ons 1910 the young sailor in Panama yellow-fever epidemic assigned to work in the wards he knew he'd catch it sooner or later then the itching started and the red rash in his crotch and ass pearling in his pants he sniffs the smell of vomit and fever shivering in yellow olive green deep mahogany and black death spasms. Rainbows in faded calendars light up and blaze across the sky. . . . Coming in for a neon landing at the Rainbow Club in Portland.

When Wilson, Chief of Security at Portland, arrived at his office, his assistant handed him a message:

"*The Billy Celeste*, U.S. Navy from 1980 has landed and requests permission to disembark."

Wilson looked at his assistant and raised an eyebrow. "Fever?"

"And how. Even the cockroaches."

Wilson reached for a standard "Quarantine and Repatriation" form. "That's Nordenholz's ship, isn't it?"

"Right."

"Miserable old bastard. One of these days he's going to find my foot up his skinny ass." He signed the form and tossed it into the Out basket.

BOOK THREE

LOCKER ROOM

It is Christmas Eve and Toby is alone in the locker room. The old YMCA building has been sold and only a few boys still stay on. They have moved into the locker room because it is warmer and the showers are there.

Now all the other boys have gone away somewhere for Christmas and Toby knows that most of them will not be coming back, since the building has to be vacated by January 18, 1924. Toby is reading *The Time Machine* by H. G. Wells.

I gave it a last tap, tried all the screws again, put one more drop of oil on the quartz rod, and sat myself in the saddle. I suppose a suicide who holds a pistol to his skull feels much the same wonder at what will come next as I felt then . . .

I seemed to reel; I felt a nightmare sensation of falling . . .

I am afraid I cannot convey the peculiar sensations of time travelling. They are excessively unpleasant. There is a feeling exactly like that one has upon a switchback— of a helpless headlong motion! I felt the same horrible anticipation, too, of an imminent smash. As I put on pace, night followed day like the flapping of a black wing . . .

The twinkling succession of darkness and light was excessively painful to the eye. . . . The sky took on a wonderful deepness of blue, a splendid luminous color like that of early twilight; the jerking sun became a streak of fire, a brilliant arch, in space; the moon a fainter fluctuating band. . . . Minute by minute the white snow flashed across the world, and vanished, and was followed by the bright, brief green of spring . . .

There is a stew simmering on a gas ring and occasionally Toby stirs it, listening to the chimes from the Salvation Army mission across the street playing "Silent Night." He remembers other Christmases, the smell of pine and plum pudding and the oil smell of his steam engine.

He had been brought up in a three-story red brick house in a middle-western town. When he was six years old his parents died, in the flu epidemic of 1918. After that, a series of uncles and foster parents took care of him.

Nobody wanted Toby for long, though he was a beautiful boy with yellow hair and huge blue eyes like deep lakes. He made people uneasy. There was a sleepy animal quiescence about him. He never talked except in answer to a question or to express a need. His silence seemed to hold a threat or a criticism, and people didn't like it.

And there was something else: Toby smelled. It was a sulfurous rank animal smell that permeated his room and drifted from his clothes. His father and mother had had the same smell about them, and they kept a number of pets: cats, raccoons, ferrets and skunks. "The little people," his mother called them. Toby took the little people with him wherever he went, and his uncle John, an executive on the way up, liked big people.

"John, we have to get rid of that boy. He smells like a polecat," Toby's aunt would say.

"Well, Martha, perhaps there's something wrong with his glands." The uncle blushed, feeling that *glands* was a dirty word. *Metabolism* would have been much better . . .

"That's not all. There's something in his room. Something he carries about with him. Some sort of *animal*."

"Now Martha. . . ."

"I tell you, John, he's *evil*. . . . Did you notice the way he was looking at Mr. Norton? Like some horrible little gnome. . . ."

Mr. Norton was John's boss. He had indeed been visibly discomfited by Toby's silent appraising stare.

Looking back, Toby could see the twinkle of Christmas-tree ornaments. Far away his father points to Betelgeuse in the night sky. The locker room holds the silence of absent male voices like a deserted gymnasium or barracks.

The boys have built a partition of beaverboard and set up their cots in this improvised room. There is a long table with initials carved in the top, folding chairs, and a few old magazines in the main room where the gas ring is located. In one corner is a withered Christmas tree that Toby pulled out of a trash can. This is part of his stage set. He is waiting for someone.

He tastes the stew. It is flat and the meat is tough and stringy. He adds two bouillon cubes. Another fifteen or twenty minutes. Meanwhile, he will take a shower. Naked, waiting for the water to heat up, he is examining the graffiti in the toilet cubicle, running his hands over phallic drawings with the impersonal interest of an antiquarian. He is a plant, an intrusion. He has never seen the other boys, a whiff of steaming pink flesh, snapping towels, purple bruises. He leans against the wall of the toilet as silver spots boil slowly in front of his eyes.

Christmas Eve, 1923: You can see the old YMCA building. Someone he carried with: Hi/ . . .

"Hi. It's me, Toby."

His father points to a few boys still staying there ... the shower's silence. Other boys have gone away. Part time in this improvised room. Building has to be vacated by the folding time machine where the gas ring is hot occasionally. Toby pulled out of the mission, stage set, other Christmases. His part is six years old in the epidemic. Toilet cubicle, his old face, remote parents. Sleepy animal whiff of naked flesh Christmas geese in the sky. Silent night for someone died waiting for the graffiti in 1918. If you ask for something solid as shirt and pants walks ... long sight you read *The Monkey's Paw*? Years over phallic drawings snapping towels and purple bruises. . . .

Toby dresses and walks back into the "living room," as they call it. A man is sitting at the table. He is thin and white-haired with blue eyes. His pants and shirt are red-and-white-striped like peppermint. A long patched coat is folded on the chair beside him. Wisps of fog drift from the lapels.

"Well, Toby, and what would you like for Christmas?"

"Well, sir, I guess people ask for a lot of silly things, so I'd like to ask your advice before making up my mind."

"Yes, Toby, people do ask for silly things. They want to live forever, forgetting or not knowing that forever is a time word and time is that which ends. They want power and money without submitting to the conditions under which power and money are granted. Now I'm not allowed to give advice but sometimes I think out loud. If you ask for something solid like power or money or a long life, you are taking a sight-unseen proposition. . . . Now, if you ask for an *ability* . . ."

"I want to learn how to travel in time."

"Well, you could do a lot worse. Makes you rich

just incidentally. But it can be dangerous. . . ."

"It is necessary to travel. It is not necessary to live."

Toby experienced a feeling of ether vertigo as he was pulled into a whirling black funnel. Far away, as if through a telescope, he could see someone sitting at a table, a slim youth of about twenty with yellow hair and brown eyes.

A fluid plop and he was inside the youth, looking out. He was sitting in a restaurant somewhere, taste of paper-thin cutlet, cold spaghetti, and sour red wine in his mouth. The waiters looked ill-tempered and tired. Now he became aware of someone sitting at an adjacent table, so obviously looking at him that they seem for a moment to be alone in the restaurant. It was a woman of about twenty-six, neither well nor poorly dressed, with an older man and woman, probably her parents. She had, Toby thought, one of the most unpleasantly intrusive faces he had ever seen, set in an oily smile or rather a knowing smirking cringe with a suffocating familiarity that pressed on his being like a predatory enveloping mollusk.

Toby began to feel quite faint. Suddenly he spoke without moving his lips: "You'll never get into a nice gentile country club with a look like that hanging out of your Jew face. . . . We like *nice* Jews with atom bombs and Jew jokes. . . ."

Dead silence, wild-eyed faces looking for the source of this outrage.

"*Ach Gott!*" A Jewish waiter slumped to the floor in a faint.

Toby shifted his attention to a table of blacks. "Yes and the right kind of darky too, singing sweet and low out under the mimosa, not feeding his black face in the same restaurant with a white man and getting his strength up to rape our grandmothers."

Next a table of Latin American diplomats.

"You greasy-assed Mexican pimps. Why don't you go back to your syphy cathouses where you belong?"

"That's telling them!" said a southern American voice.

"Go screw a mud puppy.... And if there's anything worse it's a murdering mick with a bomb in his suitcase."

A suitcase by a table of Irishmen began to tick. Toby put money on his check. He lifted his wineglass to the table of Jews: "You Jews is so warm and human. I offer to you that most beautiful of all toasts: *L'chaim!* To Life! ..."

He was moving towards the door. "You blacks got soul." As he passed the Latin Americans, he twitched his hips. "*Qué rica mamba....* When Irish eyes are smiling ..." In the doorway, Toby whipped his scarf around his neck and shouted back into the room without moving his lips, so it seemed to echo from every corner ...

"*Bugger the Queen!*"

He opened the door and heavy palpable darkness blew in with a reek of brimstone. He sprinted for the corner in a black cloud, his red scarf trailing out behind him like a burning fuse. Shouts behind him. Breaking glass.

Here was 44 Egerton Gardens. He opened the door with his key, slid in and shut the door, leaning against it. A blast outside, sirens, words in his head: "Air raid ... the blitz."

He felt his way to his room at the head of the stairs. As soon as he opened the door, the sound of breathing and the smell of sleep told him that someone else was there. He touched a shoulder.

"Hello, I'm John Everson. Hope you don't mind doubling up like this."

"It's all right." Toby stripped to his underwear and slid in beside him.

They lay there, listening to the explosions. The bombs seemed to walk in a leisurely way up and down Brompton Road. A smell in the room, not just of warm young flesh. It was a rank musky ozone smell, the smell of time travel.

Toby woke up in a dark cottage. Mother was not back yet. He was alone and very frightened. The cottage was in Gibraltar and he knew the floor plan in the dark.

He went from his room into the sitting room and looked into his mother's room. The bed was empty, as he knew it would be. The lights would not turn on. He lay down on her bed but the fear was there as well.

He went back to his room and tried to turn on the lights. None of them would turn on. Now even the light in his own room would not work.

He opened the cottage door and went out. Dawn light outside, but a heavy darkness lingered inside the cottage like a black fog. He resolved not to spend another night there.

Who would not spend another night there? He was two people—the boy who lived in the cottage and someone else.

He saw a boat. Durban to Gibraltar. A slim youth with yellow hair and brown eyes in a blue uniform and nautical hat was the first mate. Two officers and a crew of eight on the brigantine.

The boy's mother is back from the pub where she works as a barmaid. She is sprawled fully dressed on the bed in a drunken sleep. He looks around at the potted plants, a tapestry on the wall with a minaret, an ivory elephant, a glass mouse on a shelf. In the front room, a hot plate, a square yellow tea can with Chinese characters, a faucet dripping into a rusty sink. Two men are in the room: one a thin man in his thirties with a receding chin and a pasty face, and the other a priest with reddish hair and bloodshot eyes.

Slowly the boy takes inventory of the sleazy decorations, a brass bowl with cattails in it on the mantel of the non-functioning fireplace, a wobbly table with a tasseled lamp, three chairs, a couch, and an army blanket.

He is the boy, but also a concerned visitor, an uncle or godfather. He is preparing to leave. Outside the cottage is a steep weed-grown slope covered with Christmas rubbish and artificial snow. He hates to leave the boy there.

On the slope, a paper paddle wheel turns slowly in the wind. Written on the wheel: THE MISSING AND THE DEAD.

The priest is talking to the mother and the other man.

"Do be careful, and if anything goes wrong don't hesitate to contact me."

Dead fingers in smoke pointing to Gibraltar. "Captain Clark welcomes you aboard. Set your watches forward an hour." British we are, British we stay. Marmalade and tea in the shops, ivory elephants, carved ivory balls one inside the other, jade trees, Indian tapestries of tigers and minarets, watches, cameras, postcards, music boxes, rusty barbed wire, signal towers.

Coming in for a landing, he hears a tired gray priest voice:

"And how long will you be staying, Mr. Tyler?"

IT IS DIFFICULT
IN TRAIN "A"

On the train with Waring. Smell of steam, soot, and iron. The WCs are all clogged with shit. Landscape of red soil, streams, ponds, and farmhouses.

I have a little round box which contains a number of scenes on parchment-like paper that come alive as I turn the pages. Some oxen by a river mired in concrete up to the forelocks. Now four figures, two boys and two girls in eighteenth-century garb, get out of a gilded carriage. They take off their clothes, pirouetting to tinkling music-box notes.

In the train corridor, I encounter a French customs agent—a short heavyset man with a red face and bloodshot green eyes—accompanied by a tall gaunt gray-faced assistant. It seems that we are passing through a tip of French Canada and he is here to examine passports.

The door the agent is standing before opens towards him but he is pushing the other way with his shoulder, his weight preventing two conductors from opening the door from the other side. At this point, he tells his assistant to break the door down with a fire ax. I intervene to point out that the door opens towards him. He has but to pull it open. This he finally does, then upbraids me and the two conductors for blocking his way.

"*Mais je suis passager,*" I protest.

"*Quand même!*" he snaps.

Now the passengers all disembark from the train and line up with their passports in an open-air booth. The customs agent sits behind a table against a wooden partition. Every time anyone lights a cigarette a DÉFENSE DE FUMER sign appears and he looks up from the table shouting, *"Défense de fumer."*

I am first in line. The agent looks at my passport and sneers.

"Is this something of your own invention?"

I tell him it is something issued by the United States Government.

He looks at me suspiciously and says: "It says here that you live in London."

"And so?"

There is a girl behind me in line holding an American passport. I point out that my passport is the same. He snatches her passport and looks at it. Then he slaps both passports down on the table and turns to his assistant.

"Destroy these documents."

"But you can't go around destroying people's passports. Are you deranged?" I ask.

"Dérangé?" he sneers, turning now to the girl. "Is this man your accomplice?"

"Nothing of the sort! I never saw him before."

"But you travel on the same train?"

"Well, yes . . . but . . . ."

"And sit at the same table?"

"Well, yes, it so happened . . ."

"So you admit to sitting at the same table with this man you have never seen before? And perhaps you share also the same compartment? The same bed, no doubt?"

"It's not true!" she screams.

Soldiers light a wood stove. The assistant speaks: "Pardon me, sir, but my son is a collector. Could I keep one of these forgeries?"

"You may keep one. Which do you prefer?"

"Well, the girl, sir. She is prettier. My son will whack himself off looking at it, I don't mind telling you."

"Very well. Destroy the other passport."

My passport is dropped into the wood stove. He turns to the other American passengers.

"All of you now come forward and surrender your lies. Documents purportedly issued by a government which ceased to exist two hundred years ago. . . ."

A chorus of outraged protests goes up from the passengers but soldiers snatch their passports and dump them into the stove.

"Well, Mother and I want you to know we will report you to the American Consul," a tourist moans.

The officer stands up. "The currency you are carrying is of value only to a collector. I doubt if you will find one in a town of this size." He gets into the train, which starts to move.

"But what about our luggage?"

"It has been impounded. You may recover it in the capital on presentation of valid passports."

The train gathers speed. We are standing in a turn-of-the-century western town: water tower, a red dirt street, Station Hotel & Restaurant. I leave my countrymen waving credit cards and traveler's checks in front of a bland Chinese behind a counter who takes a toothpick out of his mouth, looks at the end of it, and shakes his head.

I walk along the street past a saloon and barbershop and turn into a rundown weed-grown street: Street of Missing Men. The houses on both sides look deserted. As I walk, the buildings change and the street slopes steeply down.

BATHS OPEN DAY AND NIGHT. I go into a steam room with marble benches. A boy smooth and white as alabaster beckons me and I follow him through a maze of showers and steam rooms into a waiting room and out into the street looking for a taxi on a steep stone platform over a green slope with stone steps going down.

We are looking for a Twin Taxi. He has a twin with him who is crippled, one leg in a cast. The alabaster youth sits next to me on a stone bench. He has no white to his eyes, which are a delicate egg-blue and shiny as glass. He sits there with his arm around my shoulder, talking in a strange language that sets off little cartoons and film sequences ... languid white legs flicker ... silver buttocks in a dark room. . . .

I CAN TAKE THE HUT SET
ANYWHERE

have rented a riverfront shack from someone named Camel. The river is slow and deep, half a mile wide at this point. Rotting piers along an unpaved street. Loading sheds in ruins, roofs fallen in. Standing in the middle of the street I turn now towards a row of houses. The houses are narrow and small clapboards, peeling paint, galvanized iron roofs separated by drainage ditches choked with weeds and brambles, rusty tin cans, broken stoves, pools of stagnant water running to culverts broken and blocked with refuse. I go up steep wooden steps to what had been a screened front porch. The screening is rusted through and the screen door off its hinges. I open a padlock and push the front door open. A musty smell of disuse and a sudden chill. Warm air seeps into the room behind me and where the outside air and the inside air come in contact I see a palpable haze like heat waves. The house is about twenty feet by eight feet.

On my left is a blackened kerosene stove on a shelf attached to the wall, supported in front by two two-by-fours. On the rusty burner a blue coffeepot with a hole in the bottom. Above the stove are shelves, some dented cans of beans and tomatoes, two jars of preserved fruit covered with mold. Two chairs and a wooden bedstead at the end of the room, a stepladder by the bed. To the right of the bedstead is a door which opens onto a bathroom with two oak toilet seats side by side, a bucket black with rust, a brass faucet covered with verdigris.

I go back to the street and look around. At one end the street ends in a tributary. I walk the other way and the road turns inland. There is a shack with the sign SALOON at the turning. I go in and a man with eyes the color of a gray flannel shirt looks at me and says, "What can I do for you?"

"Where can I buy tools and supplies? I just rented the Camel shack."

"Yes I know. Do with a bit of fixing up, I guess.... Far Junction ... One mile up the road."

I thank him and start walking. Dirt road, flint chips here and there, ponds on both sides. Far Junction is a few buildings and houses, a water tower and a railroad station. The tracks are weed-grown and rusty. Chickens and geese peck in the street. I go into the general store. A man with pale gray eyes and a black alpaca jacket looks up from a seat behind the counter.

"What can I do for you, young man?"

"Quite a few things. I've rented the Camel shack."

He nodded. "Do with some fixing up, I guess."

"It sure can. More than I can carry."

"You're in luck. Deliveries twice a week. Tomorrow."

I walked around pointing: copper screening, tools, tacks, hinges, two-burner kerosene stove, five gallons of kerosene, ten-gallon water container with spigot and stand, water barrel, cooking utensils, flour, bacon, lard, molasses, salt, pepper, sugar, coffee, tea, case each canned beans and canned tomatoes, broom, mop, bucket, wooden washtub, mattress, blankets, pillows, knapsack, bedroll, slicker, machete, hunting knife, six jackknives. The proprietor walks behind me writing the purchases down on a clipboard. Alligator Gladstone bag? Fifteen dollars. Why not? Jeans, shirts, socks, bandannas, underwear, shorts, pair extra walking boots, shaving kit, tooth-brush.

I pack the clothes and toilet articles into the bag. . . . fishhooks, leaders, sinkers, lines, floats, minnow seine.

Now for the guns. Colt Frontier six-inch barrel 32-20 caliber, a snub-nosed 38 inside belt holster (this I pack in the bag), double-barrel twelve-gauge shotgun. I look at the lever-action rifles.

"It would be handy to have a 32-20. Same shells for pistol and rifle. Anything around here need a heavier load?"

"Yep. Bear. It isn't often a bear attacks . . . when he does, this"—he tapped a box of 32-20 shells—"would just aggravate him."

He paused and his face darkened. "Something else needs a heavier load and longer range. . . ."

"What's that?"

"Folk across the river."

I picked up the Colt 32-20 and holster. "Any law against packing a gun in this town?"

"There's no law in this town, son. Nearest sheriff is twenty miles from here and keeps his distance."

I loaded the gun and strapped it on. I picked up the Gladstone bag.

"How much do I owe you?"

He calculated rapidly. "Two hundred dollars and forty cents plus a two-dollar delivery charge. Sorry about that. Things keep going up."

I paid him. "Much obliged. Delivery buckboard leaves at eight tomorrow morning. Best get here a bit early. Likely think of a few more things you'll need."

"Any place to stay here?"

"Yep. Saloon Hotel three doors down."

Drugstore next door. Old Chinese behind the counter. I bought tincture of iodine, shaving lotion, permanganate crys-

tals for snakebite, a tourniquet, a scalpel, a five-ounce bottle
of opium tincture, a five-ounce bottle of cannabis extract.

Saloon Hotel. The bartender had russet hair and a face
the same color. A calm slow way about him. Two drummers
at the bar drinking whiskey, talking about the rising wholesale
cost of fencing. One fat and clean-shaven, one thin with a
carefully trimmed beard. Both of them looking like they
stepped out of an old photo album. Poker game in one corner.
I buy half a pint of whiskey and a stein of beer and carry
them to a table. I measure myself some cannabis extract
and wash it down with whiskey. I pour myself another shot,
sit back and look around. A boy turns from the bar and
looks at me. He is about twenty with a wide face, eyes far
apart, dark hair and flaring ears. He has a gun at his hip.
He gives me a wide sunlit grin and I push a chair out
with one foot. He carries a glass of beer over and sits down.
We shake hands.

"I'm Noah."

"I'm Guy."

I hold up the bottle of cannabis extract. "Want some?"

He reads the label and nods. I measure it out and he
drinks it with a splash of beer. I fill two glasses with whiskey.

"I hear you've rented the Camel shack on the river,"
he says wriggling his ears.

"That's right."

"Could you do with some help fixing it up?"

"I sure could."

We drink in silence. Frogs croaking outside. It's dark
when the bottle is finished. I call to the bartender.

"Got anything to eat?"

"Passenger pigeon with corn bread, hominy grits and
fried apples."

"Two orders."

He steps to the end of the bar and taps on a green

panel. The panel opens and the Chinese from the drugstore looks out. Bartender gives him the order. When the food comes we eat ravenously. Time travel makes you hungry. After dinner we sit, observing each other with impersonal attention. I can feel the chill of silent space and for a second we see our breath in the air. One of the drummers shivers and looks around at us then turns hastily back to his whiskey.

"Shall we take a room?" I ask.

"I've got one already."

I pick up my bag. The bartender hands him a heavy brass key. Number 6, second floor. He goes in first and lights a kerosene lamp on a table by the bed. Room contains a double bed with brass bedstand, faded rose wallpaper, a wardrobe, two chairs, copper luster washstand and pitcher. I see a Gladstone bag like mine but this one has seen a lot of wear. Travel-stained, the stains unfamiliar. We take off our guns and hang them on the bedstead.

"What caliber?" I ask.

"32-20."

"Same here."

I point to a rifle in one corner: "30-30?" He nods.

We sit down on the bed and take off our boots and socks. Smell of feet and leather and swamp water.

"I'm tired," I say. "Think I'll turn in."

"Me too. I've come a long way."

He blows out the kerosene lamp. Moonlight streams in through the side window. Frogs croak. An owl hoots. A dog barks in the distance. We take off our shirts and pants and hang them on wooden pegs. He turns towards me, his shorts sticking out at the fly.

"That stuff makes me hot," he says. "Shall we camel?"

When I wake up sunlight is streaming in the front window.

We get up, wash and dress and go down to the bar

for a breakfast of ham and eggs, corn muffins and coffee. We walk up to the store, where a youth of fifteen or sixteen is loading the buckboard. He turns and holds out his hand.

"I'm Steve Ellisor."

"Noah Blake."

"Guy Star."

The boy wears a Colt Frontier at his hip.

"32-20?"

He nods. He has russet hair and skin the same color. I figure he must be the son of the saloonkeeper. I go into the store and buy a slicker, mess kit and bedroll for Guy, a two-man tent, a can of white paint with three brushes, a bushel of apples, corn on cob and three stools. We give the Ellisor boy a hand loading the gear, climb in back and sit on the stools. The boy takes the reins and we move off down the road. When we come to the turn the boy points to the saloon.

"Get some bad *hombres* in there sometimes. Not that he wants their custom. They come anyway looking for trouble."

I remember the pale gray eyes of the saloonkeeper and wonder if he is related to the store owner in Far Junction.

"Yep," the boy says, reading my mind, "brothers. Only two families hereabouts, the Bradfords and the Ellisors ... except for those who come in from outside. ..."

"Anybody else on the riverfront?"

"Two Irish and a girl if you could call her that ... end house by the inlet ... expecting more visitors in a few weeks. ..."

"These bad *hombres* you mentioned. Where they come from? ..."

"Across the river." He points. I can make out the outlines of a town through the morning river mist. "When the fog lifts you can see their fucking church sticking up." The boy spits. He stops in front of my shack.

"I could help you fix the place up. . . . Just one delivery to make down the road. . . ."

"Sure. We could do with some help. . . ."

"Would a dollar be too much?"

"Sure not."

"All right. I'll drop the gear off and be right back. . . ."

Guy and I get out with broom, mop, bucket, carbolic solution and washrags. Guy goes to river with bucket. Up steps, new hinges for screen doors, new screening for door and front porch. Unlock door which is heavy oak. Heave old stove into brambles followed by coffeepot, bean and tomato cans, preserves. Guy is back with a bucket of water into which he pours carbolic. He is mopping up bathroom and cleaning toilets while I sweep. Under the dust the floor is yellow pine in good condition. Yellow pine paneling on walls and ceiling. Trapdoor leads to attic.

Guy is cleaning table and shelves when the Ellisor boy returns with buckboard. Boy unhitches horse and hobbles the strawberry roan.

Now to unload in sequence. We don't talk, we know what to do. Water container by stove. Fill container from two five-gallon cans. Fill boiler with river water. New stove on table. Fill stove with kerosene. Fill burner under boiler with kerosene, put in new wick. Groceries and cooking utensils on shelves and stove and nails. Mattress and blankets on walnut bedstead. Trunks along wall, bedclothes packed in trunks, Gladstone bags out of the way in the attic. We take off our shirts. Steve's body is red-brown like his face. Guy's body also tanned but tanned in overlaid blotches like dab painting.

"Star tan," he tells me.

Steve and Guy start screening the porch. I take ladder outside and scrape the walls for paint. Old paint comes off easy. One wall scraped. Screen door on hinges, porch half-screened. Time for lunch. Lemonade, apples, flapjacks. Screening finished on porch. New screen for the two side windows. Scraping. Painting. No wasted movements, no getting in each other's way, no talking. Time laid out in screening, painting, putting things away in trunks, storing cases of food and ammunition in attic. At four o'clock we are looking at a neat house, white and shining like a ship in the afternoon sun. I mix a copper-luster pitcher of lemonade. We go out and sit on the porch steps. There it is in the afternoon sun, a white church steeple with a gold cross on top. I can see the mean pinched hate-filled faces of decent church-going women and lawmen with nigger notches on their guns.

Steve retrieves the bean and tomato cans I have thrown away and puts them up on a beam of the loading shed about thirty-five feet from the porch steps. He walks back towards us, pivots in a crouch, draws, aims, and fires, gun held in both hands and extended at eye level.

SPLAT

A tomato can explodes dripping tomato juice down the beam. Steve sits down. Guy stands up, draws, and aims and fires.

SPLAT

Bean can explodes.

I stand up, arms relaxed, both eyes open. Look at target. See bullet hit. Release draw mechanism. Gun jumps into my hand.

SPLAT

We fire six rounds each and reload.

Smell of black powder, smoke, beans and tomatoes. Steve gets a shovel from porch corner, walks around by side of house tapping ground with his feet. He stops and digs, fills can with earth and thick red worms. We get three lines on spools with hook, leader, float. Guy and I take our 30-30s. We walk down road to the tributary which is about forty feet wide at junction with river. As we pass the end house I see three people sitting on the porch which is overgrown with vines. A dark Irish boy grins and waves. Sitting on either side of him are a boy and girl, obviously twins. They both have casques of bright orange hair and blank inhuman expressions. They wear green shirts and pants and yellow shoes. They look at us, faces twitching. Across the inlet the road continues overgrown with weeds and bushes. I start to take out my line. The boy shakes his head.

"Catfish here."

He leads the way along a path through undergrowth by the inlet. A water moccasin thick as my arm slides into the water.

"Here."

We stop by a deep blue pool, bait hooks and drop lines in. In a few seconds floats are jerked down out of sight and we are pulling out bass and jack salmon. We are cleaning the fish when I hear a deep growl. We turn, picking up 30-30s. Twenty feet away a huge grizzly stands on his hind legs, teeth bared. Cock guns.

Click

Click

Steve slides his Colt out. We freeze and wait. The bear drops to all fours, growls and lumbers away. As we pass the end house I see that there is no one on the porch but the door is open. I call from the road.

"Want a fish?"

The dark youth comes to the door naked with a hard-on.

"Sure."

I toss him a three-pound bass. He catches it and goes back inside and I hear the fish slap flesh and then a sound neither animal nor human.

"Strange folk. Where they come from?"

Guy points to the evening star in a clear pale green sky.

"Venusians," he says matter-of-factly. "The twins don't speak English."

"You speak Venusian?"

"Enough to get by. They don't talk with the mouth. They talk with the whole body. It gives you a funny feeling."

We light kerosene lamps, cut boneless steaks off two jack salmon. While the fish cooks, Guy and I drink whiskey and lemonade.

There is a hinged table with folding legs attached to the wall opposite the stove. We sit on stools, eating the jack salmon which is perhaps the best pan fish in the world if you prefer the more delicate flavor of freshwater fish. We sit on the porch in the moonlight looking across the river.

"Be all right if they stayed there and minded their own business," Steve said.

"Ever hear about smallpox minding its own business?" Guy asks.

The boy slept between us light as a shadow. Thunder at dawn.

"Have to get started. The road floods out."

Smell of rain on horseflesh. The boy in a yellow slicker and black Stetson waves to us and whips the horse to a trot as rain sluices down in a gray wall.

We make a pot of coffee and sit down at the table. We sit there for an hour without saying anything. I am looking at two empty stools. Going zero, we call it. A gust of wind knocks at the door. I open the door and there on the porch is the boy with orange hair from End House. He is wearing a slicker and carrying a gallon can. He points to a five-gallon can of kerosene in a corner of the porch. I get a funnel and fill his can.

"Inside? Coffee?"

He steps warily into the room like a strange cat and I feel a shock of alien contact. He twitches his face into a smile and jerks a thumb at his chest.

"Pat!" He ejaculates the name from his stomach.

He throws open his slicker. He is naked except for boots and a black Stetson. He has a hard-on straight up against his stomach. He turns bright red all over, even his teeth and nails, an idiot demon from some alien hell, raw, skinned, exposed, abandoned yet joyless and painful like a prisoner holding up his manacles, or a leper showing his sores. A musky rotten smell steams off him and fills the room. I know that he is trying to show us something and this is his only way to communicate.

The words of Captain Mission came back to me.

"We offer refuge to all people everywhere who suffer under the tyranny of governments."

I wondered what tyranny had led him to leave his native planet and take refuge under the Articles.

The rain stopped in the late afternoon and we walked down to the inlet in a gray twilight and shot two wood pigeons from a dripping tree.

A sharp sickening smell. In the middle of a red carpeted room I see a plot of ground about six feet square where strange bulbous plants are growing. Centipedes are crawling among limestone rocks and from under a rock protrudes the head of a huge centipede. I arm myself with a cutlass and someone I can't see clearly picks up a piece of firewood. I kick the rock over but the centipede digs deeper and I can see that it is huge, perhaps three feet long. Now it is under my bed and I wake up screaming. I know that I must make preparations for a war I thought had ended.

e arrive at Ba'dan around midnight local time. The space front is stacked with garbage under sputtering blue arc lights. Garbage collectors' strike. Someone is always on strike in Ba'dan.

Smugglers of every variety are moored at Ba'dan. The skippers all get together at the annual Skipper Party and award a gold cup to the all-around "Vilest Skipper of the Year." Skipper Krup von Nordenholz will win hands down. There are also cops of every variety making deals with the skippers and arresting anyone who doesn't have the fix in.

We hail a cab. "Where's the action here, Pops?"

"Wal, I reckon you boys want to go to Fun City. Better pick up some artillery first."

He stops at a neon-lighted all-night gun shop. The shopkeeper has all the old western models and some of the newfangled double-action 38's. These guns shoot an aphro charge that can disable or kill. Neck and heart shots are fatal, stomach, solar plexus and genital hits are knockout shots.

Audrey selects a snub-nosed 38 in a quick-draw holster. Pu slips a 41 Derringer into his vest pocket and straps on a Smith & Wesson 44.

"It's a much better load than the 45, old sports."

Fun City is on a plateau that falls steeply on one side down to the river that separates Ba'dan from Yass-Waddah.

On this slope is a vast casbah—the houses are connected by catwalks, trapdoors, and tunnels—that contains the largest per capita criminal population ever seen anywhere. Ba'dan breaks a lot of records.

We walk into a leather bar called the Stretch Nest. A goodly crowd is there—four feet deep at the bar, waiting in line for openings at the gambling tables, going up the wide red-carpeted stairs to private hanging rooms followed by waiters with trays of drinks and buckets of champagne.

The usual costume is boots and chaps, bare ass and crotch. Some have tight-fitting chamois pants up to midthigh and shirts that come to the navel. Many are naked except for boots, gun belts, and hang-noose scarves. Nooses dangle every ten feet from a beam down the center of the room.

A hang fistfight draws a circle of cheering onlookers, as two kids smash each other in the face—lips cut, eyes black, noses broken, spurting blood. One kid is down—he tries to get up and falls on his side.

The winner bends down and ties his arms with a noose scarf. Next thing, the kid is hanged and his semen spatters the bar. The bartender wipes it off with his bar rag.

Now an old rooster, strapped into his corsets, comes in a-gunning for some kids to hang at his debutante daughter's coming-out party. He settles on Pu who has seen him a-coming and has the Derringer palmed.

"Fill your hand, you young varmint," the old gun drawls. Pu shoots him in the neck with the Derringer and he falls farting and shitting, the corsets bursting off him.

"Lucky thing he had his clothes on, old sports."

A naked fifteen-year-old sticks his head in the bar. *"The Clantons and the Earps is shooting it out at the O.K. Corral."*

A great bestial whoop goes up from the bar. The patrons shove and jostle out past hanged corpses, slipping in sperm.

And they head for the O.K. Corral ... there it is and right beside it a gallows that can service thirteen at a time.

The Clantons and the Earps walk towards each other, naked except for gun belts and boots, meeting cock to cock.

"You boys have been looking for a fight ..." Wyatt drawls. "Now we aim to give it to you." He draws and gets Billy Clanton in the crotch. Billy sags but he knocks Wyatt out with a solar-plexus shot from the ground. Doc Holliday turns sideways but Ike Clanton circles and gets him right in his skinny ass. Virgil and Guy Earp are down. The Clantons have won.

The Earps and Doc Holliday are hanged simultaneously. The crowd goes hanging mad. Gunfights all up and down the street, people sniping from windows and doorways, casting from rooftops with deep-sea fishing gear and nooses, trying to snag someone off the street.

They are lined up at the gallows. Ropes are unslung and bodies thrown aside, some of them still alive, strangled by street boys or picked up by roving Buzzard Bands.

People hang from balconies, trees, and poles. Even horses are hauled into the air, kicking and farting, while boys prance around them, showing their teeth in mimicry.

The culmination of this loutish scene is now at hand as drunken cowpokes drag screaming whores out of the cathouses.

"You've given me your last dose, you rotten slut."

"My God, they're hanging *women!*" Audrey gasps.

"Enough to turn a man to stone," drawls Captain Strobe. "Let's get *out* of here." Six youths in chaps bar the way.

"In a hurry, stranger?"

"Yes," says Audrey and he kills him with a neck shot. He flops against another boy, deflecting his aim. Audrey and Pu are unbelievable with hang-guns. The boys are all down now or dead.

We walk away and leave them, fair game for any roving band of vigilantes. Before we turn a corner, they are seized by the Hanging Fathers—naked except for their clerical collars. The Hanging Fathers represent one of the sects under the control of the Council of the Selected. They are one of the most powerful organizations in Ba'dan.

We stroll along to the amusement-park section. Here are the elevators, parachute, and roller-coaster gallows and all variations of hanging roulette. "From Russia with Love" is played like Russian roulette. You stand on the trap with the rope around your neck and you get a gun with one live load. You spin the cylinder and then, instead of putting the gun to your own head, you aim at someone in the audience—if you can draw an audience or anyone within range—and if it's the live shell, the shot springs the release. Or maybe some yokel throws a firecracker under the gallows—they'll work up to an atom bomb eventually.

Now the wall of a building flies up and there are thirteen Commies hard at it, and we take off across the park, bullets whistling all around us. We duck behind the elevator-gallows building—ten stories, three hundred feet long.

You start at the tenth floor with a rope around your neck and drop down at express speed, and when the elevator *stops* a panel flips open and you get popped. And, of course, you can play roulette on the elevators, any odds you want.

Audrey is getting that weak feeling—it's the wet dream of his adolescence, going down very fast in an elevator that suddenly stops. He didn't know what it meant then. Now he just has to try it.

So up to the tenth floor. A red-carpeted corridor runs the length of the building. On one side a Turkish bath, on the other the elevators, green lights showing when the elevator is vacant. Youths, draped in towels or naked, come out of the showers and steam room to importune in the hall.

Audrey beckons imperiously to an attendant: "Do you have a well-equipped think room?"

"Oh yes, sir. Right this way, sir. Very sensible of you, sir, if you don't mind my saying so, sir."

The youths mutter angrily. "Come up here for a free feel."

"*Hombre conejo.* . . . Fucking rabbit man."

Inside the think room, the boys put on helmets. There are dials and screens—you can call your shots. Will it be an open elevator? The moon is full. The lights of Yass-Waddah twinkle across the bay.

Audrey could throw a potent curse. Or something with mirrors and video cameras—home movies to show his friends when he has a comfortable little bungalow in a nice residential district of Ba'dan.

Everything is permitted in a think room, so Audrey simply lets himself go. An open elevator or a mirror job? Why not both, one after the other?

POP   POP   POP

He is spattering death all over Yass-Waddah across the bay. Now he reaches out for the hermaphrodites and transplants of Yass-Waddah.

Two of these creatures undulate in, trilling, "You *know* what happens *now* don't you, Audrey?"

Jerry's head is on the body of a red-haired girl and her head is on his body, long red hair down to his nipples. Audrey gets the Gorgon Queezies at the sight of them.

"We're going to *pop* you, Audrey."

An open elevator for this one.

"*Here you goooooooooo.* . . ." Her hair blows up around her head like flames from hell.

POP

Audrey is learning to relax and throw his pops. A fire starts in a warehouse across the bay.

Now for the Big Dipper, which towers eight hundred feet into the night sky, all lit up with twinkling stars. Biggest and fastest roller coaster in the solar system. Like I say, Ba'dan breaks a lot of records.

Audrey stops in a little café he just remembers, up this little street and turn right ... they sit under an arbor and order mint tea and all take a whopping dose of Itchy Tingles.

"You chaps just back up my play. Give me all your Itchy Tingle prana when I pop."

"Sure thing, old sport."

Audrey remembers a very exclusive little shop—you don't get through the door or even *find* the door unless the proprietor likes your looks. Audrey knows him from Mexico City where Audrey was a private eye in another incarnation.

Inside the shop, he buys winged-Mercury sandals and a helmet with wings from a whooping crane. He tops off the ensemble with a silver wand.

They take a private car on the Big Dipper. Audrey stands with a silver silk noose around his neck, feet apart, knees bent, riding the dips, the wand moving in front of him. Up they go now—up up up up up—Audrey is getting a hard-on ... a dizzy pause and now, the Big Dipper comes down down downdowndown and levels off. Audrey extends his arm and the wand tingles straight for the power plant of Yass-Waddah.

P O P

All the lights in Yass-Waddah go out.

A LECTURE
IS BEING GIVEN

immy Lee is checking dials. "We better get out of here fast before they get our range."

We walk over to the shooting galleries and penny arcades on the edge of the plateau. A high electric fence separates Fun City from the vast slum area in Ba'dan that stretches down to the river and extends along the river's banks.

It is 3:00 A.M., a warm electric night, violet haze in the air and the smell of sewage and Coleman lanterns. The pitchmen wear pink shirts, striped pants, and sleeve garters. They have gray night faces, cold eyes, and smooth patter.

One of the shills with a Cockney accent and a thin red acne-scarred face, standing in front of a curtained booth, makes a gesture that is unmistakably obscene and at the same time incomprehensible. Audrey is reminded of an incident from his early adolescence down on Market Street, brass knucks and crooked dice in pawnshop windows and a smooth high-yellow pitchman trying to talk him into a "museum," as he called it.

"Shows all kind masturbation and self-abuse. Young boys need it special."

Audrey does not exactly understand what the man is talking about. He turns and walks abruptly away. The mocking voice of the pitchman follows him.

"Hasta luego, amigo."

We walk on and stop in an all-night restaurant where an old Chinese serves us chili and coffee. He puts a CLOSED sign on the front door and locks it.

"Out this way. . . ."

He shows us out the back door into a weed-grown alley by the fence. Frogs are croaking and the first light of dawn mixes with the red sky. A boy pads up beside us silent as a cat.

"You come with me, mister. Somebody want to talk you."

The boy has a straw-colored face dusted with orange freckles, kinky red hair, and lustrous brown eyes. He is barefooted and dressed in khaki shorts and shirt. We walk along beside the fence.

"Here."

The boy pulls aside a piece of tar paper. A little green snake slides away. Under the paper is a rusty iron panel set in concrete. We go down a ladder and through a winding passage that smells of sewage and coal gas, out into a narrow street that looks like Algiers or Morocco.

The boy suddenly stops, sniffing like a dog. "In here, quick."

He guides us into a doorway, up stairs and a ladder onto a roof. Looking down, we see a patrol of six soldiers with machine guns checking every doorway on the street. Audrey studies the gray faces and cold fishy eyes of the soldiers.

"Junkies."

"Fuckin' Heroids—" the boy spits.

The boy guides them through a maze of roofs and cat-walks down a skylight, finally stopping in front of a metal door. He takes a little disk from his coat pocket. The disk bleeps faintly and the door opens.

A Chinese youth stands there. He is wearing a pistol in a holster at his belt. It is a bare room with a table, chairs, a gun rack, and a large map on one wall. A man turns from the map. It is Dimitri.

"Ah, Mr. Snide, or should I say Audrey Carsons, so glad to see you again." We shake hands. "And your young assistant as well." He shakes hands with Jimmy Lee. "Both somewhat altered—but none the worse for wear."

We introduce the others.

"You are welcome, gentlemen ... and now, there is much to explain." He stands before the map with a long thin hazel stick in his hand. "We are here—" he circles the area below the plateau of Fun City down along the Ba'dan riverfront. "It is known as the Casbah. Outlaws and criminals of all times and places are to be found here. The area is heavily patrolled and the soldiers, as you have observed, are all heroin addicts. Their addiction conveys immunity to the fever and assures absolute loyalty to their masters who, of course, supply them ... extra rations for arrests ... rations cut for any dereliction of duty."

"It's neat," I put in. "But couldn't they buy it somewhere else?"

"No, they could not. We control the black market. No pusher would serve them unless he is tired of living."

"But why not? If they can get it someplace else, that breaks the monopoly."

"We have other plans which you will learn in good time."

Dimitri was giving a lecture accompanied by slides and moving films:

"Ba'dan is the oldest spaceport on planet Earth and like many port towns has accreted over the centuries the worst features of many times and places. Riffraff and misfits from every corner of the galaxy have jumped ship here or emigrated to engage in various pernicious and parasitic occupations, swelling the ranks of brothel keepers, whores, pimps, swindlers, black-market operators, go-betweens and fixers. The class and occupational structure is compartmentalized like an Arab city."

Blue twilight was filling the narrow twisting alleys of the city. The stranger shivered, gathering his ragged cloak about him. Lights were going on behind latticed windows.

Here and there blue streetlights sputtered in sockets. A beggar crawled into the street, barring his way and holding forth a bowl fixed into the stump of his arm like a ladle. His legs were twisted, limp and boneless, his shaven head was fetal, his lips parted with a fetid yellow exhalation of breath. The stranger stepped by him and the beggar muttered curses in a gurgling liquid dialect that seemed to bubble up from noisome depths. The stranger felt as if he were being pelted with filth, the words sticking to the back of his cloak with a vile stench. Just ahead was a stone stairway half a house high stained with garbage and phosphorescent excrement. Beyond he could see a misty, blue-lit square. As he stepped into the square, which was littered with rubble half-buried in sand, he found himself surrounded by a gang of filthy youths about four or five feet in height, mewling and chittering and chirruping among themselves as they moved closer blocking his way and sidling in behind him. At first glance in the blue light and drifting wisps of fog the boys appeared simply as ragged hungry waifs bent on extorting what money they could from a stranger. Looking closer, he saw that they were all in some way inhuman.

Some had long red hair and sputtering green eyes and

their hands were armed with needle claws dripping fluid in the blue light. They were wearing leather jockstraps and short fur cloaks that gave off a rank smell of stale sweat and half-cured skins that billowed around them as they moved. He noted that the inside of their cloaks was faintly phosphorescent and surmised that the skins had been cured by rubbing in the phosphorescent excrement that littered the streets. The boys hissed through sharp yellow teeth with snarling smiles as the hair stood up on their heads and legs, bristling like animals. Others, completely naked despite the cold, had smooth reptilian skins, crystal disk eyes and long flexible tails tipped with points of translucent pink crystal. They swung the tails up between their legs pointing at the stranger with mocking bumps and grinds as they hissed in simulated ecstasies. Other boys had crystal fingertips, which they drew out to needles, clicking them together like tuning forks in little rhythms that set his teeth on edge.

The boys drew closer.

"Why do you block my path? I am a stranger who would pass in peace."

One boy stepped forward and bowed so that his long red hair brushed the stranger's boots in a gesture of mock servility.

"A thousand pardons, oh nobly born. But he who would pass here must pay the price of passing. This is reasonable, is it not?"

As the boy straightened up he grabbed the bottom hem of the stranger's cloak and leaping high in the air with a shrill animal cry pitched the cloak up over the stranger's head.

The other boys imitate his cry and wave their arms like the flying cloak. The stranger is now naked except for leather shorts and knee-length leather boots that cling tightly to his calves and flare up the backs of his thighs. He moves sideways, trying to keep the boys from getting behind him, and reaches for his spark gun. A boy lights on all fours like a cat, tail arched over his back. From the pointed crystal tip he quivers out a shower of red sparks that spatter the stranger's body with burning erogenous sores that twist and writhe into diseased lips whispering the sweet rotten fever words. The sparks are coming from all sides, stirring in his nipples, opening in his navel, mewling and chittering from his crotch and rectum.

Audrey woke up with a start, his phallus tight against his thermal jockstrap.

Dimitri's voice droned on, hypnotically lulling: "The area adjacent to the spaceport is an international and intergalactic zone known as Portland. Portland has its own administration, customs, and police. Biologic inspection and quarantine measures are enforced by the DNA police force. These are highly specialized officers all qualified in every branch of medicine, authorities on every disease and drug in the galaxy.

"They are armed with the most sophisticated weapons: Infra-Sound and DOR guns, fear probes, death guns that can be adjusted to kill, stun or disperse, and devices shooting tiny pellets of nerve gas and toxins.

"These officers are highly skilled interrogators, trained in telepathic techniques, equipped with the most advanced lie detectors, with readings taken from the sensitive reactions of living creatures: this flower droops at a lie, and this octopus turns a bright blue.

"In certain cases where the subject has been trained to circumvent telepathic probes and lie detectors, and where time is short (a nuclear device must be located and deactivated), the DNA interrogators have recourse to injections of stonefish venom. This poison produces the most intense pain known. It is like fire through the blood. Subjects roll around screaming.

"And here, in this syringe, is the antidote which brings immediate relief."

On screen an impassive interrogator holds up a tiny syringe filled with a blue liquid.

A man with a wrinkled old-woman face and toothless mouth was bending over him, his head ringed by a halo of blue light.

"Well, young guy, it's a good thing I happened along." He picked up the spark gun and hefted it. "Now this little trick could fetch a right price in the right place. . . ."

The stranger tried to stand up and fell backward, hitting his elbows.

"Easy does it, young feller." The man helped him to his feet. "And right this way."

Every step sent excruciating stabs of pain through his body. His throat ached and he was spitting blood. His legs felt numb and wooden. He had to lean heavily on the man's arm to keep from falling.

"Here we are." The man kicked at a strange animal in the doorway, a cross between a porcupine and a possum.

"Fucking lulow!"

The lulow snarled and scrambled away. The man inserted a rod with a pattern of holes into the lock and the door opened into a dingy hallway with stairs at the end.

He guided the stranger into a room to the right of the door. The window opening on the street was high and barred and the plaster walls were painted blue. The man lit a torch in a socket: blue light, a filthy bed, a sink, table and stools.

"No place like home, what?"

He pulled a tattered coverlet of blue velvet over the

grimy bedding and the stranger slumped down. The numbness in his legs was wearing off and he felt unbearable shootings and pricklings, like recovery from frostbite. He covered his face with his hands, groaning in agony.

The man held out a tiny syringe filled with blue liquid.

"Shoot your way to freedom, kid."

The stranger held out his shaking hands.

"Roll up your sleeve. I'll hit you."

Cool blue morning by the creek, soft remote flute calls, sad and sweet from a dying star. Phosphorescent stumps glow in the blue twilight that hangs over the streets at noon like a haze.

Red brick houses line blue canals where crocodiles play like dolphins. Lost mournful stars dim as spark boys chitter and mewl against his shoulder, a frosty luminescence off their backsides, cool remote garden, lead gutters dripping, a stone bridge where a boy stands with a sad blue monkey on his shoulder.

"Fun City is a segregated vice area occupying a plateau on the north side of the city. Here gambling houses and brothels of many times and places promise to satisfy any taste, but these establishments are, for the most part, tourist traps and clip joints with more shills and Murphy men than whores."

Audrey blinks at the screen. He must have seen Fun City through fever-tinted glasses. Seen on the screen, it is a vast composite honky-tonk, temple virgins sealed while you wait, Aztec and Egyptian sets looking like 1920s movie theaters, hula girls around swimming pools with paper palms, fan-tan games with tasseled lamps and geisha girls, New Orleans whorehouses with fake Spanish moss and houseboats on filthy lakes and canals, massage parlors, Dante's Inferno with female impersonators . . . the whole scene made in Hollywood.

"The real action is in the Casbah, but tourists are afraid to go there, scared off by horror stories concocted by the tradespeople and the Fun City shills. Addicts are routinely burned or overcharged in Fun City, so they head for the Casbah, where any drug can be had for a price.

"The Casbah is built into the hills and bluffs that slope down to the river. This vast ghetto houses fugitives and displaced persons. Outlaws in every sense, they pay no taxes and are entitled to no municipal services. Criminals and outcasts of many times and places are found here: bravos from seventeenth-century Venice, old western shootists, Indian Thuggees, assassins from Alamut, samurai, Roman gladiators, Chinese hatchet men, pirates and *pistoleros*, Mafia hit-men, dropouts from intelligence agencies and secret police."

Cameras pan old western sets, bits of ancient Rome, China, India, Japan, Persia, and medieval England.

"Over the centuries, the area has been mined with tunnels so that all the buildings interconnect. The tunnels also give access to a maze of natural caves and caverns.

"There are cable cars and wires with hand carriages and jump seats that run from one building to another. The Flying Squirrels, little people like Igor, hop from the highest bluffs in hang-gliders, skipping from roof to roof, carrying messages, drugs, and weapons.

"The Casbah spills into the river in a maze of piers, catwalks, moored boats and rafts. The tunnels at river level are half full of water, forming an underground Venice with gondolas and limestone palaces dripping with stalactites.

"Any services can be purchased in the Casbah—from assassination to such illegal operations as I.T.—Identity Transfer. There are whores, from the most sophisticated courtesans and Rems who offer wet dreams to order, to such mindless organisms as the Happy Cloak and the Siren Web.

"Any drug can be had in the Casbah for a price. Longevity drugs that require ever-increasing dosage, the addict crumbling to putrescent dust if the drug is withheld. Joy Juice: blackout in erotic convulsions and every shot takes years off the user's life-span. A Joy Juicer lasts two years on average and ends up a burnt-out idiot hulk. And Derm my God what a feeling . . . soothes your skin down to flexible marble . . . but if you don't get it . . . the irritation of the dermal nerve endings . . . well I've seen a kicking Dermy tear himself to pieces with his own hands. The Blue and the Gray, heavy metal drugs so habit-forming that a single shot results in lifelong addiction. Yes, every drug can be had here *for the price*."

"Now you take the stonefish poison. . . ." He tapped the vial of milky fluid. ". . . Like fire through the blood; morphine won't touch it, but this Blue shit is fifty times stronger. So combine the fish poison and the Blue"—he draws the milky fluid into the syringe—"for a Fire Fix!"

The stranger was running short of credits. No money for luxuries like Hot Shots. Jay had a deal going to bring in some Gray but it was dragging out and then the panic hit.

Suddenly there was no Blue in the city. Heroin just barely took the edge off like codeine with a heroin habit. The cold fire in his bones kept him in constant agony and he was bleeding through the skin: blood-sweat, it's called.

Fortunately, he had not been on long enough for the spontaneous amputations that leave arms and legs smoldering blue stumps. With the last of his credits, he went to a clinic for a deep-freeze sleep cure.

"On the south side of Ba'dan, along bluffs overlooking the river, are the vast estates of the rich, guarded by their own Special Police. Recently, sons of the rich, bored with the tinsel attractions of Fun City, began frequenting the criminal ghettos. Some of these youths are addicts and drug dealers, others are purposeful agents sounding me out with offers of aid and weapons.

"The administration, courts, and police occupy a governmental area. A pass is required for entrance. The large middle class of tradesmen, artisans, and minor functionaries occupy the middle of the city, hemmed in between Portland, Fun City, the Casbah, and the governmental area."

Camera pans a wasteland of housing projects like the drearier sections of Queens.

"Traditionally, the city of Ba'dan is ruled by a City Council in which the very wealthy hold an overwhelming majority. Now, the discontented middle class is demanding more seats in the Council. These demands are fanned by agitators under orders from the Council of the Selected with headquarters in Yass-Waddah.

"The Council of the Selected controls a number of cults that are finding adherents among the middle-class youths. These cults are basically of low-church Protestant derivation.

"Agents from the Council of the Selected are also organizing paramilitary groups and smuggling in arms. These agents operate with the connivance of the Heroid Police.

"The basic issue is a proposed Anschluss with Yass-Waddah that would leave the Council of the Selected in virtual control of both cities. This plan is supported by the middle class, who are ignorant of the intrigues of the Council to ruin Ba'dan economically and eventually to close the spaceport.

"To distract attention from these maneuvers, agents of the Council, vociferously self-righteous, call for a cleanup of Fun City, a crackdown on the Casbah, and an end to the international status of Portland. The wealthy see the Anschluss as a danger to their position, but much more vulnerable and immediately threatened are the inhabitants of the Casbah."

He is dozing off. Dry cold rasps his raw lungs . . . putting on his clothes, shivering, dropping things, cold burn in his bowels, just made the privy, a trough of smooth red stone in the hall streaks of phosphorescent shit, a smell like rotten solder, burning shivering sick, he needs the Blue Stuff. Dry blue crystals of snow on the floor stir in an eddy of wind and a crystal spark boy takes shape, naked, radiant, his long needle fingertips dripping the deadly Joy Juice, bright red hair floating about his head, disk eyes flashing erogenous luminescence, his erect phallus smooth as seashell with a tip of pink crystal, he is like some dazzlingly beautiful undersea creature dripping deadly venoms.

"Yass-Waddah, a spaceport in rivalry with Ba'dan, is a matriarchy ruled by a hereditary empress. Here men are second-class citizens who can only achieve status as courtiers, servants, shopkeepers, agents, and guards.

"Those who fall into none of these categories try frantically to ingratiate themselves as informers. No city in the cosmos is so riddled with informers as Yass-Waddah. The Ba'dan word for informer is *Yass.*

"The inner city of Yass-Waddah is forbidden to any male being, except the Green Guards, genetic eunuchs, pot-bellied but strong. They form the shock police of Yass-Waddah.

"Latterly, Her Serene Majesty, the Empress, is being pushed upstairs into the attic as the Council of the Selected moves in, backed by the powerful countesses de Vile and de Gulpa, smarting from their defeat and narrow escape in Tamaghis. They are pushing for the Anschluss, after which the Heroids and the Green Guards will wipe out Tamaghis and block the way to Waghdas forever.

"The riots we are here to foment are simply a prelude to an all-out assault on Yass-Waddah. We are pushing for a final solution. There can be no compromise. Even the memory of Yass-Waddah must be destroyed as if Yass-Waddah had never existed."

AFTERBIRTH OF DREAM

Smell of the salt marshes, slivers of ice at dawn, catwalks, towers, and wooden houses over the water where white-furred crocodiles lurk . . .

There are many albinos in the city with hair white as snow and long slanting black eyes, all pupil, like black shimmering mirrors. Many of the inhabitants change color with the seasons—being white in winter and changing in summer to a mottled green-brown.

The summers are almost tropical and the marshes bloom with a rich profusion of flowering trees and shrubs along pools and canals. Here and there patches of swamp poppies with pods big as cantaloupes bursting with reddish-brown opium.

It was a fall day, leaves turning, crisp frosty air. Most of the people were out in red hair and freckles, yellow, sepia, and orange.

Naked with the spark boy in narrow stagnant streets. Saffron smoke curls out between his legs and fades to pale yellow and violet as the boy winks and capers away.

When Audrey woke up, the smell was still there oozing from the yellow cashmere blanket that covered his naked body. He closed his eyes, remembering the arrival in Ba'dan . . . a shabby whorehouse district called Fun City where he had gone to meet his contact . . . the briefing from Dimitri during which he kept dozing off . . . dreams in which Fun City became an arena for deadly sexual games . . . encounters with the spark boys . . . addiction to a radioactive drug known as the Blues . . . the clinic . . . the doctor.

There was another body in the bed beside him. Opening his eyes and turning his head, he saw milky-white skin, amber hair, and the face of an idiot angel.

"Toby."

An English boy named Arn with a foxy, red face and a corrupt insinuating leer: "Popper Toby, we calls him. When he gets in—eat the smell of him—pops you right enough. Bit of a lark, mate."

Toby opened huge blue eyes and looked at Audrey, the pupils contracting. He kicked the blanket down and arched his body, stretching.

The room is cold with a dusting of dry snow on the floor from the round opening in the wall that serves as a window. Audrey shivers, hugging his knees against his chest.

"Oh my." Arn stands at the foot of the bed in a red turtleneck sweater, green corduroys, and sandals. "Just popped in to put some water on for tea."

Arn then lights an alcohol stove and turns back towards Toby and Audrey, peeling off his sweater and pants. "Coo . . ." he says.

A violet smoke pours from Toby's scent glands, blanketing Audrey's body with a smell of hyacinths, cyanide, and ozone. Audrey is choking, gasping, in a flash of violet light.

Audrey sits up groggily. "Where's Toby?"

Arn puts a hand on Audrey's chin, turning his head around to face a tarnished mirror on the wall above his bed: "Mirror mirror on the wall . . ."

A vertebra pops in Audrey's neck. Arn clicks his tongue. Audrey is looking into the vacant blue eyes of Toby, seeing the milky-white flesh, larval and wraithlike, clinging to his body.

Arn points to the mirror. "Gor blimey you shoulda 'eard 'im before we got together like. Right school tie 'e was." Arn says this in those clear penetrating upper-class English tones. You can hear every word fifty feet across a hotel dining room.

"You've 'eard of me, myte. *Arn the voice.* 'Absolutely breathtyking,' said a gentleman from the *Times* and the Queen dropped 'er haitches on TV. Wouldn't you?"

He tosses Audrey his underwear. "Nip into your duds, luv. Nobody is lyte for briefing. It's like rehearsals in show biz."

In the operations room, Dimitri is passing out photos and addresses for hit assignments. Arn is nowhere to be seen. Audrey is looking at the photo of the man he is to kill: a thin Italian face with protuberant yellow eyes glowing with a sulfurous hate.

"Don't looka me . . ." screams the photograph.

This will be a pleasure, Audrey thinks. I have not come justa looka you—you greasy worthless black-market wop.

Dimitri points to the map: "Right there. Runs a cigarette store. Smuggled stuff. Also an Uncle, a Broker, a Buyer. Pays off in info to operate. He's got lookouts in this kiosk and this grocery store who report any strangers in the neighborhood. Two metal detectors, here and here. He's got another in the door of his shop and a sawed-off shotgun under the counter. You pick up your gun here after you pass the first two detection points. The detector in his doorway will be disconnected."

A miniature youth, passing for an eight-year-old street boy, clicks his heels and bows. "I am the Disconnector."

"And you're just a dumb space sailor," Dimitri tells

Audrey, "looking to pick up a few cartons of smuggled cigarettes." He glances at Audrey's clothes—blue pullover, seaman's pea jacket, blue pants . . . "And here's your hat. After
you do the job on him, you walk out with your cigarettes
and go to this Chinese laundry. They'll show you out the
back way."

In the street, Toby's face is an asset. With vacant blue
eyes, yellow hair and seaman's clothes, no one could look
less like a dedicated and purposeful assassin.

He pauses frequently, looking at a map of the city which
he can't figure out how to fold up again, so he fumbles
it together and stuffs the protesting paper into his pocket.
Just a dumb fucking kid space sailor.

Now he feels the eyes from the lookouts, probing, hate-
filled, but not suspicious. Just the contempt of the angle
boys for a mark, a crumb who worka for a living. He drops
his map and as he bends down to get it, pulls a loose brick
from a wall and gets the gun. He can feel the lookout's
eyes on his ass.

"Looks like a fucking fruit—takes it up the farter."

An old Italian hag leans over a balcony: "Ha ha ha,
maricón."

The gun is a snub-nosed 38 with cyanide bullets. He
looks around, blushing, then opens the door of the shop
and goes in.

The man behind the counter looks at him. Audrey fumbles awkwardly and pulls off his hat. The man's eyes spit
hate and contempt.

"Whatta you want?"

Audrey holds the cap by the visor, moving it across
the counter within two feet of the man's chest. With smooth
fluid casual movements, he draws the gun from his waistband
and pushes it gently into the cotton lining the hat.

The vacant face of Toby ages and tightens, the eyes blazing into the Italian's face like a comet as Audrey smiles. Comprehension, then stark ugly fear, flickers into the man's eyes as he knows what is happening and knows it is too late to reach the shotgun.

Audrey shoots three times through the hat—a muffled sound like a backfire in heavy snow. The man crumples sideways, his eyes flaring out. Audrey reaches across the counter for a carton of cigarettes. He steps outside, looks around uncertainly and walks away.

In the Chinese laundry, an old Chinese is ironing a shirt. He jerks his head towards the rear of the laundry. Audrey walks through into an alley that leads to a sort of mall in sunlight.

A WALK TO THE END
OF THE WORLD

Audrey was walking on a mall in bright sunlight.
Ahead he could see mountains shrouded in mist,
brightly colored food stands, tables under umbrel-
las, waiters in red uniforms. This could be a small
resort town in Switzerland.

He was passing a huge marble snail, a bronze frog and
a beaver. Fourteen-year-old boys lounged on the statues in
studied postures, eating ice cream and looking at each other,
insulated from the passersby by some invisible barrier.

Farther on, boys in cowboy boots, Stetson hats and jeans
posed in front of a clothing store with the same stylized
unsmiling nonchalance, engaged in some timeless charade.
A boy with white-blond hair sat on a stone bridge dangling
his legs.

Audrey turned into a paved courtyard and suddenly the
air was oppressive and heavy with tropical heat. Youths in
eighteenth-century clothes lounge in cane chairs sipping rum
punch. They look cruel and languid as they caress pistol
butts in their belts with slow obscene movements.

A private eye is talking to the bartender. "What were
you doing in Bill Gray's Tropico?" It's an old western and
Clem Snide is a fabled shootist. The bar is full of black
powder smoke, the smell of entrails, blood and chili. The
walls and roof fall in.

A sweet dry wind rises from the southeast. Audrey with some last-minute purchases. Almost the same buckboard it is already taken care of Meester once he gets up beside the boy and they start off down the road where flint chips glitter in the sun. Ahead they see mountains shrouded in mist, the orange and purple sky glowing behind.

He must have dozed off while he was walking—it's known as the Walkies—you get it from space travel. You can walk and talk and get yourself around while you are sound asleep, living in a dream. The dream is made of your actual surroundings—so you don't bump into things. You just see them differently.

A ragged street urchin falls in beside him for a fraction of a second. He glances sideways and knows it is one of the miniature youths, strong and quick as little cats.

The boy flashes ahead leading the way through mirrors and walls, through shops and urinals that open into squares where street acts are in progress: minstrels, Gnaoua drums, lutes, horns, zithers, tumblers, fire eaters, jugglers, snake charmers—all blurring together.

Audrey is walking very fast to keep up with the youth's "sorcerer's gait," past a platform where several boys are doing animal copulation acts as they impersonate cats, foxes, lemurs, and horses, snorting, whinnying, growling, whimpering. The spectators roll in the street pissing with laughter.

Audrey is struck by the variety of garb and racial types that flash by like scenes glimpsed from a train window: Mongols with felt boots, eighteenth-century dandies in silk pumps and breeches, pirates with cutlasses and patches, medieval jerkins and codpieces, sharp smell of weeds from old westerns, boots and holsters, djellabas, togas, sarongs, and youths clad in a transparent fabric like flexible glass lounge about in the studied postures he had noticed in the mall—obviously there to be seen ... superb Nubians naked except for leopardskin capes and boots of hippopotamus hide ... boys in tight rubber suits with smooth poreless faces like green-white glazed terra-cotta.

"Frog boys from underground rivers ..." the guide throws over his shoulder.

Audrey notices that his guide and most of the other people he passes carry at their belts a tool like a little crowbar hooked at one end. Now a ripple passes along the street, actors and musicians are gathering up instruments and props behind him as the word moves from lip to lip.

"HIP." (Heroid Patrol)

People are dodging into doorways, prising up manhole covers with their tools, and scrambling down ladders into a maze of tunnels where the Heroids do not dare to venture. Audrey follows his guide through twisting tunnels, past youths on roller skates, scooters, and skateboards.

The tunnels open here and there into caverns where people live in stalactite-and-quartz houses and tend pools of blind fish. Up twisting iron ladders are Turkish baths, lodgings, houses and brothels. Privies open into restaurants and patios.

Down a rope ladder is a dusty gymnasium where boys are practicing with various weapons as they wait for an assignment: Jerry and Rubble Blood Pu, Cupid Mount Etna, Dahlfar, Jimmy Lee, and the Katzenjammer Kids, as we call the German boys. They drift over to greet him.

"How'd you make out with the Eyetie?"

"Easy and greasy and lots of fun ... the look on his lousy wise-guy face when he *knew*. It was tasty."

Audrey sees a number of the little people climbing up and down ropes and swinging from rings with great agility. He is amazed to see that some of them have long prehensile tails and retractable claws on their feet and hands that enable them to scramble up trees like squirrels.

As he watches, one boy drops thirty feet to the floor, lighting like a cat. The other boys are constantly trying to touch the little people but they are skittish of contact, dodging away from outstretched hands or snapping with their sharp little teeth.

All of them are expert assassins, deadly with knife and strangling cord, dropping on their victims from trees or roofs or climbing into seemingly inaccessible windows. They are also highly proficient with firearms, using a tiny revolver that shoots naillike projectiles and a rifle that shoots poison darts with a range of two hundred yards.

The subtlest assassins among them are the Dream Killers or Bangutot Boys. They have the ability to invade the REM sleep of the target, fashion themselves from the victim's erection, and grow from his sexual energy until they are solid enough to strangle him.

Audrey finds Toby in the locker room, sitting naked and pensive on a worn wooden bench. He looks up absently and pats the bench beside him. Audrey sits down and they both stare vacantly at the wall for several minutes.

Finally Audrey asks, "Is Arn around?"

Toby looks at him blankly from an empty space. "I never heard of it."

"I uh thought . . . I mean this morning . . . "

"Well, my scent glands are so potent sometimes people hallucinate," Toby tells him smugly. "Perhaps you dreamed up the whole thing."

"Well, maybe." He puts his arms around Toby's shoulders hoping to excite him so he will give out the smell which is like exquisite perfumed poppers.

Toby's cock begins to stir and stiffen as he stretches

his legs out in front of him and leans back, looking thought-fully at his toes. Two little people come in rubbing against his legs like cats. They give off a delicate sand fox smell that floats on the heavier male scents of the locker room like a pousse-café.

A thirteen-year-old in the black suit and straw hat of an English public school "fag" sticks his head in and calls to Audrey:

"The Shrink wants to see you." He pushes his eyes up at the corners to make a Chinese face and adds in falsetto, "Chop-chop!"

After a few general questions about space lag, the Doctor asks with elaborate casualness: "Would you please tell me in your own words everything you remember about this uh Arn." He glances down at a file in front of him.

Audrey tries to comply but he encounters blanks in his memory like trying to recall a dream that hovers just out of reach on the edge of perception, skittering away as you try to grasp it, erasing memory traces with a little broom that fades out, in turn wiping away footprints in distant sand.

The Doctor leans across the table and breaks an ampule under his nose. "Just relax now and breathe in deeply."

Audrey finds himself on a table looking up at masked faces.

"That's right now—count up to fifty. . . ."

When Audrey wakes up he finds a shaved spot at the back of his head that is slightly sore to his touch.

"Well, Audrey," the Doctor explains, "we've installed a *separator*. Might come in handy if you ever need to be in two places at once. . . ." He pats Audrey's shoulder. "You can leave the hospital tomorrow morning. Now I'm going to give you an injection."

The days seem to flash by like a speeded-up chase scene

in a 1920s comedy ... patrols always behind them, bullets thudding into flesh, bombs in Middletown bars and theaters and restaurants. A wake of glass, blood and brains and the hot meaty smell of entrails remind Audrey of a rabbit he had once seen dissected in biology class. A girl had fainted. He could see her slump to the floor with a soft plop.

Shatter Day always closer ...

MOVES AND CHECKS
AND SLAYS

Like many riots, the Ba'dan riots began with a "peaceful demonstration," but neither side had any intention of letting it end that way.

The Anschluss with Yass-Waddah was to be put to a plebiscite. Those most directly concerned, namely the inhabitants of the Casbah, were disfranchised. But they had obtained permission from the Town Council to make a peaceful demonstration in Courthouse Square around which most of the government buildings were located.

Meanwhile, Yass-Waddan agents were arming and organizing paramilitary forces in Middletown, intending to catch the "Arabs," as they called them, between the Heroid Police and the armed vigilantes and wipe them out. After which, they would demolish the Casbah and drop poison gas down the tunnels and occupy Portland.

Dimitri had his own plans. After delicate negotiations, he had made contacts in Portland. Portland officials are supposed to keep out of local politics except in cases of "dire emergency." But the Anschluss posed such a threat to their continued function, if not to their personal safety, as to constitute a "dire emergency" and all Dimitri asked was for a customs agent to look the other way for a few seconds when the containers of heroin for the Heroid Police were being passed through customs, while Dimitri's agents substituted identical containers filled with a short-acting opiate antagonist.

Dimitri also had promises of arms caches in the courthouse building provided by certain wealthy families who preferred to avoid more direct involvement. None of the old families wanted the Anschluss. It was a threat to their power and Yass-Waddan agents were talking openly about "parasites" and "traitors."

Audrey knew the battle plan. Even if it went according to plan, there would be close fighting and heavy casualties. So he had these special codpieces made up of a tough plasticlike material and issued them to his team, which was very good for morale. He was in charge of a commando group who were supposed to break through the line of Heroids like a football scrimmage then race upstairs to a room in the courthouse where a cache of arms was to be waiting and then take over the courthouse building.

On the appointed day, the demonstrators from the Casbah, after passing a metal detector and a hand search for weapons, made their way towards the square past snarling middies. So many things could go wrong: the guns aren't there ... they are in the wrong place ... the keys don't work.

As they filed into the square, he saw the line of impassive Heroids in front of the courthouse armed with 9-M grease guns. Sandbags and heavy machine guns on tripods were at the windows and on the roof.

The provocation was carefully planted: crowbars and a stack of cobblestones from street repairs. Audrey glanced at his watch. Two minutes to countdown.

Muscular youths snatch up cobblestones. Jeers and catcalls explode from the demonstrators. Automatic weapons are raised. This is it.

And something is happening to the Heroids. A composite groan is followed by the sound of emptying bowels and a reek of excrement. Instead of responding with deadly accurate machine-gun fire, the Heroids are going down like tenpins as the cobblestones hit. So far, Dimitri's plan is working.

On duty when there is no time for injections, the Heroids function on heroin capsules that dissolve at different rates, releasing a dosage every few hours. However, what is dissolving now is not heroin but a short-acting opiate antagonist. Withdrawal symptoms that would be severe enough spread over several days are compacted into minutes, resulting in immediate incapacity and, in many cases, death from shock and circulatory collapse.

A boy throws a football block into a Heroid in front of Audrey. The gun flies out of his hand and Audrey catches it in the air. Now they are racing for the gangway. Two Heroids in front of the main door are trying to raise their weapons. Audrey gives them a burst as he runs past.

A heavy iron door. The key works. Now down the gangway. Side door is open as it should be. Upstairs and this must be the room.

Key works and there are M-16s, ammo, grenades and grenade launchers, and a few bazookas. (The Paries he knows are equipped with the older and more cumbersome M-15s and some even with Garands.)

Immediately Audrey's team spreads out in groups of five to take over the gun emplacements in the building and on the roof. Audrey and four others fan into a room. A machine gun is on a tripod behind sandbags. The crew, sprawled on the floor and over the sandbags, is completely disabled. Two are dead.

Audrey kneels beside a young Heroid who is lying on his back, his deathly pale face covered with sweat, his pants sticking up at the fly. Audrey whips out a Syrette containing a quarter-grain of pure heroin and injects it into the boy's arm. Now the second part of Dimitri's plan is going into effect: the conversion of the Heroids. This is why he did not simply substitute a quick-acting poison for the heroin.

The boy sits up.

"Welcome to our cause, *comrade*," says Audrey.

The first shots in the area signal the Paries, under the command of General Darg, to pour out of side streets into the square, where they expect to catch the fleeing unarmed demonstrators on the flank. Instead, they run into a hail of machine-gun fire from the demonstrators who have seized weapons from the fallen Heroids. Even deadlier sniper fire strikes down from the windows and roof of the courthouse. To conserve ammunition, Audrey's commandos keep their weapons on semiautomatic, making sure of a hit with every shot.

In a few seconds, Darg's forces have suffered several hundred casualties. He hastily withdraws to seize and fortify buildings on the opposite side of the square and along the side streets leading into the square. He dispatches troops to cover the entrances from the Casbah and to patrol Fun City to prevent more men and weapons being brought into action.

By the end of the first day, the rioters are in control of most of the buildings on the south side of the square. They are, however, unable to open a passage to the Casbah.

Meanwhile, there is much rejoicing in Yass-Waddah. The courtiers are planning a torture festival for the captives, camping around in costumes and, of course, there will be a prize for the most ingenious torture device. The tortured captives will be rendered down into the most exquisite condiments and sweetmeats: raw quivering brains served with a piquant sauce, candied testicles, sweet-and-sour penis, rectums boiled in chocolate.

The Countess de Gulpa admonishes her courtiers to bear in mind that only the ringleaders deserve exemplary punishment. The rank and file will make useful slaves.

"Oh, Minny is so kind," coo the courtiers. "Minny is so kind."

Reports are coming in. The rioters have been surrounded and will surrender in a few hours. These reports have been sent out by General Darg, who is certain of a final victory and does not want the Green Guards or, worse still, a regiment of useless courtiers getting in the way and tarnishing his glory. On the other end, the reports are further falsified to curry favor with the countesses.

The Empress of Yass-Waddah holds aloof from these rejoicings. She knows that whatever the outcome of the battle, her power is gone. She is, in fact, making plans to flee the city in disguise with a handful of faithful eunuchs.

The Empress intends to leave behind a little present for the countesses, a basket of sleeping kundu.

The dreaded kundu is a species of flying scorpion. The body is covered by needle-sharp back-slanting red spines. The jaws are razor-sharp and designed for burrowing like a mole cricket's. The venom that drips from the hairs and the tail-stinger causes instant paralysis. Then the kundu sheds its wings and burrows its way up body orifices and deposits its larvae in the intestines, the liver, the kidneys and spleen so that the paralyzed victim is eaten alive. Unlike other scorpions the kundu is diurnal, remaining comatose during the cold desert nights and being slowly roused to activity by the heat of the day

Perhaps I will win the torture contest in absentia, the Empress thinks.

The second day saw substantial gains for the insurgents. The little people who can climb like monkeys, moving from roof to roof with their poison dart guns, carrying cylinders of chlorine and sulfur dioxide, flushed the Paries out of the buildings around the square, which were then occupied by the insurgents and the renegade Heroids. Darg and his troop, however, remained in occupation of the buildings along the side streets and continued to block entrances from the Casbah. Dimitri knew better than to attempt to force a passage through these narrow streets with troops on the roofs of the buildings five and six stories in height—an error that cost the police heavy casualties in the New York Draft Riots of 1863. Then rioters on the roofs of buildings along the narrow streets of lower Manhattan defeated armed police contingents with cobblestones and other missiles.

General Darg, still sure of ultimate victory, even if a long siege was involved, refused to ask for reinforcements and sent back reports that the situation was under control. However, there were still a few pockets of resistance.

The third day dawned like a bleary red eye. An old woman brought a basket of exquisite golden figs to the kitchen door of the Countess's palace. Under the figs, the kundu were still comatose from the icy chill of the night.

WILL HOLLYWOOD NEVER LEARN

In Ba'dan both sides are looking for a showdown. Darg, because he knows that he cannot conceal the actual state of affairs much longer. Dimitri, because he feels that a state of siege is not to his advantage owing to the numerical superiority of the enemy and their readier access to supplies and weapons. So both generals evoke every aid they can summon through magic rituals.

As the sun climbs higher, the square looks like Hollywood gone berserk. Roman legionnaires under Quintus Curtius are fighting French riot police. Vikings and pirates battle crusaders and Texas Rangers. Old western gunfighters shoot it out with the Black and Tans and Kenya Special Police. Hannibal's elephants charge a train of 1920s Marines on their way to protect the assets of the United Fruit Co. Battle cries and songs ring out. Peons with machetes decapitate lynch mobs ... *mucho* bouncing heads, meester. Battle cries and songs ring out with grunts and bellows, war whoops, bagpipes, the reek of horses, chili and garlic. . . .

> "La cucaracha la cucaracha
> Ya no quiere caminar
> Porque no tiene porque le falta
> Marijuana por fumar."

Pancho Villa's men shoot down a helicopter from Operation Intercept. An army of Chinese waiters charge out of a false-front chop-suey joint with meat cleavers, screaming: *"Fluck you! Fluck you! Fluck you!"* They reduce narcs and Mafiosi to hamburger. Poison darts from Indian blowguns wipe out a Klan rally. Nigger-killing southern lawmen are hacked to pieces by naked Scythians on horseback.

Audrey is in the very thick of it, changing costumes every few minutes. Now he leads a detachment of amok Malay youths with krisses against the Shah's Savak. Next Audrey, on a great black horse in medieval armor, charges down the streets of Middletown skewering religious women and lawmen on his lance. Then he is a shootist with his custom-made 44 double-action revolver leading the Wild Bunch to break up an auto-da-fé in Lima. Now he boards a Spanish man-of-war with cutlass and laser gun. Machine-gun bullets, poison darts, arrows, spears, boomerangs, bolos, throwing knives, cobblestones. Rockets whistle through the air, sharp smell of weeds and dry heat from old westerns, snow and ice with Viking ships, amok Malays trail muggy heat and jungle smells, pirates blow in with a sea wind and a whiff of rum and spices, pitchmen and camp followers spread out their wares, false-front saloons, whorehouses, taco stands, carny booths with root beer and spun sugar, sod-roofed huts serving chicha, chick-peas and roast guinea pig, street performers passing around the hat and picking pockets—pea under the shell, now you see it now you don't ... shift partners round and round—Malay youths with krisses skewering religious women, shootist with custom-made Kenya Special Police in his nostrils, southern lawmen are hacked to Hollywood and gone, and a grinning boy passes around a bloody Stetson.

"Nominate your poison, gents."

Klansmen clutch their throats and turn black.

"We don't serve niggers in here!" thunders the bartender. "Take them *outside* because they stink. Take them to the Nigger Morgue."

Boys in medieval codpieces have set up a catapult. Roman soldiers break down doors with battering rams, impervious to the bullets, which break against clear classic light with a whiff of ozone.

Raids and prisoners ... Rape of the Sabine ... Romans sweep in on a women's rally and carry the bitches away, screaming and kicking, an old western posse is lynching a Neanderthal man, KGB and CIA agents bustle scientists and enemy agents into cars or sweep down and hook them into a silent chopper like actors pulled offstage, Inquisition Police drag jet-setters out of cocktail lounges, and the Green Guards are busy with their nets.

"Oh I want that one ..." coos a courtier.

Audrey leads an army of twelve-year-old boys carrying banners of colored silk ... POLTERGEISTS OF THE WORLD UNITE!

They stand now, still as stone, in a sickening uneasy calm. As the barometer drops and drops, slowly a black cloud gathers over their heads. A little wind stirs brown hair across the mouth, blown lilacs and brown hair, ruffling through hair yellow as corn silk, through auburn, orange, russet and flame-red hair and black Pan curls. . . .

WIND   WIND   WIND

A sighing sound, a whistle, a shriek, hair standing straight up now as a black funnel whirls around their slender bodies tearing cobblestones up from the street, screaming hurricanes of broken glass as the boys ride this bucking whistling wind—it's known as a "space horse." You let it carry you all the way out, glass blizzards stripping flesh from the bones, tossing bloody bones through the air with street signs and branches, masonry, stones, and timbers—the whole city is flapping and shredding.

Thousand-mile-an-hour winds—the fences, barbed wire, and massive iron gates hemming in the Casbah are tearing loose ... flying wire decapitates screaming crowds. Pan, God of Panic, rides the wings of Death as the torn sky bends with the wind, prop sky tearing, shredding—incandescent force—the pure young purpose blazes like a comet. ...

WIND!   WIND!   WIND!

Audrey is in the eye of the hurricane, a point of lucid calm. In front of him is a dusty tube of Colgate toothpaste in the window of a Tangier shop.

Far away he sees Middletown: red brick houses, a deep clear stream, stone bridges, naked boys, high-pitched distant voices. A boy who looks familiar ... he knows the boy's name but can't remember from where exactly ... it's Dink ... Dink Rivers, the boy from Middletown.

Now Dink waves and beckons: "It's me, Audrey! I'm back!"

Audrey tries to reach him but the wind tosses Audrey about like a cork. He is fighting his way upriver through breaking ice floes ... years tearing loose.

The distant voice of the pitchman: "The age-old story of Adam and Eve ..."

Audrey finds himself in the Fun City of his dream ... can't remember exactly ... pinwheels ... shooting galleries a rural slum ... rundown houses ... rubbish ... little fields of corn and cabbage ... blotched diseased faces ... silent and intent ... all moving down a steep road of red clay ... no one seems to see him.

The road leads to a rubbly square. In the middle of the square is a platform built around a tree.

ARGUE SECOND TIME
AROUND SUCH A DEAL

On the platform is Arn as Eve with long red hair, her body covered with fever blotches. A naked youth with long yellow hair is Adam. The fever smell steams off their bodies and the crowd draws the smell in, whimpering and rubbing themselves.

Something familiar about Adam, Audrey thinks. Reminds him of something a long time ago. Why . . . it's me!

Now Arn proffers Adam an apple. The fruit is purple-red and shiny like the head of a penis. Here and there on the fruit are triangular bulges like Adam's apples and at one end is a russet rectum. *Why it's made of male flesh,* Audrey thinks.

"No! No!" Audrey screams without a throat, without a tongue.

Adam does not hear. His face wears an appalling expression of idiotic ecstasy as he bites into the apple. Audrey can feel the sugary burning-metal taste down to his quivering toes as Arn rises from his side tearing loose . . . the sweet diseased knowledge.

Eve stands there with a noose . . . bone's song burning marbled cream smashed roses . . . old story of Adam and Eve . . . how Eve was *made. Knowledge* of the blackout . . . Black Jack's Apple Tree . . . fruit made of the boy's death dangling there. It's a lovely tree, isn't it? Nets of the Green Guards fall over Audrey's head.

By noon of the third day, General Darg is ready to surrender. Knowing the treatment meted out to defeated generals in Yass-Waddah, he calculates how he can get a better deal from Dimitri. The insurgents are now in control of Ba'dan, or what is left of it. Considering the terrible fate awaiting prisoners taken by the Green Guards during the battle, Dimitri launches an immediate all-out assault on Yass-Waddah.

Audrey has been captured by the Green Guards and brought to the Countess de Gulpa's palace. She isn't going to share *this* with the courtiers.

"Hello, Audrey, I am very glad to see you here." She smiles and licks her lips, her eyes glowing with green fire. "Let me show you around."

Two massive guards flank him on either side and two walk behind. Through electrodes implanted in their brains they are telepathically controlled by the Countess.

"I'll show you my conservatory, Audrey. I'm sure you will find it interesting."

She leads the way into a red-carpeted room. There is a plastic sheet across one end where plants are growing. A horrible black smell of filth and evil fills the room, a smell of insects and rotten flowers, of unknown secretions and excrements.

"Come along, I'll show you my little plants." She stands at one end of the plastic screen, which is open and leads to a narrow path that encircles the garden. "Look there, Audrey."

Audrey sees a pink shaft growing from the ground, a penis-shaped shaft, red and purple, and as he watches, the shaft moves and pulses. The Countess leans forward with a hoe and turns the plant out of the ground. The shaft is attached to a pink sac with insect legs like a scorpion or a centipede. It scrabbles to cover itself up with dirt.

"That was once a silly boy like you, Audrey, and that's where I'm going to plant you." The Countess stands with her hand on the door. "You'll find out how it's done, Audrey. You'll have six hours to learn."

The courtiers, lounging on a colonnade high above the river, see a flotilla of boats, rafts, and landing barges approaching. This must be General Darg returning in triumph with hundreds of captives. They squirm and moan in vile anticipation, stretching forth languid fingers to a basket of golden figs warmed by the noon sun.

"My God, something's *up* me!"

The principal defense of Yass-Waddah are the towers, manned by a few skilled technicians, capable of throwing electric blasts like lightning bolts. Now the towers open fire, blowing boats out of the water.

The insurgents take heavy losses but they spread out and keep coming. Landings have been made all up and down the river and Yass-Waddah is surrounded by confused troops without a plan of attack.

The Cyclops Boys go into action. These beings have one eye in the center of the forehead. They can activate the death chakra in the back of the neck until a laser beam shoots out the third eye, cutting through stone and metal, seeking the electronic control centers of the city.

Instrument panels are blowing out, magazines exploding. The screaming crowd pours through the walls, now broken in many places.

"Death to the Council of the Selected!"

"Death to the Green Guards!"

"Death to the Foreign Sows!"

"Death to the Courtiers!"

But the courtiers are deaf to everything but their own screams as the kundu do their work.

Audrey felt the floor shift under his feet and he was standing at the epicenter of a vast web. In that moment, he knew its purpose, knew the reason for suffering, fear, sex, and death. It was all intended to keep human slaves imprisoned in physical bodies while a monstrous matador waved his cloth in the sky, sword ready for the kill.

From the depth of his horror and despair, something was breaking through like molten lava, a shock wave of uncontrollable energy. Audrey felt the chakra at the back of his neck light up and glow like a tiny crystal skull brighter and brighter. A hum filled the room and a smell of ozone.

The Countess turned from the door, eyes blazing with alertness, and Audrey saw what had happened. Her orders to the guards had not been obeyed. An interfering frequency had blanked out her control of them.

Audrey smiled and licked his lips. He started forward, hands outstretched to block a groin kick. The Countess screamed like an animal, dodged past him and out the door.

He was a step behind her as she sprinted down the corridor. He ran with inhuman speed, taking twenty feet at a stride and caught her at the end of the hall. He held her elbows pinioned, his hip against her, and grinned into her screaming face, which was losing all human semblance as he smashed her against the wall and threw his hammer-fist into her face, crushing the perfectly chiseled nose and lips that crumpled like rubber.

Now he was clawing out her eyes, which were blank and white and rubbery. Someone was shaking his shoulder.

"Mr. Carsons, what are you doing? Why, you're waking up the whole ward."

Audrey found himself looking at a ruptured pillow. A nurse stood over him.

"Just look what you've done. You've torn your pillow

to pieces." She snatched the pillow from his hands and bustled out.

The nurse returned with a new pillow. She straightened the bed and put the pillow under his head in a way that said, See that it stays there. She looked at her wristwatch. "I'll get you an injection."

Audrey lay back looking at the ceiling. He felt calm and relaxed. He must have had a nightmare. He couldn't remember what it was and it all seemed very remote and unimportant. Just a pillow. Well, he had a new pillow now. The nurse was back with a hypo on a little silver tray. He rolled back his sleeve, felt the alcohol on his arm—and the prick of the needle. GOM one quarter grain.

He woke in gray dawnlight and lay there trying to remember. When had it all started? In London with Jerry Green and John Everson. His first real habit.

He had chippied around in New York with cut shit but this was pure H dispensed by a woman doctor with a title. The Countess, they called her. If she liked you she would write for any amount of heroin and coke or both. She liked the "boys," as she called them.

Then suddenly, the terrible news. The Countess was dead of a heart attack. The Home Office was clamping down. Time to move.

So Audrey, Jerry, and John set out for Katmandu in a second-hand car that got them as far as Trieste, where they took a boat arriving in Athens in the middle of the summer.

The heat was like an oven. They finally found quarters in a hostel: a bare room with three cots. The proprietor had inquisitive unpleasant eyes. Everything about him said "police informer." But they were thin and the room was cooler than the street. The boys stripped to their underwear and sat down on the cots.

"I feel terrible," said Audrey.

"I got some kinda awful hives," said Jerry scratching at a red welt on his ribs.

"Probably just the heat and being sick," said John. "Let's see what we've got left." He stood up and swayed and put a hand to his forehead.

Audrey stood up to steady him and silver spots boiled in front of his eyes. They both sat down again, then got up very slowly and took a little Chinese H and some cotton from the knapsacks. They cooked it all together and split it.

Ten minutes later, Audrey was down with Cotton Fever. Teeth chattering, his whole body shaking, he lay on the bed, knees up to his chin, hands clenched in front of his face.

Finally, he got two Nembutals down and the shivering stopped. He went to sleep.

He dreamed he was back in Saint Louis as a child. He was eating orange ice very fast for the sharp headache and the relief that comes from sipping a little water. Just as he reached for the water, he woke up with a pounding searing headache, his body burning with fever. He knew that he was very sick, perhaps dying.

He tried to get up and fell on his knees by Jerry's bed. He shook Jerry's shoulder. The flesh was burning-hot. Jerry muttered something.

"Wake up, Jerry. We have to get help."

The door opened. The light was turned on. Three Greek cops and the proprietor were watching from the doorway. The cops pointed to the boys and said something in excited Greek. They backed out of the room stuffing handkerchiefs in front of their faces. Leaving one cop at the door, they called an ambulance.

Audrey vaguely remembered being lifted onto a stretcher by masked figures. As he was carried down the stairs, he saw words in front of his eyes: a lattice of black words on white paper shifting and rotating. He could make out the first sentence:

"The name is Clem Snide. I am a private asshole."

The nurse stood by his bed with a thermometer. She put it in his mouth and left the room. She came back with a breakfast tray. She drew out the thermometer and looked at it. "Well, almost down to normal now."

Audrey sat up in bed, drank the orange juice greedily, ate a boiled egg and a piece of toast and was drinking his coffee when Doctor Dimitri came in. The face looked familiar and seemed to stir and concentrate the vague shapes of the dream. Of course, Audrey thought. I've been delirious and he was the doctor.

"Well, I see you're a lot better. You should be out of here in a few days now."

"How long have I been here?"

"Ten days. You've been very sick."

"What was it?"

"Don't know exactly ... a virus ... new ones keep turning up. We thought at first it was scarlet fever but when there was no reaction to antibiotics, we shifted to purely symptomatic treatment. I don't mind telling you it was a close thing ... temperatures up to a hundred and six ... your two friends are here ... exactly the same syndrome."

"And I've been delirious all this time?"

"Completely. Do you remember any of it?"

"Last thing I remember is being carried out of the hostel."

"The remarkable thing is that you, Jerry, and John all seemed to be in the same delirium. I've made a few notes...." He flipped open a small loose-leaf notebook. "Does this mean anything to you? Tamaghis ... Ba'dan ... Yass-Waddah... Waghdas ... Naufana ... or Ghadis?"

"No."

"Cities of the Red Night?"

Audrey glimpsed a red sky and mud walls.... "Just a flash."

"And now, there is the matter of my fee."

"My father will pay you."

"He has already agreed to do so but he has refused to pay the hospital costs—pleading his income tax. This is awkward. However, if you will sign an agreement to pay ... your father suggests that you apply to the American Embassy for repatriation...."

The boys are at the reception desk of the hospital, signing papers. Doctor Dimitri stands there in a dark suit.

Audrey looks around: something very strange about this hospital ... for one thing, no one seems to be wearing white uniforms. Perhaps, he thinks egocentrically, they are all waiting for us to go home so they can leave—but then another shift would be coming on. In fact, he decides, this doesn't look like a hospital at all ... more like the American Embassy.

A cab pulls up under the portico. Doctor Dimitri shakes hands with a rapidly disappearing smile.

As soon as the boys are gone, he walks through a series of doors, each guarded by an armed security man who nods him through.

He is in a room with a computer panel attached to a battery of tape recorders. He flicks a switch.

"The Consul will see you now."

A black wooden slate on the desk said "Mr. Pierson." The Consul was a thin young man in a gray seersucker suit with an ascetic disdainful Wasp face and very cold gray eyes.

He stood up, shook hands without smiling, and motioned the three boys to chairs. He spoke in a cultivated academic voice from which all traces of warmth had been carefully excised. "You realize that there is a considerable hospital bill outstanding?"

"We have signed an agreement to pay."

"The Greek authorities could prevent you from leaving the country."

The three boys spoke at once:

Audrey: "It wasn't our fault. . . ."

Jerry: "We got sick. . . ."

John: "It was . . ."

Audrey: "A virus . . ."

Jerry: "A new virus." He smiled seductively at the Consul, who did not smile back.

All together: "We almost died!" They rolled their eyes back and made a death-rattle sound.

"The police found evidence of drug-taking in your room. You are lucky not to be in jail."

"We're certainly grateful to you, Mr. Pierson. And lucky to be here—like you say," said Audrey. He tried to sound impulsive and boyish but it came out all slimy and insinuating.

The others nodded in agreement.

"Don't thank me," said the Consul dryly. "It was Doctor Dimitri who put in a word with the police. He is interested in your *case*. A new virus, it seems. . . ." He looked at the boys severely, as if they had committed some gross breach of decorum.

"Doctor Dimitri is quite an influential man."

All together, plaintively: "We want to go home."

"I daresay. And who will pay for that?"

"We will—when we can," said Audrey.

The others nodded in agreement.

"And when will that be? Have you ever thought about working?" asked Mr. Pierson.

"Thought about it," said Audrey.

"In an abstract sort of way . . ." said Jerry.

"Like death and old age . . ." said John.

"Doesn't happen to people one knows . . ." said Audrey feeling like a Fitzgerald character. The sun came out from behind a cloud and filled the room with light.

The Consul leaned forward and spoke in confidential tones. "For example . . . for *example* . . . you could *work* your way home. There's a ship in Piraeus now that can use three deckhands. Any sailing experience?"

"Reef the mizzenmast!" said Audrey.

"Scuttle the bilge!" said John.

"And pour hot tar on the companionway!" said Jerry.

"Good." The Consul wrote something down on a slip of paper and passed it to Audrey. "When you get to *The Billy Celeste*, ask for Captain Nordenholz."

The boys stood up and said in chorus: "Thank you, Mr. Pierson." They flashed toothpaste smiles.

Mr. Pierson looked down at his desk and said nothing. The boys walked out.

As he stepped out of the office, Audrey got a whiff of that unmistakable hospital smell. A young man in a white coat was chatting with a nurse at the reception desk. A taxi pulled up for them at the door.

In the office, Doctor Pierson picked up the phone: "Doctor Pierson here. . . . Yes, no question about it." He picked up the slides and studied them. "B-23 all right. . . . The boy Jerry is obviously the original carrier. . . . Active? Like a plutonium pile. . . . There is, of course, the uh delicate and sensitive question of differential racial or ethnic susceptibility . . . with further research, perhaps . . . Could not commit myself on the basis of present findings . . . theoretically possible, of course. On the other hand, uncontrolled mutation cannot be ruled out . . . sure? How can I be sure? After all it's not in my district."

Late afternoon in the cabin of *The Billy Celeste.* Audrey and the boys have just signed on.

Skipper Nordenholz glanced down at the names. "Well uh Jerry, Audrey, and John . . . you have made a wise choice. I hope you are quite fit?"

"Oh yes, Captain."

"Aye aye, sir."

"The doctor said we made a *remarkable* recovery."

"Good. We will be sailing within the hour. . . . Tunis, Gibraltar . . . Lisbon for Halifax. Incidentally, we will be passing the exact spot off the Azores where *The Mary Celeste* was found in 1872—all sails set, completely undamaged, nobody on board." His green eyes glinted with irony as he smiled slightly and added, "The mystery was never solved."

"Perhaps it was just the basic mystery of life, Skipper," Audrey said cheekily. "Now you see it—now you don't."

MINUTES TO GO

We call ourselves the Destroying Angels. Our target is the rear-end of Yass-Waddah, if it could be said to have one. We feel rather like the Light Brigade. All the bad characters of history are gathered in Yass-Waddah for a last-ditch stand: the Countess de Gulpa, heavy and cold as a fish under tons of gray shale; the Countess de Vile, eyes glowing, face flushed from the ecstasy of torture; the Ugly Spirit; the Black Abbot; and the Council of the Selected—all with their guards and minions and torture chambers. How can we prevail against this wall of icy purpose?

We got the message on the teleflash from Ba'dan. Yass-Waddah has completed nuclear device ahead of schedule. All-out aid requested.

We are still 150 miles from Yass-Waddah. Four days hard marching. We don't have that much time.

Woke up in the silent wolf lope. There is the river. No sign of Yass-Waddah. I must be above or below it.

I reach the bank. Across the river I can see the rotting piers and sheds of East Ba'dan. To my right is what remains of a bridge, the upper structure rotted away, leaving only the piles protruding from green water.

I am standing where Yass-Waddah used to be. The water looks green and cold and dirty and curiously artificial, like a diorama in the Museum of Natural History.

A blond boy enters from my right where the bridge used to be, walking on the green-brown water. He moves with a stalking gait as if he were playing some part in a play, mimicking some actor with a touch of parody.

The boy is wearing a white T-shirt with a yellow calligram on the chest surrounded by a circle of yellow light, rainbow-colored at the edges. He is wearing white gym shorts and white tennis shoes.

A dark boy in identical white gym clothes is standing to my left on the bank at the top of a grassy hillock. He has planted a banner in the ground beside him and holds the shaft with one hand. The banner is the calligram in the rainbow circle stirring gently in a wind that ruffles his shorts around smooth white thighs.

The blond boy walks up from the water and stands

in front of his dark twin. The dark boy begins to talk in soft flute calls, clean and sweet and joyful with a sound like laughter, wind in the trees, birds at dawn, trickling streams. The blond boy answers in the same language, sweetly inhuman voices from a distant star.

Now I recognize the dark boy as Dink Rivers, the boy from Middletown, and the other as myself. This is a high school play. We have just taken the west side of the river. This is the conquest of Yass-Waddah.

Good evening, our chap. A good crossing. Yass-Waddah disintegrated.

A slow insouciant shrug of rocks and stones and trees spreads a golf course along the river now several hundred yards away. Two caddies stand in a sand trap. One rubs his crotch and the other makes a jack-off gesture. Music from the country club on a gust of wind. Red brick buildings, cobblestone streets. It is getting darker. Dusty ticket booth.

A sign:

The Billy Celeste High School presents:
CITIES OF THE RED NIGHT

I lead the way through rooms stacked with furniture and paintings, passageways, partitions, stairways, booths, cubicles, elevators, ramps and ladders, trunks full of costumes and old weapons, bathtubs, toilets, steam rooms, and rooms open in front. . . .

A boy jacks off on a yellow toilet seat . . . catcalls and scattered applause.

We are in a cobblestone alley. I look at my companion. He is about eighteen. He has large brown eyes with amber pupils, set to the side of his face, and a long straight Mayan nose. He is dressed in blue-and-brown-striped pants and shirt.

I open a rusty padlock into my father's workshop. We

strip and straddle a pirate chest, facing each other. His skin
is a deep brownish-purple gray underneath. A sharp musty
smell pulses from his erect phallus with its smooth purple
head. His eyes converge on me like a lizard's.

"What scene do you want me to act in?"

"Death Baby fucks the Corn God."

We open the chest. He takes out a necklace of crystal
skulls and puts it on. There is a reek of decay as he drapes
me in the golden flesh of the young Corn God.

We are in a vast loft-attic-gymnasium-warehouse. There
are chests and trunks, costumes, mirrors, and makeup. Boys
are taking out costumes, trying them on, posing and giggling
in front of mirrors, moving props and backdrops.

The warehouse seems endless. A maze of rooms and
streets, cafés, courtyards and gardens. Farm rooms, with walnut bedsteads and hooked rugs, open onto a pond where
boys fish naked on an improvised raft. A Moroccan patio
is animated with sand foxes and a boy playing a flute ...
stars like wilted gardenias across the blue night sky.

A number of performances are going on at the same
time, in many rooms, on many levels. The spectators circulate
from one stage to another, putting on costumes and makeup
to join a performance and the performers all move from
one stage to another. There are moving stages and floats,
platforms that descend from the ceiling on pulleys, doors
that pop open, and partitions that slide back.

Audrey, naked except for a sailor hat, is tipped back
balancing in a chair while he reads a comic book entitled:
"Audrey and the Pirates."

Jerry comes in naked with an envelope sealed with red
wax.

"Open it and read it to me."

"Oh sir, it's battle orders."

"Wheeeeeeeeeeee!" Audrey ejaculates.

On deck, naked tars throw their hats into the air jacking off and leaping on each other like randy dogs: "Wheeeeeeeeeeeeeee!" They scramble into uniforms as bugles call them to battle stations.

The Fever: A red silk curtain scented with rose oil, musk, sperm, rectal mucus, ozone and raw meat goes up on a hospital ward of boys covered with phosphorescent red blotches that glow and steam the fever smell off them, shuddering, squirming, shivering, eyes burning, legs up, teeth bare, whispering the ancient evil fever words.

Doctor Pierson covers his face with a handkerchief. *"Get it out of here!"*

Yen Lee looks at a painted village with his binoculars. Taped voice: "We see Tibet with the binoculars of the people."

In a stone hut, a naked boy lies on a filthy pallet. Bright red luminescent flesh-clusters glow in the dark room. He rubs the clusters with a slow idiot smile and ejaculates.

Yen Lee sags against a wall with a handkerchief in front of his face.

"It's the pickle factory."

"A health officer is on the way."

The Health Officer is on the nod on his porch over a sluggish river. The huge bloated corpse of a dead hippopotamus floats slowly by. The Health Officer is oblivious. Taped voice: "For he had a sustaining vice." On a riverbank with Ali standing over him, he looks with horror at his torn pocket and empty hand. Backdrop shifts to another bank. With the same expression, Farnsworth looks down at his naked body covered with red welts. Ali stands over him smiling, the red welts a dusky rose color on his reddish-brown skin.

Marine band plays "Semper Fi."

Picture of a privy on a door with a bronze eye under the sickle moon. Audrey, as Clem Snide the private eye, is sitting in a sunken room open at the top. The audience is looking down into the room so they can see what he is looking at: photos of Jerry—baby pictures . . . age fourteen holding up a string of cutthroat trout . . . naked with a hard-on . . . Jerry live onstage, naked with his hands tied, face and body covered with red blotches, a baneful red glow behind him. He is looking at something in front of him as his penis stirs and stiffens. Scattered applause and *olés* from the audience.

Banner headlines in red letters: MYSTERY ILLNESS SPREADS.

On a hospital bed, Jerry spreads his legs with a slow wallowing movement, showing his bright red asshole glowing, pulsing, and crinkling like a randy mollusk. He twists his head to the right, eyes sputtering green flashes as he hangs.

A sepia cutback to the hospital bed. He ejaculates, kicking his legs in the air. Jimmy Lee, as a male nurse, catches his sperm in a jar.

Thunderous applause . . . *"Olé! Olé! Olé!"*

The jar is passed to four Marine guards and rushed to a top-secret lab. A scientist looks through a microscope. He gives the OK sign.

Bouquets of roses rain on stage.

Red-letter headline: NATIONAL EMERGENCY DECLARED.

Stop lights. Quarantine posts.

Soldiers with their pants sticking out at the flies clutch their throats and fall.

Newscaster: "It is impossible to estimate the damage. Anything put out up to now is like drawing a figure out of the air."

A diseased face with a slow idiot smile is projected onto the newscaster's face from a magic lantern. . . .

"The world's population is now approximately what it was three hundred years ago."

Boys on snowshoes reach the *haman.* Steam and naked bodies fade to a misty waterfront. Opium Jones is there with patches of frost on his face as the boys sign on in the ghostly cabin of *The Great White.*

Dinner at the Pembertons. Candlelight on faces that suggest madeup corpses. Only Noah, his boyish face flushed, looks alive. The conversation is enigmatic.

"Are they doing mummies to standard?"

"This is the aunt's language."

"We still don't have the nouns."

"You need black money."

"A master's certificate to be sure. . . ."

"Suitable crops."

"Are you in salt?"

"Bring a halibut."

"Ah good the sea."

They all look at Noah, who blushes and looks down at his plate.

"Draw the spirits to the *plata.* . . ."

"The family business . . ."

"It probably belongs to the cucumbers."

"Cheers here are the nondead."

The boys are back on *The Great White.* A shout from the cabin boy brings them out on deck. Jerry, with a noose around his neck, grins a wolfish smile. Then he hangs, as the western sky lights up with the green flash.

Captured by Pirates: Boys swarm over the rail with knives in their teeth. One with an enormous black beard down to his waist swings his cutlass at imaginary opponents with animal snarls and grunts and grimaces until the crew of *The Great White* rolls on the decks, pissing in their pants with laughter.

"*Guarda costa . . .*" the boys mutter.

One puts a patch over one eye and scans the coast with an enormous wooden telescope.

Kiki fucks Jerry, pulling a red cashmere scarf tight around his neck and grinning into his face. As Jerry ejaculates, blood gushes from his nose.

Slowly, a room in an English manor house lights up. A picture on the wall shows an old gentleman wrapped in red shawls and scarves propped up in bed, with laudanum, medicine glass, tea, scones, and books on the night table beside him. Taking to his bed for the winter. . . .

A light shines on a huge four-poster bed. A man with a nightcap sits up suddenly. A naked radiant boy is standing at the foot of his bed. The man gasps, chokes, turns bright red and dies of apoplexy, blood gushing from his mouth and nose.

Cities of the Red Night: Spotlights bathe the papier-mâché walls in red light. The boys camp around putting on disease makeup. Juanito, the Master of Ceremonies, puts a red rubber flesh-cluster in his navel.

"My dear, you look like Venus de Milo with a clock in her stomach."

The boys pose with expressions of idiot lust. The spectators roll on the floor laughing. One turns blue in the face.

"*Cyanide reaction! Medics on the double!*"

Boys in white coats rush in and shoot him with a blackout dart.

Piper Boy with a bamboo flute in Lima . . . blue sky, color of his eyes. Smell of the sea. Dink is fucking Noah who turns into Audrey and Billy.

"It's me! It's me! I've landed! Hi, Bill! It's two hundred years, Bill! I've landed!"

The pilgrimage may take many lifetimes. In many rooms, on many levels, the ancient whispering stage . . .

Moving age with his binoculars, Audrey lays back in a chair masturbating. Bright pirates. Jerry comes in red wax. We see Tibet for a few seconds, people. A sepia cutback to the hospital. Depraved smile, sperm in a beaker.

He plays "Semper Fi" to four Marine guards. Baby pictures declared in red letters of cutthroat trout. Red anticipation of fever drifts from the bed. See what he is looking at onstage.

National Emergency, age fifteen, holds up a string of stoplights. Jerry's radiant ghost may take many lifetimes. Jerry, the cabin boy, stands over the hills and far away.

"Lima, flash, it's me. The Piper Boy in Lima. Dink, I've landed. Long way to find you."

Noah is in the library studying diagrams of mortars and grenades. He is drawing a cannon. A Chinese child in the doorway throws a firecracker underneath his chair. As the firecracker explodes, the cannon barrel tilts up at an angle. A backdrop of burning galleons falls in front of him.

Audrey's boys are back on deck. Gas tank explodes in Tamaghis. Flintlock rifle on the library table. Hans and Noah take off their shorts.

"Wenn nicht von vorn denn von hintern herum." If not from the front then around by the back way.

As Noah bends over, the flintlock breaks at the breech. As Noah ejaculates, breech-loading rifles pour withering fire into a column of Spanish soldiers.

A float of a Spanish galleon moves slowly and ponderously across the gymnasium floor. On the deck, we see the Inquisition with stakes and garrotes, the Conquistadores, the patróns and governors, officers and bureaucrats and their modern equivalents, *machos* and *políticos* swilling Old Parr scotch and brandishing pearl-handled 45s.

Immigration police in dark glasses ... *"Pasaporte ... Documentos ..."*

Kelley as Ah Pook, spattered with black spots of decay, is fucking the young Corn God in a pirate's chest overflowing with gold ducats and pieces of eight. As they come, a yellow haze like gaseous gold streams off them and wafts across the deck of the galleon. *Machos* clutch their throats, spit blood, and die.

Noah hangs ejaculating in the same yellow haze of magical intention. The curtain is drawn for a moment and guns are piled up in front of him—from his first cartridge rifle to M-16s and bazookas, rocket guns and field pieces.

He is lowered with a slow sinuous movement by the Juicy-Fruit Twins. The twins are naked except for their sailor hats and white sneakers.

Offstage, a voice bellows: *"All right, you jokers. ...* Battle stations."

Noah and the twins are in the gun turret making calculations, taking the range. . . .

"Yards: twenty-three thousand ... Elevation: point six . . ."

The galleon is in the cross hairs of the sight. Jerry turns bright red as he presses the Fire button. The galleon blows up and sinks into a prop sea.

Panorama of Mexico, Central and South America ... music and singing ... naked Spanish soldiers washing in a courtyard, jetting the soap around like a soccer ball and tackling each other, washing each other's backs. In trees by a river boys with idiot expressions jack off, snapping and gurgling like fish as they shake fruit into the water.

Audrey is naked against a backdrop of jungle and ruined pyramids. He gets a hard-on and levitates as it comes up. He lands from a hang-glider in a red desert.

Jerry, the cabin boy, meets him in a lizard suit that leaves his crotch and ass naked. "Me lizard boy ... very good for fuck." Rainbow colors play over his body.

Spanish galleon ... movement by the Juicy-Fruit Twins ... on the deck we see white sneakers ... bureaucrats calculating the range ... hand hair turns bright red on Fire button ... The Galleon *Pasaporte Documentos* is blown out of the water and so a vast territory as Ah Pook spatters the panorama with insurgents. All the boys in yellow haze of skintight magic transparent for a moment come to attention in a line from the first cartridge gun to M-16s ... naked haze like gold gas. . . .

"TENSHUN!"

Audrey and Noah ejaculating angels in rainbow intention. . . .

"AT EASE."

Naked soldiers sniff bazookas and field pieces. . . .

Peace does not last forever. . . .

Red Night in Tamaghis. The boys dance around a fire, throwing in screaming Sirens. The boys trill, wave nooses, and stick their tongues out.

This was but a prelude to the Ba'dan riots and the attack on Yass-Waddah. The boys change costumes, rushing from stage to stage.

The Iguana twins dance out of an Angkor Wat—Uxmal— Tenochtitlán set. The "female" twin peels off his cunt suit and they replicate a column of Viet Cong.

The Countess, with a luminous-dial alarm clock ticking in her stomach and crocodile mask, stalks Audrey with her courtiers and Green Guards. Police Boy shoots a Green Guard. Clinch Todd as Death with a scythe decapitates the Goddess Bast.

Jon Alistair Peterson, in a pink shirt with sleeve garters,

stands on a platform draped with the Star-Spangled Banner and the Union Jack. Standing on the platform with him is Nimun in an ankle-length cloak made from the skin of electric eels.

The Board enters and takes their place in a section for parents and faculty.

Peterson speaks: "Ladies and gentlemen, this character is the only survivor of a very ancient race with very strange powers. Now some of you may be taken aback by this character. . . ."

Nimun drops off his robe and stands naked. An ammoniacal fishy odor reeks off his body—a smell of some artifact for a forgotten function or a function not yet possible. His body is a terra-cotta red color with black freckles like holes in the flesh.

"And I may tell you in strictest confidence that he and he alone is responsible for the Red Night. . . ."

Jon Peterson gets younger and turns into the Piper Boy. He draws a flute from a goatskin sheath at his belt and starts to play. Nimun does a shuffling sinuous dance singing in a harsh fish language that tears the throat like sandpaper.

With a cry that seems to implode into his lungs, he throws himself backward onto a hassock, legs in the air, seizing his ankles with both hands. His exposed rectum is jet-black surrounded by erectile red hairs. The hole begins to spin with a smell of ozone and hot iron. And his body is spinning like a top, faster and faster, floating in the air above the cushion, transparent and fading, as the red sky flares behind him.

A courtier feels the perfume draining off him. . . .

"Itza . . ."

A Board member opens his mouth. . . . *"Itza . . ."* His false teeth fly out.

Wigs, clothes, chairs, props, are all draining into the spinning black disk.

"ITZA BLACK HOLE!!"

Naked bodies are sucked inexorably forward, writhing screaming like souls pulled into Hell. The lights go out and then the red sky. . . .

Lights come on to show the ruins of Ba'dan. Children play in the Casbah tunnels, posing for photos taken by German tourists with rucksacks. The old city is deserted.

A few miles upriver there is a small fishing and hunting village. Here, pilgrims can rest and outfit themselves for the journey that lies ahead.

But what of Yass-Waddah? Not a stone remains of the ancient citadel. The narrator shoves his mike at the natives who lounge in front of rundown sheds and fish from ruined piers. They shake their heads.

"Ask Old Man Brink. He'll know if anybody does."

Old Man Brink is mending a fish trap. Is it Waring or Noah Blake?

"Yass-Waddah?"

He says that many years ago, a god dreamed Yass-Waddah. The old man puts his palms together and rests his head on his hands, closing his eyes. He opens his eyes and turns his hands out. "But the dream did not please the god. So when he woke up—Yass-Waddah was gone."

A painting on screen. Sign pointing: WAGHDAS-NAUFANA-GHADIS. Road winding into the distance. Over the hills and far away. . . .

Audrey sits at a typewriter in his attic room, his back to the audience. In a bookcase to his left, we see *The Book of Knowledge, Coming of Age in Samoa, The Green Hat, The Plastic Age, All the Sad Young Men, Bar Twenty Days, Amazing Stories, Weird Tales, Adventure Stories* and a stack of *Little*

Blue Books. In front of him is the etching depicting Captain Strobe on the gallows. Audrey glances up at the picture and types:

"The Rescue."

An explosion rumbles through the warehouse. Walls and roof shake and fall on Audrey and the audience. As the warehouse collapses, it turns to dust.

The entire cast is standing in a desert landscape looking at the sunset spread across the western sky like a vast painting: the red walls of Tamaghis, the Ba'dan riots, the smoldering ruins of Yass-Waddah and Manhattan, Waghdas glimmers in the distance.

The scenes shift and change: tropical seas and green islands, a burning galleon sinks into a gray-blue sea of clouds, rivers, jungles, villages, Greek temples and there are the white frame houses of Harbor Point above the blue lake.

Port Roger shaking in the wind, fireworks displays against a luminous green sky, expanses of snow, swamps, and deserts where vast red mesas tower into the sky, fragile aircraft over burning cities, flaming arrows, dimming to mauves and grays and finally—in a last burst of light— the enigmatic face of Waring as his eyes light up in a blue flash. He bows three times and disappears into the gathering dusk.

RETURN TO PORT ROGER

This must be it. Warped planks in a tangle of trees and vines. The pool of the Palace is covered with algae. A snake slithers into the green water. Weeds grow through the rusty shell of a bucket in the *haman*. The stairs leading to the upper porch have fallen. Nothing here but the smell of empty years. How many years? I can't be sure.

I am carrying a teakwood box with a leather handle. The box is locked. I have the key but I will not open the box here. I take the path to Dink's house. Sometimes paths last longer than roads.

There it is on the beach, just as I remember it. Sand has covered the steps and drifted across the floor. Smell of nothing and nobody there. I sit down on the sand-covered steps and look out to the harbor at the ship that brought me here and that will take me away. I take out my key and open the box and leaf through the yellow pages. The last entry is from many years ago.

We were in Panama waiting for the Spanish. I am back in the fort watching the advancing soldiers through a telescope, closer and closer to death.

"Go back!" I am screaming without a throat, without a tongue—*"Get in your galleons and go back to Spain!"*

Hearing the final sonorous knell of Spain as church

bells silently implode into Sisters of Mary, Communions, Confessions . . .

"*Paco . . . Joselito . . . Enrique.*"

Father Kelley is giving them absolution. There is pain in his voice. It's too easy. Then our shells and mortars rip through them like a great iron fist. A few still take cover and return fire.

Paco catches a bullet in the chest. Sad shrinking face. He pulls my head down as the gray lips whisper—"I want the priest."

I didn't want to write about this or what followed. Guayaquil, Lima, Santiago and all the others I didn't see. The easiest victories are the most costly in the end.

I have blown a hole in time with a firecracker. Let others step through. Into what bigger and bigger firecrackers? Better weapons lead to better and better weapons, until the earth is a grenade with the fuse burning.

I remember a dream of my childhood. I am in a beautiful garden. As I reach out to touch the flowers they wither under my hands. A nightmare feeling of foreboding and desolation comes over me as a great mushroom-shaped cloud darkens the earth. A few may get through the gate in time. Like Spain, I am bound to the past.